Third Row, Second Seat

K. T. King

ISBN 978-1-63944-934-7

Contents

1. Father Spero 1

2. The Affable Eccentric 11

3. Pipe Dreams 27

4. Farewell, Peace and Quiet 31

5. The Proposal 47

6. Rejection's Pain 69

7. The String-Player's Finale 79

8. Strange Bed-Fellows 85

9. The Manila Envelope 95

10. Hemlock 36287 105

11. The Wall Talker 115

12. Taking on the Bully 119

13. Simple Patterns Stay between the Lines 127

14. Color Me Yellow 129

15. Innocence Pierces the Circle 131

16. The Cost of Dancing with the Butterflies 135

17. Roman Schmoman 149

18. What Makes Evil, Evil 157

19. Medicine for Rosie 159

20. The Bountiful Chair 167

21. The Exchange 171

22. Life in the Preserve 175

23. The Downward Spiral 183

24. Soiree Spoilers 199

25. The Broken Violin 213

26. Money Can't Buy What Money Can't Buy 233

27. The Homecoming 241

28. From This Day Forward and Beyond 251

29. Promises, Promises, Promises 255

30. Still Water 321

31. Sealed Envelopes 345

32. Home Sweet Home 361

Chapter 1

Father Spero

Throughout the night, Father Greiner prayed for God's mercy and understanding, knowing full well that what he was about to do was criminal. After years of battling the demons of guilt that goaded him day after day, he decided it was time to break all rules, cast logic to the wind, and risk whatever it took to keep a long-awaited promise he'd made to himself, "plan his own outcome."

Father Greiner checked the calendar hanging on the back of the pantry door. Today was June 16th, 1957, the day he thought would never come. From the first day of January, Greiner's daily routine began by crossing off each day with a bold black 'x,' and yesterday's 'x' was the last one. He stared at the bold red concentric circles he'd drawn one hundred ninety-six days ago and remembered the promise he'd made to himself; this time, he'd hold to it. His days of running from what he wanted for George, of doing what others commanded of him, were over. This day would present the biggest challenge of his life, and he was ready to take it on.

To preclude any errors or omissions that could possibly wreck havoc with his plans, Father Greiner itemized everything in minute detail to ensure there would be no mishaps. At the very bottom of his list one item remained unchecked—the used sign he'd confiscated from the rectory when he left the priesthood. He headed outside to retrieve it from the trunk of his car. It was just where he'd left it, inside a used brown manila envelope.

Upon request, these six-by-twelve-inch boiler-plate signs were issued to clergy, no questions asked. Generally a parishioner went to city hall, told the clerk of the court their priest or pastor sent them to pick up the signs, and was given as many as requested. These 'CLERGY' signs were printed on a sturdy off-white cardboard with bold black capital letters. Greiner removed the sign and strategically placed it so it was visibly displayed on the dashboard of his shiny black fifty-five four-door Ford sedan. He looked at his watch, noted the time, and saw that there was none to waste. He raced back to the house, grabbed the picnic basket, and placed it in the trunk. Even though the basket had an internal galvanized cooler to keep food-stuffs cold, he wrapped the basket with its contents in a thick woolen blanket for double protection. He wanted this to be a day Rosie would never forget.

According to the Pennsylvania state map, driving time to Woodside was estimated to take over an hour and a half. Something Greiner never did, was break the speed limit, today he broke them all. As he rounded the final bend in the road and reached the crest of a hill, he put his foot on the brake and stopped. It had been years since his last visit to Woodside, and the image in his memory was seemingly different from the scene he was witnessing at this moment. Greiner caught himself imagining what it would feel like to be a bird, swooping over and above this lush green hollow day after day inhaling this breath-taking view that stretched as far as his eyes could see. He put the car in neutral to let the engine idle so he could step out of the car for a moment to get a better lay of the land and view the entire complex. To see it encompassed by hills covered with dense forests standing guard to protect the vulnerable residents who lived within was like nothing he'd ever seen. To the so called normal, healthy-minded, this hollow would easily appear as a cure for anything that ails, but the locals knew otherwise. More often than not, Woodside State Hospital was referred to as "the nut house." He got back into the car, stepped on the gas, and drove towards the entrance, hoping for the best but readied for the worst. As fate would have it, his anxiety and preparation were for naught, the second the guard on duty spotted his clerical collar, he flashed a broad, tooth-less smile and waved him on through.

Father Greiner drove directly to building North One, backed into the designated slot marked 'CLERGY,' and cut the engine. He stepped out of the car and noted the parking lot was empty—a perfect scenario for carrying out his long awaited plan.

Within seconds of exiting his car, Greiner was distracted by a chorus of female voices wailing in an unintelligible language. He looked up at the second-story oversized windows covered with two-inch diamond-patterned steel grates and saw several women clambering over one another like piss-ants on an ant hill, all yammering at the same time. This vision made him uncomfortable and he rushed to get out of sight, but not before a single high-pitched voice blurted out, "Hey Father, whadda' ya' pushing today, communion or cock?" He thought to himself, "there's hope, they don't all speak the language of the insane, that one speaks filth."

Once inside, he followed the directional markers pointing to a three-sided pulpit-like monstrosity labeled 'log-in desk.' Perched atop, like a hawk stalking its prey, was Arden-Marie Whitley, relishing the vantage point from which she could readily scrutinize everyone's move. This scrawny sixty-eight-year-old woman was a sight to behold. The contrasts between her tightly-permed carrot-orange hair and white powdered wrinkled-skin accented with hot pink circles of rouge painted in the center of each cheek made her look like a mime. To make matters worse, her paper-thin lips were smeared with fire engine–red lipstick that went outside her natural lip line but didn't stop there, the greasy stuff somehow finding its way into every available crack above her upper lip, and this old broad had plenty of those. These startling contrasts made Greiner question whether she ever looked in the mirror before leaving the house every day. She was a sight to behold.

Miss Whitley, as she preferred to be called because it made her feel younger, claimed that three things kept her life in balance—smoking Camel cigarettes, chewing through six packs of Wrigley's spearmint gum a day, and her volunteer's job at Woodside. Hospital administrators respected the way she ran North One's visiting hours every Monday, Wednesday, and Friday between the hours of ten and three. It wasn't easy handling the confusion when coordinating the institution's most difficult patients and their families on visiting day. For thirty-seven years running, Miss Whitley coveted the title, "Volunteer of the Year," and to such a woman as she, life didn't get any better.

Father Greiner noted Miss Whitley's position of authority and realized that this woman could be unpredictable in determining who would or would not get a visitor permit on any given day for one reason or another. This gave him pause to question whether Whitley was really a 'volunteer' or a patient pretending to be one. He thought to himself, "This one's unstable." Before he could utter his first syllable, she looked down at him, clearly implying that she didn't recall ever seeing him there before. Patiently waiting and not getting an immediate answer, she blurted, "Are you coming to see a recently admitted patient?" His reply was equally as rude—"No."

The two then exchanged pleasantries, and in those few minutes of chit-chat back and forth, he'd hoped she'd miss the fact that he had failed to fill in all the blanks. No such luck. Whitley missed nothing. She glanced at the sign-in sheet and saw he had not followed the instructions. Her voice became dispassionate, garnering his immediate attention. "Father, you failed to sign in. I need your name, time and date, where you're going—simple stuff. It's all right there on the clip-board. Hospital rules, not mine. No exceptions, not even for priests."

Greiner's mind seized at the thought of what he was about to do. He kept reminding himself of the alias he used earlier when he telephoned the nurse on duty in the hospital's Ward Two to schedule his visit with Rosie Gradel. The deceit of his position, no longer being a priest, but pretending to be one, made him sternly aware of the ramifications should he screw up. There was no room for error. He felt awkward and uncomfortable and nervously fidgeted with his collar. Thankfully, Whitley suspected nothing. While he scribbled in the blanks on the sign-in sheet, Whitley glanced down to make sure he'd finished before dialing the number to the second floor nurse's station. Speaking into the receiver, Whitley made the call he'd long awaited, "Rosie Gradel's visitor—" she paused, and after trying a couple of times to decipher his sloppy writing, she finally spoke up. "Um—Father, would you pronounce your last name for me? I can't make out what you scribbled here, it's illegible. How'd you expect anyone to read this?" This effusive insult garnered him an attitude, and he saw these games Whitley was playing as nothing more than delay tactics. His response was derisively sarcastic.

"It's Spero—you know, like SPEAR with an O on the end."

"Father you might be a good priest, say mass well, do great at funerals, but your handwriting leaves a lot to be desired."

She spoke into the receiver pronouncing the visitor's name the way he suggested, and requesting that the floor nurse have an attendant escort the patient down to the lobby.

Greiner moved away from the desk and chose a seat near the exit. The ten-minute wait seemed endless. Between Miss Whitley's interrogation and his own uncertainties, he contemplated leaving and abandoning what was beginning to feel like a rather stupid plan. At about this same time, the tumbler's loud click diverted his attention, and a large windowless steel door leading to the lobby swung open. The moment he'd waited for had finally arrived, but nothing could have prepared him for what he saw. He couldn't believe his eyes. Standing approximately twenty feet away were two female figures, an eighteen-year-old ward attendant who was assigned the duty of accompanying Rosie to the visitor's day room, and Rosie herself. The attendant has been told a priest would be waiting for them. As the two women walked arm in arm across the granite floor in his direction, shockwaves raced down his spine, momentarily seizing his mind. He grappled to clear the ugly inescapable thoughts running through his mind; "oh to be anywhere but here right now."

It had been years since Father Greiner last saw Rosie. In fact, the last time was when he and Frank visited together. He expected that she'd aged, but nothing to this degree. Between the unsightly one-size-fits-all institutional cotton dress made of fabric resembling a flour sack, and the dreadful bowl haircut cropped off at ear's length, Rosie's appearance was beyond shocking. He gazed at the snow-white anklets inside over-sized brown institutional shoes with small zippers running up the front and questioned how the hospital expected anyone to manage walking in them. The Rosie he'd come for had dark brown silken hair with tinges of auburn-red high-lights when the sun shone on it; the woman coming towards him looked nothing like that. The only thing this lifeless gray-haired woman approaching him had in common with the Rosie he loved were those incredibly beautiful hazel-green eyes—the ones he never forgot. He looked in the eyes of the woman standing directly in front of him; the color was the same but devoid of life. It took self-control to regain his composure and express how happy he was to see her. Greiner expected a response, at the very least a "hello"—he got nothing. Where was Rosie, the one who mastered the art of listening because she cared about whatever it was you had to say, the one who always wore a broad imp-like smile that kept you trying to figure out what she'd say next, and most painfully to Greiner, the one who always shared her many kindnesses with everyone she met. He chose to ignore emotions and center instead on his long-awaited plan by repeatedly assuring himself things would be different once they were out of there.

The young attendant's mind flooded with thoughts one doesn't normally have when preparing to address a Catholic priest, at least not one as handsome as the one standing across from her. She knew she could still her tongue, but she was helpless with what flew into her mind like a wildfire, "Too bad the priesthood got you before I did! What a waste. You poor guy—just think, your old boss the Pope will never let you get married." She continued to ogle at him as if he was some movie-star she'd seen on the big screen or on the cover on one of those popular movie-star magazines she frequently read while standing in the check-out counter of the grocery store. She let go of Rosie's arm and took a stick of gum from her uniform pocket, unwrapped it, and quickly stuck it in her mouth so her breath would smell sweet when she spoke to the priest. Relentless dizzying nonsense continued to race through her mind. *Oh my God, look at those gorgeous piercing ice-blue eyes with those long black lashes—. Poor sucker doesn't even know how to flirt with them. He musta' been in the girls line by mistake when God handed those out! Only way I'd have a chance of getting those from him is if I had a kid with little holy-boy—not a half bad idea. Better find out where he's a priest. Come Sunday, I'm goin' there! Wow, look at that curly thick jet black hair. If I ran my fingers through that mop of yours while kissing that flawless baby soft skin honey, you'd give up that collar in less time than it takes me to take off my panties.* The priest saw that this attendant was somewhat distracted. To break the silence and move things along, he thanked her for bringing Rosie down to the day room. In that somewhat embarrassing moment she managed to snap back to reality and addressed Rosie. "You must be excited to have such a handsome visitor today. Maybe Father will take you to the cafeteria for lunch. I hear spaghetti's on today's menu and everybody likes spaghetti." Then, as an after-thought, she remembered what she was to tell the priest before they left. "Oh by the way, Father Spero, ward nurse said no need to hurry back. Keep her out as long as you like."

Father Greiner firmly took Rosie by the arm and thanked the attendant, and together they headed outside. In the brief time he was indoors, the grounds-maintenance crews were out and about busily weeding and watering the flower-beds that surrounded the massive brick buildings, making each one resemble a fancy hotel rather than a mental institution. In spite of the fact that the priest found himself surrounded by patients trying to engage him in small talk, his nerves remained surprisingly steady as he ignored them and approached the one lone car that awaited them.

The attendant's words, "as long as you like," resonated inside his head. "As long as you like" would only work if Rosie got into the car without a struggle. He opened the car door, and to his surprise, she got in. He closed the door, raced around to the driver's side, and quickly started up the engine. When he'd arrived earlier he purposefully backed the car into its parking space so that his exit would be swift. Retracing the route backwards in his mind he sorted it out—two left turns, then right onto the mile-long boulevard lined with arched trees that divided the hospital grounds right down the middle. This last mile was the worrisome part of this journey. He tried to make conversation by commenting to Rosie on the niceties of living in such a beautiful and meticulously maintained place. He made a second attempt to engage her in light conversation by talking about her family's gardener, who tended the gardens behind her father's hardware store when she was a young girl, but nothing. He feared the silence and what it could or could not mean, so he kept talking and answering his own questions. When he failed to get any response from Rosie, he interpreted this quietude as Rosie's need to "sit still, and just be."

Father Greiner drove cautiously to avoid garnering any attention. His eyes frenetically raced back and forth as paranoia set in and he began to fear the worst. He checked the rear-view mirror several times to see if anyone was following them. Thankfully, no one took notice as the black sedan retraced its route, eventually approaching the final hurdle, the entrance where this day began. The guard on duty smiled and nonchalantly waved good-bye. After all, he was the exception, he was clergy.

A *good-bye forever!* sigh came the moment the hollow disappeared from sight. Father Greiner denied himself the truth about Rosie's condition or that it ever really existed. After all, he had known both her and her family intimately since she was a young girl, and none of what's happened to Rosie makes any sense to him. Greiner foolishly believes he will succeed where others have failed.

The two of them cruised along with the rear windows cranked down half way, allowing a warm summer's breeze to bathe what could otherwise have felt like being cooped up in a hot box. By now they'd been driving for over an hour in silence. It was June, and summers in western Pennsylvania were notoriously known to be "hotter than hordes of hell," and this day was a testament to that. Greiner looked at his watch and knew they had about another hour's drive before they'd be home. He glanced over at Rosie and figured the stress of all that had transpired warranted a break—somewhere quiet and secluded where the two of them could unwind and have the picnic he'd prepared earlier that morning. Just then, what appeared to be an old abandoned country road on the opposite side of the highway caught his attention. He made a sharp left turn and crossed over the grassy median strip, leaving a cloud of dust behind. After driving about fifty feet or so he turned onto the dirt road he'd spotted minutes earlier. Momentarily disorientated, he couldn't remember how he got to this side of the highway or why, but nonetheless he continued driving until the main highway was no longer visible. Everything from the moment he'd awakened earlier in the day to this moment where he now had the woman of his dreams in the seat next to him clouded his thinking. Somehow he managed to locate a large shade tree to park under so they could escape the hot sun. He turned off the engine, reached over to ensure her car door was locked then wound the windows all the way down. A breeze of fresh country air blew into the car. It felt like God had turned up the fans and cooled everything down by ten degrees. At this point Greiner slid across the seat. He took hold of Rosie's hand. It was trembling, and she tried to pull away, but he held on. The trembling reminded him of another time he'd held that same little hand—the day he took her away in the cab, the day he left her at Hawthorne House, the most regretful, cowardly thing he'd ever done. He wondered if she was remembering the same incident and this was why she let out a hideous gasp when he touched her. His jaw clenched as he realized his greatest fear had come to pass. It reminded him of the women at the windows with their wails and wretched cries. Right then and there he resolved to learn the language of the troubled, even if it took the rest of his life. He finally had the woman of his dreams sitting next to him, the only one he ever coveted, the one he'd convinced himself he could fix with love and care, the now broken Rosie was finally his. If ever there was a gentle, harmless, and trusting soul, it was George Herbert Greiner. He hesitated, and chose his words carefully.

"Rosie, I know you're afraid, maybe even terrified. I am too."

The exhaustive stress in planning and executing her kidnapping had left him drained. Rosie's capture opened the floodgates on a drowning man who had decided to reclaim his life. Tears suddenly began to roll down her pale cheeks. He gently lifted her chin and wiped them away as tears poured from his own eyes. The question he asked himself was how he was going to speak to this wounded, empty soul. He decided to speak from his heart. He didn't know any other way.

"Rosie, not a day's gone by without my longing for you. For years I've begged God's forgiveness, and I believe I have His blessings or I wouldn't be here with you today. I have always loved you. First as a child forced into womanhood, and now in whatever phase of life you are in no matter the condition. Today you're going where I should have taken you a long time ago—home with me."

Greiner completely forgot about the lunch he'd prepared for this occasion. He'd gotten up early to pack the medium-sized wicker picnic basket with insulated galvanized metal lining and folding lid so he could surprise Rosie with what he'd hoped would be a special afternoon. He wanted this to be the day she would long remember. He made chipped ham sandwiches on fresh white sliced bread with crusts removed, wrapping them neatly in doubled waxed paper so they wouldn't dry out. He bought a pint of coleslaw at a local German market, knowing this was one of her family's staples eaten with most meals. He arranged canned peaches in small individual containers so she'd eat some fruit. And of course some sweet things—chocolate-iced boxed cookies, four bottles of pop—two orange and two cherry, both ones he remembered she drank as a kid, along with bottle openers, several eating utensils, napkins, and a small table cloth to spread on the grass.

Although he had no appetite, he assumed Rosie had to be starving. It was already beyond lunch-time, and he had no idea when or if she'd eaten breakfast earlier that morning, but he decided that getting her out of the car and home where she could completely relax was far more important than his previously made plan of having a silly picnic. He slid over to the driver's side of the car to regain his composure, re-started the engine, put the car into gear, and sped towards the main road. As he drove along, a haunting young voice from the winter of 1934 resounded in his ears. "Father, I have violated the seventh commandment." No need to ask himself the abject question, "why?" He knew the answer…

Chapter 2

The Affable Eccentric

On Eve-Louise Pazwalski's calendar, the New Year began December first and culminated on Christ's birthday. From December twenty-sixth to November thirtieth, she was a working fool.

Today was the first of December, and for Cordelia Jones and "Miss Eve" this was the day an annual ritual would take place at one o'clock in the afternoon.

Cordelia was a patient of Eve's late husband Dr. Thaddeus Pazwalski. On her visit earlier in the month for an infection on her hand which refused to heal, she mentioned that her husband had recently passed away, and with five children to support she stressed her need to find work as a domestic and begged the doctor for his help. As luck would have it, timing was everything. Having found herself in the midst of a rapidly growing fashion design business and giving birth to their son Francis Michael, Eve was overwhelmed. Thaddeus contacted his patient Cordelia, who was still unemployed, and arranged for her to go by their home to meet his wife Eve. Thirty-two years later, an employee named Cordelia had evolved into a loyal and trusted family companion who ran Eve's home like she was the CEO.

Cordelia's favorite, like Eve's, was everything Christmas. She knew this holiday routine like the back of her hand. Cover the three-foot-square gaming table with the white-embroidered crisply starched and ironed Irish linen cloth. Place the sterling silver tea service in the very center and, to the right of it, the hand-painted English porcelain teacup and saucer covered in brilliant red poinsettias with matching dessert plate. The white oversized linen napkin on the left, two teaspoons, and tea caddy directly in front. On the left, the lime-green satin-glass Bavarian biscuit barrel filled with fresh tea cakes. To ensure these savories were freshly baked, and not day-olds, Cordelia would stop by the pastry shop on her way to work to guarantee these specialties had just come out of the oven. Cordelia stood back to admire the festively beautiful table she'd set and thought to herself how much Miss Eve deserved this entitlement she'd created for herself and those same two guests she invited year after year—"Peace and Quiet." Tea was served promptly at one o'clock.

Within the serene confines of her mind Eve reminisced about Christmases past and the positive impact her deceased husband's family traditions had on her life. She resented growing up with atheists for parents who celebrated neither birthdays nor anniversaries, but rather landmarks of their own demise that appeared to outsiders as borderline obsessive. Both were tenured professors at the University of Pittsburgh who earned their doctorates in foreign languages. Their peers knew them as intellectual know-it-all snobs who thought they'd eaten all the brains in the world. These pretentious partners were also somewhat manic, and they operated their lives with devotion to the number seven. Each mastered *seven* languages, in addition to English, a fact which was made bluntly known to anyone who visited their domain. Required by laws of decorum, guests and company spoke the language that was paired with the current day of the week, which was bulleted on a plaque in the entry way of their home. If a visitor didn't know the language of the day they could choose one they did know. English was never an option.

These self-absorbed loons never wanted children, but ended up having what they called an 'accident' they named '*Seven*,' Eve despised being called a number, and at age nine she renamed herself Eve-Louise. Her parents indulged this name change as long as she agreed to speak the language of the day. The older Eve got, the less willing she became to participate in their nonsensical games, so they gave her an ultimatum: speak the language of the day or be ignored. Eve chose the latter.

Their plan backfired when Eve decided to go on whether or not someone spoke to her. Through silence this precocious little girl discovered imagination, and from imagination grew unparalleled creativity. A whirlwind of energy propelled this child into a self-reliant young woman who earned a doctorate degree in fashion design from her parent's alma mater, the University of Pittsburgh. It was there that she met Thaddeus Michael Pazwalski, who was studying medicine. When they both finished school, they married and started a family. Eve hated being an only child and insisted they have at least five children. In the course of ten years they produced four girls and a boy. The girl's names all began with the letter *'S'* minus the *'even'*, done purposefully to rebel against the 'stupid label' her parents placed on her rather than give her a real girl's name. The Pazwalski girls were between eighteen and twenty-three months apart. Their first born, Selene-Marie, entered the congregation of the Sisters of Charity of Seton Hill. While there she earned a master's degree in nursing from Duquesne University. Stella-Marie, who was second in line, chose to follow in her older sister's footsteps by joining this same order, but she decided that elementary education was more to her calling. Sonja-Marie, the third child, chose to become a physician like her father and attended his alma mater, she never married nor had any children. Their youngest daughter, Sophie-Marie, became pregnant at fifteen and, against her parents' wishes, ran off and married the baby's eight-teen-year old steel-mill worker father, never finishing her education. She was her parent's second biggest disappointment, and they never let her forget it. Had it not been for Sophie-Marie, who remained happily married to John 'til the day he died, Eve and Thaddeus would never have been grand-parents. Their son was the last child the couple had, the one Thaddeus favored and adored above all else in life. Everything about this little tyke fascinated and entertained him, and he in turn indulged this child's every whim. Thaddeus' greatest dream was to witness the day his son would grow up to be a physician like him and his father before him. This too was not to be. Thaddeus died when Francis, whom they chose to call Frank, was five years old.

Eve's love and passion for her husband died years before his physical body did, but being a devout Catholic and convert, divorce was never an option. His death did not remove the bitterness she harbored for his involving her in altering and ruining their oldest daughter's life. Eve was never able to forgive him, and he in turn was unable to forgive himself.

Eve had decided early on that her chosen vocation would ultimately place her in the position of being considered one of the best and most successful business-savvy women on the east coast. She knew she'd made it to the top when those with large deep pocket-books flocked to her for those original creations she skillfully designed and put together bearing the 'Madame Seven' label. There were no patterns, she didn't need or use those—a body and fabric were her patterns and two days later the garment was ready for pickup or hand-delivery, whichever the customer preferred.

Eve had the equivalent of a warehouse in one single twelve-by-eighteen-foot room lined from floor to ceiling with built-in shelves and drawers stacked with fabrics from all over the world. Most imported hand-selected silks in excess were kept on bolts in the attic and held back exclusively for key customers—much like the buttons, silk threads, and trims. Occasionally a customer brought a fabric they'd purchased elsewhere, and if Eve thought it of inferior quality or poor design, she would refuse to waste her time with it. Before taking the first step with a customer, Eve did a two-minute pencil sketch of what she thought they had in mind. If they liked the design, she'd make two or sometimes three measurements at the most—hold the fabric she selected up against the client and with scissors in hand, cut out the pieces as they would go together. If Eve thought a particular fabric for a particular design was wrong and undeserving of her label and reputation, she dissuaded the customer's choice and foisted hers on them. The fashionistas on the "who's who list"—the "socialites of socialites" wore nothing but the *Madame Seven* label, which in turn garnered Eve unfettered access into the pocket-books of the upper echelons about town who clamored to spend big dollars to have that one-of-a-kind item that she produced.

When this five-foot-five inch darling of society entered a room, heads turned. Appearance was her number one criterion, and keeping up this status required a constantly revolving wardrobe few but Eve could afford. Consistently creating the aura of allure and mystique, leaving everyone guessing which personality or character would appear next, required discipline. Once her malodorous dresses emitted remnants of stale perfume or the slightest bit of body odor, she pitched them into the trash, claiming that laundering took the life out of fibers and made clothes hang like rags. Cordelia saw this behavior as sinfully wasteful, hastily retrieving those 'Madame Seven' items from the trash before the rag man came along singing his old jingle, "rags-a-lay, rags-t-day- got any rags-t-give away." Eve happened to look out the window one morning and saw Cordelia rooting out her old dresses from the trash. She knew exactly how to handle a delicate situation without embarrassing precious Cordelia. She schemed up a plan to place the worn dresses in shopping bags and suggested that Cordelia keep them or do whatever she wanted because she had caught 'the rag man' using her originals for handkerchiefs to wipe his old nag's wet snotty nose, something her reputation couldn't afford. Cordelia graciously accepted the offer—problem solved.

Through the years, as an entrepreneur and socialite, Eve developed the habit of denying herself nothing. If she made up her mind that she had earned it, then she owned it—from choices to mistakes. Eve never dallied. When she desired to follow a new path or devotion, she gave it her all. One example, when she adopted her husband's Catholic faith she embraced every facet of the doctrine from prayers to daily mass. She yearned to make Thaddeus's family's traditions ones she could celebrate with her children so they would understand the meaning of Christ's birth, to know and love Him, ultimately knowing why they were celebrating Holy Supper on Christmas Eve. Thankfully she had Cordelia because her lackluster aptitude for cooking made it impossible to create thirteen dishes traditionally served on Christmas Eve. This task required an organized and competent cook, which Eve was not. If Eve prepared any of the Christmas meal without Cordelia's assistance, a minimum of three or four dishes were guaranteed failures. On more than one occasion the burnt travesties were so unsalvageable they defied even Cordelia's hard stance against wastefulness, and were either thrown out or thrown over the fence to the neighbor's dog, Poochie.

Eve often turned these culinary mishaps into a guessing game she played with her three grandchildren. The idea was to compete for the prize of an extra box of candies by guessing the correct estimate of the number of dishes she made out of the thirteen. This was the children's second favorite part of coming to Holy Supper—pierogis slathered with sour cream was first.

The routine was always the same: After everyone took their place at the table, Eve stood up to make a brief Christmas speech. Unsure of how her thoughts would come across to each of them, she chose her words plaintively. When the time came this year, she would focus on the responsibility of being the family leader after their father died and the family had essentially fallen apart. Breaking her stoic pose at the gaming table, Eve withdrew a handwritten draft mentally noting a few minor changes for this year's speech. Satisfied with her message Eve turned her attention back to helping Cordelia prepare for the holiday menu and her guests.

Year after year, Eve paid Cordelia a substantial bonus to make sure every Christmas was the most memorable ever. The two of them would work side by side, tirelessly emptying the butler's pantry onto the twelve foot table displaying every piece of finery from silver to crystal. The dining room was always well ahead of schedule, leaving Cordelia free to attend to matters of her own for Christmas with her family.

Even though Frank and his mother shared the same house, their erratic work schedules rarely offered them an opportunity to spend time together, and when they did, it was always brief because Eve's communication with her son always reverted back to the same subject, "Frank, when are you going to settle down and find a nice Catholic wife?" This Christmas Eve Frank suggested the two of them make time for each other and sit down at the kitchen table, and share a pot of coffee before everyone arrived. They barely had time to finish their second cup of coffee and light the Christmas tree when the first guests knocked on the door.

Frank opened the kitchen door. The first one to greet him was his sister Sophie-Marie, who adored her little brother although Frank's feelings were not mutual. "Merry Christmas, little brother, you got a kiss for me?"

"That's John's job."

"Ma, Frankie won't give his sister a Christmas kiss."

Frank's mother didn't want this to turn into some over-blown issue and stopped it then and there. "For goodness sake Frank, you ought to be glad your sister even wants one of your kisses." John was standing right next to his wife Sophie, and the smell of whiskey nearly bowled Frank over. The evening was off to a bad start. Frank held his tongue and temper, wanting nothing more than to throw John out in the snow. Instead, he treated John like he was invisible and refused to welcome him into his mother's home, Christmas Eve or not.

"Good woman yer mum is. Never minds nothin' nobody does at her place. She's the only reason I put up wit'-you 'en-that ugly disposition. My old lady drags me over here every one of them Holy Supper dinners, and damn it, this the last time I'm ever settin' foot in this palace as long as you live here!"

"Good. Just be sure and remember that when you sober up."

"Must be nice t'live off yer old lady, a real honest ta' God Polish prince, standin' right here in front a me, imagine that. Suppose I oughta' be honored t'be standin' here next t'-Prince Frank in his own little kingdom who his mummy made fer 'im."

John put one folded arm behind his back and the other across his broad midriff as one would do to ready them-selves to bow, but in his drunken foolishness, lost his balance and fell on the floor.

This angered Frank and he verbally lit into John.

"You dumb son-of-a-bitch. You better not let me see you drink another drop of anything but water. Ruin Mom's special day and I'll throw your sorry ass out in the snow and watch you freeze to death." Under normal circumstances John never knew when to leave well enough alone and keep his big mouth shut; being inebriated only worsened matters.

"Hey mummy's fairy boy, get out of my hair and go find yer-self a boyfriend since you can't find no girls 't have yah'."

"John, stop, just shut up. Maybe if you'd learned when to keep your mouth shut you'd be the boss in that mill after twenty years and not just a stooge."

"I think Santie Claus musta' left a piece a coal up yer-butt." John then let out a laugh that was hideously artificial.

Frank couldn't stand John under normal circumstances; alcohol exacerbated those.

"Stupid ass dumb kid I was, knocked up yer'sister when we was kids 'en I ended up havin' t'marry 'er. Look 'et me killin' myself 'workin' in that damn hothouse steel mill, cookin' my ass so's I come home to sleep with a damn nun. This bein' the old-man-of-the-house is bullshit. Mebbe' that's why yer old man kilt his self. He couldn't take none a younze no more."

Frank moved toward the door. He was ready to throw John out into the snow.

"You son-of-a-bitch, don't ever talk about my father. He's none of your business."

Frank grabbed John's arm and twisted it behind his back. Sophie-Marie yelled for her mother, who immediately stepped between the two men.

"Shame on you two. Show a little consideration and respect if not for yourselves then for me. Please try not to ruin my favorite day." Eve took a position at the end of the kitchen table where she spoke loudly so everyone heard her. "You've all come today to have a good time, and until the rest of the family arrives, do just that."

Frank invited his mother to join him in the butler's pantry so they could talk privately. First he apologized for upsetting her then asked if she objected to his going out for an hour, assuring her he'd be back in time for Holy Supper.

Call it female intuition but Eve suspected he was calling on a lady-friend and suggested he not go empty handed. She opened the door on the upper cabinet in the butler's pantry and selected a large gilded red oval tin filled with fancifully decorated gingerbread-men and handed it to Frank. Her remark stymied him.

"I hope the young lady likes gingerbread."

This was a jaw-dropping moment. He tried to throw her off by giving her one of those wise-guy *are you nuts?* kind of looks wondering how she could possibly know who and why, and why would she say what she just did? He tucked the tin under his arm and hastened out the door.

Frank planned to use every second of his visit with Rosie making a mental note of the time and what he had to do before heading back home. He festered over the wasted fifteen-minute trolley ride to Millbauer's Hardware Store, which was unavoidable; walking would have taken longer.

When he got off the trolley he saw Rosie chipping ice from the sidewalk. He snuck up from behind and covered her eyes, asking her to "guess who." She told him her guessing skills performed much better inside where it was warm. Assuming he'd followed her into the store, she was surprised to see he'd gone back to finish the job of removing the remainder of ice from the sidewalk. Frank finished in no time, then raced inside hoping to find Rosie warming up in the dimly lit storage room which was directly above one of two furnaces the Gradel's used to heat their three-story brick and brownstone house and business. Everyone and anyone who came to the hardware store generally found themselves gravitated to this eight-by-twelve-foot room in the back of the store. All year 'round, and especially in winter when it was cold outdoors, customers enjoyed conversing with Rosie's father, finding him to be a walking book of knowledge regarding every item carried in his store. If a customer came with a question or problem related to home repairs, Hans Gradel was the man to ask. He coached customers on how, when, where, and why they should do things as he instructed. He was knowledgeable, easily understood, carried a huge inventory, and knew the hardware business better than any of his competitors. Shoppers sought him out over other merchants knowing that if old man Gradel at Millbauer's Hardware Store didn't have it, the item didn't exist.

When Rosie's mother was a child living in Germany, her family traditionally spent the day before Christmas at various orphanages doing charitable gift giving to those less fortunate. After Elsa arrived in America she continued her family's practice, devoting the day before Christmas to those children orphaned and housed at St. Michael's Orphanage across the street from the St. Michael's Church.

When Elsa mailed Frank his December work schedule and paycheck, she included her own personal schedule so he knew when he'd not be needed. This information opened the door for him to see the love of his life, if only briefly. All he needed was ten or fifteen minutes. He had something special he wanted Rosie to have.

Before entering the storage room he unbuttoned his over-coat, readying for the moment when he'd wrap all five foot two inches of Rosie Gradel inside. The thought of snuggling tight, embracing the love of his life with not so much as a hair's spacing between, was brief. Frank savored moments like these when he gently and playfully ran his fingers through her shoulder-length dark brown silken hair, always carefully brushing it back and away from her face so he could see her beautiful hazel-green eyes that reminded him of wolves-eyes, mysteriously piercing though him like she was capable of reading his every thought. She stood motionless as he ran the tip of his tongue along the very edge of her ear, tantalizing her. Passion overcame will until it suddenly occurred to Frank that Rosie's mother could be predictably unpredictable. He stopped his playful gestures. A curtain of silence fell between them. Frank explained his action and the fact that time was running out. He picked up the tin and handed it to her.

"I thought you might enjoy sharing some of my favorite cookies."

"Are you the baker?"

"Nah, that's girl stuff. One of my mom's customers trades baking for sewing. This mother of mine managed to get a doctorate degree, but for the life of her can't read or follow recipes. The only thing my mom ever baked was cupcakes, and nobody ate them unless she was standing right there."

"What flavor were these cupcakes?"

"Orange flavor, orange color, and buried in globs of orange icing. The icing never tasted half bad, you could lick it off, but the half-baked soapy-tasting cake-part made you want to throw up."

Frank went on to tell Rosie the story of how he and Greiner lobbed those cupcakes over the fence for old man Zeigler's dog Poochie, who could catch them mid-air. He admitted that as kids they never realized those miserable things gave Poochie diarrhea. It wasn't until old man Zeigler slipped and fell on the poop, then beat the poor dog within an inch of his life, that they quit thinking this was funny. It so happened on this their last episode, Eve overheard them laughing about what they'd done. She disciplined them and vowed to never bake another anything. Life moved on.

Frank gazed at Rosie and couldn't imagine life without her. "Rosie, marry me now!"

"I keep telling you I will, but only after I finish university and earn a doctorate like my folks and yours. Can you wait that long?"

"I'll be an old man by then and you won't want me."

She took him to task. Somehow he missed the whole point of an exchange they had made weeks earlier.

"Need I remind you of our trade old man?"

She took his hand and placed it over her heart. It was pounding.

"Feel how happy it is in there Frank? That's your heart, the one you traded."

He wrestles with the notion of rejecting this childlike game but chooses instead to humor her.

"Pretty tough heart you have inside there. Thing's thumping like hell! Think you can handle it?"

Rosie looks at him, her eyes staring straight into his, "Think? I know I can. Right now that old thing is being fed nothing but love and before long you won't even recognize it, Frank."

"Do you truly believe you can change a tough old nasty heart by feeding it nothing but love, or are you trying to justify the exchange?"

"Guess we won't know until you've tried mine for a while." She paused on the chance her next statement could backfire. "What if you decide you don't like having a young girl's heart and want yours back?"

Frank thought about what he wanted to say. He placed her hand on his chest.

"Feel this young heart beat. Its voice is strong, its performance impulsive, and its love boundless. I am becoming you."

His adoring response set her mind awhirl.

Frank reached behind his shirt collar and removed the quarter-sized St. Christopher medal, a confirmation gift from his mother. He placed it on Rosie and struggled to secure the clasp. She pushed him away

"What are you doing?"

"I'm giving this to you."

"I wouldn't think of taking your St. Christopher medal."

This particular medal had been worn by three generations of Pazwalski men, supposedly to keep them from harm's way. Frank doubted the validity of this medal that failed to protect his father.

He hoped by giving it away that fate would reward him by better protecting the new recipient.

"You're the most precious thing I have. Please accept this and wear it so I don't have to worry about anything ever happening to you."

"I'm sorry, I can't take it. You shouldn't give this to me or anyone." Frank was determined to give this medal to her and knew he had to choose the right words if he expected acceptance.

"This medal holds memories I need to forgive and forget. This new heart you've given me is changing the way I look at everything. Until you, my life was going nowhere. Please keep the medal. It belongs with that nasty old heart you're working so hard to change, they go together."

They moved from the back of the store to the hallway leading outside. She clutched the St. Christopher medal in her hand.

Frank sensed hesitation.

"You don't have to wear it. I just want you to have it."

He reached inside his coat pocket and handed Rosie a small box neatly wrapped in gold foiled paper and tied with thin green grosgrain ribbon forming a single bow. Instructions were for her to place it under the tree and pretend St. Nicholas delivered it. He kissed her on the forehead then dashed out the door. He didn't want to be late for Christmas Eve dinner.

Rosie went upstairs.

When she entered her father's room, he never stirred.

No sooner had she put Frank's gift under the tree, she heard the kitchen door slam. She snatched the box and ran to her room. The jingling contents increased her anxiety to the point at which rational thinking became frenetic. She had forgotten to lock the door.

Elsa checked on her husband then headed directly to Rosie's room. When she saw the door closed, she tried the knob. By this time Rosie had locked it. This angered Elsa to the point of raving like a lunatic and screaming at the top of her lungs.

Panic engulfed Rosie. She gathered enough where-with-all to grab the small jingling box and shove it far down deep along the inside arm part of the chair in that skinny space over-stuffed chairs have on each side camouflaged and hidden by the cushion. Rosie was scared out of her wits.

"Why is this door locked?" She couldn't speak.

"Answer me young lady. Locked doors mean one thing. You are up to no good."

Rosie hesitated, "I didn't realize I'd locked it."

"Don't lie to me. You're up to something, and I'm not sure what. Believe me, I've had about as much of your insolence and defiance as I can tolerate in one day."

Earlier in the day Rosie was half an hour late and Elsa found her excuse nothing more than an un-acceptable lie.

Elsa left to make a pot of coffee. Once it began to percolate, she turned down the gas to keep it from boiling over, and headed to the cellar to check on one of the furnaces. Her husband Hans complained the house was cold.

One of the many responsibilities Frank accepted when he went to work for the Gradel's was tending the furnace's two heating systems daily, except for holidays, those were Rosie's responsibility. Today she got caught up with Frank's visit, completely forgetting about tending the furnace's condition, possibly jeopardizing her father's current failing health, sending him into shock or worse for being too cold.

Because Hans had complained to Elsa about not being able to get warm, she raced to the basement and saw the fire was nearly out. Scooping up the tiniest pieces of coal from the floor of the bin she struggled to open the two foot square steel door with glass front, throwing the small pieces onto what appeared to be several slightly red coals she hoped would re-ignite the fire. She waited several minutes until small flames began to form before adding the bucket full of larger chunks sitting next to the furnace. Once she was certain the fire would last through the night she closed the furnace door, adjusted the damper, and headed up the stairs to wash off the coal dust.

Elsa believed that her precious hands were only for playing the violin. They were never to get dirty, do menial jobs, or, most importantly, be abused. She seethed at the mere sight of coal dust on her fingers. Elsa first wet her hands before using castile soap, gently washing each finger carefully to avoid irritating her skin.

The coffee she'd set on the stove finished percolating and was ready. She poured herself a cup of plain black coffee and went into the parlor where she found Rosie standing at the window watching the falling snow. Even though Rosie was deep in thought, she sensed her mother was behind her and turned around just in time to see Elsa with arm raised, ready to throw her hot coffee in her direction. Before Elsa could let loose with the liquid, Rosie yelled, "What are you doing? What are you doing?"

Dumbfounded to hear Rosie yelling at her; she backed-off. No one, much-less her own fresh-mouthed child, ever dared speak to her in that manner. At this point Elsa was barely able to stop herself from grabbing Rosie by the neck and ripping out her tongue. Between Rosie's flippant attitude and Elsa's suspicions that she was un-able to prove Rosie had been lying to her, drove her mad. "Rosie, you think I'm a fool and don't know what you've been up to lately, but one of these days I'll catch you in these lies of yours, and you will rue the day. Two things I despise are liars and the fools who tell them." With that said, Elsa deliberately threw her cup and saucer on the floor, shattering them to pieces.

After instructing Rosie to clean up the mess, Elsa headed to her studio, deliberately slamming the door shut for Rosie's benefit. For reasons known to Elsa alone, she chose to remain secluded in silence for the rest of the day. On any given day, she never missed an opportunity to play. Of her three violins, her mother's Stradivarius was the favorite. She believed this one in particular fed her soul, and that food sustained survival and produced energy so she could capture another day to play and fulfill the void in her life that nothing else could.

Frank arrived home just in time to take off his coat and grab a place at the table. His mother had timed her schedule around his arrival. Eve looked over at Frank and gave him a broad smile like she knew where he'd been and at the same time to let him know how pleased she was to have him there. Eve took a deep breath, stood tall, looked around at the table filled with those she loved, and let her thoughts flow from her heart.

"Some of you will remember only the bad roads, the bad choices I've made in each of your lives. But given enough time, each of you will get your turn. I seriously doubt you'll only traverse the right roads and make all the right choices. Life doesn't work that way. Thank you all for coming. Enjoy your dinner and God bless you one and all." Eve felt melancholy. Father George hadn't shown up for dinner. Something had to be wrong, he never missed Holy Supper. She needed to change her mindset. After all, this was Christmas Eve and she wanted everyone to be happy and enjoy their dinner. Her mind drifted back over happenings of the last few weeks. For some reason, she couldn't stay focused on anything for longer than a few minutes. She thought about her number one rule, no work after the first of December, and how she barely managed to meet that goal for one of her preferred customers, a well-heeled socialite, Julia Levinson. In early October she'd contracted Eve to make a magenta cashmere-wool coat with collar and cuffs trimmed in black-lamb's wool. Eve suggested she put twelve of her prized imported black onyx buttons down the front, and Julia knew to trust that whatever Eve did would look magnificent. There was one caveat: it had to be ready for Chanukah. Eve readily agreed to the task despite the impending holiday season, only later realizing a potential difficulty, the onyx buttons she promised were in the unheated attic. There was a time when going up there was exciting, but not of late. This oversized third-floor room was a mass of brown carton clutter randomly stuffed, stacked, and shoved into every nook and cranny. The conglomeration of innumerable lost and forgotten items included everything from old medical books to roller skates. Mind you, Eve knew every inch of that room and threw nothing away. Gifted with a photographic memory, she could pinpoint any item within minutes. Today's find, black onyx buttons from Belgium. The sun shone through the west-end windows, brightening the room but failing to affect the frigid temperature. The wool sweater she'd put on did little to keep her warm, but hastened her need to get down the stairs where it was warmer. In her hurriedness, she knocked over a stack of boxes and a pair of knee pants fell on the floor. When she held them up a two-inch roll of tightly wadded bills fell out of the front pocket. She put the bills back into the pocket and tucked everything under one arm. With her other arm free, she was able to hold onto the rail and descend the narrow staircase.

When she reached the bottom, an unusual sense of lightheadedness came over her. She let go of the pants and buttons, slowly easing herself onto the last step. Nausea and exhaustion immobilized her but she tried not to panic. Eve looked down at the pants and buttons. She slowly picked them up one at a time, carefully folding the buttons inside the pants before laying them across her lap. Thoughts rushed to mind of a young boy who'd been beaten up by a bunch of school-yard bullies in the church playground only to be brought home by her son Frank so she could clean him up and repair his only pair of tattered pants. These were those pants.

After that fateful day, little George Greiner had become a regular guest, coming unconditionally to love and be loved. In earlier years Eve cherished being left alone, but George's daily visits changed that. Each became ever mindful of the other's presence no matter where they were in this handsome brick twelve room house. A sewing machine needle bobbed up and down at breakneck speed while pages turned and young eyes raced across printed words. No thickness of walls could barricade the invisible bridges connecting these two souls. Out of silence came trust, out of trust came love, and out of love came devotion each had for the other. This once little boy was now the new parochial vicar at St. Michael's Church, which was within view of Eve's house. For years she questioned the wisdom of making a major change so late in life to leave St. Joe's. Eve's long-suffered-knee pain, fear of falling, shortness of breath, and frequent lightheadedness forced her to renege on this self-made promise and she reluctantly accepted the fact the time had come to join the church across the street. Contrary to what she expected, the Germans of St. Michael's eagerly accepted and welcomed her, especially when she expressed willingness to do vestment alternations without charge. Prior to her arrival, no one did anything for free. That was ten years ago—ten-years gone, poof, just like that, they melted into the seven-plus-decades of life she has presently achieved with no magic markers along the way to discern one from the other. Nothing marked this year lived or distinguished this day that she had already lived. It all blended together to form a huge gray cloud, deliberately separating her from her past. *After all*, she thought to herself, *God put that cloud back there for a reason, He doesn't want me to live in yesterday, He wants me to learn from it, but to live for the "today He's given," and it's just what I've managed to do in my life.* She sighed deeply and looked at her beautiful life and thought, *This Christmas Eve Holy Supper will one day, too, be behind that cloud.* Tomorrow would be Christ's birthday, and Eve couldn't wait to attend mass in the morning. She was exhausted and retired early.

across the river, gently bobbed up and down at [illegible] while [illegible] turned and young men raced across [illegible] to thick as if walls could barricade the invisible bullets [illegible] their own souls. Out of silence came grief, out of grief came love, and out of love came devotion each had for the other. The once little girl was now the new parochial vicar at St. Michael's Church, which was within view of Eve's house. For years she questioned the wisdom of making a [illegible] change so late in life to leave St. [illegible] Eve's [illegible] knee pain, fear of falling, shortness of breath, and frequent lightheadedness forced her to forego [illegible] promise and she reluctantly accepted the fact the time had come to join the church across the street. Contrary to what she expected, the Canons of St. Michael's eagerly accepted and welcomed her, especially when she expressed willingness to [illegible] without charge. [illegible] That was ten years ago—ten years gone, poof, just like that. Eve waited [illegible] with the [illegible] along the way [illegible] one from the other. Neither marked this year lived or [illegible] had already lived. It all [illegible] together to form a large gray cloud, deliberately separating her from her past. *After all,* she thought to herself, *[illegible]* She sighed deeply and looked at her beautiful life and thought, *This Christmas and Holy Supper [illegible]* Tomorrow would be Christ's birthday, and Eve couldn't wait to attend church in the morning; she was exhausted and retired early.

Chapter 3

Pipe Dreams

A cloud of incense combined with the smell of beeswax lingered throughout the church as alter-boys extinguished candles signaling the end of ten o'clock mass.

Except for a handful of parishioners in the back of the church waiting to express holiday wishes to the priest, the church emptied quickly. Eve Louise Pazwalski purposefully waited until the line had dwindled down to her and one other.

"Merry Christmas Father Greiner, what a beautiful service! There's not another priest anywhere who can use words and move souls like you. You are a true gift from God. No doubt you could talk the devil into chasing his tail and leaving us mortals alone. I told Monsignor Mueller he better never move you from this church as long as I'm alive."

Father Greiner's response was quick. 'What did he say when you spoke to him like that?"

Eve removed the red leather glove from her right hand and held it up in the air.

"See this?" She rotated her hand so he could see the front and back of it. "Let me tell you something Father George Greiner, if Monsignor expects me to continue fitting his vestments, he'd best stay in my good graces. Thirty-eight years of dealing with thirty-three buttons on his cassock while he jumps around like a five-year-old with pinworms is not easy. Besides, the job doesn't pay a red cent." Eve firmly believed church work was not a money-making proposition from which one took money but rather the place where people gave to support the church for its good works.

Eve looked back at Father George and pondered her son's disappointing and embarrassing behavior in rushing out of church without so much as wishing him a Merry Christmas. After all, they'd been friends since childhood, but then again, none of what her son did of late made any sense. She assumed it had everything to do with not having a woman in his life, at least not one she knew of. She couldn't stop thinking about the pretty young girl Father George introduced her to, the one standing next to her in line. Oh how she wished this could be the one for her son, but she realized these mindless ideas racing around in her mind were merely pipe dreams, and she knew pipe dreams always went up in smoke.

The priest glanced at Eve and noticed she seemed to be in a stupor of some sort. "Mrs. Pazwalski, I know what you're thinking!"

Eve leaned into the priest and he leaned down to better hear what she was whispering. "Father George, unless you're a mind reader, you couldn't possibly have any idea what I'm thinking. I'm just trying to find Frank a good Catholic wife before I leave this earth. Eve turned and faced the young woman still standing next to her. Rosie knew immediately she was Frank's mother. At this juncture, not knowing how to politely excuse herself, she decided to remain quiet and listen.

Eve slowly fanned her red leather glove back and forth against the palm of her left hand, trying to decide whether or not to say what was on her mind and in her heart. "Forgive me dear if I seem a bit presumptuous, but when I saw you during mass I knew God brought you to church so my son could meet you but he left before this could happen. I wanted so much for you to be the match that I've prayed for every day at mass, and unfortunately that son of mine needs an older woman to handle the likes of him, someone his age with experience—innocence will never work!"

Eve looked Rosie over one last time and spoke with agonizing torment and sadness in her heart, "Shame you weren't born ten years earlier. You'd be perfect!"

Eve's remark caught Rosie by surprise, and she wasn't quite sure what to say or how to handle the situation, so she politely excused herself and left. As soon as Rosie was out of sight, the priest informed Eve the young lady she was talking to was the daughter of the hardware store owner where Frank worked part-time. It was at that point when Eve buttoned up her coat, put on her glove, and hastened home in the lightly falling snow.

When she walked into the kitchen, Frank's greeting was not at all what she expected. "Good God, Mom, what took you so long? Church was over an hour ago."

"For goodness sake, I told you I wasn't leaving without wishing Father George a blessed Christmas, something I figured you'd want to do as well. By the way, too bad you rushed out so fast, Father George introduced me to that lovely young lady I pointed out to you in church. Why didn't you tell me you already knew her?"

"What's to tell?"

Eve had about as much of his sarcasm as she could stand for one day and reacted much the same way when she responded. "I don't understand where this nastiness is coming from. I'm afraid you'll never change." She paused, waited, and spoke her final thought, "so much for going to church today—it obviously didn't do you any good and neither do any of the prayers I've said all these years!"

"Mom, please. You're trying to meddle in my life again and that's what makes me angry. Worry about your own life." Frank thought about his actions and regretted upsetting his mother. "I'm sorry, Mom. How about we have a cup of coffee together and talk about something else."

The opportunity to spend time together rarely happened, so this invitation from her son was like a gift, the best one he could have given her....time.

Frank saw his mother's tenderness as an unnatural act. After a lifetime of living under her roof, their relationship developed into a peculiar emotional war which Frank feared losing. Throughout his life he positioned himself inside an invisibly drawn circle and armed himself with an imaginary stick defying anyone to enter. There were no exceptions to this refusal, not even his mom.

Eve's attempts to enter proved futile. The relationship between mother and son gradually fostered criticism and bitter feelings laced with fleeting moments of kindness that created a maniacal frenzy of excuses each made to the other. Theirs was an unorthodox kind of love that began shortly after his father died.

They decided to enjoy their coffee in front of the Christmas tree where they hashed over old memories, sought out favorite ornaments hanging on the tree, and exchanged non-offensive pleasantries. It was time well spent for both.

The rest of the day remained hers to do the one thing she rarely afforded herself—sitting quietly while her mind reminisced through the roads of her life. This was her gift to self and the part of Christmas Day she enjoyed most. Eve questioned her life and where it had gone. When she attempted to put some modicum of order to those years and make sense of them all. Once again that same gray cloud separated her from her past, placed there purposefully by God, not to rob her of those treasured memories—but rather as a stop-gap to leave life where it is: in the past. Eve picked out major events she could pin-point, some good, some better left forgotten, and the lessons she learned from those life-experiences, and now, tomorrow, the twenty-sixth of December, meant a new year was once again upon her.

Chapter 4

Farewell, Peace and Quiet

The date was February 20th. Frank came home and discovered his mother's lifeless body lying on the kitchen floor. Eve Louise Pazwalski died of a massive heart attack. The first person he called to inform of his mother's death was Father Greiner, followed by a brief call to Elsa Gradel informing her that his mother died, and either Rosie would run their family business alone or they'd have to hire someone else. He had no idea when or whether he would be able to return to help them.

Father Greiner took it upon himself to inform the school administrator, Sister Mary-Agnes about Rosie's situation. Because she would be graduating at the top of her class, it was mutually agreed that her daily assignments and final exams could be done after the store closed. Tests would be supervised and administered in the evenings at the convenience of the nuns whose classes she attended.

With everything squared away with the Gradel's, Greiner went directly to the Pazwalski house where he found Frank at the kitchen table, his arms folded and his head down.

"Frank, are you alright?"

Frank lifted his head. It was obvious he'd been crying.

George Herbert Greiner entered Frank's mother's world the day her son brought him home after a schoolyard brawl. This pathetic-looking waif looked and acted like someone's piece of trash. It was Frank's mom who masterfully mended threadbare pants, remedied a broken spirit, and managed to give him worth. That was the day they became kindred souls, something Frank never knew or understood.

The saddest part of all was that death had robbed Eve of ever knowing the demure child-like woman with outstretched arms who managed to get inside Frank's circle. The good Catholic girl Eve met in church, the young one she claimed could never handle the likes of her son, did in fact fulfill her lifelong dream.

"Frank, I don't know how I'll go on without your mom, she was the only person who ever loved me, the only one."

"What are you talking about? You have an entire flock of sheep who love you, who hang on your every word."

In trying to comfort Greiner, who was an emotional wreck, Frank's choice of words fell on Greiner's ears as chaotic, nonsensical, and meaningless. Greiner needed a listener, nothing else. He needed Frank to be quiet and listen, but Frank's insensitivity to others' problems and his inability to cope with what he'd see as weaknesses, made him an asininely poor confidant who didn't know when to shut up.

"Frank, please be quiet. I need to talk. I have things to tell you, things I need off my chest and out of my mind. Please, please…don't talk."

Startled by this sudden disparate outburst from Greiner, Frank clammed up.

"Only three people knew the horrible things going on at my house…me, your mom, and God."

Greiner hated all the dirty filthy secrets. It was time Frank learned the truth. "The worst times of my life were spent inside a stupid closet. Mother would pass out and forget she locked me in there. She'd bring home strange men who cursed and beat her. I'd have to cup my hands over my ears or stick my fingers in them so not to hear. Most times I slept like a contortionist, praying she'd remember to let me out after these bums left. Sometimes she did, sometimes she didn't. If I put up a fuss or made any noise when she was forcing me in there, she'd beat me. I learned to do what I was told."

"Lucky she didn't get me for a kid. I'd have put that broom up her ass that she used when she chased us kids out of your yard."

"Please, let me talk. You need to know how this thing between your mom and me began. One day I showed up here with a bruise on my head and your mother asked what happened. When I told her, she was livid. The next time I came, she handed me a skeleton key to hide. Eve filled my belly with food and my heart with love."

Frank felt like a rotten jerk. He recalled the countless times he had taunted Greiner while they were growing up, calling him names like 'moocher' and telling him to go home and eat his own food. Frank knew full well his mother never saved leftovers. Matter of fact, most times she either threw them into the trash or fed them to the neighbor's dog. He questioned the sense in behaving the way he did all those times with Greiner. Jealousy, it was all about the 'curse of jealousy'. Frank knew early on that his mother and Greiner shared something very special, and rather than try to squeeze into what he saw as their "little circle for two," he chose to close himself off inside a circle of his own where he could decide who got in.

Frank wondered why his mother didn't send leftovers home with Greiner. At this point it didn't matter one way or the other. Ashamed by his miserable disposition and attitude in the past, Frank was more than happy to hear Greiner taking up the slack with his incessant talking.

"We had one bed. It was hers. The stinking smelly sofa was my bed except when there were no strange men for her to sleep with. On those nights she insisted I sleep with her. She claimed she was afraid.

"I frequently have this repeat nightmare. Horrible odors emanate from my bed. I get up and sniff it. I hear laughter, and sometimes it gets so bad, I can't stop it. I try covering my ears. Still it won't stop. I can't sleep. So I pray and pray and pray and eventually I fall asleep."

"You poor son-of-a-bitch, you can't be serious. What's this smell like?"

"Rotten flesh and urine, the whole thing nearly drives me mad. Sometimes the only way I can sleep is by going into a closet and curling up in a ball. Please don't tell anyone. They will think I'm insane and they'll put me away."

Frank's friends, Ray and Charlie, told him repeatedly that old lady Greiner was a drunken whore. He didn't believe them. If only he had, he might have been able to help save his friend Greiner.

"God is my salvation. I'll be eternally grateful to Him. My mother's insanity placed me in harm's way, and His divine intervention sent you along to take me home to your mother. Do you realize that Frank, or are you too stupid to put this all together?"

"Greiner, ever ask your God why He gave you such a nut case old lady?"

"Please Frank, this is difficult enough." Greiner began to sob. This in turn made Frank extremely edgy. In his world real men didn't cry, or if they did, no one saw them. Frank regained the conversation hoping to calm his friend.

"Greiner, think about this. Times were bad. She's got this extra mouth to feed, couldn't do a real kind of job, so she uses the bed. I'm not saying what she did was right, but maybe it was the only way. I don't expect you to understand what went on, you were just a little kid, but pay me the courtesy of listening, and stop interrupting."

One thing always bothered Frank, and he saw this as the perfect time to ask it.

"Why the hell did you ever have to go and be a priest?"

"I was told to. I had no choice."

"Sounds like you."

Greiner hated the seminary, but ended up a natural for the priesthood. The day he found out he was returning to St. Michael's he knew God had heard his prayers. Little did he know but his return to St. Michael's had little or nothing to do with prayer, but everything to do with his mother and the Monsignor.

In his younger years Monsignor Mueller was an affable parish priest who had a wandering eye and a lustful attraction for beautiful women. He had a sizeable family trust which supported his addiction.

George's mother was never a regular attendee of any Catholic church in particular, instead randomly picking and choosing when and where she'd go. During lunch hour, the subject of churches came up, and one of the stenographers she worked with suggested that she try attending St. Michael's ten o'clock mass to hear Father Mueller who gave great sermons. Ursula went that following Sunday. Not only did she find him alluring, she made it her business to know the exact times he said mass. After mass she'd linger behind, finding ways to engage him in conversation. He found this tempestuous beauty irresistible.

One Sunday she casually mentioned the matter of having issues with the church. He broached the idea of calling on her later that evening so they could resolve this matter. When she asked for a time, he asked that she be flexible. She waited up half the night and was just about to fall asleep when he tapped on her window.

Weeks turned into months with sporadic visits at unpredictable hours of the night. She figured he was using her, but seeing him was worth more than being used. This fatiguing schedule nearly got her fired from her secretarial job. She informed him that the affair had to end. He began bringing her cheap little trinkets and liquor to drink. The trinkets excited her, but she was unaccustomed to alcohol and hated what it did to her mind and body the next day.

The only endearing words to cross his lips were those he used when he wanted her to drink. "My black raven beauty, take a little sip and make Father happy." She would gulp it down. He'd refill it, then sit back and coyly fondle her. His sadistic mind mused over how he would take her....gently or forcefully.

In the beginning she believed submission was the way to his heart. It wasn't. His words, like his promises, proved worthless.

Seven months into their relationship, Ursula became pregnant. When she told the priest, she figured, he of all people,—a priest, would be willing to help her resolve this problem. She didn't want a baby either, but it happened. Truth be told, he was partially responsible for her being in this condition. At the very least, she expected him to show some degree of understanding, but in her wildest of dreams she never imagined he'd turn violent and yell at her demanding she "get rid of it, get an abortion." Sheer panic consumed her. With nowhere to turn, no-one to help solve this horrendous ordeal, she called her cousin Trude, who was a nurse at Mercy hospital. Growing up, she and Trude were cousins and best friends, and now her only living relative. She was certain, Trude of all people, would be willing to help. But instead, Trude ordered her out of her house, and, in no uncertain terms, told her to never come back. The two never spoke after that.

On her way home from Trude's, Ursula had stopped at the Brookline Pharmacy and pleaded her case to the pharmacist. Whatever he sold her to abort didn't work. She found herself at the mercy of none other than Father Mueller, who was more than happy to arrange for her to have that abortion. He made, paid for, and drove her to the appointment, but she ran out of the exam room the minute the doctor entered.

To her chagrin, when she exited the door at the back of the abandoned brick building where she'd been taken to have the abortion performed, Father Mueller was waiting. No sooner had she stepped outside, she knew by the look on his face, he knew she didn't have the abortion. Fearing grave danger, she turned around planning to run, but in what seemed like a split second, he flew into a raging fit of anger, coming up from behind and forcefully shoving her down the fourteen concrete steps running adjacent to the door she had just exited. The element of surprise caught her off guard. She bounced and tumbled over and over unable to stop. When she hit bottom, she lay there motionless. He raced down the steps hoping she was dead, but when he saw she wasn't, he kicked at her belly several times, causing her to scream in pain. His face turned beet red. The very sight of her enraged him to the point where sweat poured from his brow and into his glassy, protruding eyes. Wrath and indignation fueled his heartless soul. He bellowed like a castrated bull, believing this pregnancy was a strategic move on her part to bring him down for not marrying her. "You useless street whore—make another sound and I'll kick out the rest of those teeth you have left." He braced himself against the concrete wall and readied himself for one last final kick.

One of the many luxuries the Mueller family indulged their only child with while growing up were custom hand-made Italian leather shoes. Born severely pigeon-toed, his parents believed these specially made shoes would straighten out his feet, but they never did. Affordability was never an issue, and once his feet became accustomed to those he wouldn't consider wearing anything else. This time instead of the shoes being a luxury, they were a curse. Made of extremely soft leather, the soles were slightly thicker than those ballerinas wear. He approached Ursula, intending to give her lifeless body one last forceful kick, one that would cripple her enough that she'd never make it up those stairs, but instead be found dead by some vagrant. As he pulled back his right leg, he lost his balance, striking the entire frontal part of his foot on the concrete step, injuring both the ball of his foot and several toes. The pain was so excruciating that, he was barely able to ascend the fourteen steps to escape his futile attempt to wipe Ursula and her baggage from his life.

When he got to the top, he never looked back to see whether Ursula was dead or alive. She remained lying there throughout the day and on into the evening surveying the surroundings of feces, broken bottles, and trash vagrants had left behind. This hell-hole she found herself in left her with no choice but to stay put for the time being. She felt the back of her head and discovered a lump the size of an egg, obviously the result of tumbling down fourteen concrete steps. Both knees were cut and bruised, and her right wrist was definitely broken. She doubted she'd ever be able to gain enough strength to crawl up those fourteen steps. Fortunately, when he had shoved her, she had a pocketbook slung over her left fore-arm. Otherwise, she would not have had money and thus no way to get home. Ursula's head began to throb like a bad tooth-ache, and all she wanted to do was sleep. She put her purse under her head and slept until morning.

The sun rose as it had done every other day in her life, but this was one day that she wished she'd died in the night. No such luck. Intense pain seized her body and all she could think of was stopping it. At this point she had no choice but to get up those fourteen steps. Ursula surveyed the dire situation in which she found herself, and decided it was only insurmountable if she chose to stay put and die in this garbage heap. The cruelty of what Mueller had unjustifiably done fueled sufficient anger for her to begin the ascent. Imagining each step as a win against Mueller, she took her time, and by midmorning she had reached the top. Overcome with exhaustion, she had no choice but to move slowly and deliberately. She stumbled to the main street corner hoping to catch a trolley ride home, but suddenly she felt faint. Sheer resolve and fortitude proved to be just what she needed to grab onto the round steel rail running alongside the walkway. An older gentleman was walking by and saw her struggling to stand. He couldn't help noticing her debilitating condition and asked if she needed help. Ursula was in so much pain she began crying and was unable to speak. The old man took hold of her left arm and assisted her over to a nearby bench where he insisted she sit and get hold of herself. He pleaded that she see someone for the broken wrist and offered to take her to a nearby doctor. She told him she had no money, but he assured her that if she'd come with him, he would pay for the visit. The doctor's office was nearby. After a thorough physical, the cuts and bruises were cleaned and covered, the broken wrist was reset, and pain medication dispensed. Before the doctor released her, he told her he wanted to see her again in two weeks. The gentleman who'd brought her to the doctor's office not only paid for the visit, just as he'd said he would, but had also paid for two follow-up ones as well. Ursula was never able to thank or ever repay him. He left no name, no nothing—he just kept his word.

This pregnancy cost her two things: a well-paying secretarial job, and the man she loved. After George was born she worked as a domestic because she had no one to leave the child with during the day and she couldn't afford to pay for his care. Working as a domestic enabled her to take him with her. George was a well-behaved, quiet child who loved books and would sit still for hours at a time. Working as a domestic had other advantages. Ursula found that she could steal food and money from employers that they never missed. Desperate motives required desperate actions. At one point she asked Father Mueller for financial help. His solution was simple. "Put the kid in an orphanage. Then go kill yourself."

Father Mueller's name was on the monsignors' list. He had become an embarrassment to the church but no one wanted to address the matter. A move was imminent.

After he assumed his new position, Ursula Greiner tried to see him. It became impossible for anyone to get past the bulldog assistant who guarded his door. He remained steadfast in his unwillingness to see or acknowledge her.

Frank listened as Greiner recounted all of this. After a moment, Greiner picked up where he had left off.

"Mother never celebrated anything. No, I take that back, she celebrated my birthday every year by opening a new bottle of whiskey and drinking it all before two in the afternoon—the hour she claims I began ruining her life.

"My fourteenth birthday began like birthdays past, but by mid-afternoon this particular birthday, she quit drinking, got dressed, and claimed she had an important meeting with Monsignor Mueller."

When Ursula Greiner drank, a wicked woman with false courage emerged. This particular day she drank only half the bottle of whiskey before visiting the man she believed once loved her. A horrible confrontation ensued, and Ursula threatened to disclose to the bishop, or anyone else who'd care to listen, all the sordid details of what he'd done.

Greiner quoted his mother's parting words to the Monsignor.

"It's time you faced your responsibility and got this son of yours, not the 'son-of-the bitch' you've called him his entire life, into the seminary. If you know what's good for you, you'll do it."

Frank's suspicions proved right....Greiner had never wanted to be a priest. It was his old lady's idea.

"Frank, did you hear a word I said?"

"I'm listening, I'm listening!"

Several weeks before her son's ordination, Ursula forced her way back into the Monsignor's office with a manila envelope under one arm and a loaded pistol in her purse.

She laid her purse on the desk, removed the pistol, and placed it firmly against his head. She forced him to open the envelope. The contents divulged personal information he'd mistakenly left behind on one of those 'dark-of-the-night visits'. Disclosure would be his ruination. He filled out the required paper work requesting Father Greiner be sent to St. Michael's.

The only reason Ursula Greiner wanted her son returned to a local church was so he could financially take care of her. She believed he owed her that for being born.

After he finished his tale Greiner's eyes glazed over like he was in a trance. He stared straight ahead.

Frank stood up and paced back and forth. One thing still troubled him.

"Greiner, answer me this: are you happy?"

"I don't need a closet key and have my own bed. What more does a fellow need?"

Frank got the message and smiled. Greiner stood up and hugged him.

Both men were exhausted and agreed to call it a day. Frank escorted Greiner back to the rectory, where the door closed behind him and his old pal Greiner became Father Greiner, someone Frank once knew.

Frank was too wound up to asleep. He meandered up the street, chancing the neighborhood tavern might still be open. A couple of good stiff drinks were what he needed.

It was after midnight. The bar-keeper was locking up when Frank arrived and forced his way in. The bar-keeper said the place was closed, but Frank ignored him and insisted on a beer with a double whiskey chaser. Frank gulped down the shots and sat back to drink his beer.

The barkeeper noticed he had finished.

"Hey, Frankie boy, you wanna' drink, or you gonna' get the hell outta' here and go home where you belong and let me do the same? I'm tired 'en hungry 'en sure can't make money on one person nursin' drinks like a baby suckin' a boddle all night. Let's finish up 'ere boy, and get on home where you belong. Oh, by the way, hear your mum died. Sorry 'bout that."

For some reason the barkeeper's mutilation of the English language reminded him of his brother-in-law John, and, he laughed hysterically.

"What dah hell's s'damn funny, you stupid son-a-bitch?"

"You, you look like my brother-in-law John, and he's pretty stupid. Even sounds like you when he talks. So you think I'm nursin' this drink like a baby suckin' a boddle. You must be one of them damn big boys who drinks out of the glass ... right?"

Frank got off his stool, walked behind the bar, and helped himself to a bottle and a short glass. He poured in some whiskey.

"Now, let me see you drink out of a glass big boy, c'mon, show me how it's done."

The barkeeper had no choice but to drink the glass of whiskey and pray Frank would leave. Instead, Frank poured a second glass and insisted he drink it as well.

Frank filled the third glass. The bar-keeper figured he'd play along with Frank's stupid little game. He sat on the floor behind the bar and feigned inebriation. The effects of drinking two glasses of alcohol made him feel flushed. The third one put him over the edge. Smart aleck Frank decided to mimic the barkeeper.

"Next time think twice before you try and throw out a quiet, peaceful customer who sips his beer, then leaves. I think you'd rather have a real drunk like yourself lying on the floor drinkin' that shit by the glass-full than a quiet peaceful gentleman like myself sippin' that boddle. If that's what you want, you got it! A drunkard lying on the floor probably shit his pants from drinkin' too much whiskey too fast out of a glass 'en lost control of his asshole. Hope ya' lernt somethin' tonight you stupid son of a bitch!" On that note, Frank opened the door and left.

He walked up the street like the bully Frank could be when he'd been drinking, smirking to him-self because he felt he'd taken control of a testy situation when the barkeeper chose to harass him without justification. Sobriety would tell another story.

As he approached the gate leading to the alleyway along-side the house he noticed a black wreath in the center of the front door, and draped up over the top of the door frame and cascading down on each side, was a sheath of black satin fabric. The sullen presentation spoke finality.

The following morning the alarm sounded. He imagined his mother's voice. "Son, I know you heard the alarm because you shut it off. Get up. Don't want your day off to a bad start do you?"

Eve saw tardiness as a lack of self-discipline. When his alarm went off she expected him out of bed. From this day forward, the dependable yell from the bottom of the stairs would only be an echo in his mind. He got dressed and left to meet with Greiner, whose help he needed in making arrangements for Eve's funeral.

An eerie feeling came over him as he walked up the street to the rectory. Despite every attempt to disregard Greiner's inconceivable cockamamie stories, he believed it all. Greiner answered the door and ushered him directly into the kitchen. They spent an hour sorting through the myriad of details for Eve's funeral. Frank checked his watch and saw it was nearly time for the undertaker to arrive. He thanked Greiner and left.

When he entered the kitchen, Sophie-Marie and John were at the table arguing, their mouths were full of food. Sophie-Marie insisting her mother wanted to be laid out in the front room, John claiming she told him she wanted to be laid out in one of the fancy funeral homes on Main Street. Frank welcomed the opportunity to leave them to their own notions of what should and shouldn't be done, he thought to himself, *they get no vote*. The only redeeming part of his mother's passing was never facing another encounter with John. Frank went up to his room. He needed to be alone.

"Soph, yer old lady's dead 'an she don't give a shit 'bout nothin' er where da' hell ya' put 'er. Nah shut up, 'en don't start on that bidness 'a openin' the front door again."

Spring began the day Sophie-Marie started nagging John to go to her mother's to try and re-try opening the front door. As far back as Sophie-Marie could remember the solid oak front door never opened. She refused to believe John when he said the door was swollen, got varnished over too many times, and was now and forever permanently sealed shut. No matter how many spring-times went by, no matter how many times Sophie-Marie sent John to try and fix her mother's front door, the argument remained the same, the door remained the same—sealed shut.

"It ain't never gittin' open'd unless God His-self comes an'brings a shit load a mean ass devils with them forks, or d'fairies come wit-'dose magic wans. No way nobody's goin' t' loose up that door." Sophie-Marie constantly reminded her mother that it was ignorant to make guests come round the back like hired help. Eve re-assured her daughter, time and again, that nobody seemed to complain but her and John. Eve Louise Pazwalski would do in death as she did in life ... make her last visit home through the back door. She liked it that way.

The undertaker and crew arrived promptly at noon attempting to carry Eve's casket through the iron-gate that opened into the six-foot-wide alleyway running along-side the house, but the casket wouldn't fit through the narrow gate. The undertakers backed up and set the casket down on the brick sidewalk. Sophie saw the whole thing and raced inside yelling like a washer-woman.

"John, come quick 'en do something.' Mum's out here layin' on the sidewalk and it's snowin' all over her. She'll freeze out there 'less you git the gate down real fast."

As nature would have it, a light snowfall blew in and out within twenty-minutes, barely leaving a trace of having come and gone except for the water spots left atop Eve's dark mahogany casket. It was as if God Himself had sent Mother Nature to ceremoniously sprinkle holy water upon her remains.

Eve put things out of her mind over which she had no control. The day her daughter disappointingly quit school to run off and marry John and take on his name, she also took on his disgusting manner of speech. When Eve corrected her daughter, she was told to mind her own business because a neighbor told her she sounded southern.

Eve saw her family twice a year, Easter and Christmas. It was all she could stand.

Eve Louise Pazwalski's dying wish wasn't to be viewed out on the sidewalk. John struggled to get the ornate gate down, but every time Sophie-Marie opened her mouth and yelled at John he banged his cold fingers with the hammer. Frustration, combined with serenades of his wife's non-stop talking, became increasingly annoying.

"Soph' if ya' don't shut up and let me git this damn fence duhn, I'm gonna' hit choo' wit' dis hammer. Mebbe that'll shut'cha up! Aft'r I'm dun-wit choo, I'm goin' after that lazy good-fer-nothin' spoilt' brother of yerz and kill the little bastard. Younz both is a royal pain in my ass."

The outside gate opening presented the first set of problems, Frank's sisters the second. Between his wife's nagging and Stella-Marie's incessant mumbling, John lost it.

"What you over there bubblin' 'en mumbling 'bout anywayz? Speak up Stella so's we can all hear ya'. Sounds like yer sayin' them ros-rees a'ready 'en we ain't even open'd her box.'"

"I said, why do you people think they have funeral homes? We ought to forget this whole dumb arrangement and take Mom there." Frank jokingly intercepted the conversation and suggested they lay their mother out in the kitchen so John and Sophie wouldn't have far to go when they got hungry.

Eve's casket ended up in the dining room directly across from the Christmas tree she had postponed dismantling. Everyone except Frank agreed the ugly thing had to come down.

Frank pushed himself to the front of the group. "Anybody touches one bulb, one needle under that tree, one damn anything on it, I promise, they'll be in that casket with Mom. If any one of you doesn't understand or believe me, dare touch the tree and you'll understand plenty."

As gentle and nice as Frank could be with Rosie, he could be equally as mean and nasty with the rest of the world. This was one of those times everyone steered clear and kept quiet.

Eve enjoyed Christmas more than anything else in life, and spending her final hours on earth peacefully resting in front of her beloved Christmas tree was exactly what she would have wanted.

Two weeks after the funeral, Frank decided to return to his part time job at Gradel's Hardware Store. Rosie expressed her condolences and Frank told her everything except the crippling affects his mother's dead tree had on him. The inordinate undertaking of dismantling it alone was impossible. He had to somehow convince Rosie to help him.

To the day Eve died, she had refused to take down her tree. It stood in life as she stood in death, bare-naked and alone. A skeleton stripped of the flesh that once had life. As quietly as each needle fell is exactly how she stepped into death. When Frank looked at the tree he saw his mother's life as scattered piles to be gathered up and disposed of. His inability to separate the ugliness of death without this once vibrant soul from where his life began disheartened him. For the first time in his life, he questioned how he would recover and move on.

Somewhere in Frank's earlier conversation with Rosie she mentioned having an English exam later in the evening. His mental and emotional frustration over the death of his mother completely drained his where-with-all, especially when it came to the finality in having to deal with the dismantling his mother's tree. He couldn't bring himself to touch the thing much less take it down and throw it out. By inviting Rosie to see his mother's extensive collection of Christmas ornaments, Frank figured it would be the perfect ruse to get her to take down the tree for him, something he was incapable of doing on his own. Fortunately Rosie took the bait and agreed to come. She arrived on time and fore-warned Frank that the visit would necessarily be brief. With not a minute to waste he asked if she'd mind helping him. Little did he know, but the chance to handle each and every ornament excited her. She volunteered to remove if he did the wrapping and boxing up. Frank worked alongside Rosie packing as fast as he could. "Hope you realize we're putting these all away for you and the day you become that perfect little Catholic wife Mother always wanted me to marry." Rosie suspected this talk was idle chatter, masking a chore he'd put off because he couldn't do it alone, but after all it was March, the tree was dead, and just plain ugly. Time to move on…

Rosie organized the various ornaments into groups, placing the familiar bride's collection in the center of the table knowing each one of the twelve belonging to this group not only had an individual story to tell but also belonged in a special box with a designated slot specifically designed to fit each ornament. Before wrapping the last one, she stopped to share a bit of German folklore she hoped Frank might enjoy.

"See this rabbit?"

He looked at it and saw one more thing to be stashed away.

"Have you any idea what the significance of having this rabbit on your tree means?"

"Well if it's to eat all those dead needles on the floor, he's done a lousy job."

"Frank Pazwalski, how could you joke about this sweet little fellow who represents the one thing in life none of us could live without?"

What's that?"

Rosie handed the ornament to Frank.

"Hope."

He put out his hand but wasn't paying attention. In a split second the glass rabbit hit the edge of the dining room table and shattered. Minute pieces flew in every direction. Rosie stared at the shattered image lying among the needles. She was visibly upset.

"Rosie, you look like I killed that rabbit on purpose or something. It's just an ornament, and if it bothers you that much I'll buy you a bunch of them next Christmas. Think about it this way, that old rabbit is one less ornament we'll have to put away in the future. Until you pointed it out, I had no idea it existed." His words fell on deaf ears. She could not dispel her anguish.

For reasons known only to Frank, he resisted removing the needle-less dead Christmas tree from the house. Until he had Rosie by his side for some kind of moral support to help him, he was paralyzed to do anything. He could not dismantle this thing. His mother's last remaining visual imprint clung onto every fiber of his being. All of a sudden, Rosie saw sadness in Frank's eyes, and like an explosion, pent up emotions spewed out.

"Rosie, for most of my life, I trusted no one. Not even my mother. Rather than allow her to bathe me in love and tenderness, I chose to run from her. I bathed myself in the murky waters of pain. I wallowed in pools of crap and swallowed mouthfuls of bitterness. I practically drowned, and now believe I would have had it not been for her constant love and prayers. I refused to see things and people in life the way they really are, good and well intentioned. You are some kind of holy angel sent by God to touch my heart and save me. To think I never believed in Him. What a horse's ass I was."

Rosie's instructions were to be home before the eight o'clock whistle blew. This daily occurrence alerted the town's people of the time every hour on the hour, ending at midnight. She glanced at the clock on the wall and saw there was no time to waste, ten minutes 'til the eight-o'clock whistle.

"Speaking of angels, I'm sure glad this one has only eight blocks to fly instead of all the way to Heaven. Time's up you old devil—I'm leaving." Rosie was out the door and gone.

Eve willed the large brick twelve-room house, including all antiquities and contents, to Frank. Additionally she left him all of her jewelry, investments both acquired and inherited, a substantial bank account, and a gold coin collection that once belonged to her husband's grandfather.

Frank's four sisters, Selene-Marie, Stella-Marie, Sonja-Marie, and Sophie-Marie, were willed Eve's needle and thread collection, along with countless boxes of buttons. Additionally, each was left a sewing machine. They took little pride in personal appearance and refused to sew on buttons or mend torn clothing. She saw this as laziness and believed it was her obligation to see that they had the necessary tools to do these things for themselves after she was gone. None of her daughters ever claimed those items. They remained a part of the attic clutter.

Additional specifics were noted, exclusions made. Her Christmas ornament collection, along with items the girls never expressed an interest in, were left to specific individuals; George and Cordelia among those. Eve's relationship with her daughters consisted of occasional visits Christmas day, Easter Sunday, and when they needed or wanted something. The two oldest girls who'd entered the convent never came home. She found them all annoying.

Chapter 5

The Proposal

Frank opened the store, restocked shelves, and unpacked inventory. Rosie could have been late any other day, but not today. He was weeks behind in his own business of window dressing, and the merchants who used his services were now threatening to take their business elsewhere. She looked horrible. No hello, no nothing. Just two words, "I'm pregnant, I think I'm pregnant."

Frank figured something else must be wrong. No one ever got pregnant doing it one time, pregnancy didn't happen that way. And furthermore, he questioned why hadn't she mention this to him sooner. To avoid further upset and controversy, he withheld an opinion. They needed time alone where he could explain everything he felt she apparently didn't understand, but not now and not here. Contrary to what she thought, this was a serious matter he definitely wanted to address, but he was pressed for time and asked that they discuss it later. He tried to recall the date when they'd met in the church basement. Nothing made sense. She never mentioned this at Christmas-time or when they took down the tree after his mother's death.

Rosie was despondent. She trembled. She paced the floor, trying to continue without crying but couldn't. "I'm terrified, when mother learns I'm pregnant she'll send me away somewhere where you'll never find me and I'll never see you again."

"Please don't fall apart on me, please, not now. Your mother isn't going to send you anywhere without me unless she plans to kill me first. We'll work this out. Tomorrow I'll take the morning off and take you to my family doctor. He will examine you and tell us what is going on. This could be nothing at all."

Right now the notorious irrepressible ladies man had fate breathing down his neck. The last thing he needed was for Rosie to be pregnant. Not now. The more she paced the more hysterical she got. "One night, one stupid choice, and my life is ruined."

"If you are pregnant, we'll get married. It will just be sooner than we planned. This isn't the first and won't be the last time a woman had a baby without being married."

"You don't get it. I don't care about anyone else. I care about me."

Frank tried to allay Rosie's fears. "I've done plenty of things in my life I'm not proud of, but one thing I've never done is break a promise. I will never ever do that. I would die first."

Without hesitation, Frank grabbed her forearms and pulled her small frame tightly against his, kissing her repeatedly about the face and head. Between sobs she made him promise he would make the doctor's appointment first thing in the morning. Frank believed as long as he never lost her or her love, what-ifs didn't matter.

A scheduled appointment confirmed she was indeed pregnant. Outside the doctor's office Rosie fell apart. "Why has God done this to me? Why did I do that with you that night?"

Before Frank could open his mouth, she grabbed the front of his shirt and tried to shake him. "I hate you Frank Pazwalski and never want to see you again."

"Rosie, get ahold of yourself. You're carrying our baby. I don't want anything to happen to you. Tell me you understand what I'm saying!"

Her demeanor changed. The crying stopped. She went into a fit of rage about how her mother warned her time and again about men's illusive methods of seduction, and now blamed herself for not heeding those warnings. "Mother was right. Oh God, she was right. I didn't listen and look what happened. My world is crashing down around me and I can't stop or push it away. I want to die. You hear me Frank. I want this baby in me to die, too. I hate it. I hate it. I hate you, too!" She reached down and caught the inside hem of her dress and blew her nose. "I don't want to have a baby, not your baby, not anybody's baby. I don't even like babies. I wish this was all a bad dream that would be over when I blinked my eyes, but it's not a dream. It's a nightmare."

He could hardly believe his ears. For the first time since falling in love with young Rosie he willfully acknowledged their age difference. Impetuous youth marrying mature adulthood... destined to failure. Rosie's disruptive state of emotional despair was his fault. He failed her. The last thing he needed was a breakdown in communication.

"Rosie, don't talk like that. Please listen to me. We can find happiness in all of this, but we can't do it alone. I need you to be strong right now. I love you and want to take care of you and this wonderful baby inside you."

She refused to look at him. Frank adored her more than anything or anyone in his world, and seeing her agonize and suffer because of something he did, made him more determined than ever to marry her sooner than later. He gently took her chin and raised her head.

"Whatever we do, we need to do it together. You have to be strong and not fall apart. This is not a Rosie problem and it's not a Frank problem. Your pregnancy is *our* problem."

Frank assured her repeatedly that he loved her. He wiped her face with his handkerchief and kissed her forehead. She wanted desperately to believe him, "I'm sorry for all those awful things I said. I am so scared of what will happen to us. She paused briefly. "You can't tell me what will happen because you don't know. All those hopes and dreams, all the hard work to graduate at the top of my class, gone. Gone, gone, gone—for-ever gone! Do you know what they do with girls like me? They send them away, and that Frankie-dear will be the end of us."

"Rosie, we need to think about what '*we*' want to do. I want to marry you right now and move you into my house. I have a successful career along with enough money for you, me, and a whole house full of babies, not just this one."

"If you played the violin, we might have had a chance. Boy, have I ever made a mess of my life."

"Rosie, all this talk is for naught. You need to know something, I'm not afraid of your mother or your father. Tomorrow night I'm asking for you hand in marriage. If you'd like to be there, I'd love to have you. But if you join me, do not dare mention the word pregnant. They'll learn about that after we're married. All they need know is how much I love you. I promise to give you a good life with everything you could ever dream of."

Rosie's head flooded with fear and all the things that could go wrong. "I need a couple of days to think about this. Let me feel them out before you do anything.

Frank adored Rosie and wanted nothing more than to marry her—she was his life. "Rosie my love, my mind's made up. Expect me at seven tomorrow night. I'm coming to make you my bride."

The following day while Frank was working downtown setting up window dressings in Tallman's Department Store, he repeated over and over in his mind the way he'd approach those hard-nosed German's when asking for Rosie's hand in marriage. He wasn't one bit hesitant or fearful taking on either of the Gradel's. For him the hour of reckoning couldn't come soon enough.

It was exactly seven o'clock when Frank's knuckle lightly tapped on the door. Rosie's stomach churned. Her heart thumped so loud she was sure her father could hear it clear across the room. The entire time it took to walk toward the door she wished Frank would turn around and leave, but that was not how he operated. One thing Frank didn't do, he didn't break promises.

Rosie opened the door, and when she saw Frank standing on the other side of the doorway she couldn't speak. She stared at the handsomely dressed man on the other side of the doorway thinking how striking he was in his light gray pinstriped suit, fresh white starched shirt, and sporting a hand-tied-silk bow-tie in varied shades of blue that brought out the blue in his eyes. She thought he was the most gorgeous man she'd ever seen, and he was all hers. For a split second she allowed herself to believe he'd come to whisk her away into the night. Suddenly her thoughts jumbled, she questioned his reason for choosing a girl over a beautiful mature woman. She kept telling herself, *doesn't matter, he's come to get me*. Then silence.

Rosie looked at Frank, then at her father. She felt like someone had drained every ounce of blood from her body and covered her with a blanket of ice. Her color changed. A chill came over her. Frank saw what was happening to his precious Rosie. He took charge.

"Mr. Gradel, I need to talk to you and Mrs. Gradel. Is this a bad time? Would another time be better?"

Rosie's father liked Frank but had no idea why he'd come to see them. He responded, "No, is good time. Rosie, get mother."

The walk to her mother's studio was like a grueling death march in a pair of lead-bottom shoes. Her mouth was bone-dry, her tongue paralyzed, her vision blurred, and she trembled with fear. Words were nearly impossible to form.

"Mother, could you come into the kitchen? Pop and Mr. Pazwalski are in there waiting to talk to you."

"What is this about?"

"Umm, I'm not sure."

Elsa majestically entered the kitchen, placed both hands on her hips, and glared at Frank. She was obviously annoyed with his rude unscheduled visit.

"Mr. Pazwalski, what is it you want, more money? Perhaps you want to quit working for us?" Elsa waited for a response. Frank was ready and never hesitated for a second. His words came straight and simple, so there was no doubt why he'd come.

"It's none of those things. I have come to ask for your daughter's hand in marriage. I want to marry Rosie."

The lackluster expression on their stolid faces convinced Frank they'd never completely understand how he felt about their daughter. Nonetheless, he spoke from the heart. He hoped for the best and prepared for the worst.

"I am in love with your daughter, and I truly believe she loves me. After all these days and months of spending time together this was inevitable. I hope you're not naïve enough to think we worked in silence and never spoke to one another, because that's not realistic."

The look on the Gradel faces told Rosie that Frank had already said way more than he should have. Anything she added would put the final nail in this coffin she'd made for herself.

"I want to spend the rest of my life taking care of your daughter. I have enough money to give her the kind of life she deserves. I plan to send her to any university she chooses. If it means leaving the city of Pittsburgh, so be it. I'll take her to Europe if that's where she wants to go. I don't need a dime of your money. All I ask is that you give us your blessing. We love each other."

As far as Elsa was concerned, Frank's request amounted to nothing more than a foolish bunch of words. A German never married a Pole. Not even a violin-toting one. Elsa's attack—disparage Frank's character.

"You must be crazy. She's in her youth. She has a lifetime to find an old man if she wants one. Look at yourself. You're a failure. A window decorator! You want a wife? Then find yourself an old woman like you to marry. Leave our daughter alone."

Frank tried to strategize, but couldn't concentrate with her screaming. This deranged German made Greiner's old lady looked like a Sunday school teacher.

"You had some nerve doing this filthy love thing behind our backs. How could you do this to us?"

"There was no filthy love thing going on behind your back. We work hard down there in that hardware store, and always in silence."

"Oh, so we have a smart aleck 'eh? Before I would ever let her marry you, I would kill her."

Elsa approached Rosie, who remained silently staring down at the floor, grabbed a fist full of hair, and yanked her head back, forcing her to look up. Frank had never witnessed anything like this. His first impulse was to grab Elsa by the hair and throw her down the stairs. He controlled his rage, waiting to see what Rosie would say or do.

Like the tyrant she was, Elsa refused to let go of Rosie's hair. "Rosie, are you proud of yourself?"

Frank's presence gave Rosie the impetus to grab her mother's arm and simultaneously jerk her head with enough force to break free. She went directly to her father and queried him.

"Pop, you're a lot older than Mother. Your marriage is a good one, isn't it?" Rosie's word fell on deaf ears. The old man chose to ignore her.

"Please Pop, say something. Tell mom how wrong she is about Frank. You see him nearly every day and you know he's a good man. Pop, you'll let me marry Frank, won't you?"

Contrary to Rosie's hunches, Hans Gerhart stood in total agreement with his wife, the consummate provocateur. The inner turmoil of listening to everything caused Hans' blood pressure to rise. He heard his own heart beating inside his ears. He wanted the pounding to stop. He tried to stand, but as soon as he tried to lift himself up off of the seat of his chair, his weak pathetic legs began to wobble and spasm. This rapidly deteriorating condition left him barely able to stand, but he somehow managed to speak to Rosie. The tone was disgusting and moderate. "When I look into your eyes I see something different. You are changed."

The old man paused. Tears streamed down his face. His head bobbled from side to side. "The innocence is departed. Your eyes carry the look whore's use on the streets. You are no more a part of this family. I don't care where you go. No matter what he tells you, no man marries the town whore."

Frank moved within two feet of the old man. The restraint needed to keep from killing him with his bare hands left him physically drained. He resorted to verbal ferocity to make his point. "Don't ever let me hear you call Rosie a town whore. You are an ignorant, stupid old man. She's a decent and honorable young lady."

Frank glanced at Rosie, whose face appeared as white as his freshly starched shirt. "You mean, heartless, miserable son-of-a-bitch. I have half a mind to strangle you and put you out of your misery and save God the trouble."

Frank wasted no time moving in closer to the old man. In a loud boisterous voice he called him by name, something guaranteed to garner his full attention, "Hans, you apologize to her and do it right now!"

To Hans' way of thinking, Frank's speaking to him in this manner was disrespectful. He trembled all over, his head nodding uncontrollably. He began acting as if he'd been drinking. "You Polish bum. Get out of my house."

Frank made Rosie a promise that he would not leave without her. He refused to budge.

Hans extended his arms and moved forward indicating he had every intention of physically getting his hands on Frank's neck. Frank knew he was totally incapable of such an act and assumed he'd either fall over or realize he had to sit down and abandon this idiotic idea of harming him. Elsa sensed her husband was about to do something stupid and raised her voice at him, "Hans Gerhart, don't act like a fool. Sit yourself down."

Despite her warning, Hans lunged toward Frank. In his irrational and deranged state of mind, he convinced himself he was capable of taking on Frank. He somehow managed to stabilize his balance and grabbed onto Frank's neck. Even though the stroke had left his right hand virtually useless, he cupped his hands and dug his fingers into Frank's Adam's apple as hard as he could. The relentless pressure of those thumbs against Frank's windpipe called for a reaction.

"Mr. Gradel, please take your hands off me before I'm forced to push you away and possibly hurt you." The intense pressure of the old man's thumbs digging into Frank's Adams apple caused him to gasp. "You're choking me you old fool. Get your hands off my neck. Do you hear me? Let go!" Sick as he was, the old man clung on as if his hands had locked in place, unable to let go.

Frank's rage displaced restraint. He took his hands and firmly coupled them over Hans's wrists. He squeezed until Hans relinquished and his fingers became pathetic limbs. Frank forcefully thrust them down and away from him.

The old man's eyes appeared glazed and watery. He gasped for air and struggled to breathe. The extreme stress depleted every particle of energy from his being, sending his body crashing to the floor.

Elsa rushed to his motionless, rigid body lying on the floor. Her attempts to arouse a response failed. Hans's eyes remained fixed and glassy. Frank stared at the mound of silence lying on the floor and questioned how something as simple as asking for their daughter's hand in marriage could turn so ugly so fast. Nothing made sense, especially Elsa when her screams resumed.

"You murdered him! You husband killer! Are you happy now?"

Elsa kept trying to evoke a response. She glared at Frank and shrieked loud enough for the whole world to hear, "He isn't moving! Do you see him moving? What kind of an animal throws a sick, weak old man down and kills him with his bare hands? You killed Hans. I hope they put you in prison forever."

Elsa sat on the floor next to her husband in complete disbelief. Rosie stayed on the far side of the room too afraid to move. Elsa caught sight of her and screamed, "Rosie, don't just stand there like an idiot. Call for the police. Call Dr. Bauer. Do something."

Frank looked around the room unable to make sense of anything that had transpired. One thing he knew for certain, it was over. The end had come for four people that ill-fated night, and nothing would or could ever be the same. Embroiled in a nightmare of remorse, regret, and fear, Frank panicked and fled out the same door through which he entered at seven o'clock.

Rather than heed her mother's orders to call for help, Rosie began screaming as loud as she could, "Wait for me Frank. Take me with you." She attempted to catch up with him, but timing and blinding tears made it impossible. She lost sight of him but never stopped screaming, "You said you never break a promise."

Frank's mind was drowning in sea of despair. One second he'd hear Rosie's voice screaming, "Don't leave me here. Wait for me." He would start to turn around. In the flash of a second, the voice would change, and he'd hear a witch-like voice echoing inside his head—it was Elsa screeching, "You murderer, you killed my husband."

Frank fought desperately to replay the senseless chain of events hoping for different results, but each time the ending was the same. An old man was dead, and he would be named the murderer. Elsa hated him enough that she would see to it that he was put away forever just so he couldn't marry her daughter. His taking the chance to go back for Rosie would serve no purpose other than to further ruin her life along with his.

A persistent and gnawing stomachache forced him into a dark alley right around the corner from the hardware store. The excruciating cramps brought him to his knees; salty saliva drooled and pooled in his mouth, his stomach retched forcefully to expel its contents, and before he realized what had happened he was covered in vomit. Left too weak to care about going anywhere, Frank removed his vomitus-covered silk tie which now felt like a noose around his neck. He turned his wet, stained jacket inside out, and laid it down on the street so he'd have something to sit on.

For some unknown reason, this dank dark alley served as a haven for drunks and homeless men, but this night the alley's only guests were remnant smells of stale urine, Frank's fresh vomit, and a broken heart. An eerie stillness crept over him. The once street-smart Frank began to shiver. He retrieved his smelly jacket off the street and put it on. Suddenly a voice screamed, "She's dead, she's dead." In his heart he knew who "the she" was.

Rather than see whether those screams had anything to do with Rosie, he ran in the opposite direction like a demented coward incapable of looking back. Frank knew if he didn't want to keep on seeing three dead people in his mind's eye, Hans, Rosie, and himself, he had to keep running.

In the meantime a group of people waiting for a trolley gathered around the young woman lying on the street. The driver of the car emerged and someone in the crowd repeated the same scream Frank had heard just minutes before, "She's dead, you killed her!"

The driver looked down at Rosie lying on the ground, "Oh my God, she is dead. Did anyone see what happened?"

Another stranger stepped forward in defense of the driver. "Listen buddy, this isn't your fault. I saw the whole thing from across the street. Some man came rushing out the side door of that hardware store and ran west toward the alley. I got a quick glimpse of his face as he raced by me and I'll never forget the look on his face—like he seen a ghost or worse."

The driver of the car was scared and confused. "I was driving along and never saw anybody around anywhere. Next thing I know, I hear this loud thump, then a moan. I get out of my car to see what happened and see a young woman dead on the street. Oh my God, what do I do now?"

The driver of the car knelt down on the ground next to Rosie and began to cry. "He squeezed her cold hand hoping for some sign of life, and in his own fashion began to pray. "Please dear God don't let this little girl be dead. I didn't see her on this dark corner ... you have to believe me Dear Lord. You know I'd never hurt or kill anyone. Oh please Dear Lord, let her be okay."

Another onlooker approached the sobbing driver and told him what he witnessed. "Hey buddy, I'm telling you, I saw the whole thing too, and this wasn't your fault. She was running in and out of alleys and up and down these streets like a wild woman. Think maybe she was chasing after that man, you know the one that other fellow mentioned?"

The first man on the scene spoke up, "Hey everybody, she's not dead. Look, her chest is going up and down like she's trying to catch her breath or something. Let's try to get her up off the street and over under the streetlight so we can see where she got hurt." Two men were about to lift her when the driver blurted, "She moved her head. I saw it!"

The driver continued to pray while the two men moved Rosie to where they could see and try to figure out where all the blood was coming from. A deep gash above her right ear proved to be the culprit; certainly not life-threatening, but definitely in need of stitches. Several men offered handkerchiefs to tie around her head to help stop the bleeding. Her lower calf had a sizeable wound that didn't seem to want to stop bleeding. Fortunately the man who was driving the car had an old shirt in his car, which he offered so the men could make a tourniquet to stop the bleeding for the time being.

Satisfied that everything was under control, the men were now confronted with deciding what to do with this unknown young woman and the handkerchiefs on her head that were no longer dry but covered in blood.

"Don't look like any of this is the kind of thing kills a person. Think she's probably just good and shook up. Anybody got any more hankies they're willing to give up to put on this kid's cuts?"

Another passerby came forward without hesitation. "Yeah, I do. Here you can have mine." He looked down at the crumpled body lying on the sidewalk. "Oh my God, I know her. That's Rosie! I shop in her old man's hardware store right there on the corner. What the hell happened to her?"

The shaken driver of the car wanted the man who knew Rosie to know he was not responsible for what happened. "She never looked, just darted right out in front my car. I swear she didn't even stop to look before she crossed this street. I'm wondering now maybe she was trying to kill herself."

"Nah, not this kid, I've known her for years. She wouldn't do something stupid like that. Kid's a genius. Trust me, this had to be an accident."

"Thank God, I'd hate to think I might have been the one who helped her try to kill herself. Where's her family? I need to explain what happened here and let her family know I'll pay the doctor bills."

"They live upstairs over the store. Her old man had a pretty bad stroke a while back and this kid runs the place for him. Damn smart kid she is. All I can say is that she had her mind on something else and wasn't paying attention to where she was going."

The same gentleman who offered a hanky removed his coat and threw it over her. She was shivering both from the cold and shock. "Let's get her upstairs so her family can decide what to do. I'll pick her up and carry her if one of you'll lead the way."

The doors were wide open like Rosie left them when she ran out of the house chasing after Frank. The men walked inside and yelled up to the second floor, hoping someone would answer. No one acknowledged them. One of them began pounding on the wall; still nothing.

The man holding Rosie lost patience. "Don't stand down here hollering like a huckster. Go on up and see if anyone's home. If no one's there, I say we take her to the hospital. We can't just leave her down here at the bottom of the steps like a sack of potatoes. No telling what might happen. Kid could bleed to death."

The driver raced to the top of the stairs, looked inside, and ran back down to where the others stood. He told them he saw a dead man on the floor with a woman hunched over him talking in German. One of the men voiced an opinion: "Bet the guy running down the alley had something to do with all of this and that's why the old lady sent this kid running after him."

The stranger holding Rosie spoke up. "Sounds like the old lady's hands are full, but so are mine. This kid is small, but I can't stand here holding her all night. Go back up there and tell her we're bringing her up now. I'm already late for work."

Three men entered the kitchen and Elsa ignored them. The driver of the car spoke to her: "Ma'am, someone said that this young lady lives here. Is that true?"

Elsa maintained her position and refused to acknowledge his presence, not caring whatever it was he had to say. None-the-less, he babbled nervously. "Lady, I want you to know she ran in front of my car. Good thing I'm a slow driver or she might have been killed. She's got a good size gash on her head and one on her leg. We got most of the bleeding to stop and she could probably use stitches and an ice bag on it for the night. She hasn't said a word since we picked her up off the street, and she's probably mad at me for hitting her, but it was not my fault. I'll leave you my name and telephone number, call me and I'll pay the doctor bill. Tell her tomorrow how sorry I am."

The three men looked at each other, not knowing what to do with Rosie. Elsa finally spoke. "You, the one with my daughter in your arms, take her back to her room at the front of the house and put her on the bed. The rest of you have no business in here. Get out!"

The man holding Rosie in his arms followed her instructions. He readied to leave and something told him she might need help. He spoke to Elsa, "It's none of my business ma'am, but is the old man on the floor all right? Do you need help with him too?"

"No, he is fine. Kindly leave us alone and close the doors behind you."

Elsa remained on the floor next to Hans. She stroked his head. "Hans Gerhard Gradel, talk to me. You're angry with me, aren't you?"

He made no effort to answer.

"Do you hear me? Can you get up off this floor?" Still nothing, not even a blink of an eye. Elsa knew he was dead, but she didn't want to deal with it. In true Elsa fashion, she placed a pillow under his head and covered him with a blanket.

She telephoned her sister. "Rose, get over here right away. It's family business." Generally when the sisters used the words *family business*, whatever the issue, it was strictly between them.

Rose arrived by cab. The minute she entered the house and saw Hans lying on the floor, she demanded to know what happened. The two of them argued over the importance of having Dr. Bauer validate Hans's death, and Elsa informed Rose she'd called him. Elsa then gave Rose a breakdown on the sequence of events that turned a normal evening into a catastrophic one.

"Frank is to blame for all of this. He was sent by the devils of hell to marry our daughter the whore. When Hans told him to get out, he pushed him so hard he fell to the floor. Poor Hans never moved after those devil hands touched him. Frank killed him."

"Elsa, where is Rosie? You said something on the phone about her being hurt."

Rose headed in the direction of her niece's room.

"Rose, don't you dare go to her. For once in your life, mind your own business. She's fine. I called you about Hans. He's the only one who matters right now."

"Maybe we should have Dr. Bauer look at her while he's here."

"I refuse to spend one red cent on her. Besides, she is none of your concern. Do you understand me Rose?"

"Yes, Elsa, I understand all too well."

"What's taking Dr. Bauer so long? I could have carried Hans to his office faster on my back."

"Elsa you're the one who said it didn't matter, Hans is already dead. The doctor will get here when he gets here." Rose had no sooner finished making that statement when Dr. Bauer knocked. He greeted the two women, checked for Hans's vital signs, and pronounced him dead. He expressed his condolences and left.

The following morning Rose arrived before seven and entered the house via the private side door entry to the second floor. When she got to the top of the stairs and opened the kitchen door, the overwhelming concoction of sweet-smelling perfumes gagged her. She looked across the room and saw her sister sitting next to Hans' corpse whose body appeared to have been repackaged inside a fresh white sheet, painstakingly wrapped and tied with rope and doused with every conceivable bottle of fragrance in an attempt to disguise the bitter smell of death.

"Elsa, did you get hold of Father Greiner?"

"Yes. He came after you left."

"He'll be a big help. That's his job. The cemetery lots are in a registry at the back of the church. Be thinking about what you want to do."

"Rose, everything is arranged. I'm laying him out in his store. If I lay him out in the parlor his face will forever haunt me when I go there. If he's laid out down in the store, it won't matter because I've never been in there and don't ever plan to go in there after he's buried. I hate that place."

"Elsa, Hans is your husband, do what you want. Lay him out wherever, I really don't care. By the way, where is Rosie? Is something wrong with her?"

"Rose, I told you, nothing is wrong."

"Then where is she? Last night I clearly understood you to say she was hurt. Don't talk to me like you think I'm losing my mind or imagined what you said."

"I don't know where you get these crazy ideas you come up with, Rose. I never said anything about her being hurt."

"Well Elsa, something is wrong. When a girl's pop dies, and she's spent most every day of her life at his side working in the store, and you come along and tell me nothing is wrong, I think you're lying."

"Are you calling me a liar? Are you, Rose?"

"No, but I do think you owe me an explanation. Does this have anything to do with Frank, the man you said argued with Hans?"

"None of this is any of your business. Why do you insist on badgering me?"

"Because I don't believe you; I want to know where she is and what you're hiding from me."

"Rose, you have never learned how to stay out of other people's business."

Their squabbling went from snide to vicious. "Rose, mind to your own affairs. You took Emil from me when he was a mere babe, now what do you want, to steal Rosie, too?"

"Elsa, you are losing your mind. The more you talk, the more you sound like a mad woman. How dare you accuse me of stealing Emil! You threw him away when you left him with me every chance you had. Both you and Hans were glad to be rid of him. You, so you could spend time with your precious violins, and Hans, so he could live in his boring store with his boring self. Neither of you had time for anything but yourselves. I made time for that precious little boy and gave him the love he wanted, needed, and deserved. He'd have no one if it wasn't for me."

Hostility erupted in words deliberately chosen to indelibly etch and scar the other's mind. "Rose, the only person I need is dead. I don't need you, I don't need Emil, and Rosie is none of your business. I'll bury Hans. I don't want you or Emil there. Hans and I started out alone and we'll part the same way. Now get out! Don't ever call or cross the threshold of my home. You are no longer welcome."

Rose had an arrogant way of looking at people, something she'd done since childhood. This action always got under Elsa's skin and provoked her into acting irrationally.

"You hear me? As long as I live, I never want to see your face ever again. I despise you Rose Dunnigan, and as far as I'm concerned, you died today with Hans. I no longer have a sister."

"Elsa, how could you say such cruel undeserving things to me? I've been nothing but good to you. When you came to America, I took you in, let you save the money father gave you, and never charged you a single dime to live with us. Did you forget your precious Hans owned a business and a house, and not because of anything you did, but because of what I did? If it was up to you, all you'd have are those stupid violins. You only remember what you want to remember."

Elsa's retort was calculated, filled with years of disgust and animosity. "And you Rose, you'd be in an insane asylum if I hadn't made that hellish trip to America to save you and your demented, twisted mind. Hans and I were perfectly happy living and staying in Germany. Did you forget how sick in the head you were when the priest wrote our father telling him I had to come to America right away to save you? Germany was another world away, but Hans and I came for you, not for ourselves, but for you! You, too, only remember what you want to remember."

"Elsa, you are upset about Hans's death and that's why you're saying all these deplorable things right now."

"Rose, my being upset has nothing to do with Hans's death. You were a spoiled manipulative child and you grew into a spoiled and manipulative woman. I can't stand the very sight of you."

Rose walked to the door, her hand on the knob ready to depart the madness, when Elsa stormed across the room baring her exit. Elsa had more to say to Rose, but Rose wasn't having any of it. She attempted to push Elsa away but Elsa stood firm. Rose blurted out, "I don't and won't listen to another word out of that big nasty mouth of yours. Let me out of here you witch!"

Elsa had Rose exactly where she wanted, under the gun, her wicked tongue, "Father spoiled you time and again by allowing you to try new things without ever insisting you finish the ones you started. And, why? Because poor little Rose didn't like something or lost interest. And then there was 'father the fool' who never gave up hope or could spend enough money, hoping that one day you'd find something you liked or were interested in for more than a week, a month, or a year, but you never did. So what did father do? He sent you to America with more money than he ever spent on any of my violins. He supplied you with a lot of money thinking maybe America could save what he couldn't, but you failed there, too."

Elsa and Rose's mother had died in child-birth when the girls were four and six years old, leaving their father uninterested in going on in life. Loneliness exacerbated a series of already existing medical maladies, which in turn spiraled into deep depression. At this point his mother-in-law stepped in removing the girls from his home, insisting they would be returned when he proved himself a worthy father. She had no intention of raising them, and immediately placed the girls in an elite boarding school where they remained for seven years. It was during this time Elsa expressed an interest in studying the violin. A gifted child who lived to hear herself play, she rapidly exceeded all expectations and was rewarded with one of her deceased mother's Stradivariuses'. Rose, on the other-hand showed little interest in anything other than wanting to go home to be with her father. She cried for him daily, and the day she turned eleven, her father came to take her and her sister home. He was so layered with guilt over losing his girls for seven years, he vowed to spend the rest of his life and whatever monies it took making it up to them. He adored his girls. Elsa found life in music needing nothing or anything but the Stradivarius. Rose flit from pillar to post always trying new things, never finding or completing anything. As a result, Rose lacked self-confidence, had no initiative, and ended up crippled by a father who loved her so much he failed to combine discipline with that love, destroying the spirit within that makes a child's wings ready for the day they soar and fly into the winds of life.

Rose's father repeatedly blamed himself, for failing to be the father he should have been after his wife died. No matter what he did, Rose remained entirely dependent on him with no outside interests. His last resort and only solution was to send her to America to see whether a new beginning might be the answer. He bought her a ticket, and Rose was on her way to happiness. Family friends who had emigrated to America years earlier, agreed to be there to help her get situated in the small town in western Pennsylvania where they had settled.

The adjustment to being in America imploded when her father passed away six months later. She could no longer depend on him. In the beginning, like everything else in Rose's life, she was always looking for the next new thing, moving from town to town finding fault with either the people or the houses or the church or the whatever. Typical Rose, the eternal butterfly eventually settled in Pittsburgh and joined a German Catholic church. There friends introduced her to a full-blooded Irishman and confirmed bachelor named Pat Dunnigan. This gentle ladies' man was handsome, smart, had a great paying job, money in the bank, but more than anything, he was kind and soft spoken like her father. Only problem, he loved his Irish whiskey. The moment he saw Rose he told himself *she's the one*, and six months later, they married. In fast short order, Rose manipulated him in much the same way she did her father. Pat became a poor drunken fool who gave Rose any possession she wanted that he could afford. Ah, but those possessions, those wonderful endearing possessions, those things, she collected, gathered, grabbed, and suffocated herself with, ah yes, like finding '*nirvana*'. This was the one thing that could set Elsa off without reason, and today was one of those days.

"Rose, when are you ever going to learn? Things don't fulfill and make a person. If you had learned to discipline yourself and master one thing in your life, your mind would overflow with the satisfaction of knowing you accomplished something you were good at. This is what gives one peace. In turn, the world would love you for giving it the best you had to offer. You gave the world nothing and you'll get nothing back from it before you die Rose. You leave no legacy because you were too lazy to work at anything. You might think you have Emil, you might think you have that house full of things, but you have nothing I tell you, nothing! Your life, your soul, you Rose, you are filled with nothingness."

Rose's reaction to everything Elsa said was to get as far away from her as fast as she could. She gripped her purse firmly in her right hand and slammed it against the side of Elsa's face and head, throwing her off balance enough to get past her and out the door. The moment Rose was out of sight Elsa telephoned the undertaker, identified herself, gave her address, and requested a plain pine coffin be delivered to the hardware store as soon as possible, stressing that time was of the essence. Within an hour, an empty pine coffin arrived. She designated its location in the center of the store and asked the deliverymen to place it on its side. Before leaving they queried her on the whereabouts of the deceased. She arrogantly informed them they need only concern themselves with informing the undertaker that if he wanted to be paid tomorrow, he was to provide a hearse, a limousine, pall bearers, and most importantly, expected to arrive promptly at noon.

The long narrow layout of the store made it very dark inside, especially if the front blinds were drawn on the large storefront windows and the lights were turned off. Elsa found the setting ideal.

Hans's death brought on one of those formidable times when a miniscule thread of conscience broke through Elsa's tough façade, reminding her how wrong it would be to leave her husband alone during his final hours on earth. Initially she had planned to stay with him briefly, but certainly not long enough to require a chair. But, when she thought of going upstairs and dealing with her daughter, she decided that sitting next to Hans was the lesser of two evils. She walked around to the back of the store to get a chair and noticed stacks of boxes containing beeswax candles. Elsa knew her husband supplied these to the church for free from the day he bought the store from old man Millbauer. She thought about his generosity all those years and decided, right then and there, that he deserved nothing less than having every last one lit in his honor on this his last day on earth.

Elsa began the exhaustive task of gathering all the boxed candles from the rear storage room shelves, hauling them into the main part of the store where she planned to put them to good use. The endless hassle of opening what seemed like an insurmountable number of un-opened boxes of candles overwhelmed her.

Suffering from physical, mental, and emotional exhaustion, Elsa lost sight of her main agenda, locating more rope. After searching through several drawers she found exactly what she needed and headed upstairs. She went directly to Hans' corpse lying on the kitchen floor and carefully rolled him over. After wrapping the rope around his waist two times then tying a double knot to hold his rigid body secure, she dragged him to the top of the steps, positioning him so he was heading down feet first. Elsa anchored herself ten feet from the corpse clutching the rope with both hands in order to facilitate easing Hans' body slowly down the steps. Once the descent began, she managed to maintain a constant tautness, leaving out just enough line to allow gravity to do all the work. As soon as Hans' corpse reached bottom, she dragged it over next to the casket. The culmination of everything that had transpired in the last forty-eight hours sucked the very life out of her. Elsa decided to retreat to the family flat on the second floor to brew a fresh pot of strong-black-coffee and re-energize for what was yet to come. For Elsa, two cups of this black brew was pure medicine, a magic elixir capable of curing any and all ailments. This time she counted on it to aid in energizing her enough to complete the task of getting Hans' body rolled into the casket and finally hammering the nails into the lid before flipping it over. Finally, after savoring the last drops in the cup, she left it on the table and wasted no time going back downstairs to wrap-up the traumatic ordeal she'd undertaken....flipping the casket right side up. But before doing that, she needed to roll the body into the casket and nail the lid on. Unaccustomed to physical work, Elsa rolled Hans into his coffin, found a hammer and four nails, and in no time flat had secured the lid. Once that was done, she methodically executed the 'how' she'd defy this monstrous chore in front of her—flipping the casket right side up. Physically incapable of doing this alone, Elsa searched for something to assist with turning the casket. Buried in a corner at the back of the storage area behind several brooms was a five-foot-long steel pole with a pointed end. She had no idea what it was or where it came from, but she knew it had possibilities. In order for her idea to work, she had to place an object on the floor opposite from where she was standing, so the casket wouldn't just slide across the floor and away from her. The hammer used on the coffin lid was on the floor next to her foot. She returned to the storage room, grabbed a handful of six inch nails and proceeded to hammer them into the wood floor so the coffin couldn't slide. Her fragile hands began to ache and swell, but Elsa chose to ignore pain and pick up the steel pole. She gripped her fingers tightly around its core and forcefully thrust the pointed end into the floor and, in one fell-swoop, flipped it over. Aghast and surprised at seeing the casket upright, Elsa released her grip and let the pole fall to the floor. Dazed, alone, and walled in silence, Elsa was forced to face the reality of Hans' death. The woman known for having ice running through her veins underwent a transformation. Soppiness and hallucinations of Hans appearing at the side of his casket caused her to race around the store like a mad-woman being chased by his ghost. Candles, matches; both were readily accessible. Did he want her to set the place on fire? She spoke to him, but got no answer. Surely this would solve all her problems. A massive fire would rid her of the store she hated. It would rid her of Hans' dead body and a dreaded trip to the cemetery, and lastly, would eliminate dealing with her daughter upstairs in bed. At that very moment she believed she again heard Hans' voice telling her to arrange the candles randomly throughout the entire store, and when she finished doing that, he asked she light them one by one until every-one was lit. Elsa did as she was told. She began the exhaustive chore of gathering all the boxed candles from the rear storage room shelves. Once they were all in the main part of the store, she randomly placed them around the room. There were candles in every style, shape, and form. The only thing they shared in common was their color. They were all church-color-white. For the sake of convenience, the altar candles ended up on shelves or were placed in opened drawers. The top of Hans' casket dutifully displayed short prayer candles. The embossed over-sized candles able to stand alone were directly behind Hans' coffin.

In spite of being completely exhausted, Elsa raced against the 'clock of life', laboring on, lighting each and every candle in the room until it was filled with a presence of light-hearted reminiscence of days and times gone by. Times when lit candles meant dinners alone with the handsome Hans Gerhardt rushing through dinner so he could hold her in his arms and waltz gallantly around the house while humming Strauss in her ear. She stood next to Hans' casket and watched as the room became heaven-like, as if by some stroke of magic an old hardware store took on heaven-like brilliance—an ethereal light, like the one she imagined one sees when first entering heaven. Elsa fought back unwanted tears in an effort to experience seeing and being in the center of the most glowing radiant color she'd ever seen, the one called calm tranquility, the color the soul absorbs in its infancy. A gentle peacefulness calmed her frenzied mind. Elsa knew the time had come. She located a new, unopened box of matches and lit the last remaining four-foot candles next to Hans' casket. Stoic Elsa never cried, not for anyone or for any reason, but this time she lost the battle. She turned around to speak to her partner, but he was gone—off to dance alone. As morning approached a goodly number of candles had expended themselves, others flickered on leaving globs of melted beeswax, unidentifiable as nothing more than what was once is no more. The only remainder of a tribute to death and the body inside the casket were thick clouds of burnt wicks and beeswax that lingered and hung overhead like a band of ethereal angels who'd come to escort Hans off to meet his maker.

Elsa barely slept through the night, awakening hours before dawn. The first thing on her mind was a freshly brewed cup of coffee. She took one last look around the room before heading upstairs. The remaining candles depleted into modified globs of what they once were, and the notion crossed her mind how this scenario mimicked her life. She put the coffee pot on the stove then went directly to her closet and chose a simple straight black wool dress, one befitting a widow and a funeral. From lingerie to gloves, the issue was never color, Elsa wore nothing but black. This mode of dressing began when distinguished maestros like her performed on stage in formal attire, and since Elsa had become recognized as one of the leading violinists of her time, an air of superiority reigned in everything she did from dress to feeding an enormous ego.

Elsa needed to move things along so she could steal some time alone to sit quietly in a state of nothingness, a place she frequented often. A brief stop in the bathroom to freshen up and take care of personal matters and Elsa was ready to finally sit and enjoy that well-deserved cup of coffee that had finished percolating on the stove.

To preclude any delays, Elsa readied her coat, hat, gloves, and purse on a chair next to the door at the bottom of the stairs. Greiner's knock signaled the beginning of the end in the final act of one Hans Friedrich Gradel. Elsa rose straight up out of her chair and walked directly towards the door. She placed her hand on the knob, and as she opened the door, a whooshing gust of fresh cold morning air purged the room of all residual traces any angel had ever even been there. Elsa greeted Father Greiner and the undertaker, then stood back to watch the pallbearers enter and lift Hans' casket up off the floor and out to the waiting hearse. As soon as the door to the back of the hearse closed, Elsa gathered her belongings from the chair next to the door and hurried outside to join the procession, which was now ready to go.

Elsa's plans were precisely on schedule. She thanked Father Greiner for taking care of the final arrangements for her husband's burial and for respecting her wishes to keep everything private. The priest briefly discussed their schedule and couldn't perceive the notion of why no other family members were present and had to ask, "Mrs. Gradel, where is everyone? We're scheduled to leave for the church in ten minutes and no one is here. Where are your children?"

"Obviously, they are not here."

He had to ask, "Is something wrong with your children I should know about?" He could appreciate her loss, but to not even have them there made no sense whatever.

"Everything is fine, and I don't care to discuss my children."

The priest remained silent. In normal fashion, Elsa took charge.

"All night long I thought about today and how I wanted it conducted. Hans and I came to America alone, leaving everything behind. Family, friends, a beautiful house, successful careers, and together we started anew. Once again I am forced to start anew, and, in so doing, will bury Hans alone and privately. I asked my family not to be here this morning, and they are respecting my wishes. I expect you to do the same."

The hearse headed in the direction of the church and like everything Elsa had done to this point, nothing made any sense. "Driver, skip the church. Go directly to the cemetery. Father will say mass there."

The limousine driver honked his horn to get the undertaker's attention and beckoned him to pull over. At that point, Father Greiner got out and approached the hearse to apprise the driver of the change in plans he and Elsa discussed.

The caravan of two took thirty minutes to get to St. Michael's Cemetery, and in all that time Elsa never said a word. It was the end of March; dank, cold, wet, and miserable with blistering wind from the west threatening the possibility of light snow. The caravan stopped across from the gravesite, and the three of them stepped out of the car and watched as the pall-bearers carried Hans' casket to his final resting place. It was at this moment when Elsa leaned into the priest and issued her final directives.

"When you're finished saying mass, leave me alone. I prefer you wait in the car. I won't be long."

No one could have guessed Elsa's response to the calamities of the past two days any more than they could have predicted their happening. The impervious suit of armor she donned left little doubt she was anything but an enigma of great proportion and deception. Elsa never intended to be understood, nor did she care to be.

For a brief moment she revisited this last chapter in her life, how it had gone up to this point, and now how she would script the ending as she said her last good-bye.

"Hans, you didn't die yesterday. You died the day I replaced you with the violin and forced you to watch me through a window of glass. A window of glass you could touch. A window of glass that allowed music to pass through, but a window of glass that never allowed you to know the person on the other side making the music. I killed you Hans. I starved you of the most essential food of life—having someone to talk to. Now in turn, I wait to hear your voice and realize—I don't know what it sounds like"

Elsa said all she had to say and, without hesitation, turned around and walked directly to the limousine, got in unassisted, and told the driver to move on. It was what she planned to do—move on.

Chapter 6

Rejection's Pain

Rosie's lengthy absence from school had the nuns questioning Father Greiner daily; did he know anything about her missing classes for these past three weeks? Their concern was why Rosie, the top student in the school's graduating class, missed three weeks and no one knew or would give a good reason why.

Elsa figured out the reasons for her daughter's unwillingness to talk, get out of bed, or get dressed. She was pregnant. Father Greiner made several phone calls to Elsa inquiring why the store had a sign on the door that said "closed permanently," and also why Rosie wasn't in school. He was curtly told, in no uncertain terms, to "stay away."

After weeks of frustration with Rosie's refusing to cooperate or answer any of her questions, Elsa called the doctor and scheduled an appointment for him to make a house call the following afternoon. Elsa wanted answers to her suspicions.

Final diagnosis, Rosie was very pregnant and there was no way to know whether the pregnancy had brought on depression or whether the depression was an entirely separate issue. A man of few words, Dr. Bauer attributed some of Rosie's unwillingness to talk to being ashamed, embarrassed, and mostly frightened. He suggested hormonal imbalances as a known ingredient for depression in pregnant women and advised Elsa to closely monitor Rosie so that he could prescribe medication in the event that her depression worsened. Given the circumstance, knowing Elsa as well as he did, he understood Rosie not wanting to talk to her.

In order for Elsa to wash her hands of her daughter before anyone found out about the dishonor bought upon her family's name, she needed Dr. Bauer's help. "I do not deserve the kind of degradation my own flesh and blood has dragged me into, ruining my good name. I don't care what's to become of her. Just get her out of here."

"Elsa—for once, just once, could you stop and think of someone else besides yourself?"

Dr. Bauer suggested she get her family priest involved so together they could pursue the possibility of getting Rosie accepted into the Catholic Church's home for unwed mothers. Elsa was "an elitist"—a snob of the highest degree, and the solution here set her mind afire. She was enraged at the very thought of having to beg anyone for help, for nothing was as reprehensible as having an unwed daughter. Dr. Bauer thought in all his years of medical practice he'd seen everything, but nothing could have prepared him for what he'd just witnessed. He refused payment for the house call and saw himself out.

Elsa waited until the door closed before heading directly to Rosie's room, where she then wailed and berated Rosie about everything from Frank's producing a bastard child to forbidding Rosie from ever calling her "mother" for as long as she lived.

Elsa's face contorted and rapidly turned blistering red, as if she was about to have a stroke, she reverted to speaking in her native tongue. "For years I've put up with Father Greiner always acting so pious and righteous, so charitable and honorable, always showing his good side. But, I've figured him out, and he's evil, ordained by the devil."

This culmination of events led Elsa into a wild frenzy. Her voice quivered, her steely cold blue eyes bore into Rosie lying in her bed. By now all five-foot-ten inches of her were seething. "Curse him! Priest! What kind of a priest would bring a so called 'good friend,' thief, and murderer to us? Oh, that Father Greiner is just like you Rosie, 'Birds of a feather'!"

These tirades often found Elsa deliberately pausing to get the full attention of the recipient. She did this routinely with her students, knowing it would make them work harder, but this time, however, her words fell on deaf ears. "Let's see how fast the good Father can help get you into that Hawthorne House. You know, it's where the church hides their whores. Maybe he can get the bastard baby's father to drive you there. We both know a man *uses* harlots, but he never *marries* them."

Before calling the priest, Elsa paced the floor planning and thinking about what to do. Three weeks without any contact with the church was not normal for someone who never missed daily mass, and if her schedule permitted, attended twice. When she invited Father Greiner to come to her home that evening, he had no idea what to expect.

What Father Greiner found waiting for him was, the same insolent Elsa. "Dr. Bauer came and examined Rosie. She's suffering from depression, but you probably already knew that and just didn't know why. Or maybe you did know and failed to share it with me just like all the other secrets you kept about that bum we hired, you know, your trusted friend Frank."

Elsa's sharp tongue echoed words and sentiments not unlike those of his hateful mother, who always needed a whipping boy and generally targeted him. At all cost, and by his very nature, he should have avoided being in the presence of this merciless witch, who repeatedly lured him with money. He did favors for her because his mother claimed it was his responsibility to provide for her, and the salary the dioceses paid was insufficient for the life-style his mother chose.

This generous contributor to the church, the one whose pretense it was to be God-fearing when convenient, sickened him. No God-fearing human being could or would behave so wickedly.

"You and that good-for-nothing Polish bum who made Rosie pregnant are entirely to blame for the disgrace brought upon the Gradel name. Why I ever trusted the judgment of a young stupid priest is beyond me."

First she hurled insults, and right behind those, a small nicety, then, before you knew it a favor. He knew the routine well. The pieces of the puzzle all fell into place, typical Elsa. It didn't take an Einstein to figure out why she'd invited him there. She needed his help, and for the first time in his relationship with her, he was holding all the aces.

"I thought you were a smart man, you are stupid."

He thought to himself, *step number one out of the way—brace yourself Elsa, I've had it with you.*

"Stop calling me stupid and treat me with respect, or find someone else to help you." This quipped retort was not what Elsa had anticipated. She recoiled quickly and remained silent.

"Elsa, I'll handle everything and help get Rosie into Hawthorne House, but let's get one thing straight, I'm not doing this for you, I'm doing it for Rosie. And don't worry, no one there will know your daughter, and I'll see to it that she stays until the baby's born. There are plenty of good Catholic families waiting for babies, so you needn't worry what kind of people will get this child."

Greiner knew he had won both the battle and the war when he disrespectfully called her "Elsa," she was, "Mrs. Gradel" to him. Elsa seethed with anger and her face paled as she attempted to cover this annoyance using a phony voice. He knew he had her goat and silently savored every second he was able to play with her mind. He kept his tongue still, giving her all the rope she needed to hang herself with her own words.

"I can tell you right now, I don't care who gets this baby, what kind of family gets it, or what kind of people take it or even if they're Jews. Give it away as soon as it's born. Rosie doesn't deserve to see it, touch it, or have a say in what happens to it. I will sign any and all papers necessary to have Rosie's insides fixed so she can never do this again, and don't tell me they won't do it, because I've already looked into the matter and, for a price, anything can be done."

"I'm not here to argue or discuss any of what you're talking about, it doesn't concern me. I'm here because I care what happens to Rosie, which is more than you can say, Elsa. You have placed the blame for all of this on me, and I want you to know that I accept none of it. It's only out of concern for your daughter and her welfare that I'll phone Hawthorne House to see how fast they can take her in."

"Tell them I have plenty of money and you'll see how fast they take her in."

Father Greiner couldn't believe this ingrate, yet he responded coolly, "If she's accepted I'll take her there myself."

"That's the least you should do for all I've given you—not to mention all we've donated to that church of yours. I started giving them money before you ever came along. Just get her out of my house. I can barely stand the sight of her."

The priest was so incensed by Elsa's sinful heart that he refused to address her respectfully ever again, something he knew would rile her nerves and unbridle her mind. "Elsa, your daughter needs forgiveness and support from you more now than at any other time in her life. I will pray for both of you."

Elsa's unjustified ranting and raving left Father Greiner a complete mental and physical wreck. As he walked back to the rectory, Rosie's voice echoed over and over in his mind as the one he'd heard in the confessional last winter. It was as he suspected. Frank had taken from him the one thing he coveted but could never have, Rosie Gradel. He recalled clearly hearing Rosie's confession that night when she told him how she'd violated the seventh commandment, and he chose denial rather than facing his friend to tell him that what he was doing was wrong. Pain pierced Greiner's heart. He despised the skirt hypocrisy had provided him to hide beneath when he had the chance but lacked backbone to confront Frank. He hated himself.

By evening's end all the arrangements were made, the foundling home would take Rosie. Father Greiner telephoned Elsa and told her to have Rosie ready by eleven in the morning.

Elsa spent most of the night pacing the floor, randomly stopping at Rosie's door to harangue and harass her. She spilled and spewed every word that went through her head in a loud shrill voice, intended to be menacing enough to merit some response. Elsa had spent so little time with her daughter in all the years of her growing up that she knew very little about the inner workings of this extremely bright child who yearned for her mother's attention, and when she failed to get it, hollowed out a place in her mind where no one, especially Elsa, could enter.

Tonight Elsa's words fell on deaf ears. "This time you better listen to me and hear what I have to say because I'll say it only once. To start with, I am selling and giving away everything in this house. Then I am closing it up for good and going away. I came here with nothing but six trunks filled with things I treasured, and dreams of a life and legacy I would someday leave my children, you being one of them. But now, because of you, I'm forced to give up everything I've worked for and am returning to Germany to escape the disrepute and dishonor you've brought by tarnishing my name. You and that bastard baby in your belly have robbed me of my dreams. You killed me. I'm dead Rosie, you hear me! You had a chance for someone to take care of you in your life and you chose to throw it away. Now when this is over, you'll have to take care of yourself. I hope you're as ready to do that as you were to take off your pants for that good-for-nothing bum."

Rosie never stirred, and there was no way for Elsa to know whether Rosie had heard a single word. Still, Elsa being Elsa, always had the last word. "When you decide to talk, I hope there is someone who will want to listen, because it certainly won't be me!"

Elsa's determined nature, along with several pots of black coffee, kept her energized throughout the night. By morning she'd itemized and listed in specific detail every object she owned, designated where and to whom each thing would go, and lastly, she sifted through her bankbooks scrutinizing the numbers until she had accounted for every cent. The only thing left to do was arrange her departure.

The following morning Father Greiner awakened early and walked across the street, hoping to talk with Frank before taking Rosie away. He knocked several times then let himself in, as he had for the last several weeks while searching for Frank, but he was nowhere to be found. Confused and concerned as to his whereabouts, he tried calling Frank's four sisters, but none of them had seen or heard from him since their mother's funeral. Time was running out and he had obligations awaiting him. He headed back to the rectory.

The Yellow Cab Company sent out the regular driver Father Greiner requested when on official church business, the one who knew how to get places, kept his mouth shut until he got paid for the ride, and left.

When they got to the Gradel's house he asked the driver to wait while he went inside to pick up an additional passenger. Elsa opened the door and hastily ushered him into the parlor where Rosie was sitting on the sofa, dressed and waiting. The tension in the air hung like thick heavy fog. Elsa handed Father Greiner two envelopes, one with his name on it, and a larger sealed one to be given to a Sister Mary Margaret at the foundling home. It contained a lengthy letter, a promissory note, and a substantial amount of cash. However, it also contained three caveats that had to be addressed or the largest portion of monies promised would not be released.

Elsa picked up the small brown paper sack lying on the floor, which contained Rosie's two worldly possessions, her Missal and rosaries. Elsa glanced inside the bag intending to retrieve the rosaries, but for some unknown reason, hurled them back into it before shoving it up under Father Greiner's arm. "Don't leave without that bag. She'll need those if she ever expects God's forgiveness."

Father Greiner, mumbled to himself, *to think I thought my mother was insane, this witch takes the prize. Why on earth would any decent mother withhold something as sacred as rosaries from her own child?* No sooner had that thought crossed his lips when she started anew, "I'll have you know the Alexandrites in that bag were hand-selected by my grandmother, and at one time, they held special significance because all the women in our family had identical rosaries made of these precious gems. I momentarily thought about not giving those to her, but better judgment told me keeping them would only serve to remind me of someone I want no part of."

Father Greiner extended his hand to Rosie and gently urged her up off the sofa. She refused to get up.

"A taxi's waiting downstairs, we need to go now."

Rosie hung onto the seat of her chair, resisting Father Greiner's help. He leaned over, whispered something in her ear then helped her stand. The two of them walked towards the stairs and, as they readied to go out the door, Elsa slipped several loose bills into his pocket to cover the cost of the cab ride.

Father Greiner and Rosie had barely reached the bottom of the stairs before Elsa yelled down to him. "One last thing Father, I'd like you to come here a week from now, that's next Thursday." She hesitated for the sole purpose of making certain he heard Thursday. "Be here at three o'clock. Need you to sign and witness some important papers and documents."

"What kind of important papers?"

"Papers and money, both concern you and the church. Thursday's a busy day for me, so be prompt."

Elsa had an uncanny ability to recognize human frailties, and she readily recognized Father Greiner's—money. What he did with it, she never knew—certainly didn't spend it at the clothiers, perhaps some woman. No need for reaffirmation, she knew he'd be there and be on time. She closed the door and never looked out the window to see her daughter being exiled from the only home she'd ever known.

En route, Father Greiner thought about the recent series of events that had marred Rosie's life, forcing it in a direction she would never knowingly have chosen, he saw how it mirrored his own life the day his mother whisked him off to seminary. Their destinies had been determined out of desperation to bury shame, and they were the sacrificial lambs.

Assuming that this could perhaps be his last time alone with Rosie, Father Greiner took her small hand in his and nervously stroked it while trying to make small talk. Elsa's insane words, *bury shame*, played over in his mind. He inched closer to Rosie, placed his arm around her shoulder, and whispered in her ear.

"Rosie, I'm so sorry that I lied to get you out of the house, but I had no choice. I can't find Frank—I tried, and I lied when I said he was waiting in the cab. I had to get you out of that house, and taking you here is not my choice or decision. Believe me, if there were any other way to handle this situation, I'd do it. Please, please find it in your heart to forgive me, but this is the only thing we can do right now to try and straighten out what has gone wrong. I can't tell you when right now, but one day I'm coming back for you."

She sheepishly looked at Father Greiner, hating him for having tricked her into going with him. Rosie turned and looked out the window at the very moment the cab pulled up curbside to stop at the end of the walkway to the entrance of Hawthorne House.

The driver got out and walked around to Rosie's side and opened the cab door, but her rigid stillness conveyed her unwillingness to get out. He knew all about Hawthorne House and why young girls were sent there. Sensing a problem between Rosie and the priest, he obligingly took off for a walk around the block so they could resolve whatever their differences were.

The three-story brick and brownstone building resembled many throughout the city, including those in her neighborhood, but there was something sacrosanct about this one. Its long, thin inset arched windows were accented with elaborate cast concrete bonnets that stiffly stood out like a nun's habit, as if shielding stares of curious passers-by.

The entrance's recessed front doors with arched leaded-glass window over-head, showed no visible signs of life. There was a cold stillness enveloping the place. The time had come to go inside, but neither of them said a word or moved in that direction. Finally, Father Greiner got out and walked around to Rosie's side of the cab to help her out. Rosie resigned herself to the situation she'd gotten herself into and surrendered her arm to Father Greiner so they could get on with what was to be. He escorted her out of the cab and down the side-walk towards a small enclosed yard surrounding the front entrance to Hawthorne House. He leaned over and unlatched a lock on the wrought iron gate that opened onto a ten-foot-long brick walkway leading up to six eight-foot-wide concrete steps, where they stepped onto a large landing and entry to Hawthorne House. Before pressing on the buzzer, Father Greiner took one last look at Rosie, and gently squeezed her hand. He saw she'd begun to cry.

A young novitiate unlocked the door and greeted Father Greiner, completely avoiding eye contact with Rosie. Their brief exchange directed Father Greiner to the Mother Superior's office, where the two met behind closed doors while Rosie sat on a wooden bench and waited for their meeting to end. Something was said in the meeting that noticeably upset Father Greiner. He came out, handed Rosie the brown bag containing her personal effects, and left abruptly.

The Mother Superior exited the office right after Father Greiner's departure and directed Rosie to follow her down a dimly lit hallway towards a long flight of stairs, which took them up to the second floor and the room where Rosie would be hidden away until she had her baby.

"I've spoken at length with your mother about what a great disappointment you've been. If you were my daughter, I would be doing with you exactly what she's chosen to do."

The Mother Superior said all she had to say then left.

The return ride, carried Father Greiner deeper into a labyrinth of hypocrisy, twisting his thoughts and robbing him of the fortitude to turn back, to get Rosie out of there, to take charge and change the outcome of her future, or, at the very least, give her some sign of promising hope. Inside his head, nothing made sense. He couldn't erase the feeling that he'd taken her on some kind of perverse pilgrimage, where vultures raged overhead scavenging to rob her of what was rightfully hers, her child.

Chapter 7

The String-Player's Finale

In her masterfully orchestrated performance, the villainous Elsa had turned on enough charm to captivate the mighty Mephistopheles and outmaneuver the suspicious priest. "Father Greiner, you're no fool."

Elsa didn't believe a word of what she'd said about his not being a fool, but having no one left to do her dirty work, she had no choice but to keep up her ruse and patronize him to the very end.

"I asked you here because you're the one person I know I can trust."

In his formative years he tagged the Elsa's of the world "ubiquitous web weavers" who entrapped the weak of mind to use for their own preservation. He hoped this was the final piece in Elsa's "trust" game because he was about to throw this game on the floor and declare her the winner. After all, it's what she wanted, to be the winner, to come out on top. He was finished playing her games.

"Mrs. Gradel, I noticed a cab waiting out front all loaded up with a trunk and several travel bags. Are you going somewhere?"

"It's really none of your business, but since you'll be taking care of my personal affairs, I feel obligated to tell you some of what I am doing. I'm leaving America and returning to Germany, where I plan to start my life over."

The priest's feelings towards Elsa ranged from stoic dislike to passionate disdain, reinforcing all the reasons he harbored for secretly mistrusting her. A month after Elsa had arrived from Germany her younger sister Rose threw a party for some of the elites in her social circle at the William Penn Hotel so they could meet her sister, a renowned violinist. His opinion was then formed and forever remained unchanged.

"I had legal papers drawn up by my lawyer. I expect you to keep these in a safe place at the record room in the rectory. It's the least the church should do for all I've given it all these years I've been a member. These papers are duplicates. They answer any and all questions of legality my family might have regarding the decisions I've made." Father Greiner didn't understand how anyone could just up and leave everything. What Elsa was doing made absolutely no sense at all. He had to know and asked, "What's to become of this house?"

"It's been given to my dear friend, Wilhelm Steiner, to use as the Institute of Musical Art, intended only for gifted students with natural ability and a passion for serious work in the study of music. No others will be accepted. If for any reason the school should fail or the director becomes ill, passes away, you know, those kinds of tragedies we sometimes face, well..." She paused because she didn't want him to know any more of her personal business than she'd already given him, and she wasn't quite sure how to go on without making him angry enough he'd possibly refuse to help her. "Everything's in those papers you hold in your hands. I'll leave it at that."

Her collection of instruments, excluding three violins, remained with the school and became school property. Before the house furnishings were dispersed about town, the store's inventory had been sold to another merchant who removed it all down to the last nail. Several odd pieces of furniture no one seemed interested in were moved to the cellar, and the remaining smaller items were boxed up and stored in the oversized detached garage behind the house.

She instructed Father Greiner to sell the Gradel family pew and give all the proceeds to the orphan children's fund. Needless to say, none of these responsibilities belonged to him, but for this Elsa named him executor to her estate. In addition, she named him as the director of finances on the music school's board, a job for which he would receive an annual stipend.

"My children were afforded opportunities, but instead, they chose not to close their hand and take hold of what could have made a difference for them. So be it. They made their choices and must live with them, just as I am doing now in choosing to return to my homeland. I have nothing more to say, nothing more to give away, and nothing more to worry about. Life should be simple and easy now. My children never consulted me about the choices they made, and I don't expect they have any right to question mine."

Without so much as another word, Elsa turned around and walked out the door.

Father Greiner's head throbbed. This miserable woman managed to dupe him once again. Worst of all, was the unbearable humiliation of having allowed her to ever know he could be bought. He ran to the window with all her papers, yelling as loudly as he could, "I want no part of you or your stinking money," but it was too late. The cab was driving off.

Across town at Hawthorne House, Rosie remained an enigma. In the beginning the staff assumed her unwillingness to speak stemmed from embarrassment, but one nun in particular viewed it as a possible sign of depression and brought the matter to the attention of the social worker, who assumed Father Greiner might know something since he was the one who'd brought her to Hawthorne House. A lengthy conversation ensued, in which Father Greiner convinced the social worker that Rosie needed time to get over the recent death of her father, not to mention accepting the fact she was pregnant and unwed.

The matter was dropped until the staff began noticing changes in her personal habits, like bathing, missing meals, and hearing remarks from other young mothers-to-be about how they'd hear her crying in the night and pacing the floor, seemingly unable to sleep.

A meeting was called by the staff social worker to address Rosie's fate, because Hawthorne House only accepted healthy mothers, all others with afflictions of any kind were sent elsewhere. For instance, those suffering with mental disorders or severe depression were sent to St. Elizabeth's. But in Rosie's case, the Mother Superior had interceded. There would be no further discussion, the decision was final. Rosie would go nowhere until after the baby was born. Once again Elsa's money had spoken.

Sister Mary Agnes, the social worker at Hawthorne House, telephoned Father Greiner to inform him that a strong Catholic couple had been selected to adopt Rosie's baby. The position and responsibility of Hawthorne House would end after the birth of the baby, and she needed to know what arrangements the family had made for Rosie upon her release. "Can you answer this for me?"

"No, but I can tell you her only family is a brother and an aunt, but I haven't spoken to them in some time and have no idea if their future plans include Rosie. I'll need to make some inquiries and get back to you."

The social worker wasn't sure the priest understood the urgency in making arrangements for Rosie upon release. "Someone definitely needs to care for her, making certain she eats well and has medical attention for this depression. Someone needs to take responsibility for her because she's in no condition to do it alone. Remember Father, we are not a hotel or a rest home."

Father Greiner told the social worker that he would need time to get in touch with what remained of her family but he promised nothing. Elsa's ultimate revenge was to make Father Greiner pay for everything that had happened because he introduced Frank into their lives. He was barely able to tend to his morning duties, say mass, or for that matter, do much of anything without thinking about Rosie and why no one knew of Frank's whereabouts.

At one time Father Greiner and Rose Dunnigan engaged in lengthy philosophical discussions that went on all hours of the night and into the wee hours of the morning. Sadly, their friendship eroded over a simple misunderstanding. The two of them became such adversaries that Rose went so far as changing churches to avoid him.

Father Greiner never fully accepted Rose's attitude towards him as real and final, believing in his heart that she had some sort of mental disorder that zipped her in and out of these changes in her personality. Elsa argued that these changes were nothing more than left over tantrums learned in childhood to control their father who gave in to her every whim, and after that, used as a tool throughout life to get her way. Whatever the reason, whatever the excuse, this visit was one that Father Greiner dreaded almost as much as his last encounter with Elsa.

Rose anticipated his visit and prepared an assortment of teacakes and a pot of tea, hoping to get their visit off to a pleasant start. They exchanged small talk and Rose nervously flitted from subject to subject until he took charge and stated his reasons for coming. He spelled out all he knew about Elsa, Hans' death and funeral, her abrupt departure, and lastly what had happened to Rosie. When he got to the subject of Rosie, Rose's attitude visibly shifted from one of sympathy to utter disgust. Her tone spoke volumes, "Can I help, or do I want to get involved with someone who is not my responsibility, is what I ask myself. And besides, did you forget I have a husband to consult who also lives here?"

"Rose, we both know Pat has never had a say about anything that goes on in your house, and he'd be the last person to object to your helping Rosie, and she isn't even his niece."

"This matter is clearly none of Pat's concern nor is she his responsibility. And for that matter, it's none of your business either."

Father Greiner understood her perfectly. Rose did not want him to breathe a word of this scurrilous rubbish concerning a member of her family to anyone, especially not her husband. This gave him the impetus to stand up to Rose on Rosie's behalf and not leave without a commitment.

"Whose business and responsibility is Rosie? Mine? The church?" He waited briefly, prepared for any kind of argument, but got none. "Rosie is neither my responsibility nor that of the church. Like it or not, Rose, it's up to you and Emil."

For the life of him he couldn't figure out where in her twisted mind she came up with a way to justify making him responsible for her niece in any way. But Rose being Rose, she wouldn't stop her goading. "Father, you have twenty-some rooms in that huge rectory, and they're never all in use at the same time. Stick her in one of those."

Father Greiner's heart and mind weighted heavily with sadness, and a bleak darkness came over him as he pleadingly asked Rose, "What's to become of Rosie?"

"My moral constitution won't allow me to have her live here. If my neighbors or Emil's students found out about this it would mean social devastation."

When Rose got off on her high society this and that, Father Greiner tuned her out, believing in his heart that she was nothing more than a mentally twisted pretentious misfit the real ladies of social circles pooh-poohed. "Rose, listen to you! Sounds like you're more concerned about what someone thinks than the welfare of your niece!"

Rose searched for every excuse to run from this family tragedy, blaming everyone and anyone she could name. "What about the man who took her womanhood, why doesn't he take her?"

The priest had one more card to play, and he had held it for last hoping it would work. "You've been blessed with a great deal of good fortune, and all because of one woman who treated you like a daughter and named you as the sole heir to her estate when she died, yet you sit there and refuse to help a blood relative. Seems to me Rose like you're a taker, not the giver you'd like the world to think you are." He couldn't believe his ears with what came out of her mouth.

"When do you need an answer?"

"No later than tomorrow."

Chapter 8

Strange Bed-Fellows

Rose was unable to bear children, so when her sister Elsa would ask her to take her son Emil while she taught violin or had one of her frequent public performances, Rose jumped at the chance to play mother. At the age of two Emil battled severe-pneumonia, later he became susceptible to upper respiratory infections every time the weather changed. The time-consuming task involved with caring for a sick child, or having to cancel a performance every time he coughed or had difficulty breathing, made it easy to convince Hans that they should let Emil stay at her sister's during the winter months. Emil was so starved for love and attention, the mere mention of leaving Aunt Rose's and going home brought on breathing attacks the child feigned to scare his mother half-way out of her wits. This worked every time, and stays at Auntie Rose's became lengthier until he turned sixteen and refused to come home except for lessons.

Unlike her sister, Rose lived to mother Emil, which infuriated her husband Pat and made him insanely jealous. It didn't take long for Emil to figure out what was happening. This complex, spoiled young boy out-maneuvered a self-indulged woman until she became a scatter-brained puppet who managed to destroy whatever marriage she once had. The importance of motherhood fit Rose like a glove, and she thrived on those times when Emil demanded her undivided attention.

Rose loved to cook and bake and Emil loved to sit and eat—a perfect union. So when young Emil first came to live with her she created a motivational agenda where he'd perform for her for thirty minutes and afterwards they'd sit together and have teatime.

Over the years the only thing that changed in the afternoon was the length of his performances and their waist sizes. Teatime remained teatime, with Rose drifting farther and farther into her make-believe world of pretentiousness thriving on a daily concert performance by her very own personal virtuoso who succumbed to enchanting compliments used to manipulate his starving need for worth. Rose mastered the art of knowing how to use words to cajole others into doing exactly what she wanted. Daily target number one, her nephew, whose puppet strings she had wrapped around her little finger.

Rose developed a plan to persuade Emil that his younger sister Rosie was his family's problem, not hers. She methodically worked up a chart showing how much money might be required to support someone unable to care for oneself for one year. Rose listed an amount of money she was willing to contribute should Emil's expenses exceed his budget. Other-wise, she wanted no part of this shameful mess his sister had created for herself. While their tea steeped, Rose schemed up various methods she'd use to coerce Emil into her way of thinking.

"Emil, precious darling, may I pour you a cup of tea?"

"Please, Auntie dear."

"As you know, Father Greiner came by last night, and his reason for coming was rather shocking. First, your mother went back to Germany. Can you believe she would do such a thing and not tell us?"

"Good! She finally kept her word. When I was little and didn't play exactly as she demanded she'd be furious and threaten to leave me and go back to Germany, claiming I was too stupid for her to waste any more time on. All I have to say is good luck with those smart little German boys." Rose chuckled at his sense of humor.

At the early age of two and a half, Emil showed interest in the violin. By the time he was three, this child exhibited an innate talent to play by rote. Elsa decided that her little genius was ready for lessons, which began at seven in the morning before her regularly scheduled students arrived. The routine went on until Emil reached the age of four-teen. Emil was a brilliant violinist like his mother and her mother before her. He was a gifted child with perfect pitch, a natural ability, and a brilliant mind. Elsa envisioned the day when the two would perform on stages around the world, but there was one downside to all of this. Emil refused to perform for anyone except her. This behavior frustrated Elsa to the point where she determined he could never be a success unless she broke him of this nonsensical insecurity. This harsh approach of hers backfired when Emil suddenly exhibited signs of having severe breathing difficulties and repeated episodes of bed-wetting. The family physician diagnosed bronchial asthma, but the bed-wetting was unexplainable and perhaps symptomatic of something else. Elsa understood the asthma, but losing control of his bladder at his age, was unacceptable. She was so determined to break him of his "nasty habit" of wetting himself and smelling like a pig that she forced him to sleep alone on the third floor until he remained dry for a week. Interestingly, the only time Emil wet himself or had severe breathing problems was when Elsa shrieked and screamed because his technique was wrong, or the little genius went off on a tangent learning the repertoire he'd chosen rather than the one she'd assigned. Elsa was all about control and discipline, and this combination was turning her child into a neurotic.

Elsa's husband Hans was a mild-mannered, affable man, who avoided conflict of any nature, and he could no longer silently stand by while his wife mistreated their son by forcing him to sleep alone on the third floor. This cruel sadistic punishment had to stop. Elsa threw up her hands and told Hans to take over since he seemed to think he could handle the boy better. Months went by and Elsa lost all interest in doing anything with Emil, including giving him lessons. Shortly thereafter, the overnight stays to Aunt Rose's became more frequent, and that's when Emil chose to become a permanent resident.

Rose was sitting in the corner end of the davenport thinking how best to broach the subject of Rosie when Emil finished his tea, set the cup aside, and propped himself up against her with his back against her chest like she was part of the sofa. She wrapped her arms around his upper torso, held him tight, and recapped most of what Father Greiner told her regarding his mother, withholding any mention of his sister until she was sure the timing was right. Rose's greatest fear was that her niece's appalling situation had all the ear markings of possibly disrupting their personal lives. Rose Dunnigan would see to it that this would never happen.

Emil was exhausted and wanted to go to bed, but Rose wanted to prepare him somewhat for what lay ahead in the coming days and figured if she planted an idea—just a little seed, perhaps by morning he'd come up with a solution she hadn't thought of. She refused to drop the subject of his mother and, in typical Rose fashion, managed to get her last thoughts planted.

"You'll never believe what else your mother has done. She's not only left the country, but she's entrusted everything to a priest, not to her family. I say, good riddance, let the German' have her! What do you say?"

"Auntie Rose, you're repetitive and beginning to get on my nerves. I'm talked out, and whatever it is that is bothering you will have to wait. Right now I'm exhausted, I'm irritable, and more than anything else, I need my rest."

Emil curtly dismissed any further discussion on the subject matter of his mother, but Rose being Rose, the self-serving-over-indulged-Rose who never knew when to leave well enough alone, took a stab at the subject of his sister.

"Emil, listen to me and think about what I am about to ask you to do."

"If this has anything to do with that witch, I told you, I'm not interested."

"It's your sister Rosie, she's in trouble."

"What kind of trouble?"

"Rosie's pregnant and is staying in some foundling home across town for the time being. For some unknown reason Father Greiner is unwilling to share all he knows about her being there, and I don't know why or how, but somehow I suspect your mother is involved."

"Oh my God—Rosie having a baby! There's some mistake."

"That's exactly what I said when Father told me they're not sure when the baby is due, but he did mention that some couple is waiting to adopt it. Unfortunately the bigger problem is Rosie and what to do with her afterwards. Got any thoughts besides moving her here?"

"No way, I'll not have any part of that ridiculous notion. Uncle Pat's miserably unhappy having me live here. Add her to the population and see what happens, bad idea. Maybe we can find a little house to rent where she can live alone—where no one knows anything about her."

"Emil, Emil, Emil, you're mother always said you were a 'genius,' and you absolutely are."

Emil tilted his head back to read the expression on Rose's face. She lifted his chin with her hand, gently kissed his fat fluffy full lips, delighting in the moment of being the most important person in his life. Having had enough of Aunt Rose's overbearing suffocation, he pushed her away and headed off to bed.

The following morning during breakfast Rose emphasized the importance of secrecy and keeping this business about his sister between themselves. "I don't want your uncle reminding me how my high society sister's kid had an illegitimate bastard, especially since he knows how much I detest those two lazy drunken sisters of his who never clean under their filthy fingernails, always cook with a cigarette dangling out of their mouths, dropping ashes all over the food like it's seasoning and then he wonders why I take my own food, dishes, and silverware when I'm forced to go there. What an idiot! Guess if you grow up with that kind of slovenliness, you think nothing of it. Not for me! Every time I am forced to go to his sisters' place he takes the opportunity to remind me that "no one ever died from dirt."

Emil expressed disinterest in re-hashing her repetitive nonsense about Uncle Pat's sisters and abruptly told Rose he was running out of patience and boisterously told her in no uncertain terms that this "old hag issue" was nothing more than vicious gossip and of no interest to him. This got Rose's attention. She shut up and listened intently. Emil concluded that the only person who could keep this family secret was the person who brought it to them, the priest.

Later that morning Rose called Father Greiner to inform him that she and Emil had decided to rent Rosie a simple little house in another part of town, preferably on Irish or Polish hill where people wouldn't bother with a German. As well as he knew Rose Dunnigan, the last thing he anticipated was a quick positive response. Before getting too excited, he figured he'd better wait this one out because Rose's mental barometer could change in a flash. Even so, he remained cautiously optimistic.

Emil and Rose's plan was minimal. They would undertake the responsibility of caring for Rosie only until she could care for herself. Neither believed her depression was of a serious nature but was instead merely a "moody act" so that they'd feel sorry for her and the mess she made of her life.

Rose had a momentary twinge of conscience remembering the time shortly after she married Pat when she became extremely depressed, stopped eating, wouldn't get out of bed, refused to get dressed, cried all the time, and worried her husband to the point where he truly believed she might die. The doctors prescribed medication and recommended that she be put in the hospital, but instead Pat asked Father Greiner to intercede and contact her family in Germany to see whether they would be willing to come to America and help remedy the situation. Elsa and Hans gave up two very lucrative careers to come to America and possibly help save Rose.

In a blink of an eye, Rose convinced herself that her situation was altogether different, nothing like the one Rosie created by disgracing the family, then foisting this insurmountable and unresolvable situation on her and Emil. The more Rose thought, the angrier she became.

Father Greiner reluctantly agreed to help Rose, and for the next five days he exhaustively searched for a house while still maintaining his duties as a cleric. His determination paid off when a priest from St. Joseph's Church described a six-room house on Mulberry Street that his deceased mother willed to the church. It needed work and the church members hadn't decided whether to fix it up and keep it as a rental or put it up for sale.

Father Greiner called Rose to tell her about this particular house, and she insisted on seeing it immediately. After the initial inspection, she sat Emil down at the kitchen table to re-calculate their financial status. They decided to present a verbal offer to purchase. The church accepted, and the frantic chase began to get things in order.

Rose believed everything was falling into place like some divine plan and instructed Emil to go to his old house and see what was in the attic or the cellar that could be used to furnish the Mulberry Street house. If all went well and Emil found anything of use, Rose would have her handyman move it to the new location and the problem of Rosie would be solved once and for all. Emil remained the eternal pessimist and expressed grave doubt that any of this would work.

Emil kept a key to his old house, one he'd used when going back and forth between taking lessons and living with Auntie Rose. It had been several years since he'd stepped foot inside, and within seconds he realized what a horrible mistake he'd made by allowing Rose to coerce him into returning there. He unlocked the door and as soon as he stepped inside all he could think of was getting out, but he couldn't until he had done what he was sent to do. Before going down into the cellar, he walked through the house, noting a sign covered with sheeting. Several rooms had grand pianos in them, and others had various instruments left out in the open as if a group of musicians were using the place. And as far as he was concerned, he had no intention of going up into the third floor to check anything. Rose's instructions were to check out the basement, and that was where he headed. When he tried to open the door, it stuck. He put his hand on the knob and gave it a good yank, next thing he knew, the knob was in his hand. He fussed and fidgeted to get it back in place. After a great deal of frustration he opened the door, believing he heard voices. The palms of his hands broke out in a sweat. The distraction of these voices seemed to get louder with each step he took, making him nervous and uneasy. His mind swirled with confusion trying to remember why he was there. It came to him, the last thing Rose had said as he walked out the door, "Emil, be sure to take a pencil, Mr. Lewis never does anything if it isn't written down." He didn't bring a pencil.

Emil hurried down the basement stairs, reached the bottom, and did a cursory examination of the cellar's contents. Noting a pile of items neatly stashed in the corner nearest to where he stood, he recognized the furnishings, hastily turned around to escape the cellar demons, when an absolute fiasco occurred. He tripped and fell over his own feet. The struggle to get up and get moving created another onslaught of entanglements from cutting his hand to ripping out one side of his pants when the front pocket caught on a nail. This clumsy experience shook him to his very core. He fretted over going home with his fat hip poking out of his torn pants for everyone to see. More importantly, though, he realized that this was not nearly as important as locating Rose's key to check out the inside of the garage and return with a detailed list of everything he observed.

If Emil is ever the opposition, and Rose's plan is to sway his way of thinking, she picks away at him like a vulture does its prey until spineless-Emil rolls over and concedes to her every whim.

Just as he suspected, the minute he walked in the door Rose was ready and waiting to hear the verbal list. He started with naming Rosie's dark red velvet overstuffed chair and gaudy-rose-covered carpet which once belonged to Mrs. Millbauer and was given to Rosie when she moved and no longer needed them. The Millbauer's were the original owners of the hardware store, and when Mr. Millbauer died, his wife sold the business to Rosie's father before moving to another part of the city. She not only gave Rosie the rug and chair, she also gave her an antique oak dresser and matching wardrobe that Rosie had always admired. These were carelessly stacked in one corner of the cellar and covered with the carpet.

Rose could have cared less about this junk but for the savings it meant to her in both trouble and money. She was more interested in whether or not there remained anything of personal interest to her and started hammering Emil for more details. "What about the garage? Anything in there I'd be interested in?"

"Nothing I'd be interested in. Mostly I saw boxes of dishes, some clothes I think maybe belonged to Rosie, and-uh, oh yes—the family bible. I saw that too"

Rose couldn't believe what she just heard him say.

"You scatter-brain-foolish-boy…I'm so exasperated with you right now I could shake the living life out of you. How could you do this after all I've done for you—see the family bible and leave it there? Oh my God, if my father knew this he'd roll over in his grave. And dishes? What did they look like?"

After Rose's berating, Emil stumbled over describing Limoges and Bavarian sets of china he saw in boxes once belonging to Rose's great-grandmother on her mother's side. Apparently, when Elsa immigrated to America, she was to select one set and give the other to Rose. Obviously this never happened.

"I want every one of those dishes. I can't believe my sister would knowingly leave family heirlooms out there like common trash. She did this on purpose."

Rose went directly to the phone and called for a cab so she could go and gather up what was rightfully hers. She instructed Emil to call Father Greiner to inform him which things they wanted to remove from the cellar for Rosie to use, and to also let him know that she personally was taking everything in the garage. Emil had had his fill of Rose's directives and refused to call Father Greiner. Rose made the call herself.

"Father, so no one accuses me of stealing what is rightfully mine, I want you to know I'm removing my great-grandmother's dishes from the garage and am taking all of Rosie's furniture from the cellar. I have my own entry key that Elsa gave me years ago. My hired help will let themselves into the house, pick up those things we'll need to furnish Rosie's bedroom, lock the house back up, and deliver everything to Mulberry Street. Just wanted you to know you needn't bother yourself with any of this. I have everything arranged."

Father John Michael from St. Joseph's parish was next on her call list. This call would finalize everything and ready the house for its new occupant. Emil had an excruciating headache and could barely stand the sound of Rose's voice. He thought to himself, *perfect timing, she's on the phone and I'm out of here.* He went straight to his room, locked the door, and turned out the light.

The following morning at breakfast Rose and Emil set a time to inspect the house on Mulberry Street so they could prioritize those items most in need of repair in the part of the house that Rosie would occupy. The rest of the house would be left in an "as-is" condition—dirty and old, didn't matter any to Rose—she didn't plan to live there.

"Emil, the first thing you tell your sister when she arrives at this house is she better never disclose her name or where she's from to anyone ever. You instruct her on what she needs to say should anyone ask personal questions. In fact, you tell her that if she opens her mouth to anyone about anything having to do with her family, she's out on the street."

Rose and Emil never spoke about the Mulberry Street purchase, and if they did, they referenced it as "the harlot's house." Rose had her own money source and felt there was no need for her husband to know what she did or didn't do with her money. The one thing she refused to do was pay for Rosie's food. She figured she'd bought the house, the least Emil could do was buy Rosie's food until she was able to get employment. When Emil suggested they split the cost of food, she reminded him she was not a charity and expected Rosie to pay back every dime even if it meant that she had to clean toilets in the park to meet her obligation. Rose's mind flitted from one concern to the next, trying to figure out whether Rosie could conceivably get so comfortable and accustomed to being taken care of that she'd never see the need to get out and get a job. Rose's only concern was always about the money, and in this case, whether or not she'd ever see a single dime of it paid back.

"I'll never know how Father Greiner found the nerve to get me involved in this. You, yes, she's your sister. Your mother, yes, it's her daughter. But me, I'm nothing but an aunt. Your contemptible mother was in collusion with that weakling of a priest, getting him to do her dirty work. Probably gave him a lot of money. I used to like him, but not anymore. Sorry now that I went to all that trouble to have tea with him."

Rose and Emil left Mulberry Street in a taxi, arriving home in time for her to prepare lunch. Meanwhile, Emil readied to face an arduous afternoon into evening schedule of students beginning at one o'clock and ending at eight.

At approximately eight-o-five every evening, after the last student left, Rose rang a small silver dinner bell and Emil joined her at the dining room table. Tonight's dinner would be late, finishing up sometime after ten. Rose insisted that her dinner table be set with fine bone china, white Damask cloths, oversized starched napkins perfectly folded and placed on the left. The engraved silver positioned one inch from the edge of the table looked like a row of tine artillery lines. Not even the finest of aristocrats could fault Rose's table. Four crystal goblets stood to the right of the dinner plate, but the only one ever filled was the water. The other three looked great, but were rarely used. Rose's husband saw her fanaticism with setting a formal table for every dinner meal as a pretentious act, whereas she, on the other hand, grew up knowing this was how those with proper upbringing did things.

Pat eventually got pushed out of his wife's life and retired to the cellar every night to avoid hearing any of what he saw as ostentatious. Down there he'd sit on an old army cot and idle away the evening free from any conflict, listening to his radio, drinking Irish whiskey, and happy to be in his own little world away from the two of them. The following morning he'd be off to work before either of them got out of bed. As time went on, the rift between the three of them grew to disproportionate levels, with Rose and Emil on one side and Pat alone on the other.

Mid-afternoon for Emil meant teatime and a brief break from teaching. For Rose, that time gave her an opportunity to glean the undivided attention of her precious Emil. Mind you, she always wore apropos attire and posed while he did the pouring, flitting about in butterfly fashion to fetch one thing or another that she'd request, and more often than not, if she asked gently enough, he'd perform one of her favorite Wieniawski etudes. Otherwise, teatime ended, the teaching schedule resumed, and Rose did what Rose did best back in the kitchen, washing dishes for the next table setting.

Chapter 9

The Manila Envelope

Two and a half weeks later another life began at Hawthorne House.

"Rosie, listen to me. It's Dr. Penn. Can you hear me? Look at me, Rosie. I'm talking to you. I'm over here on your right side, not over there."

The doctor gently placed his hand under Rosie's chin and turned her head to face him. "Rosie, you're in heavy labor and it looks to me like this will all be over before long."

"Dr. Penn, I've noticed she doesn't look at any of us when we talk to her. At first I thought it was depression, and since then I've decided that's only part of why she hasn't spoken to any of us. I think most of her problem is shame."

"How long has this been going on?"

"Not exactly sure, but two weeks ago her parish priest came to visit and this upset her, and I asked him not to come back until after she had this baby. This late in the pregnancy, I don't think it's a good idea to upset her."

"Has she shown any signs of distress, problems with appetite, vomiting, or complaints of headaches?"

"Not that I'm aware of, but she does seem to communicate well with the head obstetrics nurse, Sister Mary-Seline." At that point the doctor requested a meeting with her.

Within minutes, she returned with Sister Mary-Seline who explained their method of crude non-verbal head-nod-shoulder-shrug communication she established so the two of them could get on during her stay at the home.

To better evaluate Rosie's problem, the concerned physician insisted that the staff maintain a ledger, as well as conduct a thorough physical exam, before anyone released her from Hawthorne House.

"One thing more, if what you're telling me is true, and if we expect this delivery to take place without complication or harm to the mother or baby, I think we need to consider having no one in the room but Sister Mary-Seline. She has an extensive background in obstetrics, and in my opinion, is amply qualified. Should complications occur, I'll be across the street at Women's Hospital and can be here in a matter of minutes."

Dr. Penn went directly to the Mother Superior's office and issued a directive that everything related to Rosie's delivery and after-care be handled by no one but Sister Mary-Seline.

This inflexibly rigid, died in the wool, "never bend the rules" Mother Superior ran Hawthorne House. This tough old bird was the one person in life you didn't want to rub the wrong way. Let there be no mistake, behind that pious-looking face lived a cold heart with little patience or regard for any un-wed mother who sinned and broke God's commandments. The doctor anticipated that she'd hear him out because she couldn't afford not to. After all, he donated valuable hours of time and his wife raised countless dollars, all to support the foundling home. He talked, she bent her rules. Sister Mary-Seline was to be the only one in the birthing room with Rosie when she gave birth.

Between running back and forth with refreshing cold compresses to keep Rosie as comfortable as possible, and giving her sips of ice water while monitoring her contractions, sister Mary-Seline waited for some kind of involvement from Rosie, but, to her chagrin, there was none. She ignored the fact that Rosie chose not to answer questions, and went on talking herself. "I'm going to ask you to do something for me, a simple request. Can or would you nod your head?"

Still nothing, but this didn't stop Sister Mary-Seline.

"Hum, so you won't nod your head and you won't talk—how very interesting. You're a jigsaw puzzle, eh! But guess what Rosie—I've got an incredible reputation for figuring out the solutions to puzzles no matter how tough. The buzz around here is you can't hear, but I think otherwise. You can hear, but don't want to talk."

Sister Mary-Seline thought she read something in Rosie's facial expression only a hearing person would respond to. "I'm right, told you I was good. I solved the puzzle!"

Rosie appeared to be off in a trance, but the nun wasn't going to let this subject die on the vine. "Rosie, you have to do something so the two of us can communicate. I want to help you. Believe me—you are going to need my help through this ordeal. Trust me, when I tell you, you can not do this all by yourself. All I am asking for is a simple yes or no answer, and I don't think that is asking, too, much. A '*yes*' or a '*no*'. If your answer's a '*no*' don't squeeze my hand. If it's a '*yes*', squeeze my hand. Now, please just try—we'll call this one a 'practice' one."

Sister waited patiently. "Good girl, it's a pretty wimpy weak squeeze, but nonetheless, I'm calling this a squeeze. Finally, we're communicating! I call this progress."

The nun took a breather, walked over to the other side of the room hoping to give Rosie time to allay any feelings of mistrust. She needed Rosie to not push her away. Mary-Seline took Rosie's hand in hers and waited. "Rosie, are you aware that this baby is about to be born?"

She wanted Rosie to squeeze on her own initiative and not because she felt pressured to obey orders. Her patience was rewarded with a barely noticeable squeeze. "Good girl, how about another one of those."

This gentle, soft-spoken woman holding her hand exhibited a kindness towards her that, to this point, no one else had. Rosie wanted to please her.

"I want you to relax and think about this baby you are about to have. Do you care if it is a boy or a girl?" Rosie gave a gentle squeeze. "That's wonderful. I'd like the baby to be a little girl. What about you?" Rosie squeezed again. This signaled that the two of them were moving in the same direction. "So we both want a little girl." Rosie looked away when squeezed the nun's hand. "I know she'll be as pretty as her Mother."

Mary-Seline noticed Rosie holding something in her left hand, carefully keeping it tucked under a fold in the cover sheet next to her hip. "What's in your hand?" Rosie raised her left hand and exposed the object in such a way that it enabled the suns rays to shine directly on it. Surprised by this sudden action, the nun's response was swift. "Looks like rosaries to me. Are those yours?"

The chameleon-like qualities each bead possessed enabled them to change from an unusual blue haze to a rose color as if magic had been performed, playfully exchanging color for color. The slightest back-and-forth movement of these intriguing gems tricked the mind into believing you momentarily caught hold of the rainbow.

Sister Mary-Seline had seen hundreds of rosaries growing up as a catholic, but none to match the likes of these. "Those are exquisite! Do you know what they are?" Rosie remained still. The nun tried not to exhibit any facial expression that might change the dynamics between them. She opened the drawer in the stand next to Rosie's bed removing a pencil and paper, "I'd be very interested to learn what this gem is. Could you write down the name of it for me?" Rosie ignored her.

When she refused the paper and pencil, Mary-Seline decided to tease her. "You won't write it down because you probably can't read or write, is that it? Ah, don't worry, lots of people can't write, and if you can't write, you can't write. Or maybe your arm's asleep right now and you'll write for me when it wakes up."

Rosie scowled.

"Oh my goodness, I was just teasing you. Honestly, I meant no harm. Something tells me you're smart as a whip."

The nun realized Rosie's hormonal levels were no doubt off the chart at this juncture and deeply regretted the ribbing. She spoke solemnly. "Have you had these a long time?" Rosie gave no response. "You're blessed to have such beautiful rosaries. Obviously, whoever gave these to you knew you were special. Don't ever forget that."

Except for an occasional gentle breeze every now and again, August was an ordinarily pleasant end to summer. Rosie was well into the seventh hour of labor, rounding into the final stages of delivery.

As in Rosie's case, Sister Mary-Seline, too, had a child taken from her when she was young. But in her particular situation, she never carried it to term because her physician father had performed an abortion, a dark-dirty-secret no one knew about other than she and her parents. Her father never told her mother that severe bleeding and other complications occurred, forcing him to sterilize her to save her life. Whether the sterilization part was true or he arbitrarily chose to do this out of anger towards his daughter for getting herself into a mess he was forced to fix, we'll never know. One thing we do know is his wife never forgave him, worse yet, he never forgave himself.

A month after the abortion, Marie-Selene was sent to a convent in western Pennsylvania where her father hoped she'd straighten out her life. The first thing she did upon arrival was change her name to Mary-Seline. She was fifteen at the time. Shortly thereafter, her father committed suicide.

Both women paid the ultimate price for wounds inflicted upon them by themselves and others for which there was no medication, no surgical removal, no love, no amount of money, absolutely nothing could eradicate the never-ending pain of having given up a part of oneself.

Mary-Seline looked at Rosie attempting to muffle any sound from the pain of the final act in the grandest performance of her life—she'd given birth to a beautiful baby girl with a great set of lungs.

"You hear that Rosie? I think we have an opera singer! You did a great job, and now I have to take the baby to the nursery and clean her up. I'll be back shortly to check on you. An aide will be in to clean you up and change the bed."

Sister Agnes was waiting in the nursery when Mary-Seline arrived with the newest member of the Hawthorne House family. "Congratulations Sister. Don't know how you did it, but you handled this difficult case well. This is confidential, but I believe you deserve to know the details on this particular girl. No doubt you're wondering why she's here instead of being over at St. E's."

"I did, but assumed Mother Superior had her reasons for not sharing any of the particulars."

"Word has it her mother made a substantial donation to Hawthorne House with the stipulation her daughter remain in this facility as an unknown. The first thing tomorrow morning she's scheduled to be sterilized. The legal papers are in my office completely filled out and signed by both she and her mother. If she were my daughter, I'd be doing the very same thing."

Sister Mary-Seline totally disagreed with Sister Agnes, but she kept her opinion to herself. She believed Rosie's mother had no justification in making a decision of this magnitude. To have her daughter sterilized and deny her the opportunity to ever have another child was wicked. Unless it meant saving the mother, sterilization under any circumstances was wrong. Mary-Seline never forgave her father for what he did. Further-more, she believed her mother could have stopped him if she wanted to but she didn't. Mary-Seline held them both responsible for ruining her life and killing the child she wanted to keep.

After completely filling out paperwork regarding Rosie and the birth of her baby, Mary-Seline delivered the packet to the main office where everything was thoroughly reviewed before the new parents were telephoned and given instructions as to when and where to come for their new baby. Along the way she stopped back to see Sister Agnes.

"In your stead, I want you to allow me to be the one to say good-bye to this little one."

"Why this 'little one' as you call her?" The social worker suspected something more was going on. "Did this mother say something during delivery I should know?"

"My reasons for doing this are purely personal, and honestly, I'm not sure I can even tell you why. Something I read in her eyes drew me to her and through them she touched my heart. I need to say good-bye to this little one, if not for her, then for me." She carefully presented her case, knowing if she used the right words and reasoning she'd win. "Is that asking too much?"

Hawthorne House's stead-fast rules were executed by the Mother Superior in charge and respectfully carried out by the entire staff. The social worker's responsibility regarding newborns carried with it many secrets and personal information kept under lock and key in the Mother Superior's files. Breaking this rule could result in severe consequences should anything go wrong. "I will consent to your request this one time, but don't make me regret this decision. And under no circumstances do you divulge what I have told you about this case. Agreed?"

After many years of working together, Sister Mary-Seline was insulted that Sister Agnes would scrutinize her to this degree, but she maintained her composure, "Of course I do. When do you suppose this baby will leave?"

"Mother Superior is making arrangements as we speak. As soon as I get the details, you can arrange your schedule. Right now would you check that new group of unwed mothers for me and make sure they're tending their duties and not finding places to hide. Seems they're a lazy lot, and I'll have none of that."

"Should I plan to meet you back in your office, say about three or so?"

"Yes, that would be fine. But in case I'm not there, wait for me. You'll need the envelope containing the birth certificate and other legal papers, and those will be locked in my desk for safe keeping up until the very last minute when the baby is ready to leave."

The more Sister Mary-Seline thought about everything Sister Agnes told her, the more emotionally embroiled she became in

Rosie's sadness. She threw objectivity to the wind, went directly to Rosie's room, closing the door and speaking as fast as she could.

She gently touched Rosie on the arm, not wanting to alarm her. "Wake up—it's me, Sister Mary-Seline." Rosie was lying on her side facing the wall, and Mary-Seline wanted her to look at her when she spoke. "I have to talk to you. Something in my heart tells me you can hear perfectly well, or I wouldn't be standing here telling you what is going to happen now that you've had your baby. Listen carefully, because I don't have much time and have to talk fast. We never know who's coming to get the baby. It could be anybody, the new mother and father or even the parish priest. The priest usually brings a nun with him to carry the baby."

She waited a minute or so, trying to assess whether Rosie was listening and comprehending everything she had to say. "We're never told how the baby will leave the foundling home, but we dress them up in one of our pretty outfits to present them to their new parents. The new parents go in a room privately, inspect the child, and if everything is acceptable and the people agree they still want to take the child, we take the baby away, remove our outfit to use again on another child in the future, and redress the baby in something the parents, the priest, or whomever comes to get the baby brings along for the child to wear home." Rosie laid there emotionless, as if in a trance. Mary-Seline proceeded to talk, hoping some of what she said got through to Rosie. "There always remains a shroud of privacy and secrecy to protect the new parents and baby. None of us ever knows anything about the babies or where they go. You have to understand, this is best for everyone because most parents don't want anyone to know the baby they have is adopted. I have no control over that." Rosie appeared tired and closed her eyes, giving Sister Mary-Seline the feeling she might well have been talking to herself all this time. In case there was a slight chance that Rosie understood any part of what she was saying, Mary-Seline kept talking. "Normally the social worker is the last one to see the baby before it leaves here, but in your baby's case, she's agreed to let me handle it. No one is to know I have told you this. Right now you're tired, confused, and sad, but I wanted you to know what is happening. If only you had trusted me enough to talk, I could have done so much more."

When Sister Mary-Seline finished talking, Rosie slowly pulled out an envelope from under the cover and handed it to her. She was stymied and wondered if Rosie heard everything she said or was merely reacting to her-mouth moving, and when it stopped, she responded. Assuming that this envelope was of a personal nature, Sister Mary-Seline quickly tucked it in her pocket before anyone entered and saw it. Unable to pierce through this patient's perplexing and guarded façade saddened her. Rosie was a difficult case, but Mary-Seline was willing to risk it all to help her.

"This is for your baby, isn't it?"

Rosie's eyes filled with tears.

"I give you my solemn promise to take care of this and no one but you and I will ever know anything about it."

A large manila envelope containing instructions on the care of newborns was given to every set of new parents upon leaving Hawthorne House. In preparation for handing baby Gradel over to whomever was coming for her, Mary-Seline took a new, unopened-manila envelope from her desk, inserted the sealed envelope Rosie had given her, and hid them in the chapel before returning to bid farewell to Rosie.

Mary-Seline's puzzle still required one last piece, saying farewell to Rosie. "You're scheduled to have hearing tests and a procedure done sometime before you leave. The doctor is worried about your depression and the fact you refuse to talk, but he'll make sure you're fine before any release is given. He will probably prescribe medicine to help you feel better before you're sent home to your family. Make sure you take the medicine he prescribes. You'll need it to get well. I won't ever see you again, which is for the best. I wish you well, and I want you to know that I will be forever grateful to God that we had this time together. Take good care of yourself and try to get some rest these next couple of days you're here. Good-bye, Rosie." Mary-Seline knew that these, her final words would make little or no sense to Rosie, but that didn't matter because they made total sense to her. "Go forward with your life, don't let this do to you what it did to me. God Bless you."

She went directly to the social worker's office and waited for Sister Agnes. While waiting there she couldn't help wondering what direction Rosie's life would travel when she left Hawthorne House.

"Mary-Seline, we've worked together a long time, and I've only seen you act like this one other time. Please tell me you're not planning to do something foolish like allowing the mother to see the baby before it leaves here." She hesitated, "You know the rules."

"You need not worry. Whatever my reason, that is certainly not one of them."

"Good, I was beginning to question my judgment in allowing you this favor. Are you sure you're not considering taking over my job as social worker instead of being the head obstetrics nurse?"

"You never know, Sister Agnes."

"The new parents apparently wanted the baby to go home in a special linen gown a relative brought back from Ireland. I understand it is absolutely gorgeous and covered in breath-taking hand-made Irish lace. They're upstairs dressing her now, and I expect one of the girls from the nursery will be bringing her down shortly."

Just then a novitiate entered the room carrying the baby. She was dressed in the most beautiful white gown with matching bonnet, and on her wee tiny feet were soft white kid shoes with a single button on each side. The novitiate complimented her on what a good girl she was and how pretty she looked then handed her to Mary-Seline.

The time had come to say good-bye. Cradling Rosie's baby tightly in her arms, Mary-Seline grabbed the manila envelope and left the social worker's office. Instead of going directly to the waiting room where she would relinquish the baby to whom-ever came for her, Mary-Seline went by way of the chapel. Once inside, she locked the door, laid baby Gradel on a pew, then raced up to the alter to retrieve the empty manila envelope she'd hidden earlier. The race was on to make the exchange. The risk she was taking, destroying an official state seal, was significant enough to lose everything she'd ever worked for. Driven by a promise to deliver this small envelope to the new would-be parents, was for her a "promise made"—and one she would not break under any circumstance.

Once the switch was made and all the contents were inside, she licked the flap and sealed the envelope. It looked just like the original minus the seal on the back, but then, no one would notice unless they were the social worker whose job this always was, and right now she was nowhere in sight. Throughout this entire time, baby Gradel never made a sound. She picked the baby up and walked to the back of the chapel, dipped her fingers in the holy water, made the sign of the cross on her forehead, and said a brief prayer for Rosie and her child. The time to part with this little one had come. She entered the room where the exchange was to take place.

"Hello Father, I'm Sister Mary-Seline. I was told you'd be here waiting for us."

The priest nodded but said nothing. Mary-Seline figured he either didn't speak or understand the same language or he felt awkward being in a place like Hawthorne House. It was anybody's guess at this point. When she handed him the large sealed manila envelope, he acted rather awkward. It was obvious to her that he was new at this game.

The distressing moment Mary-Seline dreaded all day long had come. It was time to give the baby to the young nun standing next to her. "Tell the new mommy and daddy that this little girl is healthy and strong and taking formula well. There's extra in the bag along with some instructions about the care and feeding of their newborn. I assure you this little one is perfect."

"By the way, Father, that sealed envelope you're holding in your hand contains valuable and very important papers that are to be given to the new parents. Please stress to them that these must be kept in a safe, secure place."

"I'll see they get these along with your message. Good day Sister Mary-Seline."

She was completely aghast. This young priest could speak English, but had chosen to stay in the safe zone and keep quiet. Obviously this was his first visit to a home for unwed mothers, and she sensed that picking up an illegitimate baby made him feel uncomfortable, awkward, and obviously embarrassed. She thought to herself, *young man, to be a good priest you'd better get used to doing uncomfortable, awkward, and embarrassing things, because being a priest is more than listening to confessions.* Mary-Seline followed the party of three outside and stood on the top step to watch them get settled inside their vehicle before slowly driving off. Only then did she realize, that she'd never asked the priest his name. She waved good-bye and wiped the tears from her face so no one would see she'd been crying. The day had been especially wearying, and she welcomed its end.

Chapter 10

Hemlock 36287

Every time the telephone rang, Father Greiner suspected the call could be the Mother Superior from Hawthorne House ordering him to come and collect Rosie. Once again he'd be forced to retrace the steps taken the day he brought Rosie there. The telephone kept ringing—ten, eleven, and finally on the twelfth one he picked up and heard the dreaded voice.

"Father Greiner, I want you to tell this girl's family I'm not running a boarding house here at Hawthorne House, and we need the bed this girl is occupying. I've been patient for about as long as I care to be, and am expecting you to come and get her out of here."

"I hear you, I hear you. Now you listen to me. I've had a difficult time gaining her family's cooperation and am doing everything humanly possible to help everyone involved. If that's not good enough, then I suggest you put her out on the street and see what the contributors to Hawthorne House do. And in the future when you call me I suggest you try using honey rather than vinegar."

No one spoke to the Mother Superior in that tone, nor used such a sharp tongue, and she knew she'd met her Waterloo with this particular street-wise priest. If he didn't come for Rosie, she had to figure out an alternative plan, and that could cost her the money Rosie's mother left there before her return to Germany. There was no option. Hawthorne House needed money to support unwed mothers, and she needed diplomacy when addressing the subject of how and what to do about this Rosie situation. She waited a day before re-calling him. Her approach was not far from what he expected, just packaged differently—she had one goal, and he knew what it was, he'd heard it all before. "Get Rosie out of Hawthorne House, it's not a hotel." He had no other choice but to listen.

"She appears to be mildly depressed and will be on medication when she leaves here. You must emphasize to her family that until this depression leaves, her medication has to be administered daily, and she is not to work under any circumstances until her mental state is stabilized."

"I can only pass along everything you've said. Once I turn her over to her family, it's up to them to see that she gets proper care. My hands are tied. I've done all I can do and will call you as soon as I have the answers you need."

The priest hung up the telephone and seethed with anger over Mother Superior's uncooperative disposition and urgency to get Rosie out the door. He immediately dialed Rose to relay how desperately the foundling home wanted Rosie out of there, and even offered to go and get her, but he needed to know whether Rose wanted her brought to her house or taken directly to Mulberry Street.

"Don't even think about bringing her here. I will have to do some checking around to see if my handyman has the house ready and call you back. Did they say what her condition is like?"

"She's on medication for depression and the doctor apparently believes this will help, but only if you and Emil see to it that she gets proper care and takes this medication daily. The prescribed course of treatment is rest and more rest, and absolutely no work until her present state of mind improves. Oh, and hearing tests determined no physical reason for her not being able to hear."

"Oh my God, what's this nonsense about her not being able to hear! I don't believe a word of it, not for one second. Is this something new?" The priest wished for once that Rose would deal with the here and now, but no such luck. "As far back as I can remember the girl was a consummate snoop with ears like an owl. Honest to God, with this kid it's one thing after another. We may still need a couple of days. Let me find out what stage the house is in and I'll phone you back."

Rose cracked open the door to Emil's studio and poked her head in. He was finishing up with his last student of the day. "Psst—Emil, come here a minute, I need to talk to you." Emil gave her a dirty look and told her to go away. The student had barely gone out the door when Emil entered the parlor and verbally attacked Rose. "What was so important that you would interrupt my lesson? Have you lost your mind! I've asked you time and again not to do that. What is so important that it couldn't wait three minutes?" Emil's attacking her made her both nervous and angry. Words flew uncontrollably out of her mouth.

"It's your sister. Hawthorne House is putting her out and she's not said a single word and the doctor said she isn't doing well and on top of that, she's deaf. Worst of all, if she's truly deaf she's unable to work in that condition. I have no idea what any of this means." Rose was in a quandary, and wanted this to be Emil's problem, not hers.

"Auntie Rose, if she's that bad, why don't they send her away to a place like St. Elizabeth's? Why do we have to take care of her? None of this makes sense."

"If she is crazy or something is wrong with her mind, or if she's gone deaf, I think Hawthorne House would have told Father to take her to a place for the deaf and dumb. My only concern is someone might find out about her. Think about it, Emil. Think of the damage this kind of stigma could do to our social standing? First, an illegitimate baby, then if word got out we had a crazy woman in our family in St. Elizabeth's Hospital, the hospital where they put the insane—oh, this can't be happening. No, she is not going there."

"Auntie Rose, guess we were pretty smart to buy that little house, this way no one will ever know what is going on except us. Whatever the cost, whatever measures we have to take—we have to protect our social status by handling things our way."

Emil's devious mind always worked wickedly when it came to dealing with his sister, and he came up with all sorts of "what-ifs" to convince Rose his demented sister could tell neighbors lies and stories about them. To prevent this from happening they'd isolate her. They kibitzed back and forth and concluded that Emil would be the deciding factor as to when Rosie would no longer be a threat or embarrassment to them and would no longer need to be locked up. But for the time being, they figured all these "what-ifs" were a long way off. They'd deal with those when the time came.

Rose had a tight-lipped reliable handyman, who hung onto her every word and did whatever she paid him to do. This particular day she set the stage by telling him her niece had been diagnosed as crazy enough to be put away in St. E's, and that she didn't have the heart to put her in such a dreadful place, preferring instead to keep her in a house she bought just for her over on Mulberry Street.

After she finished her pathetically warped sob story, she told him the house was in dire need of work and offered to pay him a large bonus if he agreed to do everything on the to-do list in the next couple of days. The checklist included both bizarre and some not-so-bizarre items she wanted done. Secure the door to the large bedroom on the second floor by reversing the hinges so the pins are on the outside and install a lock. Bolt and grate the second story windows so she wouldn't fall or jump out and try to kill herself.

Because the house had been neglected and vacant for some time, some of the plumbing was not functional. There was a toilet in a cubicle in the cellar, which worked fine. The main floor had a full bathroom, but that was not where Emil planned to put his sister. The second floor bathroom appeared to have been put in what was once a large hall closet, which was in the room he planned to make Rosie's bedroom. Problem solved.

Rose fretted over the impact Rosie's situation was having on her precious nephew, and she worried what possible effects this could have on his on-again, off-again asthma attacks, exacerbated by emotional distress. Then there was his career to think about, and how all this could alter her lifestyle. Their solution to every problem was to close off the world, drink pots of tea, and nibble on sweets.

"Poor dear, I can see your nerves are frazzled. Would you like me to rub you a little so you'll calm down? A good massage will do you a world of good."

"Auntie Rose, would you please?" Emil stretched out on the sofa with his head in Rose's lap and she ran her fingers through his hair, stopping occasionally to rub his temples. She looked at those fat sausage fingers and pleasantly imagined all the music they played for her enjoyment and decided to gently massage each one, stopping regularly to kiss the palms of his hands, titillating him into a state of giddy childishness. Suddenly he felt clammy, his stomach knotted, and he sat straight up. Rose figured this action was the result of too much hot tea, not enough sleep, and too many students.

"Look at you darling, no wonder you're all knotted up and sweating like a little piglet. You've got that belt so tight around your stomach it looks like a rubber band. Now lie back down and relax." She undid his belt buckle and proceeded to loosen the belt while he looked up at her like an adoring baby walrus. "My wonderful boy, what would I do without you?"

"Excuse me Auntie Rose, but I feel like I'm going to have diarrhea. All this disruption to my life is more than I can handle." Emil got up and raced to the bathroom, where he spent the next forty-five minutes doing heaven only knows what, while Auntie Rose paced the floor and waited like the bartered bride. When he finally emerged and walked into the parlor she could see he was deeply troubled. Evidently while he was in the bathroom, he had an asthma attack and decided to settle down before coming out to face Rose.

"Auntie Rose, if we don't get Rosie into that house and off my mind, I guarantee you'll end up with two of us to take care of. How would you like that?"

On hearing that, Rose called her handyman to see how many items he'd managed to check off the list. She prodded him to keep on schedule with a guarantee there was extra money in it for him if he did. As per her instructions, he had steel grates made by a local blacksmith. Those were installed from inside on both the north and south ends of the room, leaving just enough space at the top and bottom for Rosie to pull the windows up or down to get fresh air, yet narrow enough that she couldn't jump or fall out. He claimed the design worked brilliantly, and Rose seemed satisfied that this important task was off the list. Once again she reminded him he had a time limit or no bonus.

"Darling, I hate to say this, but the way I see things, you'll have to go to Mulberry Street at least once a day to medicate and feed Rosie. Last thing we need to do is give her any freedom to use the kitchen or cook anything. She's liable to burn the place down. Oh darling, all this craziness could impact your teaching schedule."

"I don't care. Anything is better than having her live here."

"Suppose she's faking this so-called illness, and drags it on longer than we're willing to play this fools game. What are we supposed to do then?"

"Auntie Rose, right now I'm only capable of thinking two months ahead." In the back of his mind he secretly held to the thought that as soon as his sister was well enough to get a job he'd convince Rose to give her that house just to get her permanently out of their lives.

"I am so proud of the way you've taken over this responsibility, which reminds me, don't dare mention a word of this to your uncle—it's none of his business."

Before Rose went to bed that night she phoned the priest and told him he couldn't bring Rosie to the house on Mulberry Street unless she was heavily sedated. Under no circumstances did she want a street scene in front of this new neighborhood because Rosie's behavior got unmanageable and out of control, thus giving way to tittle-tattle gossip about what was going on in that house. Oh no, she'd have none of that.

Their conversation ended abruptly. Father Greiner immediately telephoned the foundling home to tell them he'd be there at nine in the morning, and he requested that Rosie be given breakfast and administered a strong sedative so he and the family could ease her into her new surroundings with minimal disruption to her present state of mind.

Emil's teaching schedule was rearranged so he'd have no lessons before one o'clock that afternoon. This enabled him to have the morning free to get things organized for when his sister arrived with Father Greiner. The second part of his plan was to get there early so when Rose's bedroom furniture arrived he'd utilize all the space in the room in the best possible way. Satisfied the room was well arranged, he paid Rose's handyman and helper and showed them to the front door. As soon as the truck was out of sight, an after-thought occurred to him—could there possibly be something in one of those drawers Rosie could use to hurt herself or possibly even draw unnecessary attention from neighbors or passers-by, causing him and Rose real trouble? He snooped through all the drawers, removing things like pencils with sharp points. To save electricity, and at the same time, to keep anyone from seeing her alone at night, he removed the light bulb in her lamp. He took the stash of books in the bottom of the wardrobe and put them in the first floor hall closet. He wanted her to focus on nothing other than snapping out of this mood she was in.

The day had come for Rosie to leave the foundling home. Hopes were she'd attempt to put her life back on track, and the only person there to pick up the pieces and help was Father Greiner. Never in his life had he seen a more pitiful sight than the young woman in front of him, who appeared to have no idea where she was, who she was with, or that it even mattered. When he helped her into the cab for the ride to what was to be her new home, he couldn't look at her terribly unsteady and heavily sedated—she stumbled trying to get into the cab.

Emil stood at the window anticipating their arrival. It was ten thirty when the taxi pulled up in front of the house and stopped. Emil opened the door, but he never so much as uttered a single word. Just as he and Rose had requested, Rosie was heavily sedated, making this transition easier for everyone. If Father Greiner had not been holding onto her arm, determined not to release his firm grip until they were safely inside the house, she would have tripped over the threshold.

Once inside the front room, Father Greiner ushered Rosie to a chair so she could sit. The fact that Emil was fully aware of the seriousness of his sister's mental and physical state, and still chose to ignore her, troubled Greiner. He looked at the way Emil's eyes raced side to side like a cornered rat awaiting his first opportunity to run. Greiner began to worry whether he was doing the right thing leaving her alone with Emil? From the time Emil was a youngster Father Greiner thought he was a strange duck, but his disturbing behavior, not speaking a word to either of them, was not only rude, it was unacceptable. Ok, so maybe he didn't know what to say, but for a grown man to remain hiding behind the chair his sister was sitting in nervously fidgeting with the back of it—bizarre. How was a grown man in this state going to take on the care and responsibility of a sick sister? He wondered whether perhaps Emil was the one who needed to be medicated. This entire scenario was a disaster, but it wasn't Greiner's place to try and change matters, it was time for him to leave. He'd done all he could, the rest was up to her family.

Emil stated to Father Greiner that he had things to take care of before heading back to teach at one o'clock and asked him when he was leaving. Father Greiner got the distinct feeling that Emil wanted him out of there. He leaned over and picked up a small brown manila envelope and a brown paper sack he'd set on the floor next to the door when he and Rosie arrived, and handed them both to Emil. The smaller one contained rosary beads and a bible. The larger one, more like a brown paper sack, contained what appeared to look like a year's supply of medication with several pages of carefully laid out instructions including the physician's telephone number.

In bold red letters, could be read,

> 'PATIENT TO BE GIVEN NOTHING BUT REST, REST, AND MORE REST' IF SHE IS EVER TO GET WELL'.

One final notation in large cap letters on the bottom of the page read,

> 'PATIENT'S TEST RESULTS HAVE SHOWN SHE IS DEAF. NOTIFY PHYSICIAN IF PATIENT SHOWS ANY ADVERSE CHANGES IN BEHAVIOR.'

Father Greiner assumed it was time for him to leave if he ever expected Emil to reacquaint himself with his sister, and this could only happen if the two were left alone. But the only thing on Emil's mind was locking Rosie up before the drugs wore off and a monster emerged he'd be unable to handle.

As fate would have it everything, went as planned, no drama or mishaps that might invite any nosy neighbors to decide they wanted to be the welcoming committee coming in and possibly asking questions that were none of their business or concern.

Father Greiner leaned over and lightly kissed the top of Rosie's head. "Please take care of yourself and get well for you, for me, and for everyone who loves you. I miss the old Rosie and want her back in my life."

Emil thought it strange for a priest to do or say what he'd just witnessed, and contemplated saying to him, *if you're so concerned about her, then why'd you bring her here for us to take care of?* Instead he kept his thoughts to himself.

As difficult as it was to leave, Father Greiner turned around, took one last look at Rosie, and bid his final good-bye. His eyes overflowed with tears, knowing that his leaving her there was just another wrong added to the list of many he'd already contributed to.

Father Greiner's cab had barely driven out of sight before Emil gave Rosie a glass of water and a pink pill to swallow that was in a separate tiny envelope with instructions that read, "to be administered as soon as she arrives home." He handed her the pill and checked to make sure she'd swallowed it. "Rosie, you need to get up out of that chair." She stood up, but appeared unsteady and confused. There was no doubt in his mind that she was faking. He raised his arm and walloped her with such force that she fell to the floor.

"Get up you whore, get up before I kick the life out of you!" She heard his bellowing command, but in her drug-induced state, it meant nothing. He kicked her in the thigh, and yelled, "get up on all four and crawl like a dog if you have to!" She didn't move. "Did you hear me?" I said, "Get over to those stairs." Still—nothing. "You hear me! Get up those stairs and do it now."

Rosie struggled to comprehend his orders, and when she'd stop on a step he'd shove from behind. The brutality didn't stop until he gave the final push on the last step that sent her half way into the room. After ten minutes of observing her reaction to the new surroundings he saw no change. She remained the same—blank, dead, straight-ahead stares. And silence. Emil had no conscience about the ills of locking her in that room. He couldn't get out of there fast enough. He stood on the top step and locked the door from the outside so she couldn't get out. After checking to see that all the doors in the back of the house were secured, he headed home utterly exhausted. On the way, he summed up everything Father Greiner said about depression and discredited it all as pure hogwash. Nothing would ever convince him that his sister's problem was any different now than when they were children. Back then, if Rosie didn't get her way, she didn't talk. The family called it moodiness. He called it crazy. Day one of care giving, and already it could be declared a complete disaster. He couldn't wait to get home to Rose.

The minute he walked in the door, Rose began interrogating him. Before she could get out the first syllable, he informed her how she neglected to address one critical issue that was on the list of things to be done and that her handy-man failed to address, the claw-foot tub's drain was slow. This did not go over well with Rose when he added on the fact that he'd ordered Mr. Lewis to purchase two large wash tubs in the event they'd be needed in the future. In Emil's mind this back-up plan made perfect sense. How else was Rosie supposed to bathe? Frugal-cheap-skate-tight-wad-penny-pinching Rose thought otherwise.

"Why on earth did you tell him to waste money for something like that when I have at least five of them in the cellar and even have one of those old slop buckets down there, too. Mrs. Shubert kept all those things from the days when her husband became an invalid. No wonder the old woman was so rich when she died, she never threw anything away. Can't remember the last time I was down in that dark dingy cellar, but I'm sure they're still there." On one hand Rose knew she'd better thank him for all he'd done to help resolve the situation her sister dumped on them if she wanted him to continue going to Mulberry Street, but on the other hand, there was something about Rose that wouldn't allow her to keep her mouth shut. Between the incessant ranting about all the money her niece was costing and her verbose tongue lashings, Emil had had just about as much of Rose as he could stand. Suddenly the very sight of her repulsed him. Random thoughts of his sister's face haunted him like a monster inside his head. And then the pompous priest, who dumped her off in his care, made little sense. The act of him strangely kissing the top of his sister's head right before he left threw him for a loop. Everything that happened this day made him wish he'd never been born or that this day had ever even happened.

He pulled the cover letter out of the sack Father Greiner left with him and handed it to Rose. He had lessons to teach and no time to humor Rose or answer any questions. Besides, he wasn't interested in any doctor's opinions on what his sister did or didn't need. "According to what I read, those doctors said she needed rest."

Emil spoke like the bully he'd become, "wonder if they meant Rip Van Winkle kind of sleep, because those pills have knocked her for a loop. I'd love to be a fly on the wall to watch and see how long it takes for them to wear off. Best thing would be if those things kept her in a stupor until she snapped out of this mood, then we could open the door and say, 'good riddance, go find a job and take care of yourself.'"

Rose studied the letters, and suddenly reality set in. "Emil, from what I'm reading in this letter from the physician and all these pills prescribed for her, makes me believe she's really sick. I'm not a doctor, but I have a feeling her condition could take a long time to fix."

Chapter 11

The Wall Talker

Six weeks turned into six months. In the beginning Emil came religiously to ensure Rosie's medication was administered on time and daily. He wanted this time-consuming duty over and done with. From his point of view, Rosie seemed to be accepting her new surroundings; however, the menacing circumstances of an unwillingness to talk or answer him seemed grotesquely odd. This behavior provoked him, and he saw her attitude or lack thereof as unappreciative of his many kindnesses. As punishment, his routine visits to monitor her medication, or bring groceries, and other necessities, became less frequent. There were occasional times when she had nothing to eat, but because the medication often destroyed her appetite, food didn't matter.

When Rosie was alone, she mouthed her words, barely moving her lips like one does when praying. An idea popped into her mind and she stopped. She stood up and moved away from the overstuffed chair she'd been sitting in and stared down at the floor, lost in thought. Slowly raising her head and surveying the four walls, she turned and nodded to each section as if acknowledging a person's individual presence for the first time.

"You walls have come to mean a great deal to me since I've been here. Surprisingly, your greatest asset is being able to calm and center me when my mind gets twisted. Your silence embraces and protects me, while at the same time, keeps me prisoner. You watch me cry, listen to me think aloud, and tolerate my anger when I throw things at you. At the very least, ours is a strange relationship, but it's a crucial one if I am to remain sane while locked in this room. I am indebted to you and have no idea how to express my gratitude."

Introduction complete, she followed through by walking up to each wall, gently touching them as you would the face of a person. Her lips continued to form words without sound. "My behavior may seem silly, but after all, there's no one here but the five of us. Here we are, neither of us able to speak, yet we both have much to tell. We share silence. Mine chosen, yours given. Because you four are the experts of silence, answer me this: If in silence one isn't allowed to express the voice within, what happens? Silence, that's what happens. Unless one is allowed to express the voice within one can never know there's anything else. So, you learn to live in a world without a voice."

Rosie walked back and forth surveying her perimeters, continuing to mouth words like one does when talking to oneself. "From your appearance, I'd be willing to bet I'm the best companion you've ever had. When I look around this space I see it's rather nasty, sadly neglected, and in dire need of a major overhaul. The redressing I'm planning to shower upon your blasé appearance, along with my personal attention to detail, will make you feel special, and feeling special is something we all need."

Rosie cleared her throat and attempted to speak, but produced no sound and was satisfied there'd be no chance of speaking out of turn, stepping on toes, or disappointing anyone. The one and only time it mattered that she be heard, no one listened. When she asked permission to marry Frank, no one cared to hear a word she had to say. So be it.

Anguish, self-loathing, and guilt intensified until immense anxiety captured her whole being. She felt as though someone had punched her in the chest: she couldn't breathe. If she had listened to Frank, life would have been so different.

Rosie turned to the over-stuffed chair that had been in her room all her years growing up; she was comforted by its presence. Eager to get lost inside its deep seat, she eased onto the cushion and imagined how the thick wide arms on either side would wall her in from harm. She fell asleep; after a brief nap, she took an apple from the basket on the table and returned to the chair.

With all the consternation and confusion going on inside her head, Rosie forgot about the long lost treasure trove of buried items down near the inside bottom of each arm of this overstuffed chair. As if struck by lightning, she jumped up, threw the cushion on the floor, got down on her knees, and began digging her bony fingers into all the crevices. One after the other, lost treasures emerged. Pencils--lots of them, all hidden from Emil when they were children because he enjoyed breaking the points just to see how angry he could make her. Those beautiful pencils, those incredible instruments once abused by Emil to make her angry became the weapons she'd use to fight madness.

Chapter 12

Taking on the Bully

Rosie stalked the Victorian oak wardrobe and sized it up. It dwarfed her small five-foot frame like a bully daring to be moved. She realized its weight and awkward size required brute strength, but believed she was up to the inordinate challenge of moving it. For the better part of three hours she studied it and the scrollwork carved on the top of the drawer fronts, finally deciding that it was nothing more than a utilitarian piece of furniture storing the contents of her life. It lacked as much character as her current life.

In a moment of self-preservation, she opened the top drawer of the dresser next to the wardrobe and took out her rosary beads. As best she could figure, Emil must have placed those there because she had no recollection of ever having them on her person when she got there. How they got in that drawer, or for that matter, how she herself got in this room in this place, was a complete blur. She sat down in the overstuffed chair, repeating prayers over and over until the words became one continuous meaningless sentence, diverting her mind, drowning out fears, and temporarily putting her anxieties to rest. If she wanted to keep control of her mind and survive, she had to plan carefully, keep things in order, make good and careful choices, and above all else, find ways to keep busy. Rosie's mind consumed every object in the room; she decided that the wardrobe's utilitarian purpose afforded the most promise.

In the bottom of this particular piece were two large, deep drawers, and directly above those hung two long rectangular doors opening from the center. In order to lighten the load, in the event she ever wanted to move this piece back and forth, the contents would have to be removed.

The right-hand drawer contained two pairs of barely worn medium brown mittens made of genuine lamb with fleece lining, and one turban hat. This particular hat baffled Rosie, and she couldn't figure out how it ended up in the wardrobe with her things or even why. After all, it was a man's hat. She picked it up and examined the label. It was the hat Frank wore Christmas day when he shoveled snow off the sidewalks. How or why it ended up amongst her things didn't matter. She pressed the turban against her nose and inhaled deeply, searching for any telltale sign of Frank. But nothing—just the stale musty smell of the wardrobe's inner depths.

Rosie clutched the turban against her body. She paced back and forth across the room, trying to avoid the feelings of loneliness and desolation haunting her. Emil's demonic persecution gave her the impetus to at least try and tackle the one-hundred-forty-pound bully. She had a motive, a brilliant idea.

She got down on the floor on all fours, positioning her body so she faced the wardrobe, kneeling slightly off to the right. Next, she placed her hands palms up between the front and back right-hand side and, with brute strength, gripped the wardrobe firmly, lifting it up and away from the wall. Invigorated with fresh enthusiasm, she moved to the left side and did the same.

The piece stood out from the wall only about a foot. When she squeezed herself between it and the wall, the area felt cramped. With her back against the piece and the heels of her feet planted securely against the base of it, she extended her arms firmly against the wall and pushed slow and steady, careful not to topple it. Once she realized how easily this could be done, she returned the wardrobe to its original position and let out a sigh of relief.

By this time she was fairly well worn out and had developed an appetite. She got an apple from the basket Emil had left on the table and sat down in the over-stuffed chair. While nibbling away at her apple, an idea raced through her head. She'd already proven to herself that she could move the wardrobe, but pushing it back and realigning it against the wall in exactly the same place and position was the trick. In the bat of an eye she had the solution. Draw an outline around the piece, then fit the wardrobe inside that outline just like you'd do with a piece in a puzzle.

The excitement of the day's goings on taxed her mind and her might. Sleep came easy. The following morning she awakened clutching the hat against her chest. After she got out of bed, and before she began doing anything, she carefully hid the hat beneath the blanket at the foot of her bed so Emil wouldn't see it and possibly take it from her.

When she looked around and realized that her brother most likely wasn't coming, she relaxed. There was nothing she wanted, food or otherwise. The discovery of Frank's hat, her cleverly planned idea for telling her side of what happened—there was nothing she needed except a knife. She wondered how her wicked brother thought she was supposed to spread jam or cut cheese and sausage without one. Rosie picked off a piece of rye bread, dipped it in some plum jam, and sat in her chair staring at the wardrobe. After finishing the bread, her fingers were sticky from the jam. Rather than get up and wash them off, she ran her entire hand down inside the chair hoping to rub it off. For some unknown reason, she poked down farther than she'd intended and her middle finger struck a sharp object, causing her to recoil in pain. Whatever had stabbed her middle finger caused it to bleed. She went into the bathroom and rinsed it off. Within minutes, curiosity nagged her to go back and see what this thing was inside her chair. It was the letter opener Mrs. Millbauer had given her when she was eight years old. She remembered how she lamented over it the day Emil spitefully grabbed it from her and threw it out the window because she wouldn't give it to him. She retrieved it from the sidewalk then hid it in the chair where he'd never find it. Thankfully she'd forgotten all about it until it stuck her finger.

Rosie immediately headed for the steel grate in the front window. Her idea was to turn the letter opener into a knife by sharpening it, and the only way to do that was to draw it back and forth across the steel in a slow steady deliberate motion. She had just begun when she spotted Emil coming down the street carrying a shopping bag.

To avoid dealing with him, she sat herself on the toilet where she pretended to be having a bowel movement with all the sound effects. It worked. She outwitted him. He put her food rations on the table and blurted, "If you know what's good for you, you'll take these pills. I want you to know I've gone to a lot of trouble and expense to get these for you." He turned around, locked the door behind himself, and headed home. Normally he called her names or threw things, depending on what provoked him at that moment in time.

Emil came later and later each day. More times than not, he skipped days completely; sometimes he left extra provisions, but not always. He was as unpredictable as the weather. The one thing he never omitted was enough medication with threatening reminders: "you'd better take these pills or you'll see what's good for you." She vacillated about whether or not to take them, and often the chair got the pill and she did what she wanted.

Months rolled on with Rosie's depression worsening. Emil noted changes in her behavior and used violence to frighten and threaten her because he'd become frustrated with not knowing what else to do. He wanted rid of her and everything about her. When he had time, he'd shove her onto a chair or onto her bed to make sure she swallowed her medication, sometimes even doubling the dosage in hopes of knocking her out permanently. Rosie knew without a doubt the pills helped, but she hated how they numbed her whole being. Bad days were becoming more frequent than good ones, and today happened to be one of the better ones. Enough better that she was motivated to shove the dresser over next to the wardrobe and climb on top of it. Standing there enabled her to reach across the top of the wardrobe to touch the wall behind it.

The notion of drawing on the wall produced so much excitement she took the initiative to climb onto the top of the dresser. With the pencil held tightly between her teeth, she stood up, put the pencil in her right hand, and began drawing the first of three straight lines that would create a large rectangular page. Not only would this page fill her mind with drama, dreams, and hope, this page would also be a forever gift to the walls.

Should Emil happen to look at the wardrobe from any angle, the vertical lines had to be drawn two inches in from outer edges of the wardrobe to conceal her works in words. To accomplish this, she set the margin by placing the tip of the pencil two-inches in from the outer edge of the wardrobe, maintaining a thirty-degree angle while drawing the vertical boundary line down to the top of the baseboard. The difficult part was behind her; it was time to put everything back. This insatiable appetite to conquer the bully fueled her starving spirit and purged her mind of doubt. Where to begin? No ideas yet, but a good night's sleep is always a good start, and that was all she needed. She covered herself up with all the blankets and clung onto Frank's hat. Depression became her daily battle, and she questioned whether depression was an inherent weakness or was brought on by the insensitivities of others. These constant twisted notions and tortured mindset hauntings interrupted her sleep. Voices in the night further robbed her of proper rest. Days drifted into nights and nights drifted into days, causing her to forget what pills she took, how many she took, and whether she took any at all.

Months went by. The weather changed. Snow fell. The room got colder. Christmas came and went. Her appetite changed. Time had no value. Day and night were the same. Rosie hated her life, and Emil hated his; each grew to hate the other.

The raucous chorus of negativity Aunt Rose spewed tainted Emil. He parroted those sentiments, resenting the responsibility of caring for Rosie, both in time and money. Paranoia set in, and Emil's greatest fear was being seen by someone he knew as he came and went to the house on Mulberry Street. Consequently, his brief visits were made in the dark of night or before sunrise. Rosie preferred this schedule.

Rosie threw herself into the overstuffed chair, curled up to one side, and began gnawing at her fingernails. The desire to sleep more often and for longer periods of time recurred with greater frequency. Depression's ghouls haunted her day and night, defeating her at every turn.

It started getting dark, and it wouldn't be long before streetlights in the front of the house would be her only available light source. A rekindled fear and suspicion that Emil could return after dark pressured her to clean up her mess and put everything back where it belonged.

Just as she began to doze off in the chair, he unlocked the door. This startled her, and she decided it best to feign being asleep. He set what she supposed was food and meds on the table then walked around to the front of her chair and stood there watching her. All of a sudden he went into a maniacal tirade, yelling loudly enough that the entire city could have heard him. "Those doctors said you needed rest. I'm not buying that anymore." He dropped his cane, leaned over her small frame, grabbing both her shoulders. In one fell-swoop, he yanked her up out of the chair, shaking her small frame like she was a rag doll. She had no idea what he wanted or why he was doing this. "Talk to me!" She kept silent: she knew he was determined to get a response, and she was equally determined not to give one. Sensing the stalemate, he threw her on the floor and kicked her small frame. Rosie lay there lifeless, too frightened to move. Who could blame her? The bully in this case weighed nearly three hundred pounds.

"You lazy whore, you either clean up this stinking place or we're throwing you out. What do you do all day anyway?" She refused to acknowledge him. He lifted his arm, cane in hand, and struck her about the head and torso. Her limp body laid there. She ached from head to toe. All Emil did was make her more determined than ever to use the only weapon she had in her arsenal—silence. What she had didn't hurt physically, but it obviously did a number on his head. When they were children he knew how to play the violin, but she knew how to play with his head.

Consumed with disdain, he turned around and started to leave, but wasn't satisfied. "You lazy whore, why is it you never talk anymore? When you were a kid you never shut up. Answer me! I demand you answer me right now or I'll beat the words out of you every time I come from now on."

The streetlights outside provided enough ambient light for Emil to gather his cane, lock her in, and leave. Normally he'd come and leave a bag on the table with whatever he and Rose had on hand or didn't eat that particular day. This time he'd brought two oversized glass jars of cold tea, plus a box of loose tea, five hard German sausages, the dried ones that keep forever, black bread, two tins of biscuits, and always lots of apples. Oh, can't forget those head-numbing pills with nasty notes attached. Generally when Emil left this much food or more than one pill it meant he wouldn't be coming the following day, or maybe he'd even skip several days. Nothing made her happier. She hoped he'd never come back so she could starve to death.

The most dreaded part of life for Rosie was no longer having a purpose. She became convinced God didn't want a whore, choosing instead to believe that if she aggravated her brother to the point of exasperation he would kill her along with the monsters in her head. The enormity and fear of losing her mind was becoming real. In times past, she'd try to watch the children playing outside her north-facing window, but not of late. Their innocence and excitement once reminded her of how she was never like them because she was never allowed to be. Those little creatures fascinated her, and through observation, she learned how to pretend and be one of them, often tagging along mentally, filling in the blank parts of her life that were missing. This game sometimes entertained her for hours and helped bypass the loneliness.

Rosie spent an uncomfortably cold night in the exact spot where Emil had thrown her the night before. Sometime during sleep, she had urinated on both herself and the carpet. Try as she might, she was unable to get up off the floor. Days passed and life eluded her. Death moved on to another soul somewhere else in the world.

Rosie's body eventually healed; Emil's visitations became less frequent, but the abuse and rants didn't. In fact, they got worse. And death, well, it too avoided her. From lack of interest and sheer boredom, she paced the floor for hours on end, resulting in a clearly worn path in the carpet. Occasionally Rosie re-routed her pacing so the worn spots would not be obvious. She figured that if Emil's temper could explode over not speaking, he'd certainly stomp the snot out of her over a worn path in the carpet. Rosie's mental state was declining rapidly. The mere thought of Emil's visits set off over-whelming senses of defeat, ending in slumps of moodiness followed by severe depression. These were the times she frantically retrieved the pills she'd refused to take early on, the ones she discarded by pitching them down in the sides of her chair. They numbed that once brilliant mind that read the classics at age five. As the months and years passed--the potential to do and be anything Rosie once wanted in life, slowly vanished. She was now in physical and mental decay.

Living conditions in this hovel were a far cry from the large three-story brownstone Rosie grew up in on the South Side of the city. Passers-by referred to the residence as "The German Castle." It was an architectural masterpiece noted in the registry of Pennsylvania landmarks. The ground floor housed a large general store dealing in everything from hardware to home improvement supplies. The second and third floors were residences. Behind the house and store was a large double city lot, a third of which was taken up by an over-sized brick and stone garage. The family did not own an automobile, choosing instead to use the garage as an additional warehouse for their business. The remaining yard had a large flower garden, small pond and fountain, all for show; no one was ever noted or seen in the gardens but the gardener. The back portion of the property was enclosed with an ornate four-foot-tall black cast iron fence and gate that was kept locked at all times.

Rosie has an "ah-hah" moment. Panic sets in then grows to fear. Uncontrollable thoughts of never getting out of this horrible room, or ever going home again, cloud her mind with sadness, compelling her deeper and deeper into depression. The cycle has begun; she knows it well. Rosie falls into what she calls "the dark black hole inside her head." She screams and cries out for help, but no one comes. Emil's lashings are more bearable than the isolation and solitude he's subjected her to. She paces, she cries, she screams; nothing. Unable to tolerate another second of mind torture, she grabs several pills hoping to escape it all. Eventually she drifts off to sleep. In sleep she dreams.

When Rosie awakens, her mouth is bone dry from the medication. When she tries to move her tongue it feels like it is stuck to the bottom of her mouth, it's immobile. She tries to get the inner workings of her mouth to produce saliva, but none is to be found. By this point anxiety sets in, followed by panic and the cycle starts anew. Rosie is convinced she is dying, and for a moment or two she welcomes this escape to fall into the arms of God, but in her next breath, as if out of nowhere, comes this blast of feistiness. An angry Rosie emerges with thoughts of "not yet!" Quietude embraces her. For the first time since she was imprisoned, her mind is silent. She is convinced that this is a challenge from God to get up and do something, to start utilizing the tools she has—the pencils and the walls.

Chapter 13

Simple Patterns Stay between the Lines

Hello, dear East, West, North, and South walls, I'm Rosie Gradel. Oh, I almost forgot, you already know me and my deepest darkest secrets! Since I've spent my life living to read, and now have nothing to read, I'm forced to write what I'll call a "wall book" so I can read and reread it any time I please. This "wall book" is my legacy. If ever you want to divulge any of these personal matters I've shared with you, you can. I have nothing to hide from you. How could I? You're a little like living with God, you know everything!

I value our time together and plan to adorn you with the most beautiful patterns you've ever worn, made of simple things called words. Of course the ones I select will come from the depth of my soul to create stories that will one day be referred to as "classics." Your cooperation, in allowing me to sprawl words on you, is humbling.

My life ended the day Frank asked for my hand in marriage. I begged and pleaded for my pop to listen and hear what I had to say, but he refused. I remember everything about that day and need to tell you about this one beautiful part of my life. The sooner I get started, the sooner you'll understand why I don't belong here. I belong with him, wherever he is.

Concentration is impossible. Remembering is more difficult some days than others. Thoughts of whether I walked into this tomb-like room willingly, was dragged or carried here, or possibly given some powerful drug like the ones Emil gives me all the time, intensifies my frustration and confuses me. These vague remnants of happenings clog my mind and jam it like dead spots do with gears when parts are missing. Nothing makes sense when I feel that way; I become confused and frantic with fear of what is happening and why. My mind races out of control; madness replaces rational thought. My greatest anxiety is that my physical body won't die, but that my mind will take me to a place of no return. I pray, but nothing happens.

All those bottles of medication Emil brings are labeled, "For Depression." Actually they're all poison to turn me into a zombie. This is my definition of "depression" and why I know it now occupies every fiber of my being. I liken "depression's effects" on the mind as being similar to having been bitten by a poisonous bug whose venom paralyzes my brain, then, with slow deliberation, badgers me until helplessness causes insurmountable anguish. I surrender and wait, hoping for death to free me, but death doesn't come. This insidious "depression creature" delights in returning time and again to inoculate me with small doses of its venom, prolonging the agony, but never the full dosage needed to destroy and put me out of my misery. I tell myself, to defeat this horrible creature before it destroys me, I must shut the doors to my brain and keep it out. But nothing keeps this thing out. I've sought and searched for a blank, quiet mind, hoping to stave off this creature of depression and maybe defeat it. Sadly the mind doesn't cooperate, and like the tongue, is a formidable scavenger, searching, picking, and digging endlessly, hoping to find something of interest to feast upon. I think to myself, "ah-huh, I'll go to bed and sleep." Now what will the forager do?

Although slumber is supposed to offer repose, it doesn't. Instead, in dream-like form, sleep prostitutes itself to the night, staying the course of the day, further driving anxiety well into the darkest corners of my mind—robbing me of that which is rightfully mine. Peace, quiet, rest.

Sleep arrives with pre-set priorities and conditions of the tortured soul from earlier in the day. The contemptuous screams of the tormented soul demand attention from the dreamer, forcing him to try and make sense of what is nothing more than insignificance, seeming all too real, until recall.

In recall, twisted fragments of ideas are recognized as nothing more than the tail of a nightmarish monster whose cunning ruse is to fascinate, captivate, and entertain while erasing all evidence of the visit minutes earlier. The second sleep ends the monster escapes, but with barely enough time to erase all telltale signs of intrusion, teasing the mind and leaving it weary.

One day I aim to capture my malicious foe, the dream monster, and demand clarification of these fragments left scattered about my head. Not so easy a task, I'm afraid.

Chapter 14

Color Me Yellow

Spring started like it did every year, but for Rosie time and season no longer had meaning until this particular spring day when she awakened and looked out the front window and saw that daffodils were blooming. The school yard was ablaze in yellow, incentivizing her to open the window in hope of getting a whiff of their perfume.

The front window had been permanently nailed shut on the bottom. However, the top came down six inches. After opening it, she headed to the rear of the room knowing that window only went up six inches. She struggled to raise it. A cool spring breeze drifted in. It seemed to clear a lingering headache, and at the same time, rid the room of stale air. She knelt at the rear window for the longest time daydreaming, thinking and trying to decide whether continuing to write made any sense. For months she vacillated back and forth, wondering whether the idea was worthwhile. Eventually her self-confidence and competency eroded away. The desire to be challenged by slightly more than going to the bathroom seemed taxing. The struggles of why, what for, and who cares, played over and over in her mind.

Whether boredom or curiosity challenged her, doesn't matter. Something drove her to retrieve a pencil. The wardrobe was pulled away from the wall. Drawers were removed and inverted for her to sit on. She looked at the enormous rectangular page with multiple blank parts and chose a space directly in the center. Miniature sentences, some barely legible unless up close, were done intentionally to conserve space. On Rosie's so called "good days," writing would be emotionally taxing, but this particular day she decided to force herself to stay on task. Someone had to know what really happened, so why shouldn't the "someone" be the walls? Who were they going to tell, God? No big deal. He already knew all this. *Besides,* she thought to herself, *this will ultimately be the book I don't have. I can read and re-read this one, and no one, not even Emil, can destroy or take it away.* Being in love, oh my—there's nothing like it!

Chapter 15

Innocence Pierces the Circle

The store opened at nine in the morning and remained opened until nine at night. Weekdays were generally slower than evenings and weekends. By twelve o'clock each day I was out of school, heading to the store to relieve Frank so he could go on to what we called "his real job." When I failed to show up by three o'clock he said his heart sunk because he'd been planning to have a serious talk with me and apparently I'd thrown his schedule off track. I couldn't help notice that he acted like a silly schoolboy who'd never spoken to a girl before, so I playfully poked him in the ribs to break the tension and flirt a little. I think I was in love.

He gently took me by the arm and led me into the back room, where we could continue our conversation privately. "Rosie, I have something to tell you, and am not sure how it will effect our relationship. It could mean the end of my working here, or it could be the beginning of the rest of our lives together. You know I am in love with you. All I think about is the next time I'll get to see you. I see your face when I fall asleep and first thing when I awaken. I know who the woman is that I've been looking for all these years, and it's you. You must trust and believe me."

I never thought about how I would tell him I loved him, but it sure made it easier when he told me first. All I could think about for the rest of that day was his telling me I was the first person he'd ever loved, and the first person he'd ever said it to. I believe him today as I believed him then.

I no longer knew how to behave or what to do, and I'm sure my behavior must have seemed inappropriate at times, but I desperately wanted Frank to believe I was a woman, not a schoolgirl, and definitely worthy of his affections. Instinct told me that if I wanted to impress him with my level of maturity, I should wait and let him take the lead like in dancing.

Frank left and I ran after him to invite him back into the store to talk some more, and he told me he'd love nothing better but had an important appointment. He fidgeted with some change in his pocket and asked me if there was somewhere other than the back of the store where the two of us could go to talk privately because what he had to say to me was for my ears only, and suggested jumping a trolley and riding it to the end of the line and back. By now I had had plenty of time to digest everything he'd said, and I desperately wanted to impress upon him how grown up and capable I was of making my own decisions that I was not your average seventeen-year-old. But, the last place for any discussion was on the trolley by golly! Too many people I knew rode those things all the time. The trolley ride would never do. Once a week I went to church in the evening, lit a candle and prayed for pop, then turned around and came back home. I suggested meeting Frank outside the church afterwards but quickly retracted the idea realizing everyone there knew me too.

Frank Pazwalski had this uncanny ability of knowing how to time sound decisions, like when to move forward and take a chance, and when to back away. He asked if I knew that the church had a basement; of course, I knew about it. Everyone who went to St. Michael's knew about it. For me it was where church functions took place, but for Frank that area was the place where he and his childhood friends went to play when summer days were hot. Additionally, they enjoyed irritating the Monks, called "Brothers," who regularly ran them off. For some reason, the boys found it amusing to see them run in what they laughingly called their "brown frocks" and their "Jesus sandals."

I wasn't anxious to meet in the church basement, but instinct told me to trust him. Make no mistake, the decision to go along with his suggestion made me extremely nervous. Frank remained very matter of fact about our meeting, which is exactly what I expected. After all, he was thirty-something, educated, seemed to have plenty of money, very handsome, a great talker, dressed attractively, and I presumed by his demeanor, a real ladies man with plenty of life's experiences. I, on the other hand, was only seventeen, and (in my opinion—) not very pretty, had no money of my own, and had zero experience with boys. In fact, until Frank, I'd never even been kissed by anyone.

My youth and inexperience gave rise to twinges of jealousy. It occurred to me he may already have some "one special woman" in his life, and this was the reason for the meeting—to tell me he loved me, but wasn't really interested in a silly young schoolgirl like me. Suddenly I felt an urgency to let him know I was not a silly schoolgirl, but a mature young woman who wanted to be the only one in his life. But because I lacked experience and didn't know exactly what to say, I remained silent and hoped he'd interpret silence as a sign of maturity.

I knew meeting Frank was wrong, but I brushed aside those nagging thoughts of possibly getting caught. Don't ask me why, but I still remember being crazed with the idea of being alone with him, even at the risk of ruining everything. On that day, at the time, nothing mattered more to me than being with him. That night I closed the store, counted the money, ate dinner, and walked to the church dreading the possibility of running into someone I knew. Fortunately, that never happened.

No one had ever spoken to me as gently or tenderly as Frank, and I wasn't sure what I had done to deserve these kindnesses, but the more he talked to me, the more everything changed. I found out that being in love meant feeling lightheaded, irresponsible, and without regard for common sense. I still remember how my mind's message rallied when his words trailed into my body. I especially enjoyed hearing him say his words were for my ears only. Now I question whether or not my inexperience gave way to misinterpretation of his actions, voice inflections, and facial expressions. At this point I can no longer continue. This is far too difficult. My head hurts. I must stop.

In big bold letters Rosie scribbled, "THE END."

Chapter 16

The Cost of Dancing with Butterflies

The night we met in the church basement, Frank kept his promise and arrived half an hour earlier than me. He never went home after work, but went directly to the church hoping I'd show up early. I arrived at the scheduled time..

During the day, the temperature fell slightly—as nightfall came, the wind picked up and the weather got noticeably colder. I wondered why Frank suggested this particular place for our meeting, but the more I thought about it, the more it made sense. Church was the only place I could go alone, stay as long as I liked, and never be interrogated when I returned home.

The first thing I did when I got inside the tall iron gates surrounding the church courtyard was look for familiar faces; and fortunately, not a soul was in sight. I slipped inside the front doors of the church, made an immediate left turn, and headed directly for the secluded door tucked away in the far corner of the narthex. Frank had described it perfectly. It looked like an inconspicuous ordinary closet. I turned the knob, opened the door, and once on the other side, quickly closed it. A destabilizing blackness blinded me, and when I held up my hand, I couldn't see it in front of my face. I gripped the rail, and within a few seconds the blackness seemed to magically lift and allow my eyes to focus. I discerned a figure standing at the base of the stairs holding a candle. I recognized Frank. A calming came over me. He'd kept his promise.

The mounting tension and anxiety caused my heart to pound feverishly, making it difficult to breathe normally. But the minute Frank's hand touched mine and he helped me step off the landing at the base of the staircase, normalcy resumed. To this day, I am still awed by the picture emblazoned in my mind of this massive expanse consisting of three enormous cloistered rooms, all inter-connected with stately marble columns that ran the entire concourse of the church. Right now I don't recall the number of columns, but I do remember every one of them sat on a huge round-tiered marble base, topped with what appeared to be cast concrete angels whose only job was to brace their wings against the ceiling and support the church for eternity. Even in darkness, the magnificence of this dramatic room with twelve-foot-high ceilings and granite floors, compelled me to go from pillar to pillar, touching the solid marble columns and wrapping my arms around several as if grounding myself so I wouldn't magically float off to some distant place. I felt like a fairytale princess in a childhood tale, standing next to the most handsome prince in the world awaiting our next move.

Beyond the grand room of angels, and directly under the twenty-six–room rectory adjacent to the church, were two huge boiler rooms that housed massive coal-fueled furnaces. The things looked like they could heat the entire city as well as the church complex. To give you some sense of the size of these furnaces, it would take at least a half dozen people with outstretched arms and fingers touching, to go around each one. These monstrous coal-fueled furnaces heated gigantic water tanks holding tons of hot water that constantly circulated through pipes that ran in every direction, heating both the rectory and the church. I finally learned how the pipes that came up about eight inches off the floor under every other pew got hot enough to heat that huge church.

During winter months the nuns and brothers marched us into church daily, forbidding us to put our feet anywhere near those pipes. Occasionally somebody would slouch down in the pew and out of sight to get warm. Next thing you knew, a nun would appear out of nowhere like a frenzied devil, grab whoever it was by whatever means possible, and out of church they'd march. Soon you'd hear the kid screaming, "You're a nasty old bat—I'm gonna' freeze to death out here!" A fresh mouth plus an angry "nun" equal a punishment this kid will never forget.

The only source of light in this grand room came from a bank of twelve three-foot-wide, ten-foot-long double-hung windows. During daylight hours, I'm sure these windows provided plenty of light. But at night, these windows offered little or nothing until the city's lights came on at eight o'clock and the ambient light from those made the room aglow.

While I waited for Frank to locate a spot for us to sit and talk, every sound intensified in volume and I wondered if our entire conversation would be conducted in whispers.

Frank returned and announced he'd found a large closet at the base of the stairs, should we need a place to duck out of sight. He held out his cold nervous hand and escorted me across the room. The thought of being caught made my heart pound and my mind fizzle, and that's when I decided to be the princess and allow my heart to rule—no more nonsensical thoughts.

We meandered about for a few minutes as though we were in a park, neither of us saying a word. Then, all of a sudden, we both began whispering, and we couldn't hear or understand what the other one was saying. Frank held the candle under my chin, and stared at me. I had no idea what to expect, but something inherently told me to relax and act naturally. He let go of my hand, brushed the hair away from my ear and breathed into it, sending a cascade of shivers rippling though my body.

Frank wrapped his arms around me and pulled me closer. Everything about those first moments alone seemed awkward because I'd never been alone with a man and had no idea what to expect. His sensitivity to my uneasiness seemed genuine. I felt I could trust him and knew in my heart I wouldn't have come in the first place if I didn't.

The hardest part now is retrieving the sensations of being held securely in his arms. Time and again, memory fails me and I find it is easier to recollect words than image or touch. I clearly remember his telling me I was the only woman he ever loved.

The thought crossed my mind that he could be trying to take advantage of me, but I ignored those negative thoughts and gently pushed against him. A turbulence of emotions raced through my mind and an onslaught of mom's frequent words of warning hammered my ears. By now it was evident—I had placed myself in a compromising situation, and the sooner we finished chatting, the sooner we could leave. It was best this way.

Frank looked through the glass door of the furnace and checked the status of the fire, assuring me that someone had recently added fresh coal and no new coal or tending would be required until the middle of the night. Don't ask why, but when he professed to be an expert on furnaces and the consumption of coal required to keep one running day and night, I felt slightly more confident we'd have no surprise interruptions. The enormous responsibility of manning this complex was quite a task, and the custodian deserved the old church pew to sit on after delving into the twelve-foot-high mountain of coal in the adjacent room. Besides, the poor fellow couldn't leave until the damper got adjusted, and he couldn't do that until the fire took hold, so why not provide him a place to sit and rest.

Frank dusted off the pew with his handkerchief and invited me to sit down next to him. The overbearing heat emanating from the massive cast iron furnace radiated through the entire wing of the basement. It got so hot in there we were forced to remove our coats. I remember feeling very relaxed and sleepy. Maybe it was the heat, I'm not sure, but when Frank spoke he startled me. "Why on earth did you jump like that? Are you still so nervous?"

"Heavens no!"

I looked at Frank sitting next to me, and realized I'd thrown myself adrift in this sea of passion. As I floated aimlessly, my over-zealous heart urged me to give way and explore those waters, but my head pleaded for caution. About that time I reminded myself of the various times I explored my body in the darkness of night and instantly realized those times could never have prepared me for the sensations bombarding my body in the presence of a man, especially one I loved as much as Frank.

So many things about this night were momentous. No one other than dear sweet Mrs. Millbauer had ever touched me on the skin or held me in their arms. Certainly no one ever kissed me anywhere. Not on the arm, hand, cheek, much less mouth. The more Frank touched me, the more I desired to be touched. The sensations created from this tenderness gave way to greater demand and need for more, pushing me until I allowed myself to be swallowed up in his strong muscular arms. He squeezed me like a boa constrictor does its prey until it succumbs to defeat, weakens, and becomes immobile.

To this day I remember melting into him, my face buried against his chest, inhaling his essence. This close physical contact caused our emotions to erupt like a volcano, flailing us into a passionate frenzy of chain reactions the devil himself couldn't stop. Suddenly our mouths were open and our lips skipped and fluttered across the surface of each other's face like butterflies flitting from flower to flower on a bright summer's day, searching for the perfect spot to perch and sample the sweet nectar. Soon those joyful butterflies at play succinctly became sated and replaced with more intense passion. You could hear the fervor in our hearts as they pounded against our chest walls in what felt like an extraordinary attempt to synchronize and beat as one.

Frank's extended tongue tickled like butterfly wings, and his open mouth frenetically flit from place to place as if sampling before deciding which parts likened his fancy. The time had come for me to give myself to him.

As the sequence of events unfurled, Frank lured me along and did pretty much what he wanted, including opening the top two buttons on my blouse and manipulating his fingers until he was able to touch my breast. Suddenly, I wanted to set up rules. Frank could touch any part of my body outside my clothes, but the private parts underneath were off limits, until I reminded myself of what I wanted and dismissed the rule idea.

"Rosie, I want to see you without your clothes."

After months of working with Frank I learned he could be relentless. One way or the other, with or without my approval, he would see my naked body.

"When I am in your presence, this wild desire to touch your innocence and taste the very core of you besieges me."

My love of reading combined with conversations and whispers in the girl's lavatory at school, not to mention my adventuresome friend Madelyn, left no doubt that when this evening was over, I would no longer be a virgin.

"I want you to believe that anything and everything that happens between us tonight is one hundred percent right. There is no wrong—there never will be."

My youth and inexperience surfaced when I confessed I'd follow him to the ends of the earth if he'd promised to never set eyes on another woman as long as he lived. Rather than respond, he gently pulled me to him and brushed aside the strand of hair covering my ear, kissing the very edge of it. This action sent a complex band of electrical stimuli running through my body, tingling and taunting my mind and body until it went limp. Any slight touch afterwards caused goose bumps to rise on the surface of my skin; these silent message carriers nature deliberately released were like numbing agents that put me in a state of mindlessness where I was defenseless, bewildered, and cared not for anything. I so enjoyed where these taunts were taking me.

Frank undressed me clear down to my under garments, then stopped briefly before racing on to the second phase. I stared into the fire as he went about raising the hem of my petticoat, pulling steadily until it was up over my head and removed. Slipping his fingers under the waistband of my panties, he tugged them down and out from under me like a magician. Modestly standing back, he folded one arm across his midriff and braced the forearm of the other so it supported his chin. He studied my naked body like an art critic might do in judging a newly created work of art, and, without ever touching me, scrutinized my innocence with his eyes. My amber-cast frame stood silhouetted against the backdrop of the glowing fire, and he asked me to turn and face him instead of the fire. In my mind, allowing Frank to see me naked meant I had given myself to him completely. This unplanned escapade of lost youth and newly discovered intimacy were now part of me.

Frank lost all sense of self, randomly kissing me about the face and neck, leaving moist-wet-telltale drool—creating a map of all the "feel-

good-parts" he'd thoroughly explored, and, in the event he decided to journey back to those sites, the return route would be well marked.

Our time together evolved into a titillating sequence of events, each one beginning at the hands of a masterfully skilled man who knew how to whittle his way into my heart, reminding me over and over how we were destined to be together as one.

A couple of times he tugged and chewed at my flesh and I pulled away. His words flew on the heels of my retreat, and he had no peace until he cajoled me back by whispers of sweet nothings and how much this particular behavior was part of the normal ritual between man and woman when making love. Because I lacked experience and had no basis for comparison, I accepted his words about the importance of exploring and learning as much as possible about the other person until there were no secrets and nothing seemed strange or maniacal.

At some point, and I'm not sure when, I began to feel less embarrassed standing there in front of him completely naked, but only because it had become increasingly more important to play the part of a mature woman—the temptress. Unsophisticated in matters of womanhood, I'd grossly misjudged what Frank sought when he fell in love with me. It was not a temptress he desired; he had plenty of those. He adored my unspoiled youth, knowing he could form and meld me into the kind of woman he wanted. Unfortunately, he never achieved that goal. The only opportunity he ever had to adore my unspoiled youth came the night I stood before him in front of the fire completely naked. In my mind's eye, I don't think I'll ever forget the look on his face.

He looked at my flawless body, and described to me how privileged he felt to be able to see and touch what he considered a perfect masterpiece. He went on noting how my silken unblemished flesh appeared as though it had been poured onto a perfectly designed frame, leaving no seams or wrinkles for the eyes to fault. Positioned atop a delicate ribcage were two of the most perfectly aligned breasts he'd ever seen. This vision alone created a desire for him that he could no longer suppress.

"Rosie, you're absolutely magnificent."

He then picked up his heavy overcoat from the pew and threw it onto the hard floor before inviting me to lie down next to him. He hunched up on his elbows and leaned into me, kissing my stomach multiple times before running his tongue over and around my slightly sunken navel. The warm breath against my flesh gave way to a range of emotions, not the least of which caused pleasure.

For reasons I was incapable of understanding, he stopped as if he'd gotten a whiff of something and had to locate its source. The hunt was on and instinct told me not to budge while this demonic maniac went about sniffing the entire surface of my midriff. The combination of silence, conservative behavior, and naïveté, must have signaled I wasn't ready to be a participant, because he stopped abruptly and spoke to me.

"Rosie, correct me if I am wrong, but of late, when we would be alone in the store and you'd give off these little signals, I interpreted them to mean you wanted this every bit as much as I did."

"I do, I do want you, but only if you promise me you'll never see any other woman ever again. I have to know I'm the only woman in your life and that you will never ever leave me."

Frank wanted nothing more than to swallow beautiful young Rosie Gradel into his arms and make love to her, but recognizing the depth of innocence next to his lifetime of chasing women stopped him dead in his tracks. Frank's deep love for her far outweighed passion. He decided this was not the time or place. Not now, not today. They had the rest of their lives to relive moments like this.

By now, the fresh coal that had been added earlier caught hold and produced a roaring fire that lit the entire room and cast a warm amber glow over our naked bodies. This shocking new experience of seeing a man naked for the first time embarrassed me, yet I couldn't take my eyes off Frank's meticulously chiseled body. In my eyes, he was more perfect than Michelangelo's David. I caught on to the feelings within myself and could not quiet the temptress within.

I edged closer and whispered in his ear, stopping now and again to kiss and impishly nibble the edges of them. This playfulness caused my body to pull me next to him like some giant magnet. Suddenly I became blanketed in a shroud of shivers that began at the nape of my neck and ran down to the tips of my fingers, sending a battery of signals to Frank that I wanted him to know I too was ready. I remember needing to get my words out. It was my turn, my time to tell Frank how I felt about him.

"When I'm with you, everything feels right and good. I want these feelings we're sharing right now to be a forever thing, but can't do that unless you make me a promise."

"I'd give you the moon, the sun, and the stars if I had a way of getting up there and bringing them down to you, but since we both know that's impossible, tell me what I can give you that's realistic, and I'll promise it to you."

"Promise you'll never leave me."

He stared into my eyes and it felt like he went straight inside my mind to plant his carefully chosen words.

"The day we met I began to fall in love with you, and with every passing second my love for you grows deeper. For me, there will never be any other woman but you. You're stuck with me Miss Rosie Gradel, and I promise I'll never go anywhere unless I take you with me. And, I never make a promise I don't intend to keep."

The two of us lay side-by-side, facing each other on top of his heavy overcoat. The satin lining beneath our naked bodies enticed me to wiggle about. Frank wasted no time in taking extreme pleasure in what must have appeared to him like some horizontal dancing caper being done against the backdrop of his coat. I learned that night that he never tolerated heat very well, and when the furnace room began to feel like an oven—even for a person like me who always complained about being cold, I can only imagine what it must have done to someone like Frank. Sweat poured from his forehead and dripped onto me, and like the silly school-girl I was, I foolishly fantasized about how wonderful it would be if the droplets magically turned into glue and bound us together forever.

This is one of the gentle things Frank did to me that I think of every time I chew my nails down to the quick feeling nothing but pain. I don't know myself anymore.

He took one of my small hands in his and began gently massaging my fingers, slowly working towards the palms then back out to the tips, until the entire hand was pliable and supple. The real test of will came when he proceeded to alternate between licking and sucking each of my fingers until I turned into a muddled pile of vulnerable trust, completely void of all common sense and logic. The allure of this experience captivated my mind, taking me to a place where I had obviously never been. A place so exhilarating and safe I wanted to stay forever, but something inherently told me this place only existed for visits. Frank now had my heart, trust, and body to do whatever he desired with it. I made myself vulnerable and would do it all over again if I could.

The tips of his beautiful fingers nonchalantly danced across the surface of my abdomen. The initial touch made me uneasy, but I reminded self how much I wanted his love and obliged this next whim when his eager fingers moved brusquely, massaging and squeezing my flesh. The repetition of this playful cycle offered no resistance when he braced himself so the weight of his haunches wouldn't rest on me, and gradually lowered his body close enough to tease and cajole me with language and words I'd never heard.

Impassioned and unrestrained by his words, I initiated a kissing frenzy. He inserted his tongue in an effort to engage me in this silent language understood at the peak of emotional arousal. Without warning, my body surrendered discomfort and followed his lead in this amazing horizontal dance of love. Despite the fact we chose to do all of this on an unyielding dirt floor, we nevertheless managed to reap the grand reward of resplendent intimacy.

For several minutes after we had reached the ultimate height humans attain, that place God holds sacred where two souls meet to become one—I looked into Frank's tear-filled eyes and knew instantly that everything about us was right.

I don't ever want to forget these words he said to me that night. Today they're still mine and no one can take them away—not pills—not Emil—no one!

"You've made me the happiest man in the world tonight by becoming my wife."

"What are you talking about, your wife?"

"In my eyes, and in the eyes of your God, we're married."

He rolled over to the side of me and I don't remember now if I was nervous, happy, scared, or a combination of all those. I babbled on and on like a simpleton, and Frank placed his fingers across my lips to shush me. I still remember the time: it was only seven-fifteen. I jabbered on about nothing, making no sense what-so-ever. Frank leaned his naked body into mine and held his arm over my upper torso so I couldn't get up or away from him. I felt like I was caught in some kind of a trap. He kissed me enough times that night to last a lifetime, assuring me there was another lifetime of kisses stored in him waiting for my lips. I don't remember how long we lay there, but I do remember how wonderful it felt to be a woman.

To this day I remember how our kissing continued until I insisted he stop and get himself dressed before the custodian returned and caught us where we didn't belong.

We gathered our coats and scarves, put them on, and checked to see if there was anything left behind. Frank noticed he'd forgotten to pick his shirt up off the floor. He opened the door of the furnace and pitched it onto the hot burning coals, and in a flash, the shirt caught afire and became unrecognizable.

He took out the book of matches from his coat pocket and re-lit the candle. We raced back to the stairs, agreeing along the way, that I would leave first. Once we reached the base of the steps, Frank picked me up in his arms, lifted me off the ground, and spun around a couple of times. I begged him to put me down so I could get out of there. He kissed me one last time and my heart danced up the stairs and all the way home. Today I remember how it feels to dance.

Rosie promised herself she would never finish writing after the last entry. Time moved on and she needed something to do besides watch herself die in the hands of her own brother.

Erratic behavior… worsening mood swings…. Writing begins… writing stops…. Remembering is on again, off again… recall is sporadic…. Rosie moves the wardrobe and selects a spot in the rectangle where she'll tell more of what she remembers. Today she decides to write off to the right side of the rectangle because the sun is shining on that part and it's easier to see. No header, just very small meticulous writing. She takes her time, goes slow.

Mother will never know, but I heard everything she said, from the moment Pop attacked Frank until those kind gentlemen brought me home after I'd stupidly run in front of that automobile. I remember every word out of her mouth, the worst of them coming the day she told me never to call her mother again. I heard her fight with Aunt Rose and definitely saw Pop's casket being carried from the house. I remember hearing her map out the details to send me to Hawthorne House, and I managed to read all the legal papers she left in the parlor that her lawyers prepared. I even saw her return ticket for Germany.

Pop bought our home and business lock, stock, and barrel, from Mrs. Millbauer after her husband died. Until that time, our family lived on the third floor. Pop worked for Mr. Millbauer so he could learn the hardware business and one day own it. Once Pop bought the business with store and house combined, we moved downstairs to the second floor, occupying the entire place. Pop ran the business for a good number of years before having a stroke that left him paralyzed on one side and unable to ever work again. At the time, everyone thought he'd get better, but he never did. The responsibility of running the store became mine, along with keeping up my studies so that I could graduate with my class. Father Greiner suggested my folks lessen the burden of responsibility on me, and hire a part-time worker until Pop recovered. They were amenable to the idea and that's when he recommended Frank, his long-time friend with a business of his own with a flexible schedule. The Gradel's hired Frank with the understanding that his working for them was temporary. On those days he worked, the understanding was Frank would check in with Rosie's father before starting his hours, and at that time would be told what he was expected to do, nothing more. Frank respected Mr. Gradel's situation and didn't want him to think he was trying to run or take over his business. He had a business of his own to run and was merely doing his friend Father Greiner a favor.

Merchants all over the city of Pittsburgh knew that if you wanted customers to buy whatever it was you were selling, you hired the best, and the best was Frank. As a business savvy window dresser with an amazingly creative mind for knowing how and what to do to attract customers into a store was sheer genius. He studied what colors worked better than others and could prove to the merchant why. Frank had no competition. Store owners signed up a year in advance to guarantee a place on his busy schedule.

This fall of nineteen-something began much like last fall, except years have passed and with it went the winds of change that took my baby girl away. A day doesn't go by I don't think about what she is doing: and even though she's not with me in the physical sense, she's with me because I gave her life, and no one can take that away but God. The new mother has her in the flesh, but I will always share her soul.

The robust winds of today's fall imitate those of years past. Skies of today are still up there doing what skies do best in the fall, look dreary and overcast. The falls of yesteryear's days still get shorter, and chilled winds from the north still come from there and bring the same old message: more is on the way. Cold is to cold as old is to old, not much you can do about either one but get used to them. I despise both and will never get used to either.

This whole business of standing to write makes my back-ache and writing small to conserve space, cramps my fingers. Deprivation of sleep turns on voices in my head and I remind myself all the time, "if you don't want to go mad, hang onto the good times". Suddenly, all the misgivings I ever had about this writing idea become intolerable, and everything has to be put away right this very minute, starting with this monster wardrobe. Today I hate that thing.

The pacing began, and continued for a couple of hours before she stopped to look at her food that had been sitting out for a day. A bowl of cold Campbell's tomato soup, diluted with plenty of water to make it go farther, and a box of soda crackers. The soup tasted like soap water. She poured it down the sink. The crackers were fine, and she nibbled away at those until she'd eaten the entire box, washing them down with cold diluted tea Emil made and left in large jars. He's now leaving loose tea so she can make her own.

It rained on and off for ten days. The house was damp and cold. Emil refused to start burning the gas furnace until it got good and cold, and she knew to expect this from prior years. Earlier, he'd left her three old sweaters with a note that read, "If you're cold, put on another sweater." She put on the sweaters and returned to bed to try and get warm. The sting of her brother's persistent cruelty fueled her defenseless mental state. The persistent voice in her head nagged and nagged until she finally got out of bed and took off the sweaters because they became excessively binding and hot. She thought a warm spell came through during the night and changed the outdoor temperature dramatically, but that was not the case; she was running a temperature. She burned up during the night with fever, her throat felt like it was full of broken glass and her chest hurt when she breathed. Rosie got worse throughout the night and by morning couldn't bring herself to get out of bed. Thankfully the morning brought with it plenty of sunshine that somehow managed to warm the otherwise cold temperature.

On days when Rosie was more depressed than others, and even though medication made her groggy, she would grab whatever she felt like, often times when she did this, she slept like a dead woman. This was one of those nights. While she was asleep Emil managed to sneak in to leave clean bed linens, something he hadn't done in over six weeks. The following afternoon when she awakened, she saw them, everything changed. Fresh bed! Fresh start! An uplifted spirit filled her with enough excitement to begin moving the wardrobe. Out came the pencils. Her greatest fear was being robbed of the past, forgetting it, being robbed by a mind that seemed to be escaping beyond control. Rosie's mind raced to remember what it could while it could.

A once healthy mind found itself meandering aimlessly in search of why she was the scapegoat sent into exile living a bane existence. This perplexing situation seemed to have no resolution. Frustration allowed maniacal thoughts to run rampant, none of which would have made sense to a healthy mind, but Rosie's mind at this point was deteriorating rapidly. In the beginning of this period headaches became a daily event. At first they were annoying, and she tolerated them, but, over the course of weeks, these headaches were like nothing she'd ever experienced in her entire life. During these troublesome times Rosie ran cold water into the basin and splashed it on her face, which made her head feel somewhat better. She ripped soiled bed sheets into strips to wrap around her head thinking that cold water compresses might help the miserable pain sub-side, but nothing. When these headaches came with greater frequency her mind convinced her she was going insane. At times these headaches became so painful she'd vomit, other times they blurred her vision to near blindness. Rosie thought reliving the intimate details of her loving relationship with Frank were the cause of these antagonizing headaches, but she couldn't erase him from her mind. No matter how hard she tried, memories haunted and taunted her—twisting and turning an unrealistic photo-album of mental images into ugliness—fading like all mental photos do in time, changing what was once beautiful into nothing more than a convoluted-cockamamie bunch of nothingness. Inconsolable fear ravaged her mind—voices inside her head chastened her with demoralizing lewd obscenities that paralyzed her very core; leaving her to rot in the deepest corner of an inexplicable psyche.

Chapter 17

Roman Schmoman

Rosie's writings are becoming erratic. Placement on her so-called page is nonsensical, and her once perfect penmanship, is almost illegible. For some unknown reason Rosie chooses to use roman numerals in this series of writings. One is to assume it's because these are brief writings written at various times when the interest is there and the headaches have not begun.

IV. The last time I saw my mother she told me I was never to use the Gradel name. At the time it didn't matter because I planned to marry Frank, but since this has not happened, I am nameless. My keeper, too, shall remain nameless. He, too, has disgraced the family name by slowly killing his sister and breaking God's commandment. I denounce him as my brother, and from this day forward, dub him "Evil Emil," "Evil" for short.

V. My least favorite time of year is fall. It arrives unabashed, gradually squeezing the last ounce of life out of every living thing before sending in violent winds to shake loose then sweep away the debris it alone created. Tumultuous rains follow to bathe the nakedness left behind, audaciously holding spring responsible for refurbishing the mess it's made. The exalted spring replicates a brilliant green hue, and, once again, spring's eternal.

VI. Someone has permanently fixed the north and east windows so they never open; at least I can't operate them. The west window's top sash comes down six inches but the bottom won't budge. The south window opens six inches up from the bottom, but the top is fixed.

II. The only good thing on dark gloomy days is the variety of views the three dormers offer—all a Godsend. The varying pictures seen through the patterned iron lace curtains offer me life and some semblance of sanity. Otherwise, I'd completely lose touch. In the darkness of night I position myself off to the side of the window to observe people's behavior and remind myself Evil is the one who belongs here, not me.

VII. Ah, fall, the time of year blessed with ugly days when the sun rarely breaks through the clouds and dampness blankets my body in such a way that no matter how many layers of sweaters I don, or how tightly I wrap myself with whatever, I remain cold. The dreadful thought of spending another winter locked away beneath layers of whatever goods I heap upon myself for warmth makes me long for the grim reaper and riddance of Evil, who is exactly like our mother. Everyone knows wicked teaches wickedness.

X. On cold days it isn't uncommon for me to lounge around disgruntled, shivering half the day away. After all, harlots work the night and rest during the day. Between Evil and the girls at the foundling home, I've gained an extensive background on the subject of whores. Contrary to his thinking I am not a whore. The pathetic bully thinks he knows all, but he actually knows little else other than the violin. I promise dear walls, a day will come when he'll rue the day he broke the spirit of the soiled dove. (I don't remember why I've used these Roman numerals, but just ignore them.)

VI. If Evil would give me additional reading material other than my prayer book, which I've had completely memorized since the age of four, both in German and English, I'd at least have something to think about besides being cold and lonely. I wouldn't care what the book was about or if I'd read it before. Anything, just something to concentrate on that makes sense, rather than the circles that loop around and around inside my head, twisting and confusing me until I feel out of control. These bouts of depression occur more frequently and frighten me more than Evil. A real book to hold and read would occupy those blank spaces configured with bizarre patterns of uncertainty that cause me to feel threatened and vulnerable to the beacons of death.

XV. When depression begins, it moves into my mind slowly and gradually, seizing my entire being. My head fills with horrible thoughts and I dread the outcome, repeatedly asking myself, "what is to become of me" Think, I tell myself. Think about Frank. Believe he loved you. But I know I can't allow myself to think about someone whose broken promise resonates inside my head. I revert back to where I started. I need to hold a book, anything, just let it be a book. I try to think about something besides being held prisoner in this room, but the twisted thoughts inside my head hear demons yelling and screaming so loud, I think they're trying to burst my eardrums; instead they only leave me with headaches. The screams go over and over, "Frank lied to you. He never keeps promises and he will never come back, never."

A voice inside her head says, "Find the pills, they'll work." She takes more than prescribed dosage, crawls inside the wardrobe, and goes to sleep.

There is no activity for weeks, no writing, no bathing, nothing. The depression is worsening. Then one day, for whatever reason, writing begins again.

I am grateful to have discovered how utilitarian these walls are. They are my replacement for the books denied me. By carefully substituting this available space for pages upon pages of books I've been denied, I write to read, hoping to maintain-regain a taste of what that semblance of sanity is like.

XXII. I imagine Sister Stephanie standing behind me, checking the spelling and grammar and wondering what this is all about. Well Sister, it's about my need to read, and Evil's need to keep me from doing what I love most. He's not as smart as he thinks, because I've figured out a way to beat him at his own game in spite of his concerted efforts to deny me reading material. I'm writing my own book, that's what I'm doing. What do you think of that Sister!

VIII. My name is Rose Gradel, but everyone calls me Rosie. I've disgraced and destroyed a respectable family, and for this, I'm being punished and left alone to wait for the grim reaper and my eventual demise. No one knows me or why I am here. I suspect this action protects what remains of the Gradel family name. At first I didn't realize how I got into this strange house, but as time goes on, I remember more and more and liken being here to falling asleep and awakening in the middle of a dream turned nightmare. Still, even as I begin to remember, nothing makes sense. I remember many things and want to live in the happy past that has been taken from me, not in a future I may never see. This introduction is for clarification purposes only. I am the author of this writing and totally in control of my mind. Should there be any doubt, by any other reader than myself, I want it known that I'm not mad nor have I lost my mind. Today I am perfectly sane. My sentences and phrases will sometimes be abbreviated, but not because I lack knowledge, I must conserve space.

IX. I love my name, suits me perfectly. Often wish my hair could be the color of my name instead of brown. These days the oily nature of my hair makes it separate into clumps. I imagine I look like an old woman with long hair and see myself as ugly. I pull the strands up to my nose to smell, taste, and feel.

X. I'm recognized as being a small boned woman, about five feet two inches tall, with delicate hands and long slender fingers that are almost pointed on the ends. Oh, and I have this terrible habit of chewing my nails, and I really chew at them really bad. Lately my knuckles seem enlarged, no doubt from perhaps working my hands as though they were tools. Mother told me if I played the violin instead of doing the gardeners work, my hands would never have gotten so ugly. Had I put forth effort and learned to speak violin, I would have had beautiful hands like mother, and perhaps even someone to talk to.

Mother's life revolved around two things, herself and the violin. She avoided everything and everyone else in her life like the plague, seeing them merely as time thieves.

Mornings for her began when she wanted them to, generally when she entered the kitchen to have coffee or tea alone, uninterrupted, and always in silence. No one challenged her routine or questioned it, but respected her wishes rather than suffer her wrath. Over the years, Mother and Pop acquired unorthodox sleeping patterns and never slept in the same room or the same bed. Mother loved the night and being alone.

It was normal to find Mother playing music or reading well into the night, long after everyone else had gone to bed. This disruptive schedule suited her irascible personality, as did choosing to sleep until noon. The family became accustomed to her lack of consideration and eventually accepted it as normalcy, when it was in fact, lunacy.

Mother had a plethora of students but never taught prior to one o'clock in the afternoon, and the last lesson of the day generally ended at ten in the evening. She hated teaching but did it for the money and notoriety. Her real love was performing, and she never did it for free. She belonged to the orchestra and a string quartet. Both demanded arduous schedules of practicing and performing throughout the city. Pop and I looked forward to days when the quartet practiced in the studio because Mother's mood became affable.

As it turned out, Evil spoke violin perfectly, thus he and Mother had plenty to talk about. In fact, he spoke violin so well he ended up speaking better, faster, and more masterfully than his genius instructor. It was something to watch the two of them playing together as Evil got older and outperformed her. His short fat sausage fingers with little dimples at the base of each one would fly swiftly across those strings with speed and accuracy, leaving Mother measures behind, which became increasingly irritating to her. She never looked happier than on those nights when Evil was young and the two of them played duets. Our small family would gather in the parlor and they would play for hours until Evil begged her to quit, but she wouldn't let him. Pop and I never got involved because we would sit quietly reading and listening to the music. Fat Evil would make a mistake, and as soon as that happened, mother would hit him over the head with the backside of her bow. The first thing he did was wet him-self and then cry like a baby. I don't know if he cried because he wet himself or if he wet himself because she walloped him a good one. He seemed to sense what was coming almost like it was routine and part of his methodology to game her into quitting. "Shut up" she'd scream, "Pay closer attention to the music, think what you are doing, don't just play to play. Now do it over and over, and play those measures and phrases until you perfect them or you can't go to bed." I believe she rued the day she forced him to be such a perfectionist, because he surpassed her in reputation and ability. As time went on they were no longer partners, but became fierce competitors. Evil exceeded her every expectation from memorization to performance, and her jealousy was evident in the way she furled her brows searching for reasons to criticize him, especially after he was invited to perform with the quartet she'd been a member of for years. Evil Emil surpassed her. She created a monster who "ate her reputation!"

XI. The day Evil went to live with Aunt Rose, mother didn't speak to anyone and cancelled all lessons. She punished me and Pop by not joining us for dinner. Days went by and all her time was spent in the room she referred to as her studio; for a brief period, she even stopped going to church. When Evil left, it was like part of her died. Maybe it did. I know when my baby was taken away from me part of me died. I didn't want to eat or even talk to God, and the last thing I wanted was anyone around me. I was just like her—I wanted to be left alone. Aunt Rose took Emil, and those wicked nuns took my baby girl and they never even let me touch one of her little toes.

XII. I found my stay at the foundling home lonely. Unlike the other girls who constantly complained about all the hard work we had to do, I enjoyed being busy so I wouldn't have time to think about Frank and what lie ahead for me after the baby. I never stop thinking about him, where he is, and why we're being kept apart.

The doctors and nuns repeatedly gave me hearing tests to try and determine what caused my horrific headaches. I never spoke to anyone, never opened my mouth the entire time I was in Hawthorne House, so everyone assumed I was deaf. I didn't care and let them think what they wanted to think. They were positive about the depression, and at some point decided I was just plain crazy. I was none of those. The girls in the home gossiped about the nuns and what they did with our babies, and through listening, I learned people contributed large sums of money to the church and the home just to get one of them. If only that car had killed me, this all would have been moot.

XIII. I made a horrible mistake the night I insisted Frank ask for my hand in marriage. In hindsight, I should have listened to him, but conscience told me to do the right thing and get Pop's approval. No one cared how I felt or wanted to hear what I had to say. This devastating experience destroyed me. I had no worth after giving birth, and now no reason for living. My will to be heard is gone, therefore, no need to speak, therefore, no need for a voice. No need for anyone to know I can or can't hear either. My will to live is gone.

XIV. You dear walls probably want to know who this Mrs. Millbauer woman is. She was a kind gentle woman with the patience of a saint. When I was three years old she taught me to read, and from her, I developed a love of books that has never diminished. I love books and never seem to get my hands on enough of them. I am a voracious reader thanks to her. I wish she had never moved away, but that was not to be.

XV. When her ailing husband died, she sold the store to Pop and moved across town to live in an apartment with her maiden daughter Lela. Pop always wanted to own his own business and finally got to fulfill this dream the day Mrs. Millbauer sold him the store.

XVI. For months after Mrs. Millbauer moved, I couldn't go into the parlor. The memories and happy times we spent together were unbearable. After she left, I couldn't study or concentrate because her absence left a void in my life. Subsequent to the time my family moved downstairs to the second floor, mother consented to let me have Mrs. Millbauer's old bedroom. The only reason she agreed to this was her intense dislike for the large pink country-rose patterned wallpaper in this room. She refused to waste money repapering. Besides, she never slept with Pop, but slept in the studio with her violins.

XVII. Everyone needs a mind closet to put things in, and everyone's use for these differs. Mine has been converted into a safe haven where I go to be alone. A place no one knows better than me.

Often my mind closet becomes overloaded and requires a thorough cleaning. But rather than tackling the inevitable job right then and there, I find it easier to use excuses like, "I'm too tired" or "there's not enough time."

When confronted with the responsibility of cleaning out the back portion of the top shelf, there's no such thing as a better time because the clutter accumulates and worsens. The complicated uncertainty of what to keep or what to pitch gives way to taking the easy way out by ignoring the contents altogether.

The top shelf of my mind closet is filled beyond capacity and overburdened from the weight of all things placed upon it. I fear warping, snapping, and even possible breakage.

Life would be simple if someone other than me offered to clean out the accumulated clutter in my closet. But who would I trust to assess what is trash and what is treasure?

As the closet keeper I slam the door shut, and for the time being, convince myself the shelf can withstand more than I realize. Besides, the day may come when I have use or need for some of those pearls of wisdom in the back of the "mind closet."

Chapter 18

What Makes Evil, Evil

One day when he wasn't there I got into his room and snooped around and discovered dozens of drawings. Each one was more beautiful than the other. There were exquisitely designed and remarkably detailed plans on how he planned to make his own violin. Next to those drawings he had neat little piles of sheet music he'd either copied or composed. It all bored me, but somehow I didn't put everything back exactly the way he had it, and he tattle-tailed to mother, claiming I ruined his important papers. Mother threatened me within an inch of my life if I ever went up into to his room and touched his things ever again, but that didn't break my heart, because the entire room stunk. Evil wet his pants so many times I don't even think the mice would go up there in the dead of winter to get warm if they were freezing or to forage for food if they were starving. After the miserable smell and boring experience, I found no need to ever return to the third floor to touch or see the bore's possessions.

Aunt Rose is my mother's sister. She lived several miles away from us, and Evil frequented her house daily, namely to eat whatever she offered him. He became her all-time favorite kid, which I used to be before he came along. She fed him like he was an eating machine that would run out of fuel and die if she shut off the food supply. Evil got so fat Mother couldn't find pants to fit him and had to have them specially made.

From the beginning I believed Evil enjoyed his violin and the music it made for him, but used his devious genius to avoid all physical work. Predicated on the fact that I refused to play the violin or the piano, Mother believed her son was the perfect child and claimed I lacked discipline and direction and could never grow up to amount to much of anything. If I had chosen music over reading, my life would have gone differently.

Unlike Evil, I refused to be intimidated by that stupid violin and that dumb old piano. I enjoyed listening to music but was not interested in learning to play anything. Mother forever reminded me she had given birth to a child who lacked refinement. I ignored her words when she went off on that tirade, but Evil couldn't do that. When she'd say, "it would make me so happy if only you would do thus and such." Evil would try and so would Pop, but neither one ever quite made the grade.

One night I dreamt I saw the four of us as going down this road together. We came to a cross in the road, and with no hesitation, evil Emil turned to the right—and headed directly to Aunt Rose's. Mom chose to go straight and stay on course with her violin in tow. Pop took the easy road and turned around to head back to where he came from because it was safe and presented no new challenges. And me, I stood alone in the middle of the road screaming for them to come back and get me, but not one of them heard me. I screamed until I had no voice left.

I think Pop finally realized he was no substitute for the violin, and evil Emil couldn't take the "if only" anymore. As for me, I couldn't do for mother what she couldn't do for herself—be happy with the little things.

Chapter 19

Medicine for Rosie

I kept count of the days, and it has taken one hundred fifty-one days for me to come back to the wall. During this time I begged God to take me, to let me die, but regretfully, He doesn't want me either. No one except the devil of depression will suckle or caress me. This depression the doctors said I suffered from has no sympathy. It has no kind words. It has no understanding. It doesn't allow food to taste good. It doesn't allow sleep to come and stay long enough to complete a single dream. It doesn't allow your bodily functions to work properly. It rudely interrupts every single thought until concentration is destroyed, and no cohesive idea exists for longer than it takes to breathe a single breath. Depression doesn't know how to stop tears and is useless unless you're looking to go mad—and then, depression works perfectly.

Today the sun was shining. Rosie should have been happy, but instead she focused on the why's in her life. Why did she never try to escape this desolate dark abyss she so despised? She always knew the answer: it was fear. Rosie feared being out in the world all alone, she feared Emil's repeated beatings knowing they were undeserving, but feared being sent away to some insane asylum if she fought back, she feared being unable to care for herself, she feared the label the world would cast on her, and now if she got out of the house on Mulberry Street, where to go. To erase these irrational menacing thoughts she needed those medicines, and none was to be had. For days she tried to tell herself she could survive without those powerful drugs taken in the past, but to no avail. Unfortunately the prescriptions for Rosie's meds expired. Emil and Rose's unwillingness to spend money for medication and follow up doctor's visits to keep well informed on Rosie's mental status was deliberately ignored. Unfortunately for Rosie, she had consumed all the pills she often ditched down inside the chair because they numbed her body and all she wanted to do was sleep. She dug and searched every inch inside the old overstuffed chair, and there was not a one to be found. Sadly, a doleful Emil happened to be in the wrong place at the wrong time with nothing but a violin and an old woman living vicariously through him issuing orders which he followed. Elsa knew of what she spoke: "Rose took, Rose never gave."

XXII. I look at these Roman numerals and can't figure out for the life of me where they belong anymore. The rest of my notes are in this finely scribbled mess and lost among my thoughts. I'm confused most of the time, and only know one thing for sure: I hate Emil. I've never hated anyone in my life, but I do believe I hate him. Please dear God forgive me for those horrific thoughts I have during days here alone, but I have no room for other thoughts. These ugly ones taste like vomit in my mouth and the bitter after-taste stays to remind me how much I hate him. Emil, someday you will read this and you will know, because you will see in my handwritten words, why I hate you. It's because you did this to me. You did this to me. You did this to me.

Rosie then took her pencil and marked off a twelve-inch square section and filled it with four words: "I hate you Emil." It reminded her of times when the nuns made children write a sentence over and over when they did something they shouldn't have, or when someone got swatted across the palms of their hands for stealing or doing something wrong like writing sloppy, and the nuns would say, "this is for doing what I told you not to do, and this is for doing it when I told you not to do it, and this is for a reminder, don't ever do it again."

Rosie began sobbing uncontrollably. Writing ended right then and there. Her depression worsened, and for weeks she avoided all activities.

VII. The only way to keep track of time, that is, until you nearly go mad or don't get out of bed for days on end, is to watch the people. I now know how to tell when it is Christmas and Christmas Eve. The church bells ring, houses are brightly lit all around, and children go caroling. I am happiest then and start to make a new calendar on the wall. But then, when I don't move the wardrobe or am too tired, I lose all track of time and have to wait for another holiday. Anymore, it really doesn't matter what the day, month, or year is, because I am destined to die in this room in this house, but just don't know how or when it is supposed to happen. Only Evil knows.

VIII. Days, weeks, maybe, maybe months have gone by? I'm not sure about time anymore. Confusion seems to be a daily occurrence of late. Some days my mind just can't help me, and some days it helps me remember lots of things, and some days, nothing. Most of all, I become distressed on days like today when I want to remember something special like how it feels to dance. I think God is punishing me because I'm no good and hate Emil, and now God knows it because I wrote it all over the wall, and He saw it there. Dear Jesus, help me remember, let me remember. I scribbled all over those words about Emil and am so sorry for being no good and breaking your commandments. I'm so tired. Just plain tired. All I want to do is sleep. If the dream monster stays away I can rest, but he won't let me rest. He awakens me before dawn and then I cry all day long. Sometimes I find myself crying for no reason at all.

I am so frustrated and can't remember what I was going to write about after going to all the trouble to move this ugly wardrobe, so I broke several of those stupid pencils in half and threw them down the toilet for not helping me remember. Doesn't matter anyways, because this is no longer fun or interesting, and besides, I can't concentrate. I'm tired.

For months on end, Rosie grew more lethargic, and did little other than sit in her chair and stare into space. Occasionally she would stand at the window and do nothing but cry. She lacked the energy to care about anything, including chewing her nails and toenails. The depression worsened by the day and consumed her entire being. She couldn't focus or concentrate on a single simple thought long enough to complete it before becoming distracted. Her appetite and interest in food diminished. Sleep filled her days until nights became undistinguishable from days. On days when bright sunlight annoyed or disrupted her sleep, she gathered up her blankets, crawled inside the wardrobe, and curled up in a ball in the base of it. This became her favorite way to sleep because it was not only dark, but also, the warmest place in the room on cold days. Emil no longer mattered. In fact, nothing did. She didn't care if he found her in the wardrobe or under the bed, whether he brought food or poison, whether he struck her over the head or broke her neck. She cared about little other than wanting to die, wishing Emil would get angry enough to kill her so she could escape life and depression.

The worst part of this day was not over. Rosie's throwing pencils in the toilet caused it to overflow and flood the floor below, forcing Emil to shut off the water valve to preclude further problems. Calling in anyone to fix the problem was out of the question. He and Rose wanted no one to know their business. Solution: a used slop bucket he found in the rear of the coal cellar, which needed routine maintenance called emptying. This disgusting chore brought out the worst of Emil.

Any time he opened the door, the stench from the bucket drifted out of Rosie's room and settled like a cloud of haze at the base of the stairs and annoyed the life out of him. He would stomp up the steps and be intentionally noisy unlocking the door, wasting no time entering the room and walking over to her bedside, screaming in his loudest harshest voice.

"You lazy sow, are you deaf? I've told you a half dozen times or more—keep that slop bucket over here by the door! Time and time again I've told you not to drag it over by that window, but for some reason, you refuse to obey me. Why is it so hard for you to understand what I tell you?"

Another pause as if hoping for an answer, but Rosie says nothing and he continues his badgering. "Are you deaf, stupid, or both?"

Again he pauses. With no response from Rosie, he makes a wisecrack. "I think the only thing you know how to do is make illegitimate babies. With all the reading you did you should have learned something, but then again, you probably only read the words to get out of working and never understood a single thing on those pages because you're so stupid."

Emil leaned over and struggled with the bucket while at the same time voicing his disapproval. "You idiot, when you move it over there by the window you make twice as much work for me. Keep it where I tell you to."

With that said, he walked over to Rosie's bed and tore the covers back, leaving her completely exposed. He made a fist and struck her in the head. "Don't you lie there and pretend to be sleeping. Answer me when I speak to you! You hear me you stupid thing. Get out of that bed right now and go sit in that chair. There's no way you'll lay around and sleep while I work and lug this bucket and clean it so you can do nothing but fill it up. You hear me, get up and change the linens on this bed unless you want me to knock more sense in your head."

Emil walked towards the door in total disgust. Rosie never moved an inch, remaining frozen in a fetal position with her hands clasped together under her pillow clinging to Frank's hat inside the pillowcase.

Emil hesitated on the top step, waiting to see if Rosie would move. He was determined to prove she could hear and understand. After a few minutes he sat down and waited, listening from the other side of the door. When she failed to move, Emil lost control, and his words flew past his brain and out of his mouth.

"Keep this up you shiftless good for nothing, and you'll see where you go from here. I'll have those people from the county come get you and haul that lazy good for nothing harlot body to the insane asylum where it belongs. Nah, I take that back, you're not a harlot, you're not smart enough. You're a whore. At least a harlot makes money and supports herself, whereas a stupid whore like you gives her self away and forces me to take care of her. I sometimes think I should get something from you for all this hard work I do carrying and emptying this slop bucket, getting food and now fetching this slop bucket because you plugged up a perfectly good toilet. You know, you've never done anything right, but you better help and do what you're told unless you want sent away." His voice lowers and becomes a mumbling of indistinguishable sounds on the other side of the door.

Rosie was unable to decipher what he was saying, but knew it was nothing more than more insults. She tried desperately to ignore his words, but her efforts were in vain as phrases played over and over, etching themselves deeper and deeper into her mind. He wouldn't stop.

"Do you know how sick and tired I am of paying for everything and taking care of you? All you do is cost me time and money, not to mention the toll on my nerves." He paused a moment before going on, "Money, something you don't have one cent of because you're too lazy to get out of that bed and work." Emil's voice gets louder. "Do you hear me? I'm sick and tired of taking care of a whore who gives me no pleasure."

Balanced on the top step next to Emil is the slop bucket. The smells being emitted half craze Emil, but he re-opens the door hoping to catch Rosie out of bed. She hasn't budged. His eyes remain fixed on her as though fearful she might attempt an escape, and there he'd be toppled over, with the slop bucket dousing his entire body. With his thighs firmly planted against the bucket, he manages to hold it in place while quickly re-locking the door.

Fifteen minutes later he returned the emptied slop bucket with a fresh chloride of lime deodorizer inside the lid.

"Don't dare move this from where I put it unless you know what's good for you. Oh, and by the way, you'd better stretch out this food I brought today because I won't be here for a while. I'm sick of this routine and need a break." That said, he turned around, closed the door, locked it, and headed down the stairs.

Emil's schedule was completely erratic when it came to changing the slop bucket, making overdue times more frequent than the normal period the deodorizer was intended to last. It was obvious he despised this responsibility and postponed it as long as possible. Rosie enjoyed the fresh clean smell in the room when Emil emptied the bucket, for a brief time after the disinfectant had been replaced inside the small receptacle in the lid, the room didn't smell quite as putrid. It was amazing how those couple tablespoons of chloride of lime could neutralize the gases from all that human waste, but without a doubt, two weeks exhausted the effectiveness and the odor rapidly dulled the senses until everything smelled the same: Foul.

Emil returned a week later with fresh bed linens tucked under his fat arm and threw them on the floor, choosing to ignore the fact that Rosie had left her bed and was sitting in the chair when he ripped the soiled ones from her bed and pitched them in front of the door. When he did this, Frank's hat fell out of the pillowcase and onto the floor, but in the darkness Emil didn't see it and somehow managed to kick it under the bed.

Rosie waited until Emil secured the lock before getting up out of the chair and tiptoeing over to her bed to retrieve Frank's hat. As she stood up, she looked over the assortment of food he brought, more of the same. The only variation was new tea leaves. She picked up the linens Emil had thrown on the floor and remade her bed. In spite of a pounding headache, she slept through the night. Clean bed linens.

This particular warm spring morning, Emil arrived at Mulberry Street before dawn because he didn't want to see Rosie's face. His attitude stunk worse than the pervasive smells originating from her room which permeated every corner of the house. This particular day the stench practically knocked him over the minute he got inside.

The first thing he did was open all the windows and back door on the first floor, hoping the strong breezes would blow through and clear out the odors that had become all too familiar. He prepared Rosie's food for the day and took it up to her room. As soon as he set the tray down, he put the windows up as far as they'd go, gathered up dirty laundry, left clean linens, and snooped to see if he could figure out what she'd been up to, but not a clue.

As soon as he got downstairs, he threw her soiled smelly clothes into a paper shopping bag, and immediately washed his hands. Finally, after the third washing, he thought they were clean enough to dry off. He hesitated to pick up the shopping bag with its filthy contents, but had to in order to carry them home for Rose's maid to launder later that day. Otherwise, Rose's house would smell and this would infuriate her to no end. Before leaving the house, he covered the top of the bag with newspaper, wrapped the handles, and rewashed his hands.

Rosie could easily have slept the day away if the windows had not all been open to allow fresh breezes to blow across her face and startle her like someone throwing a bowl of cold water on her. She was convinced she'd lost her mind because she didn't remember opening a single one during the day or night. She took a deep breath and drew in as much fresh air as her lungs could hold, then slowly exhaled. The release of stale air tasted much like the room, but so did the winter doldrums. For the moment she felt cleansed.

Spring had always been, and would forever remain, her favorite time of year. At last something motivated her to get out of bed and go to the window and do something other than cry. She stood there gulping down mouthfuls of fresh air like she feared it would disappear before she got her fill. This air feast went on for about half and hour, until her soul felt thoroughly gorged. Rosie got herself a cup of tea, a slice of brown bread spread thick with butter, curled up in her chair, and slowly fed her body.

She sat there and stared at the wardrobe, and, for the first time since spring began, saw it as something other than a place to curl up and sleep. By not writing, she'd broken promises to herself. If she ever expected to have anything to read, she had to regain composure and get busy. However, circumstances changed, and for the time being, the walls no longer interested her. Everything about writing exerted more concentration and effort than she was willing to give. She finished the entire pot of tea and seemed content with life passing her by, one day at a time.

The daffodils completed another blooming cycle, signaling one less time she'd see them flower in her own life cycle. It saddened her when she thought how it would take an entire year before they'd return to bloom and brighten her days.

Chapter 20

The Bountiful Chair

Rosie lost her appetite, and began nervously biting her nails. The minute they became infected, she connected the pain with the day she discovered the pencils and dug them out from down inside the chair. She threw the cushion on the floor, and began rooting down inside the overstuffed chair where she eventually located more pencils, a birthday card, and a small sterling silver box. The box was a Christmas gift from Frank that she'd forgotten about until her fingers re-discovered it. She slowly opened the beautifully inscribed box to remove a neatly folded piece of paper that had ten gold coins on top of it. These coins once belonged to Frank's great-grandfather, like those from the collection his mother had left him when she died. Rosie ignored the card and the meaningless coins, but removed the letter, unfolding it with great care.

December 24, 1934.

"Rosie my love—this letter has taken me many hours and nearly all the paper in the house. I want to tell you what it means for me to say I love you. I have never said these three words to anyone until you captivated me, heart and soul. I am, and will forever be, yours.

As long as I live and breathe, there will never be any one but you. Should I predecease you, I will wait for you in eternity. Look for me on the other side of the rainbow. I'll be in the third row, second seat. The first seat will always be for you.

Whatever the action, whatever the reaction, everything is right when two people are committed to each other and love each other like we do. Every inhibition, every crazy position, every anything that goes on in the other's presence is right. When we're together there should never be boundaries about right and wrong, because these are the tools used to build the bridges that will make life together an eventful journey. When you completely accept this part of your mate, you see your heart's deepest emotions displayed on the most vulnerable and compromising stage, where everything is exposed and nothing is kept from the audience of two. Every performance brings down the house and gets a standing ovation. When the curtain falls, you've seen your love in their finest and best, even if their lines didn't come out exactly the way they were meant to. There's always a next time. This stage is where I have come to believe Heaven meets earth, where stars collide, and where we take solace in having found the other half of self."

Suddenly Rosie felt compelled to copy the lost letter onto the wall in case Evil decided to take away her chair—Frank's words would be gone forever.

A rush of memories flashed through her mind, and she heard Frank's voice from the other end of the room. It was loud and clear.

"Rosie, come on back here, I want to show you something."

"I know what you're up to Frank Pazwalski, you're not fooling me. You've replenished my sweet supply."

"No, never touched your sweet supply. Come over here. I want to ask you something and show you something at the same time."

Rosie went to the opposite end of her room as Frank had instructed.

"So ask your question Mr. Pazwalski. You've got my undivided attention. Why exactly did you call me back here?"

"Have you ever danced?"

"No. Never. Not the dancing type."

"Of course you're the dancing type, everyone is. Dancing is wonderful, and it's fun."

"What kind of dancing Frank?"

"All kinds, but most of all, I love to Tango. It's a beautiful dance, and very romantic. Would you like me to show you how it's done? Once you learn Rosie, you'll love it, too."

"I'm awfully clumsy."

"Good Heavens get over here and let me show you how much fun we can have together."

Rosie got nervous thinking Emil could come in at any moment and find them together. She hesitated and Frank said, "Over here Rosie, I'm waiting." Imagining they were on the wooden floor ready to start dancing, she assumed her respective position, trying desperately to concentrate, determined to catch on to this thing called the Tango. Frank's voice was clear.

"This will be one of the beautiful things we'll do together someday when the time is right. Now, keep your left hand on my shoulder, and for God's sake, relax a little."

Rosie spun herself around until the room became one big blur. She grappled with her body to maintain some semblance of balance, but it was too late. Unable to stand, she fell onto the floor and remained there, waiting for the room to stop spinning. In the midst of all this dizziness, she heard Frank's voice.

"That's it! I knew it! You're a natural."

"You know Frank, I'm feeling very dizzy right now and don't want to talk about this anymore." Rosie tried to block out his voice, but couldn't. It played over and over and over until the madness drove her to scream over and over until she barely had any voice left, "leave me alone Frank, go away and stay away!" The voice wouldn't leave. It came back and she apologized for the outburst.

"When you've danced as much as I have, and had equally as many bad partners, believe me you know a natural when you have one on your arm. And you, dear Rosie, are a natural. One thing to remember when we Tango is you must stand tall and straight. Keep that chin up because the chin keeps your posture in check and makes you look elegant. I can't help but notice you're not doing that anymore. You're slouching, and getting all hunched over. Stand up Rosie."

Rosie heard humming. She got up out of her chair and with outstretched arms glided back and forth to the music.

"Frank, I love dancing with you." Rosie listened for a moment. The music stopped. She called out to Frank, but got no answer. She aimlessly searched the room for any trace of him, begging him to come back, but to no avail. She collapsed on the floor near the south window, sobbing for him to return, but he never came. Exhaustion came instead. Rosie got Frank's hat from under her pillow, went to the back window, and threw it out through the six-inch opening. It landed on the porch roof where she could see it. From that day on she never went near the back window.

Any and every small incident intensified Rosie's deteriorating mental state. Each one lasting longer than the one before and increasing in lost periods of time where she was unable to do anything, not even get out of bed. On rare occasions, she wrote sporadic dream-like happenings, and these writings seldom made sense.

Chapter 21

The Exchange

"Frank, there are no words to aptly describe my feelings for you, and believe me, I know plenty of them. When I was about six years old, Mrs. Millbauer gave me a Webster's Elementary School Dictionary and the two of us played this game until I eventually memorized all 45,000 entries. If I put all those words together they wouldn't adequately describe what's in my heart. So, I'll choose to use the best ones I know."

I got so excited about what I wanted to say, my mind went blank and I couldn't think.

"My heart is pounding so hard, can you hear it?"

"No, Rosie, I can't. Must be I'm going deaf."

"Frank, don't make fun of me, I'm trying to be serious right now, and what I have to say is important."

As soon as I said that, I took his hand in mine, and placed it on my chest. "Can you feel my heart beating in there?"

"No, don't believe I can."

I repositioned it and repeated the question. "Here, can you feel it now?"

"Sure can. What's wrong? Why is it pounding so hard and beating so fast?"

"Because I'm excited and have something very special to give you."

He removed his hand and said, "Rosie my love, there's nothing in this world you could give me that is better than what I already have by having you in my life."

"Frank, I want desperately to give you something to always remember our first Christmas."

I waited to see what he would say or do and feared he might think I was acting like a silly schoolgirl, but he didn't say anything. I went on.

"In return for all the love you've given me, I ask you to accept my heart as my gift to you. Please accept it. It's yours forever."

He tenderly kissed me on the top of my head, obviously moved by my gesture.

I saw tears in his eyes and could tell he was deeply moved. "Thank you Rosie. I accept your generous gift and will guard it with love and protect it from harm. No one will ever take it from me."

When we were about to go our separate ways, I thought about our fifteen-year age difference and wondered whether love alone would sustain us until I caught up. I listened closely and clung onto his every word, knowing full well that living life was something I could read about all day long but, until I'd lived and experienced it like he had already done, we'd remain worlds apart. For that reason, I began to doubt my own ability to reach, touch, or even come close to catching up with the years of lost time between us. Today I finally realize why I am here and not with Frank. My being here has everything to do with God's intervention to save me from what could never be. Now I understand everything and sadly let go, because I can't hold on any longer. My fingers are tired. Good-bye Frank.

I suddenly imagined him on a train, and it was pulling out of the station as I arrived a few minutes late. I was about fifteen feet away, running as fast as I could to catch up to the moving train. Frank had already gotten on board, and I reached for his hand but couldn't grab onto it. I was too late, and for whatever reason—maybe if I had left for the station a little earlier, or if my arm were only a little longer, or I had read the schedule more carefully and not chased the wrong train, I could have caught up to him. Maybe—but maybe not.

Rosie began writing sentences one under the other rather than in paragraph form; other times, she wrote full paragraphs. Thoughts were becoming disconnected, as on the day she was hit by a car.

I thought I could dodge it before it hit me and was within seconds of making a clean escape and catching up with Frank. I wish it had hit me right smack in the middle of the street and run me over. I'd be dead, the baby would be dead, and everyone would be happy right now. Trains, trains, trains, all I can think of is missing the one Frank was on. A car struck me. It felt like a train.

All I wanted was to stop Frank from leaving me, and that's why I ran in front of the car. I wanted to catch him and tell him how desperately I wanted to go with him, but he left me there to face our problem alone. He left me with the two people who would never love me again after carrying an illegitimate child. Frank told me over and over that he would never leave me; he promised to love and care for me to his dying day.

He lied. He LIED.

He lied. I was too young and he knew all along that all he wanted was my young, innocent, loving, and forgiving heart.

He did just what Mother said. And where is he now?

He never came back to look for me.

He's dead. I am glad he is dead, because now no one can have him.

When I awaken any given morning—in whatever given month of whatever year—it's nearly always the same. This room is dark most of the time. Lately I have to resort to using the pail, sitting on it until my bottom dries, and I usually cry the entire time because the putrid stench is my body rotting. I think to myself, I stink to myself, I talk to myself, I answer myself, I go to bed in the same bed in the same room, in the same darkness, in the same clothes, in the same daylight nightlight. I drink the same tea and eat the same stale black bread. I have bad teeth. I bite my nails, I bite my skin, I pick my nose, I dig in my hair, I pull some of it out and bite it off when it annoys me I smell my fingers. I hate my hair, I hate my eyes, I hate my face, I hate my feet, I hate my stomach where babies come from. I hate me. I'm going mad. I am the animal evil Emil thinks I am. No toilet, no paper, only stinking fingers washed with cold water and Phels-Naptha soap.

"Quit faking" he screams. No one could fake this. "I don't feel sorry for you one bit Rosie. You're like Pop, you both are the same. He faked that stroke and you're faking this stupid act of… whatever it is. You're not fooling me, you're using me. Snap out of it! You're both crazy. I can't stand to look at you another second, you make me sick." Before he leaves he warns me he'll be back the next day and shoves me onto the bed before walking out and locking me in. When I pick myself up off of the bed and try to walk, I stagger. I try and try to open the door, try and try over and over again to open it, but it is locked. It's always locked.

Rosie picks away at whatever foodstuffs are available. Her appetite is poor and she's lost weight. She was always small, but now is very frail. She spends more and more time in bed, angry at Frank, believing he's gone off to work and left the baby alone. She hears the baby crying day and night. She calls out to him, but he never answers.

Could one human being ever sustain nearly eight years of being dehumanized, like Rosie had, without grievous results?

Chapter 22

Life in the Preserve

Next door to the house on Mulberry Street lived a family of three boys and their divorced mother. The youngest was a reticent child named Reggie. Early on he determined to never end up in reform school like his two older brothers and erred on the side of caution in everything he did. For some time he'd been watching the house next door and often saw Rosie standing off to the side of the window. Several times he'd caught a glimpse of her entire face. It didn't take long after hearing his mother and various neighbors gossiping about "something strange" going on in that house that Reggie decided to poke around and find out whether any of this chatter was true. However, he needed a stooge and knew exactly who she'd be.

Mind you, this little girl was a rough-and-tumble ornery kid, and Reggie figured that if anyone could get to the bottom of all the chatter his mother and others in the neighborhood shared about the person in the house next door, she'd be the one. The two playmates attended different schools, but they generally met in the playground after school. Reggie got there first, eagerly waiting to tell his friend what he'd heard.

The first words out of his mouth: "Know what we got living next door to us?"

"Why can't you use good grammar? What you got living next door to you Reggie?"

"A witch!"

"You're a liar. My mother told me a long time ago there are no such things as witches, and I believe my mother."

"Your mother doesn't know nothing, because we do so have a witch living next door, and she's real. Come on, I'll show her to you."

In an instant Reggie had her in tow and they were going to see the witch, but on this particular day Rosie was not near the window; the little girl was livid. She was sure that he'd made this up just to get her goat for all the times she's beat him up and sent him home crying. To get even, she chided him about his runny nose and the disgusting thick green mucus hanging over his upper lip he continually sucked into his mouth.

"Hey Reggie, it's snot nice to eat snot. My mother's a nurse and she says so."

"Well, your mother doesn't know nothin'. My big brother told me that if I ate snot I'd never have pimples, so go home and tell your dumb mother that, and maybe her pimples will go away."

"You dumb jerk, big people don't have pimples."

With that, she hauled off and beat the stuffing out of him, sending him home crying, and this time with a bloody snotty nose, torn shirt, and promises to never speak to him or be his friend.

Contrary to what she said about there not being such things as a witch, curiosity intervened and she meandered over to Mulberry Street on her own to check out who was right—her mother or Reggie. First she knocked on the front door several times, and when no one answered she went around to the side door and knocked on it. After not getting a response, she went to the back of the house, saw a small door to the unused coal cellar, lifted it, and let herself in to what was the furnace room with an unlocked door leading directly into the kitchen level of the house. Cautiously surveying the surroundings, she recognized the back door she'd knocked on minutes earlier when no one answered. Right then and there she would prove to Reggie that witches did not exist. With no one in sight, she yelled at the top of her voice, "Hey witch, are you home? I came to see you." Rosie heard noise and suspected it was Emil, but when she heard a child-like voice she became confused and frightened.

This child wandered through the kitchen, opening every cupboard in hopes of finding what witches ate. Instead she found ordinary cans of soup, packages of boring crackers, jars of jam, and tins of loose tea she thought looked like dead bugs. The house was eerily quiet, but this did not stop her. After finding nothing of interest on the first floor, this fearless determined kid climbed the stairs leading up to Rosie's room. When she got to the door and found it locked, she decided the witch had locked her out. "Hey witch, all my friends are gone and I have no one to play with. Will you please play with me?"

When the voice on the other side of the door wasn't Emil's, Rosie became immobilized.

"Hey witch, I know you're in there but I can't get in because this door is locked. I'm going home and ask our maid for a key and I'm coming back to get you out of your tower so we can play together and be friends."

Rosie crouched down on the floor unable to comprehend any of what was going on. At this point her mental state was rapidly deteriorating. To think or believe she had the wherewithal to suspect that Emil was doing this as a cruel trick to push her to the brink of insanity, to justify sending her away once and for all, was unrealistic. Rosie, at this point in her illness, was beyond rehabilitation.

The little girl raced home to get a closet key knowing the family housekeeper would have one. But the minute the housekeeper saw how dirty the child had gotten she chastised her and instructed her clean up before her mother got home from work. The child complied, but she was not happy.

That night before she went to bed, she removed every skeleton key from every closet door in the house and put them away for safekeeping.

The following day after school, she went out on her mission to visit the witch. This time, when she got to the front of the house, Rosie was looking out the window and—sure enough—the child spotted her. Reggie didn't lie. There really was a witch living next door to him, and nothing could stop the girl now from finding out the truth. Sheer determination, curiosity, and a pocket full of keys drove this the girl to retrace her steps back into the house, working her way back up the stairs. However, this time she noticed rather large floor grates in the center of the house that allowed heat from the furnace to radiate up through the first and second floors. She stood under the one on the first floor and yelled as loud as she could.

"Hey witch! I got those keys I promised to bring back so I can help you escape those bad people who locked you up there." Rosie recognized the voice as the same one she'd heard before. Terrified and not knowing what to do or where to go, she climbed inside the wardrobe.

Rosie barely had enough time to crouch down inside before the child reached the door and tried her keys; none worked. The key that would work was hanging on a nail right next to the door, but for some reason the girl had missed it the day before. Not this time though. She inserted the key in the lock, opened the door, and let herself in. Familiar with her surroundings from the previous day, she announced her arrival. "I know you're in here because I saw you from the street."

This child snooped around and found no one, but she wasn't ready to concede victory, especially after getting this far. "Come out come out, where ever you are! Please come and play with me. I'm really not a bad little girl, I just beat up boys like Reggie who eat snot and call my mother stupid. I'll be real good if you come out."

Rosie remained on the wardrobe floor in a fetal position, shaking all over while the child hunted for her. When the kid opened the door and said "BOO," she practically gave Rosie a heart attack. The child knew immediately that when she'd hollered "BOO" she had frightened Rosie. She then offered Rosie her hand and said, "Let me help you get out of that box." Rosie just stood there frozen, not knowing what to do. Other than her awful encounters with Emil and seeing people from her windows going about life, this was her first and only contact with another human being. "I'm really sorry I frightened you, just please don't make me go home." In child-like fashion, she gently patted the top of Rosie's hand and held onto it until Rosie got out of the wardrobe. She slowly led Rosie to the bed, where they sat down together. The little girl gave Rosie the once over. "You know you don't really look like a witch. You just have long stringy dirty hair and it stinks like witches pee, but I like you just the same. Suppose we can be friends?"

For the first time in nearly eight years someone wanted to be her friend, but Rosie's mental state of despair and disconnection from reality had reached its nadir. The child, whose parents thought she was the most perfectly brilliant child God ever created, encouraging every aspect of whatever it was she wanted to try or do, had a gift for incessant talking.

"Cat's got your tongue or something, or do you just talk witch talk?"

Rosie looked at this child as if in total disbelief, unable to understand any of what was going on.

The little girl took Rosie's hand in hers, looked her straight in the eyes, and spoke gently as if Rosie was the child and she was the one in charge. "Witchie, I'm going to the library tomorrow and find a book on how to talk witch talk, then we can be real friends forever and ever, and nobody but us will know what we are saying. I gotta' go now, but I promise to come back soon as I learn to talk like you."

As mysteriously as she had come, she disappeared. Rosie heard the door lock.

No sooner had the child gone than Rosie raced to the window to watch her run out of sight. That night, she sobbed herself to sleep thinking she'd imagined the whole thing and had gone completely mad.

Somehow this child instinctively knew not to tell anyone about her encounter with the woman she affectionately referred to as "Witchie" because this smart kid knew that if anyone found her out, she'd be restricted from going anywhere near the house on Mulberry Street.

Every Tuesday morning second graders had library science; generally the first half hour was spent on the various filing systems, and afterwards each child was permitted to borrow and sign out one book until the following Tuesday. Well, this little girl in particular had hardly been able to sleep the night before for thinking about a book she was going to borrow on "How to Talk Witch Talk." Needless to say, when this precocious child approached the librarian, it took everything the librarian had to keep from laughing. This latest request would undoubtedly be the talk of the teacher's room come lunchtime. Where the child came up with some of her ideas, no one knew. In spite of everything she did and said, the old maid teachers adored this mischief-maker because they never knew what to expect. They found her amusing.

"The library has all kinds of books, but none on 'talking witch.' Is there another book I can help you find?"

"Sure. How about one on what kind of food witches eat."

"I've been a librarian for a long time, and I can tell you for certain—we have no such book or books."

The child looked visibly upset, but the librarian needed more information to judge the seriousness of this request and perhaps talk her into another subject more suited to children. "May I ask why you need all this information about witches? You know, they do not exist, don't you?"

"Miss Twitchill, I like you a whole lot, and you're a good library teacher, but when it comes to witches, you don't know anything. They do so exist!"

Convinced the librarian knew diddle about witches, the child couldn't wait to get home and ask the housekeeper what witches ate; surely she'd know. The child followed her around the house and hounded her with one stupid question after the other. Finally the housekeeper, who knew everything but where the kid went from the time she came home from school until her mother showed up from work, told her that witches ate nasty things because they were nasty.

The child thought about the housekeeper's remark, and the only nasty things she could think of were Reggie's boogers and kaka in the toilet. She wasn't about to ask him for any of those awful things or put her hand in any kaka.

She went into the kitchen and cornered the housekeeper for a clearer definition of nasty. "Nasty is nasty, honey; you know, things like snakes and lizards, chicken heads and chickens feet, and oh yeah, can't forget guts and gizzards." Now the girl understood.

The kid marched herself up to her room, got money from her bank, and headed around the corner to Kleinhaus's Butcher Shop where she ordered two chicken feet, two gizzards, and two dead chicken heads. When old man Kleinhaus asked her why she needed these things she told the old German, and he burst out laughing. This made her angry, and she informed him that there was nothing funny about the food her witch ate. Still laughing, he went in the back of the store and threw in two chicken hearts, a duck head, a pig snout, and some innards. When she opened up her purse to pay for the items, he told her it was free.

From there she headed straight for Mulberry Street with her package of free food tucked tightly under her arm. She'd been in the house enough times to have the routine down pat, and within minutes she entered Rosie's room with feast in hand. She was so proud of herself and couldn't wait for her friend to open her gift. When Rosie refused to accept or act the slightest bit interested, the child began to cry.

"Witchie, I want you to know I went to a lot of trouble to get this for you, and it's exactly what witches eat." She put the package on the bed, untied the string, and pulled the butcher paper back. When Rosie saw the dead chicken heads, pig snout, dead duck head, and various other animal parts lying in front of her, she began to scream and beat herself atop the head while pulling at her hair and ripping her clothes.

The terrified child hovered near the floor at the end of Rosie's bed, frightfully crying and unable to understand why this new friend was so angered by her earnest attempt at doing something nice to make her happy. Rosie went to the far end of the room, and that's when the child instinctively knew to get out.

Right after the child fled, Rosie began pacing the floor and continued to pace on into the following day until she was barely able to stand. In order to lie down, she had to pick up the butcher paper containing the horrifying animal parts that were still lying on her bed and get rid of them. The only place to put them was in the toilet bowl, and because the plumbing was out of order and the package was oversized, it set in there and began to rot.

Visits from the little girl ended abruptly after the harrowing experience surrounding the gift and all the hysteria that came from a well-intended, well-thought-out effort on the child's behalf.

For days after this debacle, the child thought about what had happened and decided to never tell anyone about "Witchie" and why their friendship ended or how. In the child's mind, she was convinced no one would understand because no one believed in witches or witch talk.

Three days later, when Emil came to tend to his sister, he noticed the door unlocked but assumed he'd forgotten to lock up the time before. And now a new set of problems, new smells in the room, and for the life of him, he couldn't figure out where they were coming from or what was causing them.

Chapter 23

The Downward Spiral

Seven and a half years had passed since Emil was forced to take on the responsibility of a sister he believed used every antic known to man to pretend she was ill, when in fact in his mind he was convinced she was merely lazy.

The financial obligation and personal responsibility of caring for Rosie had taken its toll on Emil and Rose, but only because they were self-centered, stingy people who resented spending a dime on anything or anyone but themselves. For years, they refused to address Rosie's true mental state, insisting instead that it was nothing more than "a little depression like everyone has combined with a crazy mood" she couldn't keep up forever. However, they finally succumbed to the fact that Rosie was, in fact, "plain crazy."

In Aunt Rose's younger years she became the companion to a wealthy woman by the name of Gerta Shubert. As the years went by, Rose became like a daughter to her, and upon her death Rose inherited Gerta's entire estate, including the house where Emil eventually set up his studio and taught violin. A grand old brick Victorian on the main trolley line—life couldn't have been better or easier for Emil. While Auntie Rose provided the warm cozy impressive studio, the trolley delivered students to his doorstep from all over the city, and all Emil had to do was roll out of bed, walk into the studio, and make money for himself. Auntie Rose saw to it that the rest of his life was one of German royalty. His clothes were cleaned and favorite foods prepared, and all because Rose wanted a child and could never have one of her own.

When he first began teaching, Rose had an artisan design a large brass plaque inscribed with his name and profession, then had it installed at the entrance so it could be read from trolley cars and any passers-by. In Rose's mind, the day the brass plaque got bolted to the brick house was the day she permanently installed Emil. He was certain to never go home again. Rose thrived on the possibility Emil would produce the world's next Heifetz. She was so pretentious no one but Emil could stand her, and even his affection remained questionable. Theirs was an artificial admiration club closed to all others but the two of them. They were boring, selfish, and inconsiderate. Heaven forbid one or the other should die—neither would know what to do with themselves.

Emil bemoaned anything and everything he had to do in overseeing the care of his sister, especially after she plugged up the toilet making it nonfunctional. The use of the slop bucket was a disgusting job requiring additional time to empty, but the sacrifice of time and annoyance was better than having someone entering the house to do a repair and ask questions and make trouble for them.

"Auntie Rose, you have no idea how horrible it is to go there knowing I have to lug that pail down the steps and empty it. Each time I put the key into the door and start to think about having to go in there, the smell makes me want to vomit, and all I can think about is, maybe this time is the last time. We made a huge mistake not putting her in the cellar. It could have made all the difference in the world, but you were sure this was temporary and Rosie would be better—sure fooled you, Auntie Rose. Thought you said you knew people!"

"Listen dear, you were fooled by her, too, so don't go off half-cocked thinking I was the only one who misjudged this situation with your sister."

"Well Auntie Rose, your sister is no better. We have her to thank for all of this. Rosie was her problem and she chose to run away, forcing us to take on her responsibility of failed motherhood. I don't know what I would have done if you hadn't helped me."

"My darling Emil, the son I never had, why wouldn't I help you? You're all I have in this world. I think of all the happiness you've brought me from the day you were born and wonder how I can ever repay you, and now I know how I can do that. Tomorrow I'll go to the bank and transfer twenty thousand dollars into your account because you've been such a good boy. Be patient my darling, this can't last forever, and when it's over, I'll do something special for you again. But mind you, you must not breathe a word of this to your uncle. He has no idea how much money Mrs. Schubert left me, and it's none of his business."

"Auntie Rose, the money is wonderful, but back to what I was telling you. I think you're wrong. She's getting worse and could conceivably cost us all of our money by the time this is over."

"Let me tell you something my darling boy, before that happens I'll kill her with my bare hands."

"Auntie, Auntie, Auntie, listen to me, she isn't eating much these days and when I get there she's always asleep. When we first put her in the house on Mulberry Street, every once in a while she would communicate by making signs and pointing at things, sometimes she'd even move her lips at the same time. I ignored her because I thought she was playing games with me. I figured if I didn't talk or acknowledge her ridiculous mouthing of words or hand language, I'd force her to talk like a normal person. I thought she'd see I meant business and would want to get out of that room, but she doesn't want to get out of there and change or ever take care of herself—we're stuck with her."

"Emil darling, I don't see it that way. Mark my words, one of these mornings she will wake up and want out of there as much as we want her out. You must believe me, she's nothing but a lazy, shiftless, overgrown child who's spoiled and doesn't want to work. This pretending for more than seven years has turned into a waiting game, so we'll just wait and see."

"Auntie Rose, this time you're wrong, completely wrong. You've never set foot in that house. I'm the one who has gone there for the last seven-plus years, and don't forget, I take care of the bills, too."

"Now wait a minute, and please try to remember who puts in more money. It's me."

"That's not what I'm talking about Auntie Rose."

"Then what on earth are you talking about?"

"It's the actual paying those bills, the extra steps required to go there physically and pay the gas and electric company bill, then I have to get a trolley to go across the bridge to pay the water bill. All this takes time. It all takes time and effort, something you have no clue as to what it takes out of me. I hate every minute of time this takes out of my life. And what do you contribute? You open up your purse, that's easy."

"Emil darling, please, you're exhausted and not making sense. Didn't I just tell you I'm going to the bank and transferring money to your account? I'll double it, how's that?"

"Yes and that is generous, but..."

"No buts about it, I'm doing this to make up for all those extra steps you have to take that tire you out so bad. Another thing you must do is stop scheduling those out-of-town performances that obviously tire you out and make you a cranky darling."

"The out-of-town performances are the only joy in my life. Those are the times I get a break from Rosie. This whole business with my sister is killing me. I have days when I am tempted to poison her and bury her in the coal cellar, disgrace and all. I lie in bed at night wishing that when I get there she'll be dead, but that never happens."

Rose thought about everything Emil had just said. "You know what we did wrong? We outsmarted ourselves. We took everything out of that room and left it bare to the walls so she wouldn't hurt herself, and that was a big mistake."

"What do you mean, Auntie?"

"Well, if she had something like a knife, maybe she'd slit her own throat, or if she had scissors or a lamp she'd hang herself, and we wouldn't be having this discussion."

"A knife I understand. The scissors I don't."

"You dear silly boy, she could cut her bed sheets in strips and hang herself."

"Oh Auntie Rose, this is all giving me the jitters. I don't want to talk about this anymore."

"This could have been avoided had my sister not deliberately run away, sticking us with her responsibility. I hope she rots in Germany."

"Do you know for fact that's where she is, Auntie Rose?"

"Of course that's where she is! Where else would she go, up to the cemetery with your pop?"

"There's another person I wish was dead."

"Back to what I was saying, she did this to me because she believed I robbed her of you and your love, and this is her ultimate revenge. Everybody in the family knew she never wanted children, and the only reason she cared anything for you was your shared love of the violin."

Emil began having difficulty breathing, something he frequently did when upset and which generally preceded his need to urinate. Rose knew this pattern, but she was more interested in finishing what she had to say.

"Stop that, stop breathing like that and listen to me. Your mother's gauge for love was measured by loving what she loved. She never loved *you*."

Emil raced out of the room, his short body waddling from side to side, choking and gasping for air, hoping to gain Rose's sympathy while he was in the bathroom. He managed to stay in there for quite a while, and when he came out Rose was waiting.

"Auntie Rose, I'm upset because you never let me talk. And when I talk, you refuse to hear what I have to say unless it's about what you want me to play for you. Listen to me, *Rosie is worse.*"

"Ok, so she's worse today, tomorrow she'll be better. Women do that you know, they have moods that go up and down."

"Something's going on that is entirely different, nothing like what you're talking about. Today I decided to change my routine and take care of Rosie at a different time of day to see if her behavior is an act or if something else is going on. When I got to the house there was a little girl outside the house, and for the life of me I can't figure out what would possess her to throw rocks at someone's window, but that's what she was doing."

"Why wasn't she in school?"

"I have no earthly idea, juvenile delinquent I suppose."

"Did she break any glass?"

"No, thank goodness. It occurred to me that she was throwing rocks to get Rosie's attention, because I heard her say 'Witchie, come to the window.' I chased her off and told her I'd better never see her in front of this house again, or the next time I was calling the police to take her away."

"Why on earth was she calling her a witch, and how did she know Rosie was even up there?"

"Auntie Rose, I have no idea how she knew anything. The thing that bothers me more is how long this may have been going on. Today could be the first time or it could have been the twentieth—there's no way of knowing because talking to Rosie is like talking to a wall, there's no response. It's like talking to the dead. She's dead inside and out."

Rose was confused by Emil's last comment. She hadn't seen Rosie in more than seven years, and she had no idea what Emil was talking about when he described her present condition.

"I'm telling you Auntie Rose, there's a huge change in her and it isn't for the better."

Rose feared that a neighbor might call authorities, that the law would get involved and her personal family matters would be exposed. Rose suggested to Emil that if he intended to catch those brats and put a stop to their throwing rocks at her house, he should pick a day or time when they were not in school. Emil expressed how sick and tired he was of cancelling lessons and rescheduling his life around Rosie when all it did was cause him aggravation and cost him money. Pretentious Rose's only concern was maneuvering Emil into stopping a bad situation from turning into a scandalous news story for the world to see.

"You might have to sit in the living room and watch the house all day to catch the brats, and when you do, take the kid by the scruff of the neck and haul it on home to its mother. We can't afford to let this secret of ours get out. After all these years of working to protect our reputation, I'm not about to give it up now. In hindsight, we should have put her in that state hospital. Sure would have saved us a ton of money."

"How do you get this 'us'? I'm the one who has to go there all the time. All you do is open your purse once in a while and then you belly-ache about it for days."

Emil had been sold another bad bill of goods by Rose. Time and again he tried to overcome her arguments, and every time he came out the loser. This time was no different.

"Auntie Rose, I'll go Sunday and ask Rosie how long this brat has been throwing rocks at the window, maybe this time she'll tell me something. One can only hope today will be the day Rosie snaps out of this and our worries will be over, the financial bleeding will stop."

Rose relentlessly hammered away at the same issue, driving her point until she was certain to have Emil worked up enough that maybe he would follow through with what he has to do.

"Emil, darling, do you suppose she's trying to get attention from people or kids who go by the house and maybe brought this on herself? And when she gets their attention, she might tell everyone we are the crazy ones who locked her up there."

"Good God, Auntie Rose; I never thought about that possibility."

"You need to spy on that brat and get to the bottom of this before it gets out of hand. We don't need this to be public gossip or fodder for the music socialites. Something like having a sister like her could ruin your reputation in the music world." Rose manipulated Emil right into the corner she wanted him in, and once again he did what she wanted.

Emil decided that his aunt was right: he needed to go to the house, sit quietly, and wait behind those closed living room blinds hoping whoever it is shows up, and when the opportunity presents itself, put an end to it. Emil grew sweaty and nervous, but most of all, he was scared of a confrontation with this child's mother. One question resonated over and over in his mind: *Why me?*

Rose suspected that Emil could change his mind and worked up a new game plan, talking calmly as though she understood how he was feeling when all the while the only one she felt sorry for was herself.

"Emil, darling, heartache forces you to respect and treasure happy times. When you dwell on your heartaches, you become paralyzed and useless to everyone around you, and you become the heartache you despised. Accept what life sent you darling and do the best you can with it." Emil had had his fill of Rose and all her useless suggestions and never heard a word she said.

Emil chose to go on Saturday morning when school was out and the mischief-makers had plenty of time on their idle little hands. Anticipating the worst possible outcome but hoping for the best, he took music scores to study while he waited.

After he entered the back door, he picked up an old broomstick and headed up the stairs to check on his sister. He unlocked the door and covered his nose with his handkerchief. The room reeked. It was so unbearable he could hardly breathe. He approached Rosie's bed and thrashed her with the broom handle.

"Rosie, talk to me. How long has that kid been throwing rocks at the windows?"

No response whatever came from Rosie. He repeated his question, but this time his voice was stern. He struck her again.

"Rosie, look at me. I'm talking to you." She laid still, quivering all over. "Sit up and look at me."

She didn't move or acknowledge his presence.

"What is going on with you and why aren't you eating the food I bring? You're making me mad wasting food I spend hard earned money on." He figured she wouldn't answer—normal behavior for her; but of greater interest, why she wasn't eating much lately or some days not eating at all?

"I brought you a tin of crackers a week ago and you haven't opened it. I can see that you're losing weight. If you think for one minute you are going to manipulate me into another one of your stupid games, you are gravely mistaken. First, no talking; now you're not going to eat? You think you'll starve to death and punish me further by making me feel guilty. Well, little sister, it won't work. Not this time. Your trick-wickery won't work anymore, because Auntie and I have you figured out. We know you had no intentions of ever working the day you began this charade. You're lazy and useless and completely crazy—always were, we just didn't want to accept it."

The stench in the room drove him out. He wasted no time getting down the stairs to the kitchen, where he flung the back door wide open. The house needed fresh air. He was thirsty, but the smell forced him to grab a glass of water and go out under the back porch to drink it. After sitting there for more than an hour, he returned to Rosie's room to open the windows as much as he could. The slop bucket needed changing, but he figured he'd do that just before heading home. He collected her empty tea jugs and tray, and as he walked by Rosie he let out one final rant.

"If you think you're going to make us feel sorry for you, you are dead wrong. It hasn't worked in more than seven years, so give it up. You're crazy, Rosie; you hear me? You're plain crazy, and I can't stand to look at you. I wish you would starve to death. You don't appreciate anything anyone does for you and nothing seems to make you happy. Nothing I do, no matter how hard I try, seems to work with you."

To survive her brother's verbosity, she had learned a long time ago to turn a deaf ear and ignore him, but now the depression had sunk its teeth deeper into her mind and she was deteriorating rapidly. The saddest part was Emil's refusal to see or ever believe any of what was happening. "I hope the brat throws enough rocks at the window to make you good and crazy, that way you won't have to pretend anymore. You'll be legitimately insane and my job will be over. The people from the hospital for crazy people will come and take you away, and we'll all be happy. You'll be happy because you succeeded in getting someone else to take care of you, and we'll be happy because we're rid of you."

Emil took a handkerchief from his back pocket and covered his nose and mouth to defuse the putrid odors emanating from every spore attached to every surface in the room. He lost control and used profanity, something he never did.

"One more thing I'll never miss is the smell in here. It could all be avoided if you weren't so sloppy and didn't get your shit all over the place. It's one thing when I have to empty this bucket, but I'm not cleaning the floor behind you, too. I may never figure you out or ever know what's going on in that head, but one thing I do understand is this smell doesn't bother you. If it did, you wouldn't get shit all over the floor. I have got to get out before I vomit, but then my vomit might smell better than your shit." Emil wondered what it would take for her to be neater when using the slop bucket, deciding finally that it was deliberate when he had failed to fix the toilet problem she created. Nearly eight years gone, and in all this time, he still had no idea whether she could speak or hear.

Emil put his hand over his mouth and raced out of her room. All he could think of was ridding his mouth and nostrils of the lingering foul smells that returned with every breath he took. He took a kitchen chair out onto the back porch and sat for more than half an hour inhaling deep pockets of fresh air into his lungs to purge them of the possibility he might have picked up a disease from being in Rosie's room.

No more time to waste; the time to face the inevitable was here. It was time to clean the disgusting slop bucket. He started to head up the stairs, but when he heard giggling he instead turned around and went into the parlor to peeked out the window and see what was going on that was so funny. Sure enough, two children were out there throwing rocks at Rosie's window.

He suspected these were the same ones who'd been throwing rocks at the house in the past. Before he could get outside to catch them in the act, the boy ran off, but the little girl appeared fearless, even after he grabbed her by the back of her dress and demanded to know her name. Rather than answer, she kicked, screamed, and scratched at him like a feral cat. Emil recognized a raging temper; his mother had one. He knew the minute this child broke loose, turned around, and bit him right on his fat forearm that he'd met his Waterloo. In spite of the horrific pain, he managed to grab onto her a second time. This time he was determined not to let go or let her bite him a second time.

This little girl was not your ordinary well-behaved child who said "yes sir" and "no sir" like ones he was accustomed to that studied violin and practiced all the time. This one was like a wild animal. She was defiant and determined.

"Put me down you big fat man! Put me down, and do it right this minute or I'll tell my mother and she'll punch you right in the nose. She's strong and she'll beat you up. You just wait and see. She hates bullies, and you're a big fat bully."

"This isn't your house little girl and you have no business here throwing rocks at it."

"It's the witch's house and she's my friend. If she sees you being nasty to me, you just wait 'til you go to bed tonight, and when it's dark outside, she'll come inside your house and get you, you ugly fat old man."

"What's your name?"

She looked right into his big fat round face and spoke without hesitation. "None of your business."

Emil had his fill of this fresh-mouth and decided to try a scare tactic.

"Little girl I asked you once and I'll not ask you again."

She stood her ground and refused to answer.

"If you don't tell me your name or show me to your mother, I'm taking you to the police station and they'll put you in jail and throw away the key."

"Oh no they won't! You're a liar, a big fat liar. My mommy told me policemen aren't allowed to put little children in jail, they only put old men like you in there."

She looked him right in the eyes and giggled, knowing full well she had his goat. This kid was not the least bit frightened.

"Where do you live?"

"Up there in that green and white house. The one you can hardly see from here."

Emil maintained a firm grip on the back of her dress, but this feisty one somehow managed to twist around, kick him the shin, and blurt out, "that white one with dark green shutters, do you see it dummy?"

"Yes I see it, and I want you to march on up there with me right now."

Between maintaining a firm grip on the back of her dress and walking in tandem, Emil was barely able to keep pace.

"Let go of me! I told you before to get your hand off the back of me. If you tear this dress you're going to be in big trouble because my mommy will make you buy me a new one, and this dress cost a lot of money."

"You let me worry about the dress. Right now you do as I tell you, and take me to your mother or I'm taking you to juvenile hall where they lock up brats like you."

Of course the child had no idea what he was talking about when he said juvenile hall, so she ignored him and reverted back to the subject of her new dress. "If you tear any part of my brand new Sunday dress and my mother finds out, she'll have the policeman put you in jail fatso."

Emil never handled name calling well, and this was no exception. It took every ounce of self-control to keep from slapping this child across the face every time she opened her mouth, and the thought of still being a block away from her house didn't help matters.

"Where is that little boy who was throwing rocks with you?"

"He went home."

"What is his name, and where does he live?"

"His name is Julius, and he lives down there."

They got as far as the white picket fence surrounding her entire yard, and an exasperated Emil was afraid to enter the yard and march up to the front door with his hand gripping the back of the child's dress. Yet at the same time, he didn't want to let go of her and not settle the matter at hand.

"I want to talk to your mother right now about you and your bad behavior. Go get her."

"No, you're not my daddy and you can't tell me what to do, you fat ugly man."

"Listen you little brat. You either take me to your mother or I'll turn around right here and now and drag you off to the police station and leave you there. Take your pick."

At this point, Emil let go of her and, little did he know, he was about to be introduced to the most protective mother alive, a mother who would make him rue this day and the fact that he ever laid a finger on her perfect and precious child.

"OK, you wait here fatso, and don't you dare step in my yard. I'll go get my mother, but she's going to be angry with you, not me. You wait right here fat ugly. Sure you want to test my mother's Irish temper today?"

The child assumed Emil would let her go, but he didn't. "'You'll be sorry,' Daddy always says, 'You don't want to test Mother's Irish temper honey 'cause it's really bad.'"

"Well little girl, I got news for you, she obviously has no idea what it's like to cross a German. We're real nasty."

"My mother will pluck your head off just like she does those chickens on my uncle's farm."

Just then, the child's mother heard the commotion in her front yard and came bounding out the front door, down the front steps two at a time, strode right up to the gate at the entrance of her yard where Emil was holding onto her daughter, and shouted in his face. "What in the hell is going on here, and what are you doing to my angel you fool? Let go of her before I grab the back of your fat head and rip it off."

Seeing the rage in her mother's eyes, the child began to scream at the top of her lungs. "Mama, this mean fat ugly man said I had bad behavior. Is that like his bad breath?"

"Hush Honey, I want to hear what this man has to say for himself."

She turned to Emil. "I asked you, what in the hell are you doing to her, and what is this all about?"

Emil was trembling, his German courage having slipped to nil. Even his German mother couldn't have prepared him for the likes of this Irishwoman. "I, uh, I uh—live in that brown house on the other side of the schoolyard." Emil paused as if he wasn't sure of anything at this point. "It's the one you can barely see from here. I don't know whether or not you are aware of what your child does when she's out of your sight, but she's not the angel you think she is. She throws rocks in my windows and at my house, and it has to stop."

"You know what? I don't believe you."

"Why would I be standing here, and why would I lie about something like that? Would you like it if I came up here and threw rocks at your windows, would you, huh?"

"No I wouldn't like you throwing rocks at my windows or at my house you fool."

"You need to know she isn't doing this alone. She has help from a companion who is equally as guilty, and I plan to go to his house as soon as this brat tells me where he lives. I have a sister who is there most of the day alone, and she isn't well. They could not only break a window, but a rock could go through the window and hurt her. Is that what you want, to encourage your child to go around hurting people?"

"Honey, did you throw rocks at this man's house today?"

"No, Mama, I didn't throw any rocks at this fat ugly man's house today."

The child's mother spoke to her in the softest and dearest voice imaginable, "Honey, could you please apologize to this man for mother for what you just said?"

"I'm sorry."

She queried the child again in the same sweet tone, "Did you ever throw rocks at this mans house?"

"One time I did."

"Oh, Honey, I'm disappointed in you, and you don't want to disappoint Mama, do you?"

Emil was disgusted with this mother's lack of discipline and was anxious to resolve the problem and, at the same time, find out who her accomplice was. He asked the child again, but this time, in front of the mother. "Where does this boy Julius live?"

"I don't know for sure."

"Honey, did Julius throw the rocks or did you?"

"Julius threw the rocks. I didn't throw any."

Emil saw that the mother was refusing to let her child tell the truth and was determined to catch her in a lie. "It sounds to me like you are saying you didn't throw any today, but that you have thrown rocks at my house other times, is that right, little girl? Did you ever throw rocks at my house?"

"Uh huh, I already told you I did. Didn't you listen?"

"When did you throw rocks at my house?"

"The other day, but not today. Today I only went to see my friend 'Witchie' because I had to tell her something and she wouldn't come to the window for me."

Emil thought about Aunt Rose and the comments she had made earlier about drawing attention to Rosie's situation and raising the possibility of trouble from the authorities.

"Lady, you'd better keep this child away from my house, and I had better never see her there again. The next time I catch her throwing a rock at my house, or even so much as standing in front of it, I am calling the police, and the next time, I won't be this nice."

He started to turn around, but stopped short—there was one more thing on his mind. "I'd like to suggest something to you, something you ought to seriously consider. To avoid this problem in the future, I think you might want to keep this spoiled child in her own yard where she belongs. You might also try teaching her some manners and respect while you have her gated in there—she has neither."

"You fat ugly bastard! Get the hell out of my yard before I take you by the back of the shirt and throw you out myself. You're lucky I didn't call the police because you put your fat ugly hands on my child! No matter what she did, you had no business to lay a finger on her—I think you're mentally deranged."

Emil had had about as much abuse as he could stand from one half-crazed woman. He turned around and began to walk away, but she wasn't through. She whipped open the gate and chased after him. Within seconds she'd managed to get ahead of him and face him dead on with her arms spread wide so he couldn't move past her. The kid knew what she was saying when she had quoted her daddy.

"Anyone who would treat a child like you treated our precious little girl should be shot dead! You big fat slob, you ought to be ashamed of yourself picking on a child—go pick on someone your own size. You're damn lucky my husband isn't here. He'd beat you to a pulp and roll your fat ass down the hill where it belongs. Don't you ever come here and tell me where my child can or can't go. The last time I checked, this was a free country and we can go wherever we like. Let me remind you stupid, you don't own these streets—they belong to the city and all the people in it. By the way, not only are you fat and ugly, you stink, too."

That evening when the child's father came home from work, her mother was anxiously waiting to talk with him. During the day she had a great deal of time to fester over this unpleasant incident, and she had made up her mind—they were moving. This was no longer the kind of neighborhood to raise her child, and besides, they were making good money and could afford to live wherever they liked.

This headstrong Irish woman was educated, and she worked as registered nurse until the child had come into their lives. At that time, they had agreed that she would take a sabbatical until their precious little girl entered first grade and then decide at that time whether or not she would resume her career. The time schedule was delayed by a year, and they hired a housekeeper to care for the child for a couple of hours a day up until the mother returned from work.

When her husband came home that evening, she was waiting on the front porch; as soon as he got out of his car, she started telling him about the event of the day.

"I had an awful experience today with a man who lives on Mulberry Street. You wouldn't believe how he mishandled our precious baby by dragging her home by the scruff of the neck as if she was some sort of animal. He practically lifted her off the ground. When I saw him holding her by the back of her dress, I was livid. The stupid son of a bitch is lucky I didn't get one of those operating room knives I have and cut him in a million pieces. I can tell you this much, dear—he'll be sorry if he ever comes near our yard again, no matter what our precious does. I want to move and I want to do it as soon as we can sell this house and get out of here."

"Honey, please calm down. Let me get a cold beer, then I'll join you out here on the porch and we'll talk about this. I can see you are upset, and when you or anyone is this upset, you can't think rationally."

He looked at his adoring wife and said, "I love you, you wild little Irish woman. How about my kiss? You got yourself so worked up you forgot it."

She leaned towards him and gave him a big hug and a kiss, just as she'd done every day when he came home from work. Then he asked, "Where's that other little darling of mine?"

"Upstairs playing with her doll house. God I love that kid. Isn't she the most perfect thing God ever made?"

"Sure is, and looks just like her mommy, but not quite as Irish."

"Now what was that remark supposed to mean?"

"Doesn't quite know how to get her dander up yet, but she's got a good teacher and that's all I care about."

"Let me tell you something, dear, she's smart as a whip and twice as quick."

"Let's get back to this house business."

"I never did like it here. I only moved here because your uncle died and left us this place, and it was free. I have nothing in common with any of our neighbors, and think it's time to move on with our lives. Are you with me or not?"

"Oh my, oh my, dear wifey, I can't believe you are this upset. Why didn't you call me at the office or call the police? Why did you let this jerk get away with what he did?"

"I didn't let him get away with anything and almost plucked his stupid head off. I could tell he'd never met an Irish woman the likes of me, and I'll bet you a new house that he'll never forget me either. He was the strangest man I've ever met, and he gave me the creeps. Only hope our little precious doesn't have nightmares over seeing his ugly face. I didn't even want to get near him. The smell of that man is still lingering in my nose. He dragged our precious baby home and told me she'd thrown rocks at his house. Can you imagine she'd ever do anything so impossible? I'll bet she couldn't even throw a ball much less a rock."

The two of them discussed the possibility of selling their house and possibly moving to suburbia where her Auntie Maeve lives. The husband had a promotion in the works, which meant more money and the possibility of his wife staying home with their little angel.

"I'll think about this not working, not sure about that one. This next time I want her to go to a Catholic school. No more public schools."

"I agree. But if you recall, you were the one who wanted her to go across the street to school so you could keep an eye on her."

"I know, but the next house we buy will be right across the street from the school too, but this time it will be a Catholic school."

He wanted nothing more than to keep the gals in his life happy; if it meant a move, they'd move. A call followed to Auntie Maeve to keep her eyes open for a house in her area.

Chapter 24

Soiree Spoilers

The confrontation Emil had with that mother and her child was disconcerting, and he couldn't wait to get home. After locking the doors to the house on Mulberry Street, all he could think about was Aunt Rose and what her solution would be for his racing heart, sweaty palms, and unsteady nerves.

The trolley dropped him off right in front of Rose's house, and as soon as he entered the parlor he saw her sitting on the sofa waiting. She patted the spot next to her where she wanted him to sit. He plopped himself down and leaned against her.

In anticipation of his arrival, and whether or not he was able to quell the situation with whoever was throwing rocks at the house, she had prepared a pot of tea and set a tray of sweet cakes and small watercress sandwiches where he'd be sitting.

"I keep telling you, there's been a change in her behavior. Lately, and right after I get to the house and am getting food ready to take up to her, I hear her crying through the grate in the floor. This crying is more frequent and not normal. It's more like a wounded animal sound, and amplifies from that top floor down to the kitchen and scares me to half to death. At first I didn't think much of these sounds and figured she was doing it for my benefit, but lately I'm not sure. This has been going on for the past four months, maybe longer. The other thing I noticed is she's lost weight. I think that's because she hardly eats, and when she does, she picks at her food like a bird. She refuses to comb her hair or clean herself. After all, she has no excuse, there's a sink basin and tub with running water. At first I ignored these issues because I was sure she was doing it to irritate me, but now I'm not sure. Sometimes I think I am the one going mad and she is the sane one."

"Emil, Emil, Emil, what am I to do with you? There's nothing wrong with that girl, she's crazy like a fox, just like her mother. Don't you let her trick you, you hear me?"

"Auntie Rose, you are not listening to me. I keep telling you, we have a problem and it's not those brats throwing rocks at the windows. A while back, I tried to give Rosie a haircut because her hair was long and stringy, but she wouldn't cooperate. You have no idea how ugly it is with bald patches all over. I thought it would be easier for her to take care of it if was short. The time after that when I went to see her, I took the scissors in my pocket. When I got up to her room I told her to sit down so I could cut it and she pushed me away. As tiny as she is, she is very strong."

"Darling, you're not afraid of her are you?"

"Of course I am. You would be too, if you saw her."

"Listen to me, you just have to show her who's boss, and that's all there is to it."

"The last time I tried, I failed. I don't care what she looks like or how long and stringy that hair gets. It's no wonder the kids call her a witch; she looks like one."

While Emil vented his concern and frustration, Rose poured tea and served up a plate of neatly arranged teacakes and sandwiches and handed them to him as if she hadn't heard a word of what he said. The sight of food combined with Rose's voice and mind-pictures of his sister displeased him. All he could think of was running as far away as he could and being left alone. Rose wanted into his world, and she could see he was pushing her away. She chose Emil's favorite teacup to serve tea, hoping it would lift his spirit, but he pushed it away. Unsatisfied with not being able to get him to behave the way he always did in her presence, she wouldn't shut up. He tucked one corner of the linen napkin in the front of himself like a bib and began shoving the delicate sandwiches into his mouth practically whole, while talking at the same time. Under normal circumstances Rose would go into hysterics with this type of slovenly rude behavior, but today was not an ordinary day. She ignored his ill-mannered behavior as he spoke with a mouth full of food spurting out between words. The trade-off to hear what happened mattered more to her than any manners.

"Speaking of witches, I caught one of those brats today, and what a spoiled one it was."

"I'll bet it was a boy. I hope you took him home to his mother."

"It wasn't a boy at all. It was a girl, and I'm guessing she was between six and eight years old and have no idea why a child would do something like that. When I was that age it would never have occurred to me to throw rocks at someone's house. This matter is well behind us though, and I don't anticipate any problems in the future."

"Good for you. I knew you could take care of this."

"I only caught the girl, the boy got away. I think I scared her and hopefully she'll warn the others with that big mouth she has and they'll all stay away. Auntie Rose, I'd like to see how you would have handled this fresh-mouthed kid. If she were mine, she wouldn't be able to sit down for a month of Sundays."

"I'm sure you did just fine, and it doesn't sound to me like you need anyone's help."

"All I want is peace and quiet and to be left alone. I have enough problems with Rosie and don't need additional ones from any authorities who might come snooping around to see what's going on. Next thing you know, the neighbors will be spreading stories about us all over the city, especially once they find out how famous I am."

Rose wanted to hear about Rosie's present condition. The two of them discussed the length of time they believe they've put up with what they refer to as a "charade" and how Rosie took advantage of their generosity. Because of their unwillingness to accept the severity of Rosie's depression in the beginning, when the doctors had prescribed medication and instructions to keep abreast of her progress or lack thereof, these twisted minds had ended up bringing upon Rosie, and upon themselves, a sequence of events that could otherwise have been prevented.

Emil told Rose in no uncertain terms how disgusted he was with his sister's newest and latest trick of doing her business down the outside of the pail, creating a huge mess and making more work for him. Rose's alibi for not sending her maid there years ago was because she was a gossip and Rose didn't want the business of Rosie out in the public domain. She told Emil he either had to break Rosie of this habit, clean it up himself, or make his sister clean it up; those were his choices.

Emil tried to explain to Rose how mentally distressing and physically exhausted he was, explaining that he didn't know how much longer this could go on. He confessed how he avoids going there as much as he can, leaving more food hoping it lasts until next time. Finally, Emil admitted that he's contemplated poisoning her. Those words to someone like Rose, who has lived a well-heeled life, who's never worked, and has always had someone take care of her in much the same manner as they've done with Rosie, are merely words falling on deaf ears. She has no earthly idea what he is talking about nor does she give two hoots. Emil asks Rose: when is enough enough? Is enough enough day after day? Week after week? Year after year? When? He told himself that the time is never and chose to sit in silence. Rose never heard a word he said; her mind was off on a tangent, planning the soiree she's hosting for Emil's quartet.

Two weeks passed and Emil made his routine visits to Rosie, doing less and less to accommodate her needs each time. Years of caring for his sister had churned a fantasy into an obsession to kill her, but he was too lily-livered to go through anything so bizarre and unrealistic.

It was Tuesday morning, and Emil had decided to take care of his chores at Rosie's earlier than normal because he had a full teaching schedule in the afternoon followed by rehearsal with the string quartet at Rose's in the evening; a busy week in general.

In an effort to maneuver her way into the musician's circle and impress upon them how much class and good breeding she and Emil shared, Rose fussed and prepared special delights to serve that evening. It had been raining off and on all morning when Rose called for a cab and asked that they send her favorite driver, who was accustomed to her shopping habits and acted more like a personal chauffeur than an ordinary cabbie. Without question or comment, this particular gentleman took her about town to the various specialty shops in order to get the ingredients and foodstuffs for the evening's social hour; for this, Rose tipped him well.

Emil's day began with shopping for foodstuffs and necessities his sister needed to carry her over for the duration of the week. The weather forecast called for rain, and fortunately he'd taken an umbrella. He was within a block of Mulberry Street when a torrential downpour soaked both him and the shopping bag he'd loaded with enough foodstuffs to last over a week. Barely able to hold on to everything with the winds that accompanied the rain, the bag tore, dumping the contents all over the street. Mumbling to himself about how much he hated having his sister, he picked up what he could and then continued on. He entered the house, and it was dismally quiet. A disquieting silence. A frightening quiet. Emil found himself torn between being excited and full of guilt and went to see for himself what was going on. Something was different up there.

Once upstairs, he looked around and could see human excrement everywhere, along with a bundle of something resembling a dead animal.

"Rosie, what have you done? Look at this mess you've made." Emil had never witnessed anything like this, and didn't know what to do. "After all I've done for you how could you do this? How do you expect me to clean this up?"

Emil decided that, because she made the mess, she could clean it up.

He looked at Rosie lying in her bed, frozen in position and lost in time. Reality had totally escaped her world, and nothing Emil did or said made any difference or even mattered, not even when he lost control and screamed like a tyrannical maniac. "I'm not cleaning up this mess, you are! Did you hear me? You are cleaning up this shit! You made this mess, you clean it up."

Emil covered his nose and mouth with his handkerchief and walked over to Rosie's bed; he was determined to control his temper, but he failed miserably. "I've been far more generous, lenient, and kind to you than you deserve. I thought if I were too tough you would break, but there is no breaking you, you break everyone else. You break hearts and destroy people's lives. First you destroyed our family, now you are destroying me. I should never have agreed to this job of caring for you. Think about it, not even your own mother wanted you after what you did to our family. Wicked woman couldn't get far enough away and stuck me and Rose with you."

The combination of exasperation and hysteria brought on a coughing frenzy that set Emil's heart pounding so hard he questioned whether or not he might be having a heart attack. He knew he had to get away from Rosie. He left the room to collect his thoughts and to decide how to recoup control without drama and emotion. An hour went by but nothing changed; Emil was more determined than ever to get Rosie up and out of that bed.

"Do you know what Elsa did to get away from you? She went back to Germany. Think that's far enough away Rosie? Huh? Get up out of that bed you whore."

The rain had stopped and the sun managed to brighten what was otherwise a miserable day. Emil went over to Rosie's bed, spitefully kicked the side of the mattress, hoping to evoke something, anything—just some sign of life. Nothing. He opened all the windows throughout the house to let in as much fresh air as possible before returning to Rosie's bedside.

"I said, get up! Get up before I pick you up and throw you out of there. Do you think you'll spend the rest of your life in that bed loafing while I'll stand by and clean up this shit? You're crazy. I'm not going to do that. Think I'll poison you and put you out of your misery. How would you like that Rosie? How'd you like a big fat bowl of poison? Then maybe we can finally have peace in our lives. Talk to me, you whore. Talk! I know you can talk. Do you talk to those kids outside? You must talk to them, or why else would they come around? Are you telling them lies about me and Auntie Rose? You better never let me hear you say anything about us or I'll beat you within an inch of your life." After years of these mindless threats, Emil knew full well Rosie wouldn't speak, but nonetheless he never stopped trying to force a response.

A strong breeze of fresh air swept in from the north end of the room, flowing over and out the south end, yet even mother nature couldn't dispel the odors clinging on to everything. Emil scrounged up two old buckets, several rags, and two bars of Octagon soap. He lugged everything up the stairs, put it all front of Rosie's bed, and let her know in no uncertain terms how there was no excuse not to have the mess she made cleaned up before he returned the next day.

Emil left the house on Mulberry Street in such a hurry that he forgot his umbrella, and halfway to the trolley he was drenched by another downpour. He believed a black cloud was definitely following him.

He arrived home in time to find Rose in the kitchen preparing for the quartet's practice session, which she'd managed to turn into a soirée. He was in no humor to see or talk to anyone, wanting more than anything to cancel everything. Rose, on the other hand, was in a great mood, singing opera arias with her horrible voice and sounding much like a wounded alley cat. She'd waited all day to show Emil all she'd done for him. Instead of showing appreciation, he said nothing. This ingratitude did not set well with Rose.

Emil had more on his mind than what Rose was doing in her kitchen. He needed empathy. "Auntie Rose, you wouldn't believe the newest game Rosie is playing—it's called throwing shit all over the room."

"Emil, you know I detest foul language, and that word is particularly repugnant. Don't ever use it in front of me again. You hear me? You know I find people who talk like that abhorrent, so why would you use that kind of language in my presence?"

Rose was the one person Emil counted on to defend him to the death, and she failed by attacking him in his most vulnerable of moments. Suddenly something triggered his intrinsic sense of what Rose was all about, and for the first time in his life he saw her for who she was.

"Rose, don't you dare talk to me about my language. If you had the job of going there just once, I wonder what kind of language you'd use."

Rose expected Emil to cower like he normally did when reprimanded, but this time he asserted himself and acted distinctly rebellious, inconsistent with the Emil she thought she knew. She wanted to tell him what she thought of his attitude, but he continued talking before she could get a word in edgewise and never stopped until he had said all he had to say.

"The responsibility of my sister has consumed me. I have no life. I died the day I was given Rosie to care for. Sure you helped financially, but that was easy. Anytime you can buy your way out of anything and never give up an ounce of energy or sweat, you take the easy way out, and you were smart Rose—once again you let money do your dirty work for you.

"You never had to make one trip in the cold to deliver so much as a can of tea leaves—instead, you bought the water. You never had to shovel the walk to get to the door—you bought the shovel so I could do it. You never hauled the pails of water so she could bathe in that galvanized tub when the tub drain wouldn't work—you bought the pails so I could do it. Big deal, you paid the water bill. You never had to clean the slop bucket for her to shit in, because you chose to never set foot in that house. Heaven forbid anybody you know should see you coming or going there.

"You did nothing but provide money. Had it been up to you, Rosie would have starved to death. You never brought her one morsel of food. Everything that had to be done for that girl, I did. No one helped me. Not one time, not one day did I get a break. When I wasn't there, I was forced to think about when I had to return. I lived with this nightmare day in and day out. I dreamt about it. I ate my meals with it. I taught my students with it. It never went away. Rosie never went away. She wouldn't get well and she wouldn't die. There was no escape. I too have spent years locked up in that attic with Rosie. Neither one of us is free—we're both prisoners of life's disappointments. I've done it all, but at the same time, I've done nothing with all these wasted years. And you Rose, have some nerve talking to me about my language."

"You apologize to me right this minute, Emil Gerhardt Gradel. You have no right to speak to me like that after all I've done for you. You hear me? You apologize!"

"I'll never make another apology to anyone for anything. I've apologized to everyone my entire life. I apologized to my mother because I could never play quite well enough for her. I apologized to my father because I wouldn't allow him to teach me what he knew and loved best, music theory, because I thought mother was better at it, but she wasn't. I apologized to the kids at school no matter what they did to me, because I was the fat kid with no friends who carried his violin case everywhere to feel important. I apologized to the nuns at school for being late because I was too ashamed to tell them the truth. The real reason I was late, I'd wet myself then had to wash out my pants by hand so mother wouldn't punish me for wetting myself. Most times I'd go off to school with them soaking wet. I smelled.

"Now I know the truth. The kids were right when they said I smelled. Rosie was right when she said I smelled. You, on the other hand, lied to me when you said I didn't smell. I still smell, but not like a little boy who wet his pants—it's a different kind of smell. It's a rotten smell that emanates from within. The smell people have who are without a heart—rotting, dying slowly. The worst kind of lingering smell a human can have is when the flesh rots because there is no soul to feed it and keep it healthy. I have no soul. I have no feelings. I have no care. I am full of hatred, and I smell. I became so used to my own rotten stench that my nose became desensitized. I now can smell myself and I now know what drove the world away. I'm exhausted, Rose. I'm going up to my room. Don't bother me. I'll not be eating dinner with you this evening."

"But what about your guests and all the preparation I've done for this evening?"

"What about them, Rose?" He gave no pause or opportunity for her to answer but instead answered for her. "If you're so concerned about them showing up and embarrassing you that I'm not here or that I was rude and didn't call, then feel free to call them yourself. I don't care."

Rose jumped at the chance to cancel everything rather than be embarrassed by what people would say.

"You know, Emil, this is your responsibility not mine, and it's you who needs the money and a job, not me. I have plenty of money."

"Rose, with you it's always been about money. Never about kindness or love or caring. It's control. It's whose life you can run, and ultimately what works best for Rose.

"I'm almost thirty years old, and for the first time in my life I know the only one who cares what happens to Emil—it's Emil. Emil will be the only one who can love Emil—and if Emil doesn't love Emil, nobody else will. But you know what, Rose? I don't know how to love Emil because I know too much about him that's wrong and can't be fixed. Poor Emil, I don't even think I can love him."

Rose looked at Emil, and the look in his eyes frightened her. She questioned whether he might be possessed because nothing he said or did made sense.

Emil walked up close to Rose, and put his face within inches of hers and said, "Right now look at him."

She looked the opposite direction.

"You can't look at him because you know I'm right. I see how much love you have for me—it's so great you can't talk and you can't look me in the eyes."

Emil felt passionate about the things he was saying—words and emotions withheld throughout his life because he was afraid to speak up to defend his own principals and values. Instead he had allowed Rose to dominate and direct his life without question. Emil no longer wanted or needed Rose in his life. "Rose, the love was never there, in fact, it didn't exist. If you loved me as you say, you would not have spent a lifetime trying to buy me. A price tag was put on me the day I moved here and there were always paybacks. The price increased each time you did something for me, like providing me with a studio right on the main trolley line, so everyone could see that brass plaque on the front of your house." Emil paused to gather his thoughts.

"No, your buying me began way before that. You bought me the day I was born to a self-indulged woman you knew loved the violin more than life itself. You bought me by showering a fat smelly little boy with little boy fantasies of sugar cakes and treats, and allowing him to do anything that went against his mother's grain. You bought me at the expense of the most priceless thing you had, your sister's friendship. You bought me at the expense of your husband who adored you and was put out of his own house, forced to drink in local saloons to drown his loneliness and sleep in the cellar alone. For what? So you could have me to yourself. You bought me by shutting out Rosie and forcing her to be alone when she desperately needed nothing more than to be loved. She didn't need our money and what it could do for her. She needed us. You bought me, you own me, now what do you do with this statue you own?"

Emil slept very little that night, tossing and turning and thinking about Rosie's deteriorating situation and what he had to do to possibly turn things around. He wanted to go there in the middle of the night, but he knew that might frighten her; besides, he wouldn't be able to see a thing because there was no electricity in her room. He waited for daybreak and was out of the house before anyone awakened.

He entered the house on Mulberry Street quietly in case Rosie was sleeping and tiptoed up the stairs to see if she had done what he asked her to do. He unlocked the door, and when he entered the room Rosie was sitting in her chair with her back to him. For the first time in more than seven years, he spoke gently.

"Rosie, it's me; it's Emil. You didn't clean up like I asked you to do. What's wrong with you? How could you stand this smell?"

Right after he said, "what's wrong with you," he was sorry he'd said that. His next remark was sympathetic. "Oh, Rosie, look, you've wet your bed, just like I used to do when I was a little boy and mom got so mad at me. I used to hate when she screamed at me for wetting my bed. I wanted to stay in it facing the wall just like you did with me two days ago when I screamed at you. I can't scream any more Rosie. I have nothing left to scream with. Like you, that voice is gone. I'm tired."

He looked at the bed and immediately knew why she was sitting in the chair and was sorry for all those times he'd been so cruel. His entire demeanor changed; the guilt was intense, and he fought back tears.

"Rosie, you pooed in your bed. Gosh I wish you hadn't done that."

Emil walked over to where she was sitting and knelt down on the floor in front of her so he could see her face.

"Rosie, Rosie, Rosie, if I'd only done things differently you and I wouldn't be sitting here like this facing what looks to me like an improbable situation, one which I've helped create. What have I done to you? You don't have to answer because I already know.

"When you threw your shit all over this room, I deserved to have it thrown all over me for all the ugly things I did to you. I never took you outside for fresh air or even for a walk in the back yard. I could have, but didn't. There is no excuse, and I'm beyond sorry.

"I knew how much you loved books, yet I never allowed you to read. You loved flowers, yet I never stopped and even picked you a dandelion off the street. You loved your God and going to daily mass, and I never took you to church.

"I didn't even feed you well. There were days when I didn't feel like coming here so I didn't, and on those days you had nothing to eat. It was wrong. Everything in our life was wrong.

"I had a chance to make life better for you and didn't do that. Saying I'm sorry will not change what has happened, but you must believe how truly ashamed I am." Emil buried his face in his hands and sobbed, stopping intermittently to plead for forgiveness.

Rosie never moved from the chair or acknowledged his presence, and he chose not to disturb her.

After nine pails of water, and endless counts of rag wringing, Emil managed to clean up the majority of the mess Rosie made. While he was cleaning it appeared as though Rosie was totally unaware she's had diarrhea. The stench was so ghastly it could have awakened the dead. But in Rosie's case, she seemed oblivious that anything had happened. He went over to her bed and thought how he would lift her lifeless body and clean up yet another mess.

To ease the removal of her soiled dress, underwear, and bed linens, he gently placed his hand behind Rosie's back and elevated her into a sitting position. The embarrassingly challenging job of taking off soiled underpants to clean dried feces from his sister's irritated skin was the last thing he'd ever imagined he'd ever have to do. The urge to leave and never look back crossed his mind, but instead he swallowed hard, redirected his thoughts, and did what he had to do.

Emil found the task of taking care of his sister's personal needs the most difficult challenge of his life and by far the most humiliating thing he ever had to do. It was beyond embarrassment and mentally exhausting. The day had just begun, and the inordinate amount of work required to make Rosie's room somewhat habitable drained the very life out of him. He was totally unaccustomed and incapable of physical work—something he never had to do.

Emil was completely wasted, but before departing he was forced to tackle one last task. He had to dispose of the soiled linens, cleaning rags, and Rosie's disgusting clothes. He found an old cardboard box, put the items in it, and then tied everything up with a piece of old clothesline. It was heavy and awkward going down the steps, but he managed to get it out of the house. Between strong soap and water and wringing out wet rags, Emil's hands were painfully irritated.

"Rosie, I'm about to leave. I have to go teach violin today, but I'll be back as soon as I am finished, and I'll bring you some fresh hot soup. Aunt Rose's maid comes today and I'll have her cook something special for you. Please try to get out of bed for me. Please Rosie—you have to do that if you want to get better."

It was almost five o'clock in the afternoon when Emil returned with two shopping bags filled with soaps, multiple sets of clean bed linens, towels, and foodstuffs he'd taken from Rose's larder.

"Rosie, I can't stay long. I have more students coming in one hour, but I wanted you to have some hot soup—I thought it might give you a little energy and strength. Please try to at least eat some of it."

Emil had no idea what was going on inside his sister's head or if she was even able to hear, but he kept on talking anyway. He begged her to eat some small amount of anything and told her when he'd return. His demeanor changed to kind and gentle. "I need you to stand up and sit in your chair for me so I can change your soiled bed linens."

Until he extended his arm, she didn't move, but as soon as he coaxed her to get up she did. He led her over to the chair and worked quickly to remake the bed before suggesting she get up and move around a bit.

Emil got ready to walk to the door but made sure she understood his plans first. "I'm leaving right now because I have to teach today. I'll see you tomorrow, and maybe if you're up to it we'll go outside for a walk."

When he looked at her he realized how awful her hair looked and made a suggestion. "I'll bring scissors tomorrow and cut your hair so you look pretty when we go for that walk. Good-bye Rosie. Don't forget to eat your soup, it's delicious."

Emil finished out his day in the studio with no breaks. As soon as the last student left he headed for Rosie's with additional linen's. He was anxious to see how she was doing now that he had changed his ways. When he entered his room, she had a surprise for him.

"Rosie, what have you done?" The soup he had brought was spilled all over the room, and from the size of this mess it look as if she hadn't eaten a single drop. Seeing what she had done made him angry, and it took everything he had to control his temper when he looked around.

"Oh Rosie, you wet your bed again, too. Why did you do this? I know you know better. Please don't make me sorry that I'm doing nice things for you by doing nasty things like this to me. My nerves are shot. I'm short on patience. This is not the time to be testy with me—not now, Rosie. I'm sorry, but you'll have to live with this mess today because I don't have time to clean it up. I have one late lesson tonight, and this student is one of my best."

He didn't feel like apologizing, but he did so to avoid creating more anguish. "I'm sorry, but I can't help you today. This is your mess, and this time Rosie you'll have to clean it up. I'll get you plenty of water, soap, and rags, to make cleaning up easier. I planned to cut your hair today, but I'm too upset to even think about doing it now; maybe tomorrow. And please, Rosie, clean this up."

Later that evening after his student left, Emil approached his aunt. The verbal exchange they'd had earlier weighed heavily on his mind and made an uncomfortable situation worse. When he spoke, he addressed her sternly by her name and specifically omitted the title "Auntie."

"Rose, I won't be having dinner with you. I have no appetite, I'm exhausted, and right now the only thing I want to do is sleep."

"Emil, you and I need to talk. First of all, when you speak to me you address me as Auntie Rose, not Rose. Secondly, you've managed to avoid me these last two days, but sooner or later we are bound to run on to each living under the same roof, and I won't tolerate your acting like a child in my house. This walking around and sulking is beginning to irritate me."

"Rose, I've said all I have to say. I'm exhausted, and I don't know how much longer I can continue the pace I've been keeping before I can no longer function in any capacity. For some reason you refuse to understand this about me."

Rose knew every facet of Emil's stubborn personality, and she made one last attempt at resolution. "Emil, if you and I don't discuss our differences right now, we never will."

"Rose, I've said all I have to say and regret nothing. My entire life I've suppressed how I think, feel, or wanted things done, because everything had to be your way. Well those days are gone, and I'm no longer your little boy."

"Emil, I don't know what has gotten into you. I've devoted my entire life to giving you anything you wanted."

"You're right, Rose; you gave me anything I wanted, but you also gave me things I never wanted. Everything you gave had strings attached that enabled you to yank back whatever it was you gave anytime you wanted. With you, Rose, there was always the piper to be paid, and with far more than you ever gave away. You were a shrewd, wicked woman, and I was too young and naïve to recognize what was underneath that facade I so lovingly called Auntie Rose. From this day forward, you will be known only as 'Rose.'"

Rose panicked at the thought of living out the rest of her life without her beloved Emil and tried another approach, hoping his behavior was nothing more than a bad case of nerves and exhaustion. "Emil, Emil, Emil, what has come over you?" She studied his face, waiting to see if he was going to answer her question, but he said nothing. Rose went on, "I no longer recognize the person standing before me, and I am not sure I want a person like that living in my house."

"Fine, Rose; I'll move in with Rosie. It will save me a great deal of time, I'll be free for the first time in my life, and I'll be the master of my domain. Believe me, I won't starve. I'm an excellent musician and no one can take that away from me. Elsa did one good thing for me, she made me the best I could be, and I am good. I never thought so before this week, but this week I learned a great deal about myself and am reminded of the day you told me to look out another window in life because the one I was looking through was covered with dirty, filthy heartaches. Sure, a different window might give me another perspective, but it never gets rid of the heartaches, it just briefly distracts the mind. I've discarded those rose-colored glasses you had me wear, and now when I look out those windows I cleaned with my tears, I see clearly and I want to live with Rosie."

"You can't leave here. What will you do with your students? They can't go to that horrible house to take lessons."

"Of course I can leave. Again you didn't listen to me. I told you, I am an excellent teacher, and serious students don't care what a studio looks like, they want to learn what I know, not see where I live."

"I'll give you the benefit of knowing you're upset and let this pass."

"Rose, this will be the last night I will ever spend in this house."

Chapter 25

The Broken Violin

The following day Emil awakened before dawn and headed for Mulberry Street. He was anxious to move and make the transition as simple as possible for both himself and his students.

The first place he went when he entered the house was up to Rosie's room. He slowly opened the door so as not to alarm her, but she never stirred. He approached the side of her bed and gently tapped her on the shoulder. The last thing he wanted to do was startle her. He spoke softly.

"Rosie, wake up, it's me, your brother Emil." He waited for a response but got nothing. He tried several more times but when she refused to acknowledge even so much as his presence, he lost his temper and began to yell at the top of his voice. When she still didn't move, he decided she was doing this on purpose because he'd told her to clean up her mess and she was getting even with him. Angered and frustrated with being subjugated to a doting fat aunt who bought and owned his very soul, Emil no longer knew who he was or how he got to this point in his life. His mind spun in circles, twisting one thought into the other until nothing made sense. Thoughts spun around and around in his head until he believed he heard his mother's voice. She grabbed a fistful of his hair and shrieked at him in German. He thought to himself, *when will this witch give up and stop banging me on my shoulder with her bow.* He cupped his ears and yelled for her to "shut up and go away," something he wished he could have said when he was a kid but never dared do lest she'd open a window and throw him out of it. Emil hated this cruel and abusive so-called mother, who with the help of a fat lonely sister somehow managed to turn a perfectly kind and sensitive individual into the monster he had become.

In what seemed like a split second, and for no reason whatsoever, everything about Rosie's inaction set him off into a frenzy. Resentment outweighed human decency. By this point he was so deranged, so lost in anger and resentment, he had no idea what he was even doing. In a fit of rage, he lunged to the side of her bed and forcefully grabbed her thin frail arm and yanked her straight up out of the bed and down onto the floor. Rosie was stunned, confused, and unable to move. She just laid there and cried.

"It looks to me like you never even attempted to clean up this soup mess you made. What is wrong with you? That was perfectly good soup, and what did you do with it? You threw it all over the room like a spoiled brat." He stopped talking just long enough to gather his thoughts. "With you it's always one thing or another." At then he bellowed, "I hope you're listening to me! All I've done for years is clean up the messes you've made out of your life. Rosie I can't take this anymore. Do you hear me? I can't take it! I'm a broken man."

Emil was mentally and physically spent. His voice was gone from yelling, his clothes were covered in perspiration, and his entire body ached like he'd walked all the way from Aunt Rose's house. Emil was ready to collapse, and he didn't care where. It could be on anything anywhere, just so it was close—a chair, the bed, the floor—it didn't matter. Rosie remained frozen on the floor, her bed was empty—he chose it and plopped himself down onto a urine soaked mattress. The smell of urine blasted him in the nose like a gallon of ammonia. He leapt up off the bed, looked down at his sister lying there, and began to weep uncontrollably. Apparently sometime during the night Rosie had wet her bed again, and suddenly the mental image of her lying in the middle of a urine-soaked bed upset him. He mustered the energy to go downstairs to get clean linens, towels, and a basin of warm water and a bar of soap. After several failed attempts to get a response, he placed a clean dry towel on her chair before gently placing his arms under her small, wet-smelling frame and carefully lifted her into the overstuffed chair. Rosie never stirred. Emil thought about how and what he'd said and knew his delivery couldn't have been worse. *Why on God's green earth did I say such a stupid-wicked thing?* He spoke to Rosie and apologized. "I am so ashamed of myself, but I don't know how to talk to you. I never did. My first words should have been—'good morning Rosie.' I'm so sorry. Please let me help you." Emil regretted ever mentioning the soup issue. His eyes welled up with tears. By now he'd put two and two together and realized how grossly inept he was at understanding anything in his sister's life, either past or present. Communication with Rosie never existed, and now when he desperately needed to make things right between them he had no idea where to begin. Emil hoped by speaking softly he might elicit a response and find out what he was doing wrong. He pleaded repeatedly, but Rosie remained still and unwilling to respond.

"Please, please, please roll over for me. I need you to hear what I have to say. Please Rosie, please. I'm begging you."

Emil gently rolled Rosie over so he could see her face and recalled the countless times his hostility rained down on her life. He was unabashedly ashamed of the monster he'd become and told her in no uncertain terms he would never harm so much as a hair on her head or ever leave her until she was completely well. The following day he set up her bedroom on the floor below with his room next to hers so she would never be left alone. There would be no more cold food, no more eating alone in her room; instead, they would eat together at the kitchen table. No more jars of water to drink from. No more pails. No more of any of that. The shame he felt was menacing, and for the first time Emil's eyes were open to the damage done to Rosie.

Once was bad enough, but being forced to bathe and change Rosie a second time required patience. He was beyond embarrassment and moved quickly to change the bed, thoroughly wash and cut Rosie's hair, give her a sponge bath, and cover her nakedness. Her hair dangled in her eyes filled with sadness, and Emil decided to temporarily tie it back with a piece of butcher's string until he had a chance to go shopping for some pretty pink ribbon. While he cleaned the soup Rosie had thrown all over the room, he thought of possibly trying to get her to go downstairs to her new room and wondered whether she could handle a flight of stairs. Emil recognized how desperately ill his sister had become and the gruesome contributions he had made to that.

If he had stood up to Rose and heeded doctor's orders instead of denying Rosie the care she deserved, this madness could have been avoided, distress eliminated, and life for everyone would be considerably different; but when you're Emil, you back down from Rose—it's what everyone did.

"I miss the Rosie I once knew, and I want her back in my life. Please come back into this shell of a body and back to the real world. Please little sister—please hear me and let me help you." Pausing to give her time to process what he said, he spoke from his heart. "From now on, I'll be here to care for you, and I'll see to it that you get well, Rosie. And maybe when you're better and you feel like it, you can get a job and, who knows, maybe even get married someday. Won't that be nice Rosie?"

After years of little or no ventilation throughout the house, the interior was saturated with spores attached to just about every surface imaginable. Emil opened windows and doors hoping to get a strong cross-wind blowing that would ventilate the house and eventually rid it of the lingering odors. Right after that, Emil sat down and wrote each of his students a personal letter informing them that a family crisis required his taking a sabbatical. He walked to the corner mailbox, dropped the letters in the slot, and hurried back to tend to Rosie. During the time he was gone, she never moved. Emil gently took hold of her arm and encouraged her to stand. In her seemingly dazed state of mind she allowed Emil to lead her down the steps one at a time and into a kitchen she never knew existed. Before inviting her to join him at the table, Emil took her to the bathroom to use the toilet, offered his hand to help her stand, and from there they went into the kitchen where he sat her in a chair facing the backyard. He wanted her to relax and see something other than his face. In those twenty minutes or so it took to prepare fresh lemonade he talked aloud to her. When he finished he filled a glass and placed it in front of her, but she seemed unresponsive and made no attempt to taste it, preferring to stare off into space. Emil mustered up self-control, promising himself not to say an unkind anything and to take everything slow. He got up out of his chair, walked around to where his sister sat, and lifted the glass to her lips. She refused to open her mouth. Obviously aggravated by this display of rejection, he put the glass back on the table and promised to take her back to her room only after she tasted his lemonade. Again he put the glass to her lips, but this time she opened her mouth and managed to drink half. When she did what he told her to do, Emil wondered if she was following orders or reading his lips. After all these years he had assumed that one of several things was going on. Either her hearing was erratic and that drove her mad, or she faked it all. He set the glass on the table then escorted Rosie back to her room. She gravitated to the overstuffed chair he remembered seeing her sit in as a child and rarely without a book in hand, reading to her heart's content.

No one knew better than Emil how Rosie lived to read, and the mere fact that he denied her this simple pleasure all those years initiated pangs of guilt for removing this one simple harmless joy from her life. He and Rose surmised that if Rosie had nothing better to do than read, she'd just sit on her bottom and do nothing all day long but read her life away, never thinking about getting well and out of there to get a job. He nearly tripped over his fat flat feet rushing downstairs to the front room closet where he ransacked through several boxes of books stacked off to one side. Emil knelt on the floor and unearthed a favorite of Rosie's, and spoke aloud to himself, "Oh my God, why didn't I think of this before now? Maybe if I get her to start reading again I'll turn this thing around. I've got to get her to read." Emil held the book in one hand and held onto the closet door jam, laboring to balance himself and get up off the floor at the same time, shamefully berating himself for denying her this or any book. A sick, sour feeling came over him as he examined the small, leather-bound maroon book in his hand, one he'd seen in Rosie's small hands many times, a beautiful collection of *Andersen's Fairy Tales* translated from the original of Hans Christian Andersen. As he flipped through the pages he came upon a handmade bookmarker she'd made to mark this, her favorite nighttime reading event, "What the Moon Saw." Rosie discovered these tales in her third year of school, repeatedly borrowing it from the library until no one else could get hold of it. The nuns told her that other children had the right to read it, too, and that she could no longer borrow it. As a result, that Christmas, Rosie was given the book as a gift, but Emil couldn't recall who had given it to her until he read the inscription inside the front cover:

To Rosie Gradel, St. Michael's brightest star and most outstanding pupil. We want you to enjoy your very own copy of your favorite book.

Emil's heart pounded, and with each thump came a jolt to remind him of all the cruel, unnecessary wounds he had inflicted on an innocent, undeserving body and mind. The humiliation for wrongdoings committed against his sister weighed on him; he could barely climb the stairs.

He lowered his head and handed the book off to her from the side because he was unable to look her in the eyes. She remained emotionless. "You sure look pretty sitting in that chair with a book in your hands. While you stay up here and familiarize yourself with your old favorites, I'm going downstairs to decide what to make us for dinner."

The kitchen was void of foodstuffs, and Emil knew he had to leave the house to go shopping. He nervously secured both the lock to the front door as well as Rosie's room to preclude any problems from arising during his absence.

Emil was concerned about leaving his sister alone, but at the same time he had to get out and get groceries. The big question on his mind was remembering her favorite foods, ones to hopefully stimulate an appetite and help regain some of the lost weight. Of equal importance, surprises and presents she doesn't expect, something to light up her eyes.

First stop, the drug store to purchase a large bar of rose-scented soap from France. Then dash directly across the street to the confectioner's to purchase a bag of licorice and an assortment of penny candies in a separate bag. Next, two other purchases, a dozen fancy tea cakes and a pound of Belgian chocolates like those Aunt Rose frequently hid away for her own consumption. Emil was reminded how much Uncle Pat adored Rosie yet couldn't stand to be in the same room with him. Every time Rosie came to visit, Uncle Pat slipped her a couple of Rose's Belgian chocolates on her way out the front door, knowing that this irritated Rose.

Emil experienced sheer delight while thinking about the purchase of a new wool sweater for Rosie from one of the better clothier's on Main Street. Winter was coming and nothing but the finest boiled wool in a small size to fit her slight frame. Pink, her favorite color, would be best. After years of wearing rags, new cotton undergarments were a must, several pairs of socks to keep her feet warm, and lastly a navy blue wool skirt to go with the sweater he'd chosen.

After the purchase he informed the merchant that it was for someone special and asked these be put in a box and tied with a ribbon. Emil could hardly wait to get home.

The final stop was a preferred grocer where he picked out an assortment of fresh breads, a tin of crackers, a few fresh fruits, some vegetables, and a variety of fresh German sausages. As he scuttled back to Mulberry Street lugging a shopping bag in each hand, all he could think of was how happy all of his effort would make Rosie.

He hurried upstairs to check on her, and the minute he got inside he saw that everything remained exactly as it was when he left. She never opened the book.

Rosie's predictably unpredictable behavior made him extremely frustrated, and for the life of him he had no idea what he'd done wrong or why she remained upset with him. After all, he did try to make up to her by apologizing and doing nice things, like telling her multiple times how sorry he was—what else did she want from him?

Emil removed the gift-box from the shopping bag and handed it to her. Surely this gesture and effort to please would make up for some of his past nastiness, but this too failed. Rosie maintained the same blank stare and never so much as blinked an eye.

He then took out the small brown bag of penny candies, hoping she'd recognize its contents and not be able to resist the temptation to open it—still nothing.

He opened the chocolates and removed a piece from the box. It was set in a small brown crinkle-edged wrapper, delicately painted on the top with a small design. Emil passed it under her nose, hoping the aroma of chocolate would elicit a response—still nothing. That's when he decided to go downstairs and purposefully leave the door to her room unlocked, hoping to encourage her to roam freely around the house or even join him in the kitchen.

Emil's unprecedented desire to make Rosie's favorite meal of potato pancakes with canned applesauce and fresh German sausage caused much agony as he fretted over whether or not his final presentation would appeal to her appetite. Using cookware and utensils that had been left in the kitchen by the previous occupant, Emil managed to prepare dinner. The meal ended up taking longer to prepare than he'd planned, because he couldn't get the hang of grating raw potatoes while keeping his knuckles out of the way.

The aroma of frying pancakes drifted through the register in the center of the house, permeating Rosie's room. Dinner was ready, and for the very first time in his life Emil made a complete meal without anyone's help. He proudly rushed upstairs to get his dinner partner.

"Rosie, I've got your favorite dinner ready, potato pancakes with applesauce and German sausage. Can you get up and come down to eat with me? I would really like your company."

Emil became grossly disappointed by his miserably failed attempts to improve things between the two of them. So she wouldn't have to look up to him, he got down on the floor next to her and spoke gently, begging her to listen.

"The only face I've seen at meals for this last part of my life is Aunt Rose's. I think you'll be lots better company and prettier, too. Please come sit at the table with me and taste my dinner. I don't want to eat alone."

No sooner had the words "eat alone" rolled off his lips and he realized what he said was exactly what he had done to Rosie. He was sorrowful and ashamed. When he spoke his voice reflected sincerity. "Can I help you get up?"

Emil pulled her by the arm in an effort to try and help her up out of the chair, but she held on, obviously not interested in joining the enemy. He took hold of her hands and, working with one at a time, gently pried each of her fingers loose until she relinquished and stood up. As soon as she stood up he noticed she'd wet in the chair. Emil knew this accident could have been prevented had he hired someone to repair her nonfunctioning commode. The chair would wait, but the dinner couldn't—it was getting cold and all he was interested in was getting her to eat something. He never mentioned what she did.

Emil again sat Rosie in a chair facing the backyard. He placed a napkin on her lap before sitting down himself. He chatted about what it was like to cook when you're not a cook and how difficult cooking is, and then he asked if she would please try his slightly rubbery but tasty potato pancakes. In an effort to move things along before her dinner got too cold to eat, he got out of his chair to cut up her pancakes and sausage into bite size pieces.

"Why aren't you eating, Rosie? You have to eat or you're going to get real sick. A body can't go on for three days without eating you know. You're beginning to worry me."

Ever mindful of the lump in his throat and the fact that he could burst into tears at the slightest mishap, he went on trying to explain to her how important it was that she eat for him. Suddenly the dam erupted and Emil began to cry. Embarrassed that his sister should see him falling apart and losing control, he grabbed a dishrag to wipe away the tears.

"You're getting so thin and frail, and I'm afraid you'll die and I don't want you to die. You have got to eat."

He pushed his dish aside, left the table once again to go around to where she was sitting, and sternly told her to open her mouth, then forced food into it. She began to gag on the first bite and he scolded her, reminding her he'd tasted his cooking and it didn't warrant gagging. His gentle persistence and patience finally paid off when she swallowed several bites of pancake for him. Emil was so proud of his achievement and knew this was an omen; they were on their way to getting back on track.

"Rosie, if you don't eat, you'll get real sick, and you could die. I told you before and am telling you again, I don't want you to die.

You're all I have left in the whole world, and I want you to get better. If you don't eat and something awful happens to you, I don't know what I would do."

Emil was satisfied. Rosie managed to eat a lot more than he'd expected, but she looked tired. Before he took her back upstairs, he insisted she use the bathroom, but she barely produced a trickle. She exited the bathroom and the two of them ascended the stairs, Emil once again expressing regrets and accepting blame for what he and Rose did to bring about this extreme sadness, all of which could have been avoided with kindness and not bitterness.

Upon entering her room, the first thing Rosie did was head for her chair to sit down, but Emil asked her to sit on the edge of the bed until he washed off the cushion. The combination of soapy water and urine saturated it and he took it outdoors to dry in the hot sun and replaced it temporarily with a chair from the kitchen so Rosie had something to sit on. Emil returned to the kitchen, picked up her unfinished plate of food, and carried it upstairs, hoping something would appeal to her as the day wore on. Before he left Rosie's room, he asked her to take a bite of sausage and pleaded several times over for her to do this for him. He had the fork loaded with a small piece and as soon as she opened her mouth he got very excited and had to comment. "The butcher made this, and if it tastes bad, he gets all the credit."

Rosie chewed the sausage slowly and eventually swallowed it. Emil watched and waited, then several minutes later, put another piece into her mouth, which she also ate, but again, very slowly.

"Rosie, if you allow me to keep doing good things for you, little by little, I'll undo the bad I did all these years. I want you to know how much I appreciate everything you did for me today by coming downstairs to eat the first dinner I ever made. You made me feel like I wasn't the failure Rose said I'd be without her in my life."

Before he left he explained once again that he'd be downstairs if she needed him and that all she had to do was pound on the floor and he'd be right by her side. He told her he would never again lock her door, and that she could come and go freely and use the downstairs bathroom whenever she needed. First thing Monday morning he would call the plumber to overhaul the bathroom in her room.

"There's so much we have to talk about, but I don't want to be the one always talking, especially because I was never any good with words or much of a talker. The violin was my voice, and for my entire life it spoke for me—leaving me in some ways much like you, unable to speak."

After Rosie fell asleep, Emil got blankets and a pillow and slept on the floor next to her bed, hoping this act would begin building trust, something he knew he had to earn. The next morning he awakened before her and remained quiet.

The first sign of life came when she opened her eyes and Emil told her how much difficulty he had falling and staying asleep, because he couldn't decide whether the floor was too hard or the smell in the room was too putrid. He came to the conclusion that without basic hygiene, years of neglecting to keep after routine cleanliness, everything from walls to furniture were ruined. The only fix was to move Rosie downstairs and completely redo the entire third floor from top to bottom.

The month was September, and it was a gorgeous day. The sun was shining, the sky was a brilliant azure blue, filled with big puffy clouds, and the temperature was perfect. Nothing could make the day better except moving Rosie out of that room—but first things first.

During the night he had put a great deal of thought and planning into how he would make this transition alone. He figured that if he braced himself in front of each piece of furniture and slide-bounced down the steps until he got to the landing, pushing and heaving the rest of the way would be doable.

His choice for Rosie's new bedroom was the room in the rear of the house facing south. It had the biggest windows, and the view was spectacular.

The first item pitched down the steps was the cushion from Rosie's overstuffed chair. Next came the chair itself, with Emil braced in front of it. Both survived the move without a major catastrophe. The night table and bulb-less lamp, along with drawers from the dresser and wardrobe containing Rosie's clothes and sundry other things, all followed. Emil was exhausted from all this physical exertion but remained resolute. He determined that neither of them would spend another night in that myriad of horrific sensory tortures, where taste and smell blended until all discernable distinction to separate the two was completely destroyed, and the only way to guarantee that was to finish the move before nightfall. Rosie ignored the entire process and never stirred from the edge of the bed until Emil asked her to sit in the kitchen chair.

Once the mattress, bed springs, bed linens, head board, foot board and side-rails were in what was to be Rosie's new room and he had reassembled everything, Emil returned upstairs to get his sister so she could see her new room.

Emil had never done this kind of heavy work before and decided to call it a day. The brute force required to physically do more than lift a violin from its case took its toll on his fleshy body until no part seemed spared. He ached all over. His hands were covered with cuts and bruises, flaking and cracking from being in and out of buckets of harsh soapy water. He no longer recognized his hands and wondered if they'd ever be able to play again. The rest of everything that didn't get done could wait, right now all he wanted to do was sit down, get something to eat, and steep a pot of tea and invite Rosie to join him. Then afterwards they could go see her new room. For the life of him he couldn't get her to get out of the kitchen chair. After much coaxing it was evident that Rosie was not the least bit interested in seeing anything or going to the kitchen to have tea or, for that matter, to move out of her chair. Emil had no idea what was going on inside her head or why there were times she'd do things for him and other times she'd stare blankly off into space. This time when he asked her to come with him she followed him down to the second floor where he set up her bed. No matter how much he wheedled, she stayed outside the room refusing to enter. Eventually, before day's end he was able to gently nudge her into the room, but she just stood there looking like a lost bewildered child.

"This is your new room, the one where you'll be staying from now on. You'll like it a lot better and I want you to know I'm never locking the doors ever again. What do you think of that! I'll bring the remaining dresser and wardrobe down here tomorrow so you'll feel right at home with your own things. I'd do it today but I'm too tired to even lift my fat feet. Let's go eat."

Emil prepared the tea, buttered a slice of rye bread and spread it with jam before placing it on a plate in front of her. When she made no attempt to even sip her tea, even when he put the cup to her lips, Emil got a strange sinking feeling and saw there was something terribly different about her. At first he tried to console himself that exhaustion made him imagine things, but in his gut he knew otherwise. He decided to go see Dr. Bauer and find out what he might give Rosie to get her to eat. He knew Rose frequently took tonics for different ailments, and he thought maybe that was what Rosie needed.

"Rosie, this not eating is worrisome, especially because you're withering before my very eyes. I had hoped to go outside with you and sit out on the porch, but I think we'll postpone that for now; it's more important I go see Dr. Bauer and ask him to make a house call. But I promise, we'll do it tomorrow. Let me take you back up to your room. Your bed is back together and maybe you can rest while I'm out. I won't be gone long."

Thirty minutes later Emil returned from visiting the family doctor and spoke to her in an almost childlike manner. "Rosie, I went to Dr. Bauer's office and he's agreed to make a house call first thing tomorrow morning and fix you up good as new. Rose always said he was the smartest doctor in the whole city, probably had everything to do with the fact he was German, I'm sure. So long as he fixes you, I'll be happy." He held the cup up to her lips and tried to get her to sip some tea, but she turned her head away.

"Come on now, I'll hold the cup to your lips and you just sip the tea. It's cold, but you must drink something because I won't leave until you do, so it's either drink the tea or put up with me sitting here all day holding this cup to your lips." Rosie held her ground and wouldn't drink the tea. "So you're going to be stubborn, eh? You always were good at getting your own way by holding out longer than anyone else in the family. This time, Rosie, I'm going to win." He exerted enough pressure against her barely open mouth to force her to swallow some tea he'd made then went downstairs to the front room where he set up a music stand, chose his favorite violin, and began performing Wieniawski's second violin concerto in D minor, hoping that perhaps music would bring life back into an otherwise eerily silent house. His playing went on for hours, and when he stopped to check on Rosie he found her fast asleep on top of the bedcover in exactly the same place and position as when he had left hours earlier. A dread came over him. His greatest fear had come to pass—*Rosie was gone.* Any effort to try and save her was in vain; it was too little, too late. Emil raced to see Dr. Bauer, this time begging the doctor to come immediately—tomorrow might be too late. Dr. Bauer agreed to come at eight o'clock that evening after his office closed.

Emil hurried back home to give Rosie the good news, but she never acknowledged him. He sat at the foot of her bed and observed this motionless person staring off into a place where he was not included. For the next three hours he sat clinging to the side-rail of her bed, waiting for Dr. Bauer. During that entire time, he had nothing to do but think and face the bitter truth: *This was his fault.*

Emil knew the prognosis before the doctor arrived. There were no surprises when Dr. Bauer chastised him for not recognizing the severity of his sister's rapidly declining mental and physical health. Dr. Bauer could not fathom how anyone could look at Rosie all this time he was with her and not see she that was malnourished and dehydrated. Furthermore, he admonished him on the possibility of further internal deterioration or damage to her organs if he didn't get a constant stream of fluids going immediately. Emil avoided eye contact with Dr. Bauer, who was livid with Emil for allowing Rosie's condition to worsen to this degree before seeking help.

"How could you let your sister get this sick before calling for me? I would have come here anytime of day or night, and you know that Emil. What you have done here is unforgivable. What has happened to Rosie did not happen overnight; what I see here could have been avoided with proper care and medication. Allowing this to happen to this brilliant young lady is both stupid and inexcusable on your part, and I will never forgive you for this. God help you, I hope you'll be able to sleep nights for all you've not done for her that you should have."

Dr. Bauer told Emil he would attempt to make arrangements for Rosie to be taken to the local hospital to stabilize her current most obvious condition, dehydration. If this were not possible, he would be forced to wait until morning and have Rosie taken directly to Woodside Mental Hospital, which was beyond the city limits.

Emil listened intently as Dr. Bauer explained the severity of Rosie's complex situation and the circumstances involved in trying to recover all she'd lost and why the regular hospitals would only be a temporary lifeline until she could be moved to a mental institution where he hoped they could still save her. Before leaving, Dr. Bauer gave Emil instructions.

"In the meantime, while I try and make arrangements, I want you to get Rosie to drink something. It doesn't have to be water, it can be anything liquid, just get it down her. I don't care what it is. It can be broth, tea, any liquid she wants, just get fluids into her. I don't give a damn if you have to sit by her bedside all night long and do it drop by drop with an eyedropper. Do you understand me, Emil Gerhardt Gradel?"

"Yes, sir."

"Then do it, don't just sit there. Move!"

Emil went to the kitchen and stood in front of the sink, unable to think of what a liquid was. His mind froze and he couldn't get it to remember anything Dr. Bauer told him to do or what it was he was ordered to give his sister. He began to cry, and suddenly it came to him, broth, tea, any liquid she wants. He grabbed a glass of water and a rag and raced into Rosie's bedroom. Dr. Bauer was gently stroking Rosie's head, speaking softly.

"Rosie dear, you are going to be fine, I'll see to that. Sometime between tonight and tomorrow morning we're going to get you out of here and take you to a hospital where you can get well. In the meantime, you must listen to me and drink whatever it is you like, but you must drink something."

With no telephone in the house, Dr. Bauer was forced to leave and return to his office to try and make arrangements to have Rosie admitted to the hospital. Unsuccessful in his attempts to have her admitted that evening, arrangements were made to have her picked up by ambulance first thing in the morning and taken directly to Woodside.

Dr. Bauer made a second trip back to Mulberry Street that night to inform Emil that he needed to have Rosie awake and ready to leave by seven o'clock in the morning. Once again, he stressed how crucial it was to get liquids into her.

"Don't forget Emil, throughout the night I don't want you to let her fall sleep without forcing liquids into her. If you don't manage to get liquids into her, she will die. If you don't want that on your conscience in addition to whatever else it was you did to drive her to this point, then force her to drink. Good night"

Dr. Bauer saw himself out.

Emil remained awake the entire night and never left Rosie's side except for occasional trips to the kitchen to replenish glasses of fresh water. At first he wet the corner of the rag and let water droplets fall onto Rosie's mouth, but he found that more water fell on her than in her.

It occurred to him that maybe the easiest solution lie in something as simple as droplets of water from a piece of ice. He went to the icebox and got a small chunk, and as it melted he'd return to the kitchen to get another chip.

Emil tirelessly pried Rosie's lips apart while holding the small chunks of ice over her lips, allowing the droplets to fall one by one into her mouth, dabbing away those she failed to swallow.

As the rag absorbed the run-off droplets from the corners of Rosie's mouth, Emil would occasionally take it and lay it across her forehead, hoping to make her feel better.

Looking at Rosie lying there, he couldn't fathom how any of this had happened and why. As her sole remaining family member he kept remembering what Dr. Bauer said: "When they come for Rosie tomorrow you'll have to sign papers committing her to Woodside. Don't hesitate, just sign them and get her committed so she can begin to get well."

The words *committed* and *committing* resonated through his mind. Over and over with each droplet that fell on Rosie's lips came intense guilt. Astronomical peaks and valleys of emotions gathered momentum, resulting in volcanic eruptions of tears and voices inside his head that admonished him for destroying the soul of the person lying before him.

Once in the middle of the night he was able to get Rosie to drink an inch of milk from the glass and, for a split second, foolishly hoped this might be a miracle—a turning point. There was no miracle, no turning point, just a temporary fix with him holding his finger in the dike, waiting for morning. Emil no longer was able to secure himself against the ravages of the sea of guilt coming towards him.

After faithfully executing Dr. Bauer's orders to keep Rosie alive throughout the night and into morning, Emil could barely keep his eyes open. The last hour before dawn, he fell asleep at the foot of Rosie's bed, but he hardly got any sleep before the alarm went off. He immediately got up and began gathering Rosie's clothes so he could have her ready to leave for the hospital.

He leaned over and gently tapped her on the shoulder, careful not to startle her.

"It's morning Rosie. You have to get up, go to the bathroom, and come let me help you get dressed. You're going to the hospital this morning."

Rosie rolled over, sat up slowly, and with Emil's help stood by the edge of the bed. It was then that Emil noticed the bed was wet. Unlike times in the past when he would have berated and admonished her for such behavior, this didn't matter. In fact, it never did. Nothing mattered anymore other than fixing what he'd broken.

"You're going away for a while, but you won't be there forever, just until you're well again. The place where you are going is a rest hospital where they cook good food, not awful pancakes like I make, and maybe the cooks there can get you to eat again so you can get strong and healthy."

Emil was nervous and never stopped talking the entire time he was brushing her hair and getting ready to tie it back with the ribbon he'd bought. He jumped from subject to subject.

"I remember when we were little, you were never sick. I want you to get strong again Rosie, and in this special hospital they'll help you get that way. And when you're strong, you'll get well. At this place they know how to fix people like you—I don't."

The two of them sat side by side on the edge of Rosie's bed, Emil completely devastated by the thought of what was to be. He patted her shoulder as if to touch the broken side of her, and for the first time in his life he felt genuine love.

"I can't fix anything but my violin, and we both know you're not a violin. If I could have one wish, today or any day, I'd wish you were my violin—then I could fix what I broke a long time ago." Still sitting side by side on the bed, Emil clutched Rosie's hand, unwilling to let go a minute before he had to.

The knock at the door announced the ambulance arrived right on time. The dreaded moment had come just as Dr. Bauer had said it would.

Emil would have preferred to have his last memorable picture of his sister be one of a happier nature, but it was not to be—not today. He surveyed her from head to toe making sure he hadn't forgotten anything that might be important to Rosie.

He selected a plain cotton dress with pockets in the front so she could keep her rosaries in there along with the St. Christopher medal he'd found under her pillow when he moved her bed. He remembered how special the rosaries were to her and assumed the medal would hold equally as much importance when she got well.

Rosie had one pair of shoes, but he thought the bed slippers with anklets to keep her feet warm a better choice for a hospital stay.

He felt sure she wouldn't want to go out without under panties so he put them on in spite of feeling extremely embarrassed, making sure to turn his head to the side and feeling his way rather than looking directly at her.

The new rose-colored sweater was the last item he put on. He looked at her and thought how much more like a little girl she appeared than like the young woman she'd grown up to be.

The ribbon he'd put in her hair managed to stay in place but looked lopsided, and just as he began to straighten it out a second stronger knock at the front door interrupted him in this their final moments alone.

He promptly opened the front door and four men in white coats and pants greeted him. The first two men handed Emil commitment papers to sign. The other two attendants were brief but explained to Emil that the ride to Woodside was a long one, and that Rosie would be given a sedative as soon as they got her into the ambulance. This sedative would keep her from being upset or anxious until they arrived at the hospital's center where a doctor would examine her and determine her status and where she'd be sent within the hospital complex.

Emil agreed to everything they were doing until he saw the jacket. Dr. Bauer had never mentioned any straight jacket, and when Emil saw the men putting her in it, he began to scream for them to stop and, for the first time, watched Rosie react to something objectionable.

As weak as she was, she tried desperately to fight their attempts but quickly submitted to their strength and ability to overtake her. The men nicely explained how this didn't hurt and was being done for her safety—to immobilize her arms so she wouldn't injure herself.

Rosie glanced at Emil as they took her all tightly secured on the stretcher from her room and down the hall towards the front of the house and out to the waiting ambulance. A small crowd had gathered to see what the commotion was all about, but mostly to see what an ambulance was doing in front of the house that never generated any activity and looked vacant. One of the people in the crowd asked the attendants what had happened and they remained silent, going about their business of securing Rosie for a safe journey to where she could get the help she so desperately needed.

Emil stood behind the closed front door and waited until he heard the hum of the ambulance engine fade into the distance before locking it and walking back to Rosie's new room, the one she never really had a chance to see furnished with most of her things.

He climbed the stairs to what had been Rosie's home for the last seven-plus years and opened the door. An accumulation of rotten odors flooded his nostrils and lungs like the tail end of a typhoon. In a single day he managed to foil his brain into thinking the smells weren't all that bad, but the minute he opened the door the stench practically propelled him down the stairs.

The thought of facing Rose when he went to collect his personal property was no match, even when put up against the rotten odors in Rosie's old room. The encounter, however brief, would be more than he bargained for, especially knowing there would be questions he wouldn't want to answer. Before he left Mulberry Street, he promised himself he would not tell Rose any more than where Rosie was.

"Rose, I've not come to disturb you, I've only come for my personal things and don't plan to be here very long. Uncle Pat can now have you all to himself. I hope it isn't too late for that poor fellow to enjoy his remaining years with you, because you are all he has, and he is all you have. You two started out together, and here you are, ending up the same way, just as it should be. I'm sorry for everything I denied him. Please tell him that for me when he comes home tonight.

"This is the last time I ever plan to see you Rose. I will manage to take care of myself just fine, and if you have any financial quibbles with me, do it via the United States Postal Service. I no longer have the responsibility of Rosie, a mental hospital does. There they will attempt to succeed where you and I failed. I'm going back to Mulberry Street and wait for Rosie to get well. And when she is well, I can and will take care of her. Good bye, Rose. I have nothing to thank you for."

As soon as Emil returned to the house on Mulberry Street he opened every window plus the rear door to let in fresh air, hoping to flush out the putrid-foul odors passing down from the open floor register grate in Rosie's room. He planned to keep the windows wide open day and night until he'd diminished the lingering odors to a more tolerable level. The old lady who once lived in the house left a thirty-six inch square table out on the back porch. Emil lugged it up to Rosie's old room and turned it upside down over the grate to block off the airflow.

Rosie's wardrobe and dresser remained on the upper floor and needed to be moved into her new room. Because he'd closed off the register and decided to permanently seal off the entire staircase and top floor, he needed to move those two pieces sooner than later. Determined to tackle this oversized piece, he pulled it from the wall one side at a time, bracing himself as he shoved it across the varnished wood floor. Before reaching the landing at the top of the stairs to survey the situation and plan his next move, he turned around and noticed a large shadow on the wall where the wardrobe once stood. This curious shadow was not the kind of pattern formed by light passing behind an object—this was different. He got closer to the wall and discovered a faint outline, meticulously drawn to create boundary lines containing a collection of rectangles and squares, and directly in the center in an approximate ten-by-twelve-inch rectangle was a pencil-drawn portrait. At first glance it looked like a Van Gogh but was, in fact, a self-drawn portrait of Rosie. This collection of distinctly blocked off sections varied in size, and each contained miniscule hand-written words carefully placed close together to optimize space and create a magnificent masterpiece on what would otherwise have been nothing more than a dull boring wall of nothingness.

Questions began clamoring around inside his head, like how she reached the very top of the outline with nothing to stand on—the wardrobe was more than six feet tall! Where did the pencils come from? He was aware his father's business sold them in bulk, but he didn't recall seeing any when Rosie's furniture was delivered; it didn't make sense. How did she move this monstrous wardrobe? Best he could figure it was at least three feet wide and not easy to grab onto. When and at what time of day did she do all this? What in God's world possessed her to do this, and how did she manage to do it all without ever being caught in the act? How did she do a self-portrait with exact likeness to herself? Emil was in complete awe of the talent required to create this masterpiece with nothing more than simple pencils, a blank wall, and desperation.

The meticulous printing within each rectangle and square looked as if Rosie had ripped pages straight out of a book and pasted them on the wall. He marveled at the discipline required to keep her writing in straight lines while maintaining intricate detail. Emil stepped back to witness Rosie's massive amazing undertaking in its entirety. He picked random sections to read, obviously invading her guarded writings, and here Emil would learn the consequences of being a snoop.

Chapter 26

Money Can't Buy What Money Can't Buy

Father Greiner was sitting at his desk working on Sunday's sermon and wasn't making much headway. His stomach kept gnawing, trying to let him know it was time to stop and eat dinner, but he wanted to finish writing and quit for the day. The sermon was about the unpredictability of life. Suddenly he was interrupted by the telephone's intermittent ring, signaling that this party line call was for him. He put down his pencil and answered the phone: "Hello?."

At first, silence. He waited a few seconds thinking he had a bad connection and tried a second time. "Hello? But this time he spoke louder in case the person on the other end might have a bad connection and unable to hear him. Abruptly the voice on the other end began shrieking and talking at such a rapid pace the words came out garbled and incoherent.

"Hello, and please, whoever you are, speak slowly and distinctly so I can understand you."

"Fine, I will," the woman curtly replied.

"Who is this?" asked Father Greiner.

"It's Rose, Rose Dunnigan. Father, surely you remember me. Who on earth did you think this was?"

"Well, Rose Dunnigan, you must admit, it's been years since we last spoke and, with this bad connection, I didn't recognize your voice. How are you, and why all the screaming?"

"Father, I don't have time for small talk or sarcasm." Her voice began to climb the vocal scale, teetering on the brink of hysteria.

"Please just listen to me," he began. "If you want my help or if you want me to talk to you, you must speak so I can understand you. What is it that you want from me Rose?"

Rose hesitated a moment. This subject was one of grave personal content and she was not interested in discussing it over the telephone where someone might eavesdrop and glean any particulars.

"It's about young Rosie Gradel."

Rose had a suspicious nature and trusted no one. She spoke just above a whisper, in case someone might be listening in on the party line conversation. "Rosie's done it again—disgraced and shamed her family."

At this point Rose lost control of her emotions and spouted more than she normally would have had circumstances been different.

"I don't know what's gotten into that girl. She had a chance to change her attitude, straighten out her life, but instead she decided to get revenge and punish us."

"How did she do that Rose?"

Rose flew into a vocal tirade. "She's gone crazy, and we had to have her taken to the insane asylum today. The girl went completely 'cuckoo-cuckoo'—off her rocker, and no one is to blame but Rosie; she did this all by herself. I washed my hands of this whole mess a long time ago, so no one can say I had any part in this."

"When did all this happen and how?"

"If you're insinuating I had anything to do with this, you're totally out of line. Rosie hasn't been right since giving up that bastard's baby she had, and if you hadn't introduced that Frank Pazwalski to my sister when Hans had his stroke, none of this would have happened. It's your fault, too, Father. Need I remind you, you told Hans about all the things he could do, how honest and decent he was, makes me wonder if you know the meaning of those words. You call getting an innocent girl pregnant, then leaving without so much as a telltale sign of where or why, decent? In my world, we call these worthless bums." Rose regretted running her mouth without thinking of the possibility a party liner, also known by her as the whole world, might have been listening in on all of this conversation.

"How you can blame any of this on me, after all I did to help you and your family, is preposterous."

"I'm sorry Father, I shouldn't have said some of those things, but right now I don't know what to do or where to turn."

"Rose, where is Rosie now?"

"They took her to that crazy house—Woodside. Ever hear of it?"

"Yes. Did anyone go with her?"

"No Father, no one went with her. Emil tells me that men from the hospital came, drugged her, then put her in a straight-jacket, and off they went. Thank God I can finally put a stop to the drain she's put on my pocket book. I knew I'd made a mistake the day I divulged to the family that I received a rather large inheritance from Mrs. Shubert when she died, and ever since, they think I'm their personal piggy-bank. Those days are done—over—finished—gone."

"Rose, Rose, Rose, this is not about money. This is about your niece's life and what has happened to her."

"Oh for crying out loud, stop this righteous pious talk. You might fool a lot of people, but you don't fool an old fool like me. You're just as culpable in all of this as anyone. If I've told Emil once I've told him fifty times, Rosie has been off her rocker for a long time—just put her away. But no, he thought he could spare the family further embarrassment and shame by taking care of her on his own. He gave up every spare minute in his life to go there and take care of her just so he could keep her crazy business private. Lots of good it did waiting on her and taking care of her these past seven plus years. I say enough is enough and I'm glad this nightmare is over."

Rose still hadn't discussed the real reason for her call.

"Father Greiner, I need to talk to you about other issues I don't care to discuss over the telephone. Could I come by the rectory tonight? I have no one else I trust to keep matters confidential."

After all the things he heard Rose say, he'd had his fill of her. "Rose, I'm in complete shock and disbelief over what has happened to Rosie and why. Please don't come here, not tonight, not now. I need time alone. I'm gravely upset, deeply saddened, and for some reason, you refuse to understand. With you Rose, nothing ever changes, it's still the same old business, Rose only thinks about Rose."

The nonsensical-noise-babbling about his being culpable played over and over, going round and round in his head. When Rose said culpable, his first response to himself was, *she doesn't know what she's talking about*. As hard as he tried to deny her accusation, the word rushed back into his head. *Culpable.* Rose was right, oh my God, she was right, but not for the reason she stated. He realized Rosie's illness was serious the day he brought her to Mulberry Street to be buried like some dirty filthy secret, yet he took her there anyway. She didn't belong in Hawthorne House and she didn't belong on Mulberry Street. Sadly, he always knew how he felt about Rosie, had the wherewithal to save her, and didn't because he was gutless. Rose was right, he was as culpable as anyone, maybe even more so because Rosie trusted the family priest to be her last saving grace, her last hope. Admittedly, he was worse than Frank, Frank ran because he thought he'd be held for murder. Greiner ran like the rest of her family, and for this he was culpable. Self-loathing consumed him. One day he has to right this wrong.

"You didn't answer me Father. When can I come see you? Tomorrow, a couple of days from now, when? Will you call and tell me?"

He had no interest, nor did he want any part of her, her melodramatic family drama, or her phone number, and furthermore, didn't care if he ever saw her again. His response was clipped—"what's your number?"

By his response, Rose sensed he was brushing her off, and questioned whether or not he'd return her call. She cleared her throat, "my number is Hemlock 3-0687—did you write that down?"

He sat there and listened to her babble, and thought to himself, *why am I putting up with all of this—after all, she no longer belongs to my parish and I owe her nothing. Besides, she has a parish priest, why doesn't she call him if this matter is so important, why's she bothering me?*

Father Greiner couldn't believe the gall of Rose Dunnigan and hung up without so much as a good-bye. He loathed himself for not seeing her for who and what she was: a selfish, wicked, and inhumane woman.

Father Greiner's conversation with Rose Dunnigan, the grim reaper of news, had put him in a complete stupor. Time passed, darkness set in outside, the city streetlights came on, and he lost all sense of time. When Father Greiner needed a break from parishioners, he'd sit in his office in darkness staring at night-time light patterns as they danced through the venetian blinds creating patterns on the floor. This mindless gazing momentarily dispelled any half-cracked notions running the gambit of his mind, and then, just like that, those hauntingly dark thoughts of Rosie Gradel crept back into his brain. Why couldn't he stop this? What was it about her that eerily crept into the hollows of his mind? He knew the answer, he always did: denial. What could he have done differently when he was involved with her family years ago that could have changed the course of events in her life? He closed his eyes to put this unsightly mess to rest, but culpability had found itself a home.

Between the doorbell's nonstop ringing and torturous thoughts racing around in his head, he wished he was anywhere but the rectory. He sat perfectly still. Because it was dark inside, he figured no one could see him sitting alone in the darkness, but he had failed to think how the streetlight outside his office lit it up. He was clearly visible and had no way out without being seen. His heart raced, and he broke out in a nervous sweat and thought he'd better move fast and slither down off the chair, onto the floor, and crawl into the near-by hallway where he'd be out of sight. But just then, the person at the door began simultaneously pounding on the door and ringing the doorbell, as if the devil himself were after them. Yet as suddenly as the frantic pounding had started, and the ringing of the doorbell began, it stopped. He thought the person at the door had gone away, deciding there was nobody in the rectory, when suddenly a face appeared in the window. From where he sat, he could see the outline of a woman peering in as if she knew who she was searching for and didn't care if she awakened God Himself.

She cupped both hands on the sides of her temporal area and spotted the priest sitting in the chair. He feigned sleep and that's when the pounding resumed, but this time, on the glass. It was so hard it surely could have shattered the glass. He kept his head down as if asleep. Suddenly the face had a voice and it began to scream as the fists pounded on the glass.

"Open up this damned rectory and talk to me. I see you in there, so don't you dare act like you don't hear me!"

He recognized the voice, but not the tone nor language. Rose Dunnigan never used profanity. She could see him, and he had to respond before she did something stupid like break the glass and cut herself.

"Oh God, please let this be a bad dream and make her go away." Rose was acting bizarre, and he knew that if he didn't let her in, she'd remain until he did. He lifted his head slowly as if awakening from a sound sleep, grabbed onto both arms of the chair and stood up. He could no longer ignore Rose Dunnigan. He reached for the crucifix at the end of his rosaries and begged God's forgiveness. "I am so ashamed for having taken money for work done under the guise of being a priest. If I could give it all back and not be in this predicament I would do so. I am so sorry Dear

Lord. Please, please forgive me for succumbing to these human frailties. Please, dear Lord, give me the strength and stability I need to serve you at this time. I am overcome with human frailties, desperately in need of your Divine guidance. I need to quell these emotions and listen. Please, please help me serve this your child in Rose with true and kind words."

Father Greiner hastened to reach the front door before his unwelcomed visitor had a chance to arouse the entire neighborhood with her maniacal screaming. Before him stood a woman he'd known for many years but suddenly didn't recognize. Her eyes were wild and cold. Her hair was disheveled and her clothes appeared as if she had slept in them. She had obviously been drinking, another thing Rose never did. He knew Pat to be a heavy drinker, but Rose strongly objected and never hesitated to tell him when she thought he'd reached his limit, always respectful of her wishes he'd stop. Although after Emil moved in and usurped Rose's time and attention, she became less interested in Pat and what he drank or did with his life and more interested in Emil and spending as much time with him as he gave her.

Uncertain of how to handle Rose in her condition, he reached out, but she was incoherent, out of control, and screaming at the top of her lungs. "Father, I knew you would never call me back, I knew it by the tone of your voice when I called you. You're blaming me for Rosie and what happened and none of it's my fault. It's her fault. She was a sneaky kind of kid you couldn't trust, that's why I never liked her. She killed Hans and destroyed our family."

With that said, she pushed past the priest, and entered the rectory causing him to lose his balance and fall down. He tried to grab hold of the rail to the stairs but fell onto the steps. It took several minutes for him to regain his composure. Rose, in her drunken stupor, tripped on the edge of the carpet, hit her head on the corner of the office wall, and fell to the floor. He stumbled over her to turn on the lights before running to the kitchen to get a towel and cold water. She laid there motionless with blood running from a deep gash on the side of her head. He thought about calling for help, but this was supposedly a serious fragile matter and of such great personal secrecy, he decided to take matters into his own hands. He wet the towel and cleaned up the wound, finding far more blood than damage to Rose's head. He located a small pillow to elevate her head and explain what happened, but before he could complete the sentence, Rose was asleep on the floor where she had fallen. He got a small blanket, covered her, and left her there to sleep off the alcohol and ugliness of the day. Morning would bring a new beginning for everyone. He considered calling Pat to tell him of his wife's whereabouts, but decided one o'clock in the morning was not the time to call anyone. He dispelled every thought that went round and round in his head, and focused instead on the spoiled child inside an adult mind and body that lie motionless out in the hallway. Her father and Pat were to blame for giving everything and expecting nothing, one taking over where the other left off. By merely accepting what was taught, she ended up acquiring qualities society dislikes but never sees in itself yet is quick to judge. Rose wanted what most of us want—love and acceptance; but without learning the importance of virtue, she lived a meaningless existence, surrounded by materialism.

Chapter 27

The Homecoming

After Frank had been gone for some time, two of his old grade-school chums met up and queried each other about his whereabouts. His pal Charlie volunteered to go by his house and check on him but gave up after several attempts. Another one of his friends worked on Main Street and checked with old man Fleishmann, who said Frank never showed up for work anymore so he hired another guy to do his window dressings.

No one understood this leaving without anyone knowing, especially his best buddies. Where did he go? Surely his sister would know of his whereabouts. They even kicked around the possibility that he had died and no one told them, or—worse yet, had killed himself like his father and the family kept it secret like they did when Doc Pazwalski died.

"Ray, you don't really think he got one of those broads pregnant down at the club and she came after him to get married, so he went and took the bridge just like his old man?"

"Who the hell knows, I just know he's nowhere to be found and that's not like Frank. I ask around about him everywhere and nobody's seen him. Can't figure what the hell's going on. Nothin' makes sense."

"Charlie, last time I saw him was back in February, and I thought there was something different about Frank, but I sort of felt it was a happy good change."

"Hell, this is already September and no one has seen him. Let's go see his fat-ass sister Sophie and see if she knows where he is."

Frank's two friends jumped in Ray's car and went to see Frank's sister. When they got there she told them she had no idea where her brother was or where he went, why he quit his work, or how long he'd actually been gone.

The only concrete thing she had to go on was what her husband John told her the night he came home from the Falcon Club where he and Frank got drunk together. Frank's friends knew Frank despised John, so his getting drunk with John was totally out of character. Nothing made sense.

"My John's drunk most all the time and I don't listen to half of what he tells me when he's like that 'cause most of it's booze talkin', but John kept sayin' over and over how Frank ran his mouth 'bout two people and a kid dyin' and how it wasn't his fault, and he wasn't stickin' around to take the blame."

Ray was one of Frank's best pals and couldn't go along with this story because none of it made any more sense than the woman telling it. The two men were stunned by what they heard, and didn't remember ever hearing anything about two people and a kid dying mysteriously or being killed. They bought the daily Post-Gazette, and there was never any mention in the headlines even remotely close to what Sophie concocted. They rehashed everything a second time and concluded she was just like Frank always said, as nuts as her old man. The unforgivable part was Frank's willingness to leave without so much as, a 'good-bye'. Best friends didn't do that to each other.

The two of them drove away from Sophie's, unable to make sense of what they'd heard. Charlie reminisced about the good-and the bad, the happy and the-sad times these childhood friends had shared with Frank. Charlie knew wherever Frank was he was right with the world, it's who he was.

When they were kids Ray and Charlie never told Frank how they felt about his friend Greiner, knowing he always protected him. Back then the kids joked about why Greiner went to be a priest and decided it was because he was afraid of everything from girls to shadows, had a nut for a mother who hated all of them, but hated Frank worst of all.

In the end everyone knew how bad it was for Greiner in that crazy house. In the summer the boys would stand outside their kitchen window just to see and hear all the crazy stuff his old lady would do to the poor kid. He never knew they saw what went on and they swore to never tell anyone. The two of them recalled the time they were about twelve years old and Frank told them about the day old lady Greiner was so loaded she could hardly stand up and tried to chase him out of her yard waving a broom. He said he turned around, ripped the broom out of her hands, and told her she was nuts and mean as cat turds.

The boys were in high school and talked all the time about Greiner's mother and how miserable she made his life, telling him horrible things about women, like never trust them. She made him go to mass and do all that good Catholic stuff, and then the poor kid got shipped off to minor seminary in the middle of the night.

Charlie was feeling melancholy about the three of them and how their lives went off in different directions, how they ended up unable to find the missing part, Frank. Both friends were trying to figure out what went so wrong in Frank's life that he would just up and disappear like Greiner the time Greiner disappeared. The two of them kicked around all sorts of ideas, including one Frank had never told either Charlie or Ray until this one night. Ray recalled how it all went down.

"Yeah, Frank, what? Thought best pals didn't have secrets."

"Ray, if you're going to act like a jackass, then I'm not telling you anything serious. You're pissing me off and if you keep this up I'm going to punch you in the mouth and then you won't be able to run that mouth enough to chew gravy. This is serious stuff."

"OK, OK, tough guy Frank, what's this serious crap you want to tell us?"

"I'm not the tough guy you think you knew all these years."

"Charlie, you think Frank lost it?"

"Could be Ray, I never saw this side of him, all soupy and soft. Maybe he's gone off to join Greiner and be a priest too. Nah, on second thought, it's got to be a woman. Nobody loves chasing skirts more than Frank. Maybe this is what's messing up his head. Guess since he's gone we'll never know now, will we? Besides women, Frank's got a soft side, not many people know that about him, but think about that time he told us how he cried and we didn't believe him."

"Did you guys know that the only time in my life anybody ever saw me cry was the day Greiner went to be a priest?

"No shit, you mean you never ever cried when we were kids? Ever get a whipping?

"Charlie you asshole, shut up and listen."

"I always felt in my heart that he was going off to minor seminary for all the wrong reasons. He never stood up for himself or for any of his ideas. It was always do what his mother wanted, because if he didn't, she'd bawl her eyes out and scream for her old man who was dead. She'd talk to him and all sorts of weird stuff. She'd even set the table and put whatever little bit of food they shared on a plate for the old man and pretend he was having dinner with her and Greiner. That nut-case

would even make Greiner talk to his dead old man. I know this for a fact because I used to stand outside their window and watch this shit. That's why I'd wait outside and never go in that house. Holy crap, there was no way I was going in there to join them and talk to a dead man's ghost or whatever the hell the two of them talked to. Poor Greiner would talk to his old man like he was really there. It was weird as shit, the whole thing. I was afraid of that crazy old woman too, just like Greiner was, so I never stayed around to see what or who the hell ate the food on the dish. I'd wait a while after I'd watched them do this weird shit, then stand out by the gate and call him. One Wednesday night I went there to see him because I thought he might be all by himself and I thought we'd hang out in the street and kick a ball. His old lady usually worked Wednesday nights cleaning this restaurant place and she always came home snookered. Well for some reason, she didn't work that night. Lucky me, I didn't go to the front door, always looked in the kitchen window first to see if she was there. There she was, wailing her head off and poor Greiner was standing by the table and he was naked. Can you believe that, a big boy ten years old standing there naked in front of his old lady. He wouldn't talk to her and she kept telling him to answer her. When he just stood there, the old bat grabbed him and shoved him into the closet then locked the latch on the outside. I could hear Greiner sobbing and begging to be let out and all she could do was wail for the old man to hurry and eat his dinner and do something with that useless boy Herbert. Often wondered what the shit she would have done had she had me for a kid. I'll tell you one thing for sure, there is no way that I would have stood there naked and not done something to her when she started that screaming. I would have pissed on her leg and run away or taken the bridge like my old man did! Old bat was lucky to have a great kid like Greiner. He was a swell little guy and so smart. Pissed her off when I called him Greiner. Old hag never figured out I called her baby Greiner for a reason, to help him be tough and not a sissy. I so desperately wanted him to stand up for himself and he never did. No matter what I did or however hard I tried, I never could change him. She thought I was stupid and didn't know Griener's real name was George. Why the hell would you give a kid a weird name like George any-ways? To make matters worse, she stuck poor Greiner with the middle name Herbert. I ask you, why would you name a kid George Herbert unless you wanted him to grow up and be as weird as his name? Then the poor sucker comes along, and right before he's confirmed, his old lady puts pressure on him to use the name Heinreich. Greiner wanted the confirmation name Michael after our school. The old bat claimed she hated the name Michael because that was her father's name and he was mean. I'll bet her old man's name was Heinreich. I'd also be willing to bet some lover dumped that old bat and his name was Michael. Tell me if that isn't a nut-case reason for not letting a kid pick his own confirmation name, "mama doesn't like it." Remember when we were up in the playground before confirmation and we picked out confirmation names, and he picked Michael because he thought it was a strong name. Poor guy couldn't even pick a stupid confirmation name he liked. Everything had to be her way or she'd start that wailing for the old man business. Greiner would do anything to keep peace. He always did what everybody else wanted, never what Greiner wanted. At home it was the old lady, at school it was what the kids wanted, at church it was what Father John Albert wanted, it was never what Greiner wanted. His old lady reminded Greiner all the time that he promised her when he was a little boy he'd be a priest. Tell me, what the hell did a little kid know about being a priest and living that weird—as---shit life they live? I was his only friend and felt sorry for the way his mother treated him, and that's why I fought his battles, because he couldn't. He wasn't a fighter and would never even try to defend himself against the likes of bullies like us. He'd just let everybody beat the shit out of him, rip up his clothes, and steal his schoolwork and he would never say a word. I was the only one who knew all this about him and never told anyone except my mom. When this shit happened I'd have to take him home to my old lady to fix up his clothes before nut-case got home and found out. It was so weird how afraid he was for her to find out the kids beat him up and tore his clothes because he was so smart yet weird at the same time. The old bat hated me because I called him Greiner, and all I ever did was be like a big brother and best buddy. I took better care and was kinder to him than she ever was. I know I'm the only person who really loved him. He had no idea what being a priest meant. What a waste of his life, and his old lady had the nerve to say I'd be a worthless bum. Do you guys remember that? What's worthless is wasting a person like Greiner who had no say in what he'd be when he grew up. With his brains he could have been anything he wanted to be."

"Wow Frank, I had no idea all this was going on inside you all these years. Guess we never knew you as well as we thought we did."

"Frank, you're too serious tonight, maybe we ought to take you back home, cream-puff."

"Eh Charlie, don't you ever know when to shut up. Frank's spilling his guts and you don't want to listen, you just want to talk and be the same old smart-ass."

The two friends lit up a cigarette, talking, interrupting, and recalling the night they all went out in Ray's five-dollar car, hoping to evoke a word or thought that could offer up a clue as to what could have happened to Frank.

"Hell, I just saw what Frank's leaving did to us two, I'd never do something like that. The only thing I really don't understand is, Frank. I've been thinking about this, you don't suppose he did something stupid like join the Army and maybe thought we'd ride his ass for doing it?"

Ray thought a second or two, "Aw shit, Frank would never do anything that dumb, join up with the Army----nah, bad idea. Ten minutes talking to that lame-brain sister of Frank's and suddenly you end up talking just as nuts as that loopy loony woman.

"Suppose I'm right Ray an' he did do something like that."

"Frank in the Army taking orders doesn't make sense. He only gave orders, never took them from nobody."

"Ray, with that guy, unless they make him head sergeant, it'll never work. It just won't work. 'Nah', you're right, no Army marching for that rebel."

"For Frank's sake, if that's where he is, let's hope he's the head order-giver, be right up his alley. I will never forget when we were kids and voted him to be our gang leader then he turned around and made us all into his little stooges. Remember how we followed him like he was some general? To think about it now all he was, was a general pain in the ass. Bet there aren't many fellas' be any better than him conning guys. Frank's a survivor."

For Sophie, the visit from Frank's buddies had rekindled concerns about her brother and whether or not there was any truth in what John told her the night he got drunk with Frank. She tried to put the pieces together about her brother and a crazy-wild story John told her in his inebriated state, but nothing made sense that night. Sophie remembered waiting in the kitchen for John the next morning, questioning him about the subject he'd rambled on about the night before. He repeated it verbatim, and after John left for work she raced over to her mother's house to question Frank as to whether or not any of what John told her was true. By the time she got there, Frank was gone. She worried about her brother and what would happen to him if he had in fact killed two people and was running away. The whole thing made her cry. Then there was the call to her sisters and concern for what might have happened and what should be done with their mother's house sitting empty. None of this interested or concerned them in the least.

Sophie was the family's nosey-busy-body-worrier who annoyed the life out of her mother Eve her entire life. She was the only one who had a key to what was once her mother's house. She found a letter on the kitchen table with a list of instructions, the first of which was, the house would sit empty, period. Frank noted that the house was his, willed to him by his mother; under any and all circumstances no one was to touch the house or anything in it. No one. Taxes were paid two years in advance and future taxes would be solely his responsibility. Lastly, no one need get into his business or worry about his where-about.

***

1946

"Major Pazwalski, a phone call for you in my office."

"Thank you sir, who is it?"

"Got no idea, sounds like a young lady's voice."

"Don't know as I know any young ladies."

"Well, she knows you Major. Specifically asked for you by name, and yours is not a name a young lady would make up. You either know someone with a name like yours or you don't, and she knows and wants to speak with you."

Frank couldn't imagine who was on the other end of the phone.

"Hello, this is Major Pazwalski."

"Uncle Frank, it's you, it's really you! It's wonderful to hear your voice. This is Anna, your niece."

"How did you find me?"

"Aunt Stella got the idea to go down to the tax office to make sure the taxes were paid on Busha's house after everyone tried to find you and no one had word of where you were or if you were even alive. Her main concern was that if the tax bill didn't get paid Busha's house would go up for sale on the courthouse steps. Guess the tax people had your address because that's where Stella got it. Then mum heard how the Red Cross helps find people and she took a chance and called them with that address and now I found you!"

"Good old Stella still doesn't know how to mind her own business. How are you Anna, and how's your family?"

"They're doing fine. Mom took it real hard when dad died, but she's doing better now."

"When did he die?"

"June twenty-third. Had a heart attack and dropped dead at work."

"As you know, the two of us never got along very well, but I'm sorry to hear the old boy's dead."

"Thanks Uncle Frank. Why did you leave here like you did?"

"Too many reasons to talk about, Anna, and I really don't care to talk about this right now."

"I'm getting married October thirty-first. Can you come?"

"I'm not sure."

"Please tell me you'll come! You're my Godfather and you were always my favorite man in the world next to my daddy. Please come home and give me away on my wedding day. If daddy were here he could do it, but he isn't and there's no one else."

"I don't know if I can get away, Anna. I'm on a very important assignment right now and don't know if I can make that kind of a commitment."

"Uncle Frank, I've never asked you for anything ever, and this is the only thing I'll ever ask you to do for me."

"Let me look into it and see if the Army will give me the time to come home for a couple of days. I'll have to get back to you."

"Uncle Frank, it would mean the world to me if you gave me away on my wedding day. You'll love the guy I'm going to marry. He's just like you in lots of ways and I really love him."

"Anna, I can't make any promises right now, but I'll see what I can do and try to get back to you soon. When is the date again, did you say October twenty-first?"

"No, October thirty-first. Uncle Frank, you have to try to come home, besides it's been eight years since you were home, and we all miss you. Everyone in the family misses you. Even your house misses you. Please try Uncle Frank. Please."

"I will, Anna, I honestly will. I miss all of you, too. I'll call you before the weekend and let you know if it's possible for me to come."

"I'll be saying my prayers and rosaries every day that God will make it happen. I love you, Uncle Frank. Goodbye."

"Good-bye, Anna."

"Was I right, Major? Was that a young voice and was it a mistake or was it for you?"

"Yes sir, it was a young voice and it was for me alright."

"Who was it?"

"My niece and Godchild who's getting married the end of October, wants me to give her away. I told her not to count on my doing anything because my schedule wouldn't allow for time away right now."

"Major, I'll personally see to it that you get the time off to go. I think a break would be in order. No one can keep up the pace and schedule you've been keeping of late, not good for anyone. I say, take this break and get away. I can handle everything until you get back. Let's not disappoint the young lady. Call her back and let her know you'll be there for her big day."

"Thanks Colonel. I haven't been home in eight years, and maybe it's time."

Frank wasn't sure the decision to go home was a good one, but he knew that sooner or later he had to check his house, and face his reasons for running away. It was time.

"Hello, Anna, this is Uncle Frank, I'll be honored to give you away. I got time off to come home for your wedding."

"Uncle Frank, I can't believe God answered my prayers this fast. I didn't even have time to get out my rosaries. This is great news. Father Greiner is going to marry us and he's been asking me who would give the bride away. Now, I can tell him it's my Uncle Frank. Wait 'til I tell mom and all your sisters. They'll be so surprised to find out I was the one who got you back home. Please take good care of yourself and thanks, Uncle Frank, thanks. I really love you. Goodbye."

"I love you too, Anna."

Frank hung up the phone and just sat in the swivel chair thinking about the past eight years and where they'd gone.

It seemed impossible that the little girl he used to hold on his lap could be getting married, when it seemed not long ago she was one of the kids at the family gatherings grabbing her share of the special treats under the Christmas tree along with her siblings.

The big problem was always the same, where everyone would sit and how none of the kids was ever happy with where they had to sit—this one always wanting to sit next to Uncle Frank. Simple things, and now, that was all gone. Life moved on and that little girl, all grown up, would now take her mother's place and show up with her kids on Christmas Day, and those kids would fight over which chair they would sit on and give his sister Sophie an opportunity to experience the same raft of nonsense his mother got. Frank thought how sad it was that his mother wouldn't be around to see the bickering come back and play on his sister. He was sure his mother would be amused at the whole scene.

Chapter 28

From this Day Forward and Beyond

Frank was thirty-three when he left Pittsburgh, and now, eight years later, returning home for the first time, gave rise to wondering if he hadn't made a big mistake in accepting his niece's request to give her away. There was no way to separate home without remembering Rosie and their baby, her dad Hans, his mother Eve-Louise, and now John, all dead.

He wondered what other surprises awaited his return, like the condition of his house and what might have to be done after being locked up with no one living in it for eight years. One thing he knew for certain about it, the taxes were always paid on time. His emotions were twisted about having left it unoccupied, and he wondered whether or not somebody ought to live in it or maybe consider selling it. After all, he had no intentions of ever coming back to Pittsburgh.

It seemed selfish for it to sit empty all this time, and now that Anna was getting married, maybe he should offer to let her live in it until he decided what he wanted to do when he was through with the Army.

Thoughts drifted to times gone by, and Frank thought about Rosie as he had every day. It was generally in the quiet of evening that he missed her most, and now, going home, the entire hell would begin anew.

He regretted reacting out of frustration and anger the night he ran out of the Gradel house, rather than thinking through the consequences of his actions that fateful day. If he could be given the chance to replay this part of his life he would right his wrongs, but reality rarely traverses the course in life that fantasy entices with wishful thinking.

Frank doubted he could ever forgive himself for the incident that caused the death of his beloved Rosie and their baby. If only he hadn't raced out of the Gradel house like a mad man. Had he taken the time to think rationally, and taken Rosie with him, she'd be alive.

After the loss of Rosie, life held very little meaning. Day after day Frank went through the motions of living, but in actuality, he behaved as though he had an appointment with the grim reaper who was the only one who could grant him peace of mind and heart. The dream of once again being united with his beloved Rosie and their child was tempting, but it was not enough to lead him to commit suicide like his father.

He forced himself to think about something other than the negatives of going home. From time to time he toyed with the idea of a visit, but at the last minute, he always scrapped his plans.

Frank went back to his office and retrieved the classified documents from the safe that he'd been translating when Anna's phone call came in. He made some additions and corrections, returned them to the safe and called it a day.

He went back to his quarters and readied for bed. Before turning in for the night, he carefully took a piece of paper out of his wallet. It contained words he'd written and hesitated to give Rosie because he wasn't sure of its correctness.

He thought about how much he still loved her and all those times he teased her about their age difference and the possibility of his dying first. "If I die before you, I'll wait for you in eternity. Look for me at the end of the rainbow, third row second seat. I'll save the first seat for you."

One of those times she had teasingly said, "Why can't we sit together in the front row?"

His reply—"My mother's had the first two rows reserved so the sinners in our family could be right up front under God's watchful eye."

Frank visualized happier times and imagined that he could hear her laughter. Her predeceasing him was not in the plans. He read the letter this time, but most times he just said the words as if they were a prayer.

My dearest Rosie—You asked me to put on paper what I have in my heart. Let's see how bad I brutalize what I once learned in literature class:

I liken your inner beauty to dusk
Before darkness of night,
You calm and quiet my soul,
With gentleness
You captivate me.
Each passing day you earn trust
From me to willfully succumb, no longer fearing darkness
Or dreading tomorrows
Once filled with emptiness.
As moonlight gives brilliance to darkness,
The lost soul within
No longer fears the labyrinth of night,
For courage moves fear beyond boundaries,
And therein resides my inner strength in thee.

Chapter 29

Promises, Promises, Promises

October 30, 1946.

"Mom, have you heard from Uncle Frank? Last time I talked to him he said he'd come, but that was more than a month ago and I haven't heard a word from him since."

"Anna, he'll be here. When he tells ya' somethin', that guy don't never go back on his word. Trust me, he's been like that since he was a kid, and like they say, 'tigers don't change them stripes.' Hey, my little brother don't show, I'll give ya' away."

"Mom, stop talking crazy, Mom's don't give daughters away. Maybe I ought to ask Uncle Paul just in case."

"Anna you're gettin' on my nerves real bad. Sure'll be nice to get this all over with."

"But what if he's hurt I didn't ask him in the beginning and won't like being second best."

"Anna, it's the day before the weddin' and I know yer' nervous, but yer' drivin' me nuts. Go do somethin', go some place, get outa' the damn house. I can't take this nervous naggin-'en- talkin' all the damn time. Did you finish cleaning up the kitchen over to Uncle Frank's house like I asked you? You can bet he'll wanna' stay there no matter how filthy it is or did you get it cleaned up?"

"I still have to sweep the floor and wash and dust a couple of little things."

"Did ya' take them clean blankets out from our house and take 'em down there? An' don't forget to put sheets on the bed."

"I already did all those things and now you're getting on my nerves treating me like a kid. I'm going over to Uncle Frank's and don't know when I'll be back."

"Sure ya' don't want no help?"

"No, I want to be alone. I'm, too, nervous and don't want us to fight, and that will happen if we go to grandma's house together. I'll be back when I'm done."

Anna walked slowly to her grandmother's old house, recalling all those after school and after church visits when the two of them shared secrets and had tea before grandmother took her to the attic to go through her favorite boxes of buttons to pick out ones she wanted on her next new dress. She adored her grandmother who was now gone, like all those pretty little dresses with all the fancy buttons.

Anna opened the side gate to the alley entrance of what was once her grandmother's house. When she put the key in the door, she found it unlocked and assumed that it was carelessness on her part for having so much on her mind these past weeks, and promised herself to be more careful in the future.

As she entered the side door to the kitchen, a surprise awaited her. It was Frank. Her eyes filled with tears and she raced over to where he was standing and gave him a hug.

"When did you get here?"

"Late last night, came in on the ten-thirty train."

"I thought maybe you'd forgotten, or would ignore all of us again and decide not to come home. Wait 'til Mom hears you're here! Boy, am I going to be in trouble, I was supposed to have your house all cleaned up before you got here."

"The house is fine Anna and looks better than I thought it would."

"When did you say you got here Uncle Frank?"

"Last night."

"Oh that's right, I'm so excited I'm not thinking straight. Why didn't you come up to the house?"

"I was tired and needed to rest after that long train ride, and more than anything, I needed to be alone. Eight years is a long time to be away from anything."

"Eight years too long, Uncle Frank. When Mom hears you're here, she'll be so happy. She's really missed you, Uncle Frank, more than anyone else in the family. She says rosaries for you all the time. You have to go up and see her right now."

"Anna, I know you're excited, as well you should be. Tomorrow's your big day, but please, please don't tell anyone I'm here, not just yet. I'm not ready to try and explain to everyone where I've been all these years. Tomorrow will be soon enough to answer questions. Kindly give me this day to sit here in this house and just be. I need that."

"I'll do anything you want Uncle Frank. I'm so happy you're here I'll do anything you ask. You've made this the happiest, best day ever."

"I'm glad I've made someone this happy, and I'm glad it's you. Of all the members in our family, you always were my favorite, and don't worry about doing anything else. For as much time as I'll be spending here, the house and everything in it looks great."

"Aw thanks Uncle Frank, I tried real hard because I wanted Busha to be proud of how nice I fixed up her house for you."

"Anna, do me a favor."

"Sure Uncle Frank, whatever you want."

"How about I give you a shopping list and some money and you pick up a few things I need, like cold cuts, coffee cakes, coffee, milk, bread of course, and, um, some beer and anything else you think I could use these next couple of days I'm here."

"I'd be happy to do that for you."

"Your doing this eliminates the possibility of my running into people I know, explaining where I've been and what I've been doing, and I don't want to see people today."

"I understand. Don't worry, I won't tell a soul you're here."

"Thanks Anna."

"Father Greiner will be so happy you're here. He just asked me at church on Sunday if I had heard from you yet, and if you were still going to be able to come. I told him I hadn't heard a thing. He looked disappointed, too."

"Ten dollars sound like enough money to get all that?"

"Obviously you don't shop much! This is plenty Uncle Frank. Besides, we'll have lots of food at the reception hall with plenty left over I'm sure, and we can bring some of it over here for you to snack on. How long are you staying?"

"Three days, then I'll be heading back on the train. There's one thing I need to talk to you about. Where are you and your husband planning to live? By the way, what's his name?"

"John, we went to St. Michael's together."

"What's his last name? Maybe I know his family."

"You wouldn't know them. They used to live down near 22nd Street. His last name is Meinhardt. They moved up here on the hill after you left."

"Does he have a good job so he can take good care of you?"

"Right now he works in the mill and hates it, but he's saving his money to go to college to study engineering and almost has enough saved up. He's really smart and I know he'll be a great engineer. I plan to work until he gets his degree, and after that, we'll see where life takes us. "We were going to live with mom until we saved enough money to rent or buy a house somewhere in this neighborhood. We like it here real well."

"I have an idea. How would you and John like to live in this house for free until I decide what I want to do? I don't like leaving it sit empty like I've done all these years, and besides, it needs cleaning and fixing up. I'll pay for the paint and any other supplies you need and even pay the taxes. In a situation like this, we both win. You live here and save your money, and my house is taken care of. How's that sound?"

"Uncle Frank, it's a dream! Are you sure, or are you teasing me like you did when I was a kid?

"No Anna, I'm not teasing, I would never tease about something like this."

I can't believe you're going to let me live in Busha's house. I never expected anything like this to ever happen—I never did. Is this a dream, or are you really here and making me this offer?"

"It's not a dream. You're a great kid and you never took anything for granted or expected life owed you anything. You were different from anyone else in the family and that's what I liked about you. The house is yours until I come back. The only problem is I don't know when that will be."

"I don't care when that is Uncle Frank. I'd give up this house next week, tomorrow, anytime, if it meant you'd come home for good and I could see you whenever I wanted."

"You're a special kid whose values and judgment are so well entrenched Anna. You make me proud to be your uncle. This John better take good care of you or he'll have me to answer to. Be sure and tell him that for me."

"Uncle Frank, I'm going to go to the store before mom comes looking for me and discovers you. This list won't take me long. Then if it is okay with you, can I tell John about the offer you made for us to live here? He won't breathe a word to anyone."

"Sure Anna, but please don't let anyone else know I'm here. I'll see them all tomorrow, and that's soon enough."

"Uncle Frank, I'm so happy. You'll never know how happy you've made me today."

"Oh yes I do, I can see it in your eyes and hear it in your voice. I'm glad I could do this for both of us."

Anna picked up the items Frank requested, delivered them to his house, and left quietly once she saw he was asleep on the sun-porch. When she arrived home her mother was busy ironing, and she announced she was going over to her fiancée's house.

"Anna, don't dare go see John unless you want bad luck, and that's what'll happen if ya' see the groom the day before the weddin'."

"No, it's bad luck to see him on the day of the wedding before you take your vows."

"Damn it, I'm tellin' you and you're not listenin', Anna. I'm telling you, you can't go'en see'm today. You want bad luck? What if luck turns bad right after you go see'm today and yer Uncle Frank don't show up. That what the hell you want?"

"No Mom I don't want Uncle Frank not to show up. I don't want bad luck today, tomorrow, or any other day. Mostly I don't want us to fight my last day in your home."

"Did you finish cleanin' Busha's house and do a good job?"

"It's perfect."

"I seen how you measure perfect. You're like your grandma and tend t'be messy like her. Maybe I oughta' go down t'inspect what you did."

"Mom, you don't need to go inspect anything. I'm telling you it's perfect, and that should be good enough. I'm not a little girl anymore. I'm a grown woman and I'm getting married tomorrow. Please don't insult me and check up on the kind of job I did. Are you planning to come inspect my house after I'm married too?"

"What in the world's gotten into you? I sure don't like'a snappy-fresh-mouthed kid and this isn't like you. Suppose your attitude's bad 'cause you haven't heard from Frank? If he doesn't come by the end o' the day, you'd better be thinking how you're going t'ask Uncle Paul to give you away and you'd better have some damn good reason why you waited to the last minute."

"Mom, I'm holding out for Uncle Frank. My money's on him. He'll be here by tomorrow to show up for the wedding. If he doesn't make it, I'll grab the first man I see and ask him to walk me down the aisle and give me away. I'm sure there will be someone at the church besides Uncle Paul who can give me away. Besides, he's usually had a few whiskeys and he won't know or care that I asked him to give me away at the last minute."

"You sure got a fast smart mouth today. One thing for sure, that John'll never win a fight with the likes 'a yer fast mouth. I feel sorry for 'im, has no idea what he's in for."

The day was October 31, 1946, the day Frank's niece was to be married, and the reason he'd come home for the first time in eight years. The return was a dreadful mistake, and he wished he'd never agreed to coming.

The family was waiting for Frank who failed to join them. Instead, he remained in seclusion at his mother's house.

"Told you your Uncle Frank wouldn't show up. I'll never understand 'im if I live t'be a' hundred."

"Mom, I'm going over to Busha's house to see if he's there. Maybe he came in late and didn't want to bother us."

"Go ahead, get disappointed early s'ya' can find a substitute to stand in for that good for nothin' uncle. Hope you 'kin find someone this late t'give ya' away. I told ya' not to wait 'til the last minute, but ya' had all the answers. If ya' don't care, why the hell should I?"

"I'll be back as soon as I see if he is there."

"I don't want t'be here when ya'come home cryin' about that shiftless no-show, then I'm goin' over t'the church basement an see if them women need help with the food for the reception. I want this t'be perfect so them German's on his side don't say we don't know how t'give a good party. After that, I'm gettin' this hair fixed."

Anna raced over to her grandmother's house to see what had happened to Frank and whether he changed his mind. She let herself in with her own key and looked for Frank.

"Uncle Frank, are you up? Are you in here? Where are you hiding?"

"Yes, Anna, I'm up and I'm here and I'm not hiding from you. But if you were your mother I wouldn't have been here. I will see her at the church and that'll be soon enough. I just don't want to be interrogated before the wedding. I anticipate the badgering I'll get at the reception will be an emotional train wreck. Sorry Anna, you'll have to excuse me, I need to be alone."

"I know Uncle Frank, there's sadness in your eyes. Maybe I shouldn't have asked you to come back after all this time away."

"By the way, I plan to wear my uniform to give you away—is that OK with you or would you rather I wore something else?"

"Uncle Frank, I'd love you to wear your uniform. I'm so proud of your being in the army and it doesn't matter what you wear; besides, I love men in uniforms. Wait 'til mom sees you walking down the aisle with me on your arm, bet her chin will drop clear to the floor."

"One thing your mom always did was annoy the hell out of me the way she got into everybody's business, and sounds like with your dad gone she'll get worse."

"She's been hassling me for the last three days about who I am going to have give me away because she's sure you'll be a 'no show.' All I've heard for these last eight years is what a loser you are and how you got everything of grandma's and then left her house and all she worked for to sit there and rot."

"Well, we're going to show her a real reliable Uncle Frank who made a promise to his favorite niece and kept it, right Anna?"

"You betcha' Uncle Frank. I'm so glad I never told her how I found you and that you're the one giving me away. The idea of surprising the family when they see us strolling down the aisle together makes me think we'd better hope no one has a weak heart because this surprise will be a real shocker, especially to mom, and I'm not sure I'm ready to be an orphan."

"Your mother's too mean to have a heart attack. Remember, I knew her my whole life, and as a kid she tried to run my life. Drove her nuts because I'd tell her she wasn't my mother and didn't have to listen to her. Always told your grandma I'd turn out to be good for nothing and right about now she's thinking I'm still the uncontrollable brat, not worth a damn, a real loser, and off somewhere in the world lying in a ditch drunk and passed out."

"Uncle Frank, I don't think she thinks you're a loser, she's disappointed like the rest of the family because none of us ever hears from you anymore, sort of like you abandoned us. All that matters is you're here, today's my wedding day, and everybody's going to have a swell time."

"What time should I be at the back of the church to walk you down the aisle?"

"The ceremony start's at five o'clock, so be there five minutes early. Everyone will be seated and they won't see you until you and I walk down the aisle. See you in the back of the church."

"Where's the reception?"

"It's downstairs, in the basement of the church, Uncle Frank. First we'll have dinner then afterwards a polka band's going to show up so we can have music and dancing, and there will be lots to drink, and a cake to cut, and the bride's dance. Oh God, I can hardly wait."

Frank's face turned ashen and Anna couldn't imagine what was wrong. When she saw perspiration rolling off his forehead she feared something horrible was happening and ushered him to a chair and hurriedly unbuttoned the top button on his shirt.

Anna thought Frank was having a heart attack and panicked when she saw him gasping for air and having difficulty breathing.

Lightheadedness forced him to put his head between his knees to avoid passing out.

The memories of an evening spent in these same surroundings, with the love of his life, threw him back to a time and place he never wanted to see or think about. Tension mounted, and the grieving process began anew as though the experience had been yesterday.

After all these years, after all the pain of losing Rosie, nothing could have prepared him for a wedding reception in a place he worked so long and hard to erase. The mental stamina required for him to endure walking down those stairs to the wedding reception was incomprehensible.

Suddenly the rendezvous with Rosie in the church basement the night he married her in his heart were all there, in full color, with all the emotions, sounds, and smells. Today he was expected to witness the marriage and celebration of his niece, and he wanted no part of it.

This marriage today should have been his and Rosie's, and he begrudged the fact it wasn't. By agreeing to give Anna away, he'd placed himself in a quandary and couldn't think of a viable solution except to leave town.

Frank wondered whether accepting Anna's request had everything to do with wanting to get caught by the police and finally put an end to running from the law for the murder of Rosie and her dad. If he left town, no one would ever know he'd been there but Anna, but he fretted over how she'd handle his breaking a promise on the most important day of her life.

Frank knew himself, and the only way to keep his promise to Anna was to have a couple of stiff drinks to calm his unsteady nerves. He chose a small tavern on the corner of Main Street where no one would recognize him and interrogate him on where he'd been all this time.

The place was dark and dimly lit. Frank quietly took a seat at the far end of the bar, hoping no one would notice him or go out of their way to engage in conversation with a man who obviously wanted to be left alone.

He ordered two shots and a beer chaser, guzzled them down without a moment's hesitation, and then ordered a second round.

The effects of the alcohol began to soothe his jittery nerves. A general feeling of malaise preceded intoxication of mind and spirit, and Frank prescribed another dose of self-medication—he was ailing.

When he requested more, the barkeeper refused, and this made him angry. By now Frank had been there quite some time, and with nothing in his stomach but alcohol he immediately felt the effects and lost all sense of time. He got up to go to the toilet and could barely get up off the stool or stand without wobbling.

The barkeeper couldn't help notice how inebriated the officer in uniform had become and decided to not serve him anymore liquor; instead, tried to engage him in conversation about the war. Frank refused to participate in anything other than being served and being nasty. When the barkeeper saw Frank struggling to maintain balance, he decided, nasty or not, he needed to call a cab and get him out of his bar.

"Soldier, can I help you get to wherever it is you got to go?"

Frank's foul mood and sarcasm were uncalled for. "Mind your own business. All I need from you is the time."

"Sir it's quarter to four."

Frank knew he had to be at the church by five of five, but could barely make it to the door. When he finally reached it, he fumbled with the doorknob and eventually managed to get outside where he hailed a cab and asked to be taken home. He managed to remain unnoticed even as he exited the cab and swerved up and down the sidewalk to his house.

The kitchen clock stopped running years ago and when he glanced at it, it read one o'clock. Being drunk, Frank lost all sense of time and didn't think to check his watch, figuring he had hours before he needed to show up at the church. Because this was his first return home in eight years, he wandered aimlessly about the house, bouncing from wall to wall and eventually ending up in the living room he despised and hadn't entered since his father's wake. The haunting memory of that day was one he could never shake, but now that he was totally inebriated he felt brave and sat on the sofa. It didn't take long before he tilted over and passed out.

At ten o'clock Frank awakened and sat straight up in the darkness completely disoriented, unable to figure out how he got into this room and why it was so dark.

He nervously fumbled for the light switch and turned it on. When he looked at his watch it was after ten. He had missed the ceremony.

By now the family conversation centered on him, and every negative thing they could think or say about him he'd already said to himself. He was a rotten loser, a spoiled brat, a bum, a louse, and a lying promise-breaker who managed to ruin the most memorable day of Anna's life. At this point, nothing he or anyone could say or do would change a thing. He was what he was—no good.

The effects of the alcohol hadn't nearly begun to wear off, because when he tried to stand his legs were unsteady. To make matters worse, his head spun around with dizzying force.

Frank barely managed to make it to the kitchen sink before splattering vomit all over it and himself. Time after time he doused his face with cold water, thinking it would help him feel better, but nothing seemed to work. He made a pot of black coffee and drank most of it before gathering up enough courage to face his family, apologize to Anna, and take whatever they dished out. Then, he would give Anna the keys to his house and leave town. In that order.

He weaved his way across the street and towards the church, debating whether or not he should turn around and head right for the train station, and that's when he ran smack into Greiner, who had just left the reception.

"Frank, it's you? It's you! Oh my God in Heaven, it is you! I am so happy to see you. What happened?"

With this said, he wrapped his arms around his dear friend to give him a big old bear hug, and that's when the smell of a combination of whiskey and residual vomit blasted him in the face. Frank was in no condition to be seeing anyone, not now.

"Yeah, Greiner, it's me, but I wish I was somebody else and somewhere else. Seems the only thing I've mastered in life is making one mistake after the other. Sure would be nice to know what the hell your God has in mind, keeping a lousy son of a bitch like me alive. For what, I ask you? I told Anna I would be here for her today and I got so drunk I passed out and missed the wedding. All I ever do is disappoint people who trust me. I'm a carbon copy of my dad. He was a loser, and so am I."

"Frank you're not a loser, you're just really drunk and this is whiskey talking."

"If I'm not a loser, then I'm one sorry son of a bitch with a head full of pretty ugly pictures of myself."

"Frank, don't you think everyone has pictures in their heads that aren't pretty? You're a smart man, figure it out."

"Greiner, there you go, just like when we were kids, thinking you could fix everyone by talking. Always thinking, always talking, always scheming, out-smarting your opponent with that brain. Good old Greiner, you never changed. Always trying to make everyone feel good about themselves, but never thought about how Greiner felt or what Greiner really wanted."

"Frank, that's not so."

"Greiner, you're full of crap because you admitted the truth to me the night my mother died. Or did you forget?"

"That's not true."

"Isn't it Greiner? Well, I know you better than you know yourself, you poor son of a bitch. I know for fact you never had a chance to be what you wanted to be. Shit, you didn't even get to pick your own confirmation name. Your old lady picked it. You are what someone else wanted George Herbert to be. Between that fake uncle of yours, the almighty monsignor who fathered you, who was always farting under his black robes smelling like he shit himself, and your old lady chasing all your friends out of your life with her broom, you had no choice but to do what they wanted. Greiner, you would have been one hell of a dad to a bunch of kids. And what a great husband you would have been!"

"I am a father, a father to every kid in this parish, and a good one at that."

"Greiner, there's no sense talking to you, you just don't want to get what I'm trying to say. You don't want to hear me and what I'm saying."

Frank began to cry and put his arms around his old friend.

"Greiner, I can't even count on one hand the people in my life I truly love or ever loved. You are one of them. First, I loved my dad and he robbed me of ever getting to know him when he killed himself. Then I allowed myself to love my mother and she robbed me. You know how she robbed me? She robbed me by not demanding respect, respect she rightfully deserved. And lastly, there was Rosie. Oh, how I loved and adored her."

No sooner had those words fallen from his lips and he realized what he'd admitted to Greiner. The two shared many things, but never his relationship with Rosie.

"I know you did Frank."

"How the hell do you know about me and Rosie?"

"In your present condition, I think it's best we discuss Rosie another time."

"Greiner, no! Now that I've opened my mouth, I need to talk about this and get it off my chest. How about you doing your priestly job and listen to my confessions."

Greiner looked at his friend, who seemed to be carrying the weight of the world on his shoulders, and wanted to help him, but the middle of the street was not the place and Frank seemed unwilling to move.

"No one will ever appreciate the depth of my love, not even you. I wish I'd died with her, and that way, we could have gone beyond the rainbow together. Now she and our baby are there and all alone."

Frank reeked of booze, and the booze played havoc with twisted, unfounded, and convoluted ideas that made no sense.

"Greiner, how the hell can I get to the other side of the rainbow to be with her?"

"Frank, you're talking crazy. Listen to me—Rosie is not dead! She's just very sick and in a special hospital."

"What the hell are you talking about, Greiner? What the hell is a special hospital? Next, you'll be telling me it's a little place in heaven with angels and all that bullshit. She's dead damn it. I know because I was there."

"I'm trying to tell you, she is not dead.'

"But I saw a car hit her just as I began to run up the alley."

"Frank, listen to me."

"No, you listen to me. I'm doing the talking, because I was there and you weren't and I saw and heard what happened."

"Fair enough, I'll listen."

"The night I asked old man Gradel for Rosie's hand in marriage, he tried to strangle me. I asked him to stop, but he refused, and that's when I took both his hands and firmly pushed them away, hoping he'd give up. But something happened and he lost his balance. Next thing I knew he was on the floor, the old lady was screaming I killed him, I killed her Hans. All I could think was run far and run fast or get blamed for something I didn't do. Poor Rosie kept screaming for me to wait for her, but like a coward, I ran off and left her there. Best I could figure, she must have come after me. I don't know, but I didn't hear her. I dashed down the first alley I could find. I heard car brakes screech then this loud horrible moan. I can't get it out of my mind. I hear it all the time. It must have been Rosie's last breath before she died. To this day, I still can't delete those sounds from my memory. Honest to God Greiner, I wanted to turn around, cross the street, and pick her up, but I couldn't bare the pain or thought of touching her dead flesh. I was a coward.

"I associated touching her dead body to the time I touched my father lying in his casket in the living room. So help me God, I tried to go to her but was paralyzed by the cold chill of a thermometer being jammed into my heart by the grim reaper to destroy what little heart I had left. My greatest regret was not going back to pick up my Rosie to say good-bye to her and our baby. I should have been the one to die and not Rosie and our baby. Tell me you understand why I didn't go back. Greiner, please tell me it was ok, that your God will forgive me. I didn't mean to kill any of them. You know me—I'm a lot of things, but not a killer. I'm exhausted and need to be with Rosie so I can tell her how sorry I am for what I did to her and our baby. Maybe then I'll have peace and the running will end."

The more Frank talked the more Greiner realized how ill informed he was about what had really happened to Rosie and what had transpired in the years he's been gone.

"Frank, let's go in the rectory. I don't like talking out here on the street. Will you please come inside with me? I miss you my dearest old friend, and I have so much I need to tell you. Please come inside."

Father Greiner took Frank by the arm and supported him as the two of them walked to the rectory. Greiner entered first, put on a light, and the two of them went into the library where they could sit and talk privately. He invited Frank to sit in his favorite chair so he could fully relax and get comfortable, because he certainly looked like he could use it.

"Could I offer you a cup of coffee before we begin?"

"Thanks, Greiner, sounds good, but what I really need is a stiff drink. Got any booze in this place besides Communion wine?"

"Yes, I have a bottle of unopened whiskey upstairs in my closet one of the parishioners gave me years ago."

"Go get it Greiner, I need a stiff one."

Greiner knew this was not the time for more drinking. His mother was a drunk, and he recognized the familiar patterns of behavior seeping into every word out of Frank's mouth choosing to ignore his request.

"Frank, I need you to tell me what happened that night, and then, I need to tell you what I know. It is important we talk, but for now, I think it best you stop drinking. Please Frank, please don't drink any more tonight."

"Greiner, if it was anyone else but you, who never gets to have his way about anything I'd tell you to go to hell. But for you old buddy, I'll not drink another drop. But when this conversation is over, we're opening that bottle you got stashed away."

"As soon as we're done, it's all yours."

Greiner began telling Frank the hard cold facts of what, where, and why Rosie is where she is. He spoke slowly, knowing that the news would be shocking and not at all what Frank would expect. Rosie is not dead, but gravely ill.

In his wildest of dreams, Frank could only wish for news like this. *Rosie alive*'—two words spinning round and round in his head like a record out of control on an old Victrola. He tried to make sense of Greiner's farfetched, surreal words. His heart raced, his hands trembled, and tears of mixed emotions ran down his cheeks.

Greiner proceeded to tell Frank that Rosie hasn't spoken since the day he left and that his return is possibly the one and only way to save her. He confronted Frank on his reason for coming to Pittsburgh in the first place, a wedding. He emphasized to Frank the fact that he never attended it, but did run into him on the street, and this encounter led to plans for visiting Rosie. Frank remained skeptical and queried Greiner whether he was taking him to a cemetery to see her grave and this was his way of going about it. Greiner, running short on patience, explained to Frank how messed up his head is from drinking and, for the last and final time, told him they were not going to any cemetery. Exasperated with all this back and forth over whether or not Rosie was or wasn't alive had pushed Greiner to the point where he wanted to pick Frank up by the scruff of the neck and shake the living daylight out of him. In any given situation, good or bad, Greiner always maintained a calm gentle spirit, but frustration with his old pal was emotionally taxing. Frank never expected the news thrust upon him like a slap in the face and was equally upset. As badly as he wanted to see the only woman he ever loved, he had apprehensions, and he labored to explain to Greiner why.

"I promised her over and over I'd never ever leave her. Then when I got her pregnant, I wanted to make everything right and begged her to run off and marry me, but she panicked and wouldn't listen. I assured her I could provide a good life for her and the baby, but she insisted we go to those two impossible unforgiving people to get their blessings. Instead of blessings we got dealt the worst cards in the deck, losing hands, and you wonder why I never believed in that God of yours. Well this kind of shit happening is just one more reason why I don't believe in your God or pray to Him for anything."

"Frank, we're not discussing God and what He did or didn't do."

"Well, I am. I take back some of what I said about your God. I started to believe in Him after I fell in love with Rosie because I was so grateful He gave her to me. And then, just like that He took her away like He took everything else away. Greiner, why the hell did He leave me you? Guess because you're the only person left in my life who can save my ass from the devil who's been running me ragged. I need you Greiner, please don't give up on me, not now. You're all I have left."

Frank sobbed uncontrollably. The emotional trauma from the day's events had taken their toll, the alcohol had dulled his mind, his tongue had lost its way, and his heartstrings had nothing to wrap around.

In those quiet times before sleep comes, Greiner would often lie still and recall childhood bullies, wondering what purpose the Lord had in mind when He created them, and never took for granted the day He sent "Frank the tough guy" into his life. This time, a different band of bullies had come and gone, leaving "Frank the tough guy" strewn about life's floor, and this time He sent in "Greiner the weakling" to teach him he was no different from Frank. Frank was just a better bluffer.

"Sitting here looking at you, I see our unique differences as not so much in our hearts and minds but in the immeasurable thickness of our skin. In your case Frank, I hope age has made yours the thickness of leather, because you're going to need it."

The two old friends sat pensively for the longest time. Before long Frank dozed off in a sitting position, his head fell forward, gave a jerk, and his neck gave way to the weight of his head. Suddenly his head popped up as though someone had smacked him. He rubbed his eyes, looked seemingly confused for a few seconds before realizing where he was. He stared at Greiner and stated he wanted to go see Rosie right then and there. Habituated to his position in the army with assignments all over the world, accustomed to entering places any time of day or night without advance anything, he assumed this request not unreasonable. Yet this was not the army, and Woodside didn't operate on his watch. Greiner explained hospital protocol to him.

"We can't show up without checking first to see if she's allowed visitors, and if so, when. The upside to all of this is that, because I am who I am, we'll have a much easier time seeing her without much advance notice or a lot of hassle. I can wander in and out of most places most of the time without question, one of the good parts of being a priest. Nonetheless, I'll call first thing in the morning and then come over to your house and give you the details. How's that?"

"Sounds like a loose-lip dream. I want to believe with all my heart this is all true, but I'm so afraid I'll awaken in the morning and learn its nothing—nothing more than bullshit and booze."

"I understand where you're coming from, and believe me, if I were in your shoes, I'd be apprehensive, too. But put all that doubt aside and give me a chance to prove you wrong."

Frank listened but still had difficulty dismissing the pictures and sounds locked in his memory of the night he believed Rosie died.

"It's really late and I need to go home and try to make sense out of this day and everything that's transpired."

Greiner knew Frank well and knew he hadn't forgotten about the booze upstairs in his closet he'd mentioned earlier, but he didn't want Frank to drink another drop and never offered it to him. They had a big day ahead, and Greiner didn't want it ruined.

"Come on, I'll walk you home."

"Trust me, I can find my way. It's just up the block, and don't worry—I won't get lost."

"I know you won't get lost. I'm just afraid you'll start drinking again or worse—go to the church basement and make a complete fool of yourself. The wedding is over and no one missed you except Anna, and she'll get over your absence."

"Greiner, I have no intention of going to the church tonight."

"Step number one in the right direction. Next one is for you to get a good night's rest."

"I will. But when I get up, first thing I want to do is be on the first train out of here. I have this nonsensical wishful notion that seeing Rosie might possibly be the beginning of starting our lives over, but my gut tells me it'll never happen. I believe when the opportunity first came with me and Rosie and I had that chance to close my fist and grab hold of our situation, I failed to close my fist and grab it. But instead, like the romantic I'd become because of how deeply I loved her, like nothing or anyone I've ever loved or ever will, I stupidly let Rosie convince me to do the romantic bit of asking her folks for her hand in marriage. I will never forgive myself and know I no longer belong here.

"Rosie needs you, and I need you. You can't go anywhere."

"Yeah, I understand you, Greiner. You want me to go with you to see Rosie, but I don't know which Rosie you mean—some Rosie or a Rosie. I'll be at my house until five o'clock tomorrow night. Our government is sending me on an important assignment overseas and I have to be back at camp by Wednesday. Right now I just want to sleep."

Greiner retrieved Frank's jacket and they stood at the front door. As Frank was about to exit, Greiner stalled him.

"Frank, I have an idea. Why not stay here instead of going back to your house, that way you won't risk running into anyone in your family. I'll go to your house in the morning, get your clothes and suitcase, and that way we'll get to spend some extra time together. Heaven only knows when I'll ever see you again. Please stay here in the rectory. We've got lots of room, and it would please me to have you stay."

"Greiner, I know what you're doing. You want to stand guard over me so I can't go anywhere or do anything but sleep and rest. Good old 'scaredy cat' Greiner, afraid someone will get hurt or in trouble. Don't take a chance. Make the sure bet or don't make it. There is no such thing as a sure bet, Greiner. I can still get drunk even if I stay here. I'll drink all the damn communion wine and then what will those poor good little Catholics do on Sunday morning when you serve them watered down wine, not be forgiven for their sins? Greiner, I'm not even safe here."

"I'll take my chances, Frank. You take my room and I'll sleep in one of the guest rooms. And by the way, I'm taking that bottle of booze to bed with me, that way I'll know you'll be protected from yourself."

Frank was too tired to argue and agreed to stay the night. Greiner familiarized Frank with the bathroom's location, took him to his room, and then went on down the hall to one of the guest rooms where he planned to sleep.

Fearful that Frank may decide to leave during the night and rob Rosie of the only remaining chance she had of getting well, he prayed Frank would pass out and not awaken until morning.

His prayer went unanswered when he heard a loud noise at three thirty in the morning, sounding like someone had fallen. He scrambled out of bed and raced down the hall in the direction of the noise and found Frank in pool of vomit.

Frank had awakened from a sound sleep with excruciating abdominal pain, intense cramping, and nausea. All he could think of was making it to the toilet, but being disorientated and in unfamiliar surroundings made that feat impossible. Frank apologized profusely and offered to clean up the mess, but before he said another word Greiner went to the basement, retrieved a pail, filled it with soapy hot water, grabbed plenty of rags from the housekeeper's collection, and cleaned Frank's mess.

Greiner finished up, put everything away, and by the time he returned Frank was propped up against the bathroom wall in a sitting position, sound asleep. Greiner nudged him, helped him up, then took him back to his room and put a towel on his pillow in case he felt like throwing up again. Greiner loved Frank, but not enough to go through the exercise of cleaning up vomit a second time. Once was enough.

The two slept soundly until morning. Greiner awakened first and immediately began making arrangements for them to go to the hospital. Fortunately he had a light schedule planned with mostly paperwork and a school pageant, which he could get another priest to attend in his stead.

Train service to the hospital grounds ran daily; however, their schedule was not compatible with the limited time Frank had remaining before he had to catch his train back to camp. After several phone calls Father Greiner found a parishioner with an automobile who was more than willing to take him to the hospital. He masterfully juggled his schedule to accommodate everyone involved, phoned the hospital to explain his relationship to Rosie Gradel, requesting visitation rights that morning, and was told to come ahead. He called the parishioner back and asked to be picked up at eight o'clock.

Greiner went into Frank's room and found him sitting on the edge of his bed complaining of a pounding headache and not feeling like he was up to going anywhere.

Greiner rarely lost patience, but Frank had pushed him beyond his breaking point. He placed both his hands on Frank's shoulders and shook him as hard as he could, looked him right in the eyes, and began yelling with a full unwavering voice.

"Frank, I've had about as much of your nonsense as I am willing to take. Listen to me and hear what I have to say because I'm only going to say this once. We, you and I, are going to the hospital. A car and driver will be here to pick us up in thirty minutes, which is plenty of time for you to get off that bed, clean up, and be downstairs dressed and ready to go. There's a razor in the bathroom. Shave, comb your hair, and try to look and act decent. Rosie knows I am coming and she will be waiting for me. What she doesn't know is that you are coming. And Frank, you will be coming with me if I have to find one of your infamous broom handles and beat you over the head with it until I knock you out. I don't want to hear another word out of you until we are in that car heading for the hospital. I'll be downstairs in my office waiting. Get ready as quickly as you can."

Frank walked into Greiner's office just as their ride arrived. The two friends climbed in the back seat of the 1940 Packard and headed south to Woodside State Hospital. For the first fifteen minutes or so of the trip, neither one spoke a word, each thinking the other caused the misunderstanding. The first leg of the trip was dominated by silence until Greiner couldn't stand it any longer and offered his apology.

"I'm sorry for the way I spoke to you this morning, but I knew it was imperative to get your attention with our limited time schedule and all we have to squeeze into it."

"None of this is your fault. I'm the one who should be apologizing for being such a stupid jerk when all you've done is try to help me. Tell me about Rosie."

"Sadly, I lost touch with the family, and they with me. As a result, I don't have much to tell. This thing with Rosie and her family is too complex and painful for me to get into right now. Between the parishioners, the hectic church school schedule, and my demanding mother, I don't have the time to go see anyone."

"Greiner, because Rosie isn't dead and wasn't killed, whatever happened to our baby?"

"First off, you were nowhere to be found when this baby was born. The stigma, disgrace, and shock her family suffered was real to them. They were proud Germans who never thought they'd face this kind of disappointment, having a daughter pregnant out of wedlock. This didn't happen to families like theirs—it happened to low-class families, not educated affluent ones like theirs. Elsa had no idea what to do with Rosie or where to send her to bury this secret, so she called me. I connected with the right people and made arrangements for her to get into Hawthorne House, where their dirty little secret was safe. Rosie stayed there, and after the baby was born she gave it up for adoption. If you hadn't run off like you did, things would have been altogether different. You were the only man she ever knew or loved, and I believe whole-heartedly that disappointment is what broke her heart. She couldn't handle losing you, then the baby, and in the end she allowed her mind to go and do whatever it took to bury her pain."

Frank had seen his share of young men in the army suffer mental breakdowns and questioned Greiner whether this is what has happened to Rosie, but Greiner claimed otherwise, choosing to believe Frank was the medicine she needed. Frank remained doubtful.

Greiner thought about the blood on his hands, beginning with the day he had introduced Frank to the Gradels. As her priest and father confessor, he was privy to every aspect of Rosie's involvement with Frank from the outset and was in the perfect position to have altered the course of events by putting an end to her relationship with an older man, but he had done nothing.

He thought about his cowardice the day he'd dumped Rosie off at Hawthorne House and the missed opportunity to direct the cabbie to keep driving straight out of town and not stop until he crossed the state line. Once there, he could have married Rosie and made things right. But, because he feared the consequences of acting on impulse—following his heart—he delivered her on a silver platter to the vultures of life whose sole expertise lie in picking at vulnerability until nothing was left.

"You know what Greiner? I will never forgive myself for violating Rosie, but she was the one woman every man dreams of finding. When she came along, it was like this great force possessed me and I lost all sense of what was right or wrong."

Greiner recognized how desperately Frank loved Rosie, but secretly, so did he.

"I have another plaguing question. Did I kill her father that night when I pushed him off me?"

"No, Elsa told me Hans had a stroke after that incident, and that's what killed him. The events were unrelated. If it had been your push that killed him, believe me, you would not be sitting next to me. Elsa would have hunted you down like a wild dog and you'd either be sitting in jail rotting away or put to death inside a gas chamber. She's an enigma who seeks ultimate revenge on any and all who dare cross her. And, in her book, that's a definite no-no."

"I never liked Rosie's parents—thought they were the coldest people I'd ever met. When I worked for Elsa, she treated me like I was the dirt beneath her shoes and it was obvious she couldn't stand me. Where is she now?"

"Elsa went back to Germany. Believe me, at first I didn't get it. In her mind she was truly disgraced and dishonored by what happened to Rosie and wanted to be as far away as possible. I'm not saying she was right; I'm saying when your faith is as strong as Elsa's and your mother's, they have principles that you do not violate. Yep, I'll give you that Elsa was nasty, ugly, mean, selfish, ... you name it, the list goes on and on. But, whatever else you thought about her, she practiced life as strictly as she lived it, no room for nonsense. So when this happened, it was the end. She gave the house to one of her music students to set up a music school and gave away everything except a few hand selected items left in the cellar.

Strange things—she went to the trouble of leaving Rosie's bedroom suite down there, yet never even said good-bye to her when she left. In fact, I wonder if Rosie knows her mother's gone. Elsa never said good-bye to anyone, not even her sister or Emil.

The only way I gained any knowledge about her departure was because she needed a safe place to plunk legal papers regarding personal affairs, and she knew I'd never look at them. Most normal people leave those documents with their lawyers, but for some reason she didn't trust the person who drew them up and stuck me with them."

Frank wasn't sure where Greiner's cockamamie ideas about Elsa came from or why he would take up for her knowing how much he despised her and what she did. All this nonsense Greiner spewed unnerved him, and he passed it off as "Greiner's being Greiner" and let it go.

"Know what I'm counting on Frank? Rosie seeing you elicits a response, and she starts talking again."

"What do you mean by again? She never shut up. The girl talked all the time."

"She hasn't spoken since the night of the accident."

"Why Greiner, why? What the hell's going on?"

"No one seems to know Frank. It's a mystery, and for whatever reason, she won't talk."

"*Is she deaf?*"

"I asked this question and was told the doctors find no physical evidence nor give any concrete reasons why she shouldn't be able to speak or hear. Some think it might have to do with that car accident and possibly a brain injury, but there's no definitive diagnosis because the patterns and results are inconsistent every time they retest her. More and more they are leaning to depression as the culprit, but they won't commit to that either."

"How long has she been in this hospital?"

"Not all that long. It was only after Rosie was committed that I learned the ugly truth about Emil and Rose. There's not enough time right now to go into detail about what the two of them did or didn't do for her, but they're not alone in their mishandling of Rosie. You, me, her mother—doesn't matter, we all had a part."

Greiner's mind trumpeted one thought after the other trying to dispel his part in the blame game thinking how everyone thinks he or she knows who's to blame, when in fact nobody knows the exact time things go wrong—good and bad happen, planned and unplanned. If not for happenings taking place, life would be a mundane existence, and in Greiner's case life with Ursula was anything but mundane.

Frank would never accept blame for something he knew nothing about. In his mind, he believed Rosie was struck and killed by a car and died alone on the street like a lost dog. If anyone thought his life had value for him, they were gravely mistaken. After joining the army he volunteered for life-threatening assignments no one else would do because without Rosie life had no meaning. He refused to give a damn what others did, including Greiner. Although he had no idea how involved Greiner was with Elsa, Rose, or Emil, none of it was of interest to him. The only thing Frank cared about was a lifelong friendship ending over something neither of them could ever resolve without differences.

"Feels like we've been in this car seven hours the way that old fellow drives. Think you could ask him to speed it up a little?"

Frank thought about what he'd said about the old gentleman and felt bad. After all, giving up his day to drive all that distance, using his own car and fuel, was a true act of kindness, and the least Frank should be is grateful. The car rounded the final bend in the road, and the driver took the next sharp right turn. Out of nowhere there stood a small city of brick buildings, each one in pristine condition, giving the visitors the sense they'd arrived at a prestigious resort rather than a state mental institution. To gain entry onto hospital grounds, a visitation permit was required. This driver regularly volunteered to bring priests to visit parishioners and knew to follow entry protocol.

On the long drive there was plenty of time for Frank to think how, in one short week, fate had managed to turn his life upside-down with a simple telephone call asking him to come home for a family wedding, which he ended up missing entirely, only to be inside a stranger's car with Greiner on his way to see someone he believed was dead. Nothing in any of this made sense, unless this sequence of events was a good omen, but a nagging inside his head echoed otherwise. Fortunately for Frank, awareness and appreciation of the beautiful surroundings captured his attention for a brief moment, clearing his head. His eyes feasted on how neatly the streets and grounds of this magnificent city were impeccably groomed. It was evident that management took pride in planning and selecting the colors and varieties of flowers, exercising steadfast discipline in overseeing planting each row perfectly straight, like soldiers standing in review. The hedges and bushes were snipped and trimmed to look like barber's shears had produced fresh haircuts; not a leaf was out of place. All the grassy areas and knolls were cut and edged with precision, appearing as though each blade's height was measured before cut. The place was picture-perfect.

The driver was directed to North One, where new admissions were placed until their diagnosis was finalized. He found a shaded spot to park before stepping out to open the doors for his passengers. Frank hesitated, but finally he got out of the car, stood straight, and looked around, not saying a word. Greiner gave him all the time needed knowing this was going to be a bitter pill to swallow, seeing Rosie for the first time since the night he believed she died. His noticeably steely blue eyes stared straight ahead at the long lofty windows, huge screened verandas, and landscaped grounds, and he thought how it mimicked heaven in some peaceful, quiet, serene way, but in a split second, those pictures no longer allowed him to see beauty. Instead, he saw mind jails, mind prisons, mind confinement, and mind confusion for any person looking out those lofty windows. The place felt like hell. Nothing changed from when he was a kid—still the same rules. Stay sick, stay inside. Get better, go outside. Stay inside, stay sick. Go outside, get better. The word *outside* played over and over. As the two men walked down the sidewalk leading to the building, Greiner led the way and Frank followed. Despite the bars and grates, Frank wanted to believe he was entering a safe protected zone in this pristine resort where guests just came to visit but, at some point, could leave.

Many of the patients from North One were sitting in rockers on the front veranda, getting fresh air and enjoying a perfect fall day. There was a slight nip in the air and some had on coats and sweaters; others had blankets over their legs and sat silently rocking back and forth, not seeming to harbor a care in the world, content in their own solitude. Few patients ever acknowledged an arriving guest or fellow patient, but for one exception—the woman sitting guard in a rocker right next to the door. She jumped up the minute she saw the two of them and held the door until they were both inside.

"Hi Father, Hi Mr. Man, you come to see me?"

Father Greiner looked right at the woman and engaged in conversation. Frank wanted no part of being there or talking to anyone other than Rosie.

"Of course I did."

"You want to come sit by me Father? You can sit right here in this empty rocker."

"I can't now, but as soon as I take care of some personal business, I'll come sit with you."

"Good Father, I have lots of sins I can tell you about. We'll talk about my sins, ok?"

"We'll talk about anything you like."

"I'll wait right here for you. Don't you forget me like everybody forgets me. You won't forget me will you Father? Fathers always remember everything, don't they? You remember my sins?"

"See you in a little while. Now you go sit down, and I'll be back shortly."

The woman did as she was told, rocking fervently, smiling broadly. She had a visitor.

The combination of patients inaudibly talking to themselves in nonsensical dialogue and being interrupted at the door had made Frank uneasy, and he couldn't wait to get inside to escape the madness. Once the doors closed behind him, his mood declined significantly. The tension mounted and he wanted to be back out on the porch, talking to the woman with the sins. The bizarre screams, the crying voices, and the nonsensical moaning never ceased. For the unsuspecting visitor, these goings on were out of the ordinary and distracting. One had to labor to focus while signing in.

The aid at the information desk asked a series of questions beginning with names and relationship to patient. Did the patient expect your visit? If it was not a normal visiting day and normal visiting hours, did the doctor approve the visit? Priests were exceptions and had no rules unless the patient had ECT that day, then there were no exceptions—the patient saw no one.

Hospital procedure, everyone signed in, everyone got a pass to pin on their lapel, and everyone was escorted to a day room where they sat and waited until an attendant returned with the patient they'd come to see. No visitor was allowed beyond the locked doors leading into the hospital itself. Escorted patients were permitted outside with visitors to sit on the veranda, to meander-hospital grounds, or, as a genuine treat, to have lunch in the cafeteria.

Waiting to see Rosie made Frank visibly disturbed. The more nervous he became, the worse his hands sweat. He wanted to get out and run as fast as he could and never look back.

Greiner sensed Frank's anguish and invited him to sit down and try to relax, but the recurring cries and moans made it nearly impossible to stave off the urge to run. If Rosie didn't show up soon he knew it would all be over.

The sound of keys clanking together drew his attention to a door not far from where he sat, followed by a turning of the tumbler as the door opened. An attendant dressed in white stood proudly next to Rosie with her hand on her shoulder, thrilled to see that Rosie had visitors.

"Go on honey, go on over there and see your guests. I'll wait over here for you until you're ready to go back upstairs. But right now, you have a good time with your friends."

Frank couldn't take his eyes off Rosie. Eight years had taken their toll, and she looked like someone else the way they'd cropped her hair, straight and short. He supposed the haircuts were done in this fashion because hospital staff didn't have time to fuss with making anyone beautiful; the purpose here was to make people well. He pondered the "one size fits all" simple cotton hospital dress with no identifiable style, white nondescript tiny print fabric that lacked personality or description, low maintenance, no ironing, no time for nonsense. In order not to lose sense of why he was in this place, he kept his mind still and focused—this is an institution for making people well; nothing more, nothing less.

The nurse-attendant spoke softly to Rosie, but neither Frank nor Father Greiner could hear what she said. When Rosie still hesitated, the nurse returned, took her by the hand, and nudged her along. Frank stood up first and Father Greiner followed; neither said a word, waiting for Rosie to speak first. It appeared to Frank that she did not recognize either of them, because she made no effort to acknowledge their presence. Bewildered by this reticence on her part, Frank suspected embarrassment as the reason for her silence. He took charge and spoke first, but very slowly—ignoring how she looked, whether or not she spoke, none of that mattered. The mere presence of witnessing the only woman he ever loved standing before him, alive and not dead, was all that mattered. "Rosie…Rosie…Rosie, oh how I've missed you. Not a day's gone by, not a night I go to bed without talking to you. Oh….how I love you—to think I thought you were dead, but you're not. You're very much alive." Pools of tears caused his eyes to fill and overflow, blurring his vision to the point where he was unable to focus or see anything but a huge magnified glassy impression, making Rosie appear larger than life. Frank stood motionless and apprehensive, refusing to blink, knowing that the second he did his eyes would clear and he'd be forced to accept the grim reality of what stood before him, a sick and tortured woman. The presence of this once-vital woman, who now appeared completely expressionless and fixed like a statue of stone, engulfed him in pain. If only the blur could last forever, maybe it would be an easier picture to carry away with him and hold next to his heart. Rosie never blinked an eye or made any attempt to move. This terrified him and gave rise to further concern over the status of her condition. The attendant never left them alone during the entire visit, managing to remain close by without crowding Rosie. It was evident that she hoped this visit would evoke some kind of response the doctors could deem positive.

Unable to keep his hands to himself, Frank acted on impulse and grabbed Rosie. He began to shake her uncontrollably, as if he believed she might be lost somewhere inside or perhaps succumbed to a deep kind of sleep. Sadly, the shaking conjured up no reaction whatsoever.

Frank held her tightly in his arms and sobbed until a torrent of tears washed down his face and onto Rosie. He clutched her near lifeless rag doll body in his arms, and squeezed tightly. She never acknowledged him. Frank deliberately hesitated to relinquish her tiny frail frame from his intense grip knowing this was not the beginning but a time he would only hold onto in memory. The end had come. Frank stepped back to study the only woman he would always love, and for a second or two he contemplated racing out of the room. But something made him stop, and when he gazed at Rosie and realized she was the heartbreaking result of his raging temper and running away once before, he knew that this was not the time for a repeat performance.

The attendant pulled Frank aside and told him in no uncertain terms that his actions were uncalled for, and remarked that any further upset or display like the one just exhibited would end the visit. Father Greiner acted as the mediator and explained to the attendant the circumstances between Frank and Rosie. Frank apologized for his disruptive behavior and pleaded for a few minutes alone in the far corner of the room where there would be no distractions. Convinced that Frank's intentions were not intended to harm Rosie but were instead an impulsive response to mere frustration, she honored his request. Frank took Rosie by the arm and slowly led her to a bench at the far end of the day room. She offered no resistance when he directed her where to sit and then sat down alongside her, perfectly positioned so that when he turned they were facing with knees touching. He took her small hands in his and looked directly into her eyes to begin a one-sided conversation, choosing his words carefully and speaking slowly and softly.

"Do you remember the first time you saw me?"

He paused briefly, giving Rosie time to feel comfortable and trusting in his presence.

"I remember the first time I ever saw you, and I will never forget it. It is such a beautiful picture that I carry it with me everywhere I go. Today I got a new picture to carry with me, and it's a picture of a gorgeous living Rosie.

"All these years I believed you were dead, but yesterday I learned from Father Greiner that you were alive. At first I didn't believe him and thought he was lying, but when I stopped to think, it didn't make sense for him to lie to me about something he knew was significant and could change my life. You are the only one who could possibly know how much I love you, because we shared the truest and purest love and became one."

Frank stopped talking for a brief moment and took his right hand and put it under Rosie's chin, lifting her head gently; while stroking the back of her head with his other hand he continued talking.

"I loved you then, I love you now, and I'll love you to the day I die. There will never be another love for me as long as I live."

He leaned forward to get a little closer and kissed her on the forehead, as he had done so many times in the past. Sitting back on the bench and holding her hands in his, he asked. "Can you hear me?"

Rosie looked straight away.

"Father Greiner told me the doctors claim you can't hear and have no explanation why you can't hear, and no one has heard you speak since the accident. Rosie, are you not talking because you can't, or is it because you don't want to?"

Frank paused and waited for some simple response. There was none.

"If you're not talking because you don't want to, I understand. You're entitled to do anything you like, you've been through a horrible nightmare and I don't think I could have survived it any better than you. Can I tell you something? If you talk to me, I will never tell a soul. I'll keep your secret, and I'll treasure every word you utter and never let anyone know I heard you. For the rest of our lives, we'll only need to talk to each other, you and me. That way, I can protect you from words that can pierce your heart, and I can stop pain from ever touching your life again. I'll devote my life to you and never leave your side."

He couldn't help but think about the promise he'd broken when he left her back with her parents, and over and over in his mind he was reminded of why she had no reason to trust anything he said or did now or in the future. Rosie's head drooped, her shoulders tightened, and Frank sensed a change in her demeanor.

"Rosie, please look at me, don't look down at the floor. I want to see into your soul like I used to do; I want to see the expression in your eyes when I talk to you. How else can I possibly know in my heart whether you're hearing me?"

He looked right at her and spoke in a disciplining manner.

"Rosie, you can hear me, I know you can. And what's more, I know you understand everything I am saying. But, for some reason or another, you don't want anyone to know you can hear. Listen to me."

Knowing he had to earn her trust all over again, he had an idea he wanted to share and thought he'd try talking her through it.

"I'll even talk to the world for you if you want and keep it from our doorstep, never allowing anyone or anything to ever hurt you again as long as we both live. Please give me a second chance and let me right the wrongs I've done. You don't belong here! You belong with me so I can take care of you and protect you like I always wanted to do."

Suddenly Frank noticed Rosie fidgeting in her seat, then as if on purpose, she turned her head to the side so he couldn't see her face. Her eyes glazed over and appeared to be filled with tears, but they never overflowed the lower eyelid. She looked down at the floor, and Frank sensed a definite sadness blanketing her; he knew this was not his imagination.

"Rosie, I upset you, and I'm sorry. I didn't come here to do that, but I know you can hear me. I know it, and no one will tell me otherwise."

His convictions were greater and stronger than ever that she heard every word. He *knew* she understood.

"What has happened to you in these last eight years? What?"

She remained silent, almost catatonic, staring down at the floor.

"Who did this to you? Tell me and I'll kill the son of a bitch with my bare hands."

Rosie stood up on her own and headed towards the door and the awaiting attendant.

Frank had no idea what caused her to get up and leave abruptly on her own, but he was positive it was something he had said.

Everything that happened reinforced what he knew in his heart, Rosie hated profanity; she had heard what she didn't like and this was her way of telling him. His first thoughts were to share what happened with her doctors, but the fear of breaching another promise told him not to say a word to anyone. Like Rosie, he remained silent.

Frank frantically searched his mind for clues to what Rosie might have been thinking and figured maybe the only way to understand any of this was if he came back to Pittsburgh where he could see Rosie daily, as often and as much as needed, until he could take her away from this place. The screams, the sounds, the loneliness, the doors within doors always locked, the mindless wandering of everyone except the staff; it was all overwhelming and frightening. He could see this was no place for Rosie, but for now it would have to be.

Frank's thoughts became disjointed, and for a fleeting moment he wanted nothing in life but to be able to free Rosie of this life sentence to which she had committed herself. As his mind filled with doubt and fear and wondered—if Rosie locked all the doors to her mind, could anyone ever open them? One consistent notion relentlessly hammered his mind. Rosie had gone beyond the rainbow.

The nurse-attendant busied herself chatting with other nurses, and somehow she missed the moment when Rosie stood up and walked back to the door, waiting to be taken back upstairs. Within a minute or so she spotted Rosie standing at the locked doors and went directly to her.

"Appears you're finished visiting and are ready to go back upstairs. I sure hope you had a nice visit with your guests."

On Ward B most of the staff assumed Rosie might be deaf, and the nurses often touched her as a way of getting her attention and looked at her when they spoke in the event she read lips. Most times this practice got a response.

"Before we go up, your priest mentioned something about communion and seeing you. I'm going to go get him. Please wait right here and I'll be right back."

Rosie stood facing the door with her back to Frank and waited as she was told. The attendant walked over to the far end of the room where Frank sat motionless and dazed from everything that transpired between him and Rosie. He never noticed the attendant's presence; she startled him when she spoke.

"Do you know where Father is?"

"Yes, I do."

"Will you please get him for me? He mentioned something about wanting to see Rosie before he left, and I think that would be very nice."

"Before I get Father Greiner, would you be kind enough to give me a run down on visiting hours?"

"Visiting days are Tuesday and Thursday afternoons between one and four o'clock in the afternoon. If the patient has a specific problem, let's say for example Rosie has to undergo ECT treatment—there would absolutely be no visiting under any circumstances. I recommend you call before visiting. Things change around here daily. And by the way, how did your visit with Rosie go?"

"It went fine for me, but she didn't respond to anything I said and so I have no idea how it was for her."

"Maybe the next time you'll have a better visit and she'll feel more comfortable around you. I see by the uniform you are in the Army. Are you close by, or are you stationed far away?"

"For the time being I'm stationed in Illinois, but soon on my way to Europe."

"Do you get back this way very often?"

"Unfortunately not. This is the first time I've been back in years.

"Well, I'm sure anytime a handsome soldier can come back and visit Rosie, it'll make her happy and us, too. We all enjoy having visitors, and according to our records, you two gentlemen are the only ones who've come to see her."

"Are you sure no one else has ever visited her?"

"Yes, I'm positive. Checked the ward records before we came down. No one except you and the priest has shown any interest in her. She's a lovely, quiet patient, always willing to help, and never bothers anyone. You hardly know she's around. The staff loves Rosie. When a patient is sick or just coming out of ECT she's a great help to us and would have made an excellent nurse." She paused, "Who knows, someday if she gets well, and gets herself out of here, maybe she can still do something with her life. We just never know what the future holds around here. This place is full of surprises."

Frank liked this woman and felt grateful that Rosie had someone who exhibited sincere kindness and understanding towards her since she was alone. He went outside to get Greiner.

"Greiner, the nurse in there said you mentioned you wanted to see Rosie before we left. They're waiting for you back by the same door they brought Rosie into the day room through. By the way, I'm ready to leave whenever you are."

"This won't take long. You can either wait in the car or sit outside somewhere."

Father Greiner approached the two women and spoke to Rosie. "Do you suppose you can spend a little time with me before I leave?" He stopped then directed the rest of his comments to the nurse.

"Could you leave us alone for a few minutes, I'd like to talk to Rosie."

"Of course, I'll be over on the other side of the room—just come get me when you're through."

Greiner led Rosie to a quiet place in the day room, and they sat down next to each other.

"I know this had to be a traumatic day for you, seeing Frank again. I'm sorry if I've made another mistake by introducing him back into your life, but I did it because I care what happens to you—always have and always will.

All any of us wants is for you to get well and find your way out of this depression. We never lose hope. If we lose that, we've lost everything. You must never give up, and you must never lose hope; most of all, you must never lose your faith in God. Please let us help you help yourself, and don't shut us out. We love and miss you, Rosie."

The longer he remained in this place the more difficult it became for him to maintain control of his emotions. He was forcibly fighting back tears and focusing intently to maintain control and not upset Rosie. He saw that she looked tired and decided not to hassle her with communion; instead, held her delicate hands in his and prayed aloud. She appeared to be listening.

When he finished, he gently squeezed her hands in his, let go, and beckoned to the nurse. He was ready to leave.

"This young lady looks very tired to me, and I hope it's not because we overstayed our visit."

"Has nothing to do with your overstaying. It's simply exhausting for patients when visitors come because they work so hard to be on their best behavior. No sense to making the visitor mad or upset, they might never come back and see us, right Rosie girl?" The nurse looked at Rosie and kept talking and answering her own questions like this was their normal routine.

"Rosie, you ready to go back upstairs and take a nap? I'm ready if you're ready."

The nurse-attendant turned towards Father Greiner and spoke just above a whisper,

"Father, could you wait just a few minutes longer for me to come back down? We have something of Rosie's locked in safe-keeping and the ward nurse wants it out of here before it's lost or stolen. We think it might have sentimental value or even be a family heirloom. Usually a family member comes and we send these kinds of things home with them, but since Rosie hasn't had any visitors except you two today, would you mind keeping it in a safe place for her? Maybe at the church?"

"Of course, I'd be more than happy to do that for her."

He looked at Rosie, who had not taken her eyes off him, "Goodbye Rosie, I hope you get well real soon so I can take you home."

Rosie turned around, the nurse gently put her hand on Rosie's shoulder, and together they disappeared behind the locked doors.

It didn't take long before the nurse-attendant returned with a white letter-sized envelope with the flap tucked inside. Father Greiner felt the coin like object and chain inside, but he couldn't imagine what it was. The attendant saw he was perplexed about the contents.

"Go ahead, you can open it. It's a medal, a gold one on a gold chain." Father Greiner opened the envelope to see what kind of medal it was.

"It's a Saint Christopher medal."

He paused briefly and thought about where he'd seen it.

"I know I've seen this medal before, but right now it escapes me. Guess I've had a full day like Rosie, and I'm tired. Be assured I'll keep it safe for her."

He put the envelope in his jacket pocket and remembered he'd forgotten to thank her.

"I must get going, but before I do, I want you to know how much I appreciate all you are doing for Rosie. With caring people like you, she's sure to get better. God bless you."

"Well thank you Father. We do our best, but nothing works like family members who come see them, too. It's the best medicine of all."

Father Greiner exited the building and walked towards the parked car. The driver was there, but no Frank. When he inquired where Frank had gone, the driver had no idea.

The man had brought a large brown paper sack containing sandwiches and fruit for all of them; he offered Father Greiner something to eat. The two men found a bench near the parking lot, sat down, and shared the assortment of foodstuffs. Neither had much to say to the other, and when they'd finished eating Father Greiner became concerned because there was no sign of Frank anywhere.

Imagining how upset Frank had to be, seeing Rosie in her present condition and in these surroundings, Father Greiner got nervous and feared Frank might do something stupid. He lowered his head, immersed himself in prayer, and never noticed Frank when he reappeared.

"Frank, where have you been? I've been worried about you and couldn't imagine what happened."

"I had to go back. I had something that belonged to Rosie."

"Did you get to see her again?"

"No, I had the receptionist have the nurse come down so I could speak to her. I explained I had something belonging to Rosie and wanted her to have it. She agreed to give it to her so long as it didn't harm her."

"Did you think about what this might do to her depression?"

"Greiner, trust me, this won't upset her. If anything, it will probably help."

"Do you think the nurse will give it to her?"

"I don't see why not—it's just a piece of paper, an old letter."

"Is this the letter you told me about?"

"Yes. Do you think for a minute I'd give her something that would upset her? It' just a simple letter and belongs to her."

"Frank, I don't understand why any of this happened, but one thing for sure, we can't lose hope."

"Hope is why I went back. Like you, I keep hoping for a miracle. Maybe this letter could be it. Something has to bring her out of this depression. I want her out of this horrible place."

After Frank's visit with Rosie he doubted she had the stamina and will to survive becoming just another face in the myriad of ones locked within these confines. He knew the old Rosie would claw her way out and never allow herself to be awash in this deep sea of depression, but that Rosie was, as he originally believed, dead.

The turmoil inside his head, with all the "maybe ifs," caused his head to pound when he added up his contributions to her breakdown. Maybe if he had written the letter like he promised, maybe if he'd not gotten her pregnant, maybe if he hadn't run off in a fit of rage, maybe if he'd kept his promise to never leave her, maybe if her father had said "yes, marry my daughter," none of this would have happened, but no amount of "maybe ifs" could justify breaking a promise. Frank knew without a doubt that he was as guilty as anyone for Rosie's being in this place.

"So, when you went in, how did she react when you handed her the letter?"

"She didn't react because I didn't get to see her. The nurse came down and I gave it to her."

"I'm sure they'll read it before giving it to her to make sure it doesn't contain anything that would upset her. Does it bother you to know that something so personal might be intercepted along the way like that?"

"No. That letter is threadbare and as fragile as she is. I've carried it around in my wallet for eight years, and every once in a while I physically remove it from my wallet and read it before I go to bed. Most times though, I read in it my mind—I have it memorized. I did this religiously because I was falling apart and was trying to hold on to any part of her, even if was just in a memory. Those words I wrote her are scribed in my brain. You know, Greiner, one way or the other, I read that letter every night before falling asleep—like a prayer."

"Speaking of prayer, do you ever pray to our Heavenly Father from the bottom of your heart and ask for His divine intervention?"

"Greiner, knock off the bullshit. I don't have a heart. I gave mine away eight years ago to the only fool who would take it, an innocent and foolish Rosie Gradel who didn't have a clue what she was getting. Precious innocence and naiveté—never a match for the likes of an old codger like me. My heart was a piece of shit. I promised it to every whore in town who would sleep with me and didn't care if they slept with me for fifteen minutes or two years. Didn't matter, I wasn't in love with any of them. All I wanted to do was use them to make myself feel good, even if it cost a piece of my heart. What the hell did I care? I didn't have use for it, and it worked better than money. It was meaningless."

"Frank when you talk like this, I don't believe any of it, it's all rhetoric because you still want the world to think you're the tough guy you're not."

"By the time I gave my heart to Rosie it was worthless. It was tired, worn out, full of bitterness, infected with disease, and dying. Can you believe this one? The kid begged me to trade hearts with her, and I let her talk me into it. She actually asked for my heart and I gave it to her. Taking it was like receiving a gift from the devil himself. It was a mistake. Mine was a bad heart and should never have been given to anyone. Look what happened to her—it destroyed her. The only thing that should have been done with that heart was to bury it. Even your God couldn't save a heart like that."

Frank's nervous babbling upset Greiner, and he resented his constant rejections of God every time he broached the subject.

"Frank, what do you say we get going? You have a train to catch this evening, and the gentleman who brought us is ready to leave. I feel bad we've used up his entire day."

"I can't get that picture of Rosie out of my mind and have to go back and see her one more time—just one more time before we leave.

"Frank, I seriously think we ought to consider leaving right now before you do something you'll be sorry for."

"I don't give a damn if they arrest me or lock me up in this place, I have to see her."

"Frank, you're losing control and I'm beginning to believe I made a mistake bringing you here."

"I'm going in there and won't be long. Give me about twenty minutes or so."

"Frank, you're pushing your luck bothering that nurse for the third time and not thinking rationally. You have a train to catch, too."

"I don't give a damn if I miss the train and the Army puts me in jail. I have to go back in there once more." Frank waited for Greiner to physically try to stop him, but that didn't happen. "What if I go back this time and Rosie says my name? Do you have any idea what that one word would mean to me?"

"Frank, I think you're making a big mistake, but obviously you won't listen and I can't stop you any more than I can get you to listen."

Frank recklessly ran down the walkway, bumping into people and not stopping to say excuse me, I'm sorry, just rudeness. The receptionist recognized Frank and didn't ask him to sign in for the third time, but asked if he had a problem.

He explained his being in the Army and having to return in the evening, leaving the country within the week, and stressed he'd forgotten to tell Rosie something important. She asked him to take a seat then inquired by phone whether Rosie could be brought back down to the day room for what might be a final visit.

The sounds and cries within his mind were so hauntingly eerie that Frank wanted to cover his ears and run as far away as his legs would take him, but instead he paced the floor like a caged animal.

After a fifteen-minute wait, the attendant returned with Rosie and explained to him how Rosie remained extremely pensive and seemingly quite upset ever since she left the day room earlier. Frank knew the attendant was sympathetic to his cause and had fulfilled Frank's request out of the kindness of her heart. He noticed the letter in Rosie's pocket and had no idea whether she had read it, but he was pleased that the nurse had seen fit to honor his plea and give it to her.

He looked at Rosie, and this time he was able to see her without the outside interferences of cries and moans and realized any attempt to reach her was futile. He thanked the nurse for allowing him this one last goodbye before turning around and walking away. Frank never looked back—he didn't want his mind's eye to carry around a picture of a stranger for the rest of his life. This third and final run back to North One confirmed what Frank already knew—he woman brought down for the third time wasn't responding to him because she was unmistakably someone else called Rosie Gradel. The Rosie he loved was gone—she died eight years ago.

Frank met up with Greiner and the driver of the car, who were ready to get on the road and head back. Each one climbed into his respective seat and within minutes they were on their way back to the city. In the first part of the ride home neither one knew what to say to the other.

Father Greiner occupied himself by mentally organizing church business and mapping out schedules for after Frank left. He reached in his jacket for his little black book and realized he'd forgotten about the medal in the envelope; in a flash, he remembered where he'd seen it.

"Frank, with all the excitement and confusion I forgot to tell you what happened today. The nurse gave me something of Rosie's to put in safe-keeping because she worried it might get lost or stolen in the hospital. I think it's your St. Christopher medal. Do you know anything about this?"

"Yeah, I do. I gave it to her because I wanted her to have it. Honest to God, I can't believe she managed to hang onto it all this time. This is unbelievable."

"Well apparently she did, and now I'm giving it back to its rightful owner."

"I don't want the damn thing, Greiner. Do whatever you want with it."

"Frank, you're upset right now, and I understand this has been a long hard day, but please take it. Think about all those years growing up and how special this was to you because it was the only thing of your father's you had left."

"Give me the damn thing, just give it to me. I'll take care of it."

The car slowed up and stopped in front of the rectory. Both men remained in the back seat, neither of them making an attempt to exit.

The elderly gentleman came around to Father Greiner's side of the car and opened the door for him. When Greiner got out and thanked him for his generosity, the old man said he was happy to be of service.

Frank let himself out of the car and walked over first to slip several bills into the older gentleman's hand for his act of kindness, then embraced his dearest old friend and thanked him for releasing him from the prison he'd been in for these past eight years. A certain foreboding ran through his veins as he reluctantly released Greiner, knowing this meant an end to this portion of his life and the possibility of never seeing him again.

"Greiner, I want you to know I'll always love you no matter what you do or where you are."

"Frank, please give me your address before you leave. I don't want to lose touch like this ever again. You are the most important person in my life, in spite of that horrible mouth and bad language." That said, both of them laughed and Greiner went on talking.

"You're like an ingredient in a recipe when one thing's missing, the things a flop, like those orange cupcakes your mom made us." Both of them chuckled and remembered with fondness those times when Frank's mother made her infamous cupcakes no one wanted to eat.

"In my life you'll always be the main ingredient, and with you missing, I am so forlorn. Bad mouth and all, I love you my friend. Always will." As almost an after-thought, Greiner remembered he'd forgotten to get Frank's address, not just for personal reasons, but also to let him know Rosie's status should there be any changes. Frank acknowledged he'd be grateful to learn of any progress in her wellness.

Greiner handed him a pencil and piece of paper. Frank jotted down a current general post office mailing address, explaining that his job took him all over the world doing classified work for the government but not to worry because eventually, one way or the other, he'd catch up with his mail, and his mail would catch up with him. Greiner went into his office and retrieved his small black book and transferred the address so it wouldn't get lost. He asked his friend to promise to keep in touch and keep him apprised of any future plans. Frank agreed to do that and asked Greiner not to tell anyone about Rosie, especially none of his family members, because he felt it was none of their business. Finally, Frank asked for one other thing—he asked that Greiner not give anyone his address or tell anyone where he was.

"What are your plans now that you've found Rosie and know she's not dead?"

"I have no idea. My mind is a muddled mess, lumps stuck in my throat feel like something is trying to choke the life out of me, and to make matters worse, I can't get the pictures of what I saw today out of my mind. Today was a dream come true and a nightmare all twisted into one. Something is seriously going on inside Rosie—her doors are closed, and I don't think she'll ever let anyone in ever again. Greiner, let's not fool ourselves—she's never leaving that place."

"Frank, you're wrong. Rosie will come out of there if I have to take her out myself."

"Greiner, the eternal dreamer, thinks he'll ride in on the wings of some angel, swoop down, and take Rosie out of that living hell she's in. For God's sake pal, it ain't gonna happen. I've seen guys in the Army go off like her, and those poor bastards never get better."

"I'm telling you, I know her, and she's different."

"Greiner, the nice guy, the optimist, the dreamer who wants to make everyone happy, do and say what everyone wants to hear, anything that will save the rotten world. You hear me, she's never getting better."

Everything seemed topsy-turvy, and Frank became increasingly unhappy, mentally blaming Greiner for his disappointment. On the drive towards Woodside, he had imagined a blissfully happy reunion with the only woman he'd ever loved. He knew the minute Rosie set eyes on him she'd snap out of this depression thing and the two of them would pick up where they'd left off. When this didn't occur, he became increasingly angry, blaming Greiner, who he thought should have known better and left well enough alone. Frank festered over why Greiner didn't think before taking him to Woodside, knowing full well it would bring nothing but grievous pain.

"I'm telling you Greiner, she's left her body just like the dead do. She's gone and left this shell, or whatever you want to call it. That was not Rosie. I don't know the woman we saw today, but whoever she is, she was sent here by your God to remind us what we all did to Rosie. She's a real-life ghost, and I think each and every one of us is responsible, including the ghost."

The increased hostility Frank exhibited concerned Greiner, and he questioned where this would end. "Had I known you'd be this pessimistic, I would never have taken you to see her. The more you talk, the more I wish you'd shut up, because I believe she'll get better and get out of there."

"Dream, Greiner, dream, and maybe talk to your God, but I'm telling you, there's nothing left."

Frank stared off into space, totally disengaged and obviously distressed, trying to dissect what set of circumstances could have sent her into this death spiral, whether it was by choice or her body caving to an internal chemistry waiting to defeat her at the first opportunity. No one could go on pleasing everyone all the time like she did. Frank saw this unselfish act as giving permission to chip away little pieces of love from her heart, which was obviously fine with her, but what he observed was failure of takers to replace love for love. In Frank's way of thinking, if you can accept you can repay, whether it be a dinner or love—it's what you did. Frank questioned the doctors, hospital confinement, ECT, all of it—doubting any of anything would fix the broken Rosie. He told Greiner what a huge mistake it was and how desperately he regretted ever answering the telephone call beckoning him home, wishing it had never happened.

Greiner was deeply troubled by Frank's words and attitude and knew there was nothing left to say. "I don't know what I should or shouldn't say to you anymore. Seems the only thing I'm sure of is our need to pray and believe in the Almighty God who loves us and answers our prayers. I can't make you believe, but I will pray for you and for Rosie everyday of my mortal life. Don't forget to write to me once in a while."

"Greiner, I'm not a writer, couldn't even keep a promise to Rosie, why the hell would you want me to make another promise I might not keep?"

"I'll settle for a postcard."

"I have to get going. Some things I have to take care of before I leave."

"If there is anything I can do for you back here, let me know. I'll help any way I can."

"I know you will Greiner. Take care of yourself and don't let those sheep in your flock lead you down any wrong paths. Never know where the big bad wolf might be hiding."

Frank picked up his coat, but he couldn't look at Greiner. His eyes were filled with tears and he questioned why he was ever born, tossing around the reality of life without Rosie after finding her alive. His thoughts drifted to his father and the profound loneliness he must have felt the day he took his life. Suddenly, and for the first time, he understood why his father committed suicide.

Before zipping up his duffel bag, Frank took one final look around the house for any personal items he might have missed. The house was clear of his belongings; not a sign or trace that he'd ever been there. Reassured and comforted, knowing his niece would live in the house until he decided what he wanted to do with his life. He locked the door and promised himself he would never return to this house.

Preoccupied with making one last stop before heading to the station to catch the last train to Illinois, he raced to catch the trolley to the 22nd Street Bridge. He hadn't eaten all day, but the thought of food repulsed him.

Frank got off the stop where the street met the entrance onto the bridge. A hawker was stopped with his wagon, trying to sell the remaining produce on it before calling it a day. The hawker attempted to interest Frank in buying some apples, but Frank told him he didn't have any money. The hawker threw an apple at Frank and said, "hey good American soldier boy, 'dis apple be good for you, make your teece nice and vite."

Catching the apple with one hand, Frank flattened out his palm and held it directly in front of the horse's mouth, waiting for him to eat it.

"Looks like this horse needs white teeth more than I do."

That said, he turned around and continued on and over the bridge. He hurried along and walked the fifty or so yards it took to get to the spot where his father supposedly took his life.

A kid never forgets a spot like this, because his mother wouldn't let him. Every year on the anniversary of his death, Eve took little Frankie by the hand and walked silently to the very spot from where the husband and father of her children leapt to his death. Eve got over her husband's death long before the day of the funeral. Her sham of a marriage to Dr. Thadeus Pazwalski survived because he clung on. Divorce was never an option for this devout Catholic. But, there was always intense grief and respect, and an elaborate bouquet of flowers dropped into the river grave he had created for himself. She never let go of her little Frankie's hand while forcing him to repeat whatever prayer she was reciting.

As Frank got older, he refused to participate in this annual ceremony that his mother perpetrated, whether he went or she went alone to stand high above the river and pray into the darkness. Now, standing there alone, he laughed aloud, thinking how comforting it would be to be smothered by her love. He looked up and down the bridge, but she was nowhere to be seen.

Between exhaustion and the emotional roller coaster ride of the unprecedented events of the day, he began talking to his dead mother in soft prayer-like whispers, much like the ones he'd heard her say during those rituals she had taken him to every year.

"Mom, I never told you how much I loved you because I never knew I did—I did love you. And oh how proud I was of you!

"I can still see your face in my mind's eye and was afraid I'd forgotten what you looked like, but I haven't.

"I thought you needed me the most, but I was wrong. Moms don't need kids—they're nothing but work, worry, and grief. But kids, on the other hand, need their moms and never outgrow them. I see that now and wish I could have seen it then.

"Please Mom—hold my hand just this one last time."

He froze. It was already dark outside and the wind was whipping about, but he held tightly onto the rail with one hand while pretending to hold his mother's hand with the other, managing to look up and down the bridge. There wasn't a soul in sight.

Occasionally, a car would go by and the headlights would identify his standing there in a ghost-like form, but he remained motionless.

He pondered and listened to the quiet peaceful sounds of the wind and water engulfing him. The most pronounced ones came from the rippling water beneath, as if calling and promising to lull him into the most restful sleep he'd ever know. A long restful sleep where he could be with his father and be one with him. No one fully appreciated how dreadfully Frank missed his father. He couldn't help wonder how different life might have been had his father lived.

In the loudest voice he could muster he screamed to the water below, "Pop, why the consequences in life? Why?"

Frank stared down into the dark abyss below and wondered if his father was in a place protected from life's ups and downs. He thought how sick to death he was of the gigantic roller coaster rides in his own life that made him want to retch his guts and purge all that was wrong and couldn't.

Frenetically, Frank's mind tugged and pulled like a piece of taffy stuck to a slab of marble. Was his father like a ship in a storm, tossing back and forth never finding calm waters—eternally lost and thrashed about in the sea of darkness and death?

He thought, for just an instant, that he heard a voice, but he didn't recognize it. Trying desperately to identify it made him miss what was being said. Abruptly he turned around in the direction of the voice, certain he could identify whoever it was.

He stood motionless, waiting for the person to repeat their message, but this time he thought he'd listen more intently and catch the words. The silence was deafening. Once again he screamed as loud as possible, "What the hell do you want from me?"

Still no vocal response. Recognizing this was merely a figment of his imagination, and no one was there, he refocused on the water and stared into its darkness, mesmerized by its mysterious sounds. Again, he thought he heard the voice, but this time he was pretty sure it was his father.

"Pop, that you?"

Certain his father was calling him, he awaited the answer.

"Pop, want me to join you in that pitiful boat caught in those murky river waters going nowhere?"

Still no voice came back. Where was that voice he'd just heard? Where did it go? Frank's patience and frustration mounted. He awaited an answer. "I said—you want me to come down there and be with you?"

He waited a few seconds, fumbled to locate the medal in his pocket, and pulled it out with the chain still attached. Holding it up in the air over the river below, screaming at the top of his lungs, Frank wrestled with his words.

"Is this what you're looking for old man? Is this what you want or do you want me?"

Now hysterical and the center of his own drama, his voice blared. "You couldn't want me! You know how I know that?" He paused to fuel his argument. "Because if you wanted me so bad, you would never have left me like you did."

With that said, Frank threw the medal, chain and all, into the river below. Even though his voice was hoarse and barely audible, this confrontation with his father wasn't over. "You've gotten as much of my ass as you're getting old man. I'm not getting in that boat with you, you hear me? The only thing I'm giving you now is your medal back. That's all I owe you, nothing more.

"You bled the life out of me when I was an innocent babe. No wonder I never knew what love meant. No wonder I never knew how to stop taking or when it was time to give back. How could I?

"You robbed me of the only chance I had to learn and understand how man manipulates this delicate balance of playing fair in the game of love. Oh sure, mom loved me, but it wasn't the same kind of love a pop gives his kid. You always called me your little angel. How could you do what you did if I was truly your little angel?

"My wings were tiny and frail and I was just learning to fly when you burdened me with the weight of your suicide, crippling my wings and breaking my spirit. After that I never quite flew the same. Oh sure I tried, but something was always missing.

"I was a mere babe, an innocent kid who desperately needed direction. I don't need you any more and I sure as hell don't need your dumb damn medal. Take it, and get the hell out of my life you son of a bitch. I hate you, and I hate everything you did to all of us the day you left us here on the bridge.

"You're a thief who robbed everyone whose life supposedly meant anything to you. First you robbed yourself by missing life, then you robbed mom by taking away her lifelong mate, and lastly, you robbed the girls and me of a pop.

"You didn't earn the right to rest in peace, you deserve to be floating down there for eternity, all confused and tossed about—lost in time like you left the rest of us to do here.

"Sure hope you enjoy your medal—it belongs with you. It's all yours, and is the last thing you'll ever get from me."

Frank's face was beet-red, but as soon as he'd finished his excoriations it paled quickly. The constraints he placed upon himself to withhold this bitterness dissipated, and for the first time he felt exhilarated.

The pressure and need to bury years of pain had finally been removed from his shoulders. Lightheadedness surrounded him and he thought for a moment that he might faint. He grabbed onto a lamppost and collected himself. Passers-by looked at him strangely, assuming he was drunk. He glared back and bellowed out, "What the hell you looking at?"

He thought how unjust his life seemed and reckoned he'd been born under an unlucky star, because nothing about this day made sense. None and nothing mattered for Frank Pazwalski. Life no longer held special meaning or direction, and for a fleeting moment he considered going back and joining his father, but realized his father's solution to problems was a stupid one.

There was still time, and he decided to walk to the train station. Hopefully, moving—just moving *forward*—would calm his jittery nerves. He paced himself and scrutinized shop windows along the way. It reminded him of those yesterdays when he raced up and down these avenues, known as the best window display man in the business. His reputation began when he was nearing the end of his third year at the university and working part-time. The creativity and talent he exhibited gave rise to greater demand for his services, and this in turn fueled his oversized ego, and he quit to pursue his dream of being the best that money could buy. It broke his mother's heart the day he announced he wouldn't be returning to school but would instead start his own business.

This was a high time in his life when everything he touched turned to gold. Life was perfect. Perfect career, plenty of money for good times, and few responsibilities. What more could a young guy want? Perhaps one special woman, but he could never find her.

As he approached age thirty-two, he met that one special woman and fell in love for the first time.

Frank stood silently looking up at the sky, lost in time and space. A broad smile crossed his face—he felt composed, but then suddenly the smile disappeared. He realized he'd experienced love with the most perfect woman, but his love came and went like any season in any given year. He questioned how long it would take for his mind to erase memories of her so they blended like the seasons, one into the other, leaving no distinguishing markers.

He remembered a time when he brought Rosie to see the window displays he'd done for the Christmas holidays. His eyes blurred as he recalled the excitement of holding hands while walking up the back alley paralleling Main Street, hoping to steal minutes alone from anyone who might recognize or catch them together.

Chills ran down his spine as he fished into his memory to retrieve the emotions that ran through his body the night they strolled through the snow together, her giggling when he wrapped his unbuttoned coat around her tiny body and pulled her tightly next to him to kiss her, and how silly he acted buttoning his coat so the two of them could pretend to be trapped inside for a few minutes. He was grateful he'd taken the initiative to invite her to sneak out and join him in the thrill of walking in the snow together, or else he'd have missed that as well.

Burdened with a heavy heart, Frank cried most of the way to the train. Years of pent up emotions poured out of his eyes and heart, and he could barely see where he was going, bumping into people and cursing as though the recklessness was their fault. He thought about the only two times before this day when his heart had given way to tears—the day his pop died, and the day Greiner became a priest.

His heart was ever mindful of Rosie. In time, memories of her would blend and mellow to become part of a total blur—indistinguishable, meaningless, and he hoped no longer painful.

He arrived at the train station, headed straight for platform number three, handed the conductor his ticket, and seated himself next to a window at the very back of the car.

People were waving to loved ones on board the train, some happy and some sad. Frank closed his eyes and welcomed the chance to run away from this ongoing saga that managed to consume his life, rob him of joy, and banish him with heaviness of heart. All he wanted was to be left alone and not think about anything but closing his eyes and getting some rest.

Two weeks after Frank and Father Greiner visited Rosie, her mental health declined and the nurses noticed severe regression. This behavior was confirmed by an attendant who stated that Rosie was wrapping her excrement in her cupped hand and cradling it next to her body like a baby. This behavior concerned the ward nurse, who chose to take Rosie aside and get to the bottom of whatever brought this about and what could be done to put an end to it.

"Rosie, ever since your friend and the priest came to see you, your behavior has changed and not for the better. Your depression is back, getting worse by the day. You're not eating, and the night nurse brought to my attention you're not sleeping well. These things cannot continue and we may have to up your dosage of medication which I hate to do. We'll see what Dr. Wolfe has to say when he comes this week.

"The other disturbing issue is this need to save your bowel movements. People don't do that, Rosie. Hiding your bowel movements from everyone then carrying them around in a towel, sitting in the rocker and pretending you have a baby in there makes no sense. It's nasty and dirty. You don't have a baby Rosie—you never had a baby. Why are you doing this?

"It's filthy and dirty to play with your feces, and you have to stop doing this before it makes you sick. Do you want us to have to give you ECT?" She paused a minute hoping her words sunk in and Rosie might be listening. "It's what's going to happen to you, Rosie, mark my words. We're going to be forced to take severe action if you don't stop. I know you understand and can hear me. The doctors don't believe it, but I know otherwise. You understand and hear everything you want to hear."

The nurse got up close to Rosie's face and shook her finger.

"Now you listen to me, Rosie Gradel. If this doesn't stop, it's ECT for you and you know what that's like because I've watched you care for patients in the day room when they've undergone it, and it's no fun. None of us likes cleaning you up with this mess all over your hands and I don't want you to have to go through ECT—so stop doing this!"

A daily chart of Rosie's behavior was posted in the nurse's station, noting that there were no changes. Rosie continued to save each bowel movement, carefully placing it in her cupped hand, wrapping it in a towel as if it were a child, positioning it next to her body, and carrying it around like a real baby. Often times she'd smile and caress it, and upon occasion even kiss it. Other times she'd move her mouth like she was talking to it. Patients would scream and call her crazy, then tell the nurses Rosie smelled like poop, and that's when the staff would investigate and learn Rosie had repeated this undesirable act.

After a reasonable period of time, with no improvement in her condition, doctors decided to schedule a series of electro convulsive shock treatments to stabilize her moods, create memory loss, and disorientate her enough to hopefully eliminate the severe depression that added to this undesirable behavior. The same nurse who'd taken her aside weeks earlier wanted Rosie to understand that the shock treatment was not a punishment but something to help her get well. She was apologetic as she handed her a gown and led her into her office to talk privately.

"The doctors think ECT can help you. It doesn't hurt, and many times it helps patients like you get better. In fact, some get well enough to go home."

Rosie appeared confused, as if in another world. It was apparent to the nurse that Rosie hadn't heard a word. There were times the staff concluded Rosie could understand and hear everything she wanted, yet other times it was a conundrum.

"You're scheduled to receive your first treatment this morning at eleven o'clock in another part of the hospital where you've never been. The doctors and nurses there are very good, and they will take good care of you for me. Just think, you could be better by Christmas, and who knows, maybe even go home to your family."

A nurse and a male attendant from the ECT lab arrived with a wheel chair. The attendant waited at the nurse's station while the nurse retrieved Rosie from the day room.

"Come along, Rosie. You're going to get to relax and take a ride, and we're going to do all the work."

Rosie climbed into the wheelchair, and the three of them disappeared behind several sets of locked doors and down a long covered hallway connecting the two buildings.

***

Rosie completed the series ECT treatments. The regression and severe depression improved, she ate and slept without the aid of medication, and she no longer saved her excrement—clearly positive signs, but still she didn't speak.

For the first time since her arrival at Woodside, Rosie developed a friendship with a woman named Maisy, better known as the boss of the day room.

Maisy's greatest pleasure came from assigning seats to patients in order for her to perform operatic arias. This interesting character was rarely challenged because of her stature, headstrong nature, and aggressive behavior. If a patient refused to sit where they were told, Maisy would yank their hair for not minding. The nurses constantly warned her to stop, but such threats fell on deaf ears.

As the result of being diagnosed as retarded, and dismissed from school for behavioral problems, Maisy's grandmother decided to homeschool her precious granddaughter. The adoring grandmother who raised Maisy couldn't sing worth a hoot, but she played piano and loved opera. Early on, she recognized Maisy's ability to sing, and exposed her to the likes of Puccini, Mozart,

Strauss, and others, until the child mimicked and sung arias on command. Her repertoire was endless. To the day Granny died, she had refuted Maisy's diagnosis.

The loyalty and devotion between Maisy and Rosie confused the entire staff. They were complete opposites. Maisy was three times the size of Rosie, never shut up, and minded everyone's business but her own. Rosie, on the other hand, was miniature in size, never opened her mouth, could care less about anyone's business, but insisted on everyone's cleanliness. The two of them communicated well, and Maisy protected Rosie every minute of her waking day.

Chaos arose on days that ECT was administered because the results affect the patient's entire psyche. Coordination becomes haywire, confusion paramount, and excruciating headaches flare up that oftentimes result in nausea and vomiting. Drool runs freely from patient's mouths, soaking the front of their gowns, creating moisture that often causes rashes to those with sensitive skin. The loss of bodily functions requires constant changes of clothing with repeated showers to cleanse the excrement. In general, these days overwhelm the staff and patience wears thin.

Time and again Rosie could be found assisting the nurses by wiping patient's faces, creating bibs out of towels to catch the drool so the fronts of their gowns would not become soaked to the skin, or holding their hands to quell their fears. Seeing all of this, one could only question whether Rosie's loss was physiological or psychological.

Maisy was an addicted smoker who introduced Rosie to this habit shortly after they met. Every afternoon at one o'clock, Rosie would join her wardmates to hand roll and enjoy a smoke.

The rule of one cigarette per patient prevailed, and the fun began once the attendant lit each one with a match. For those who indulged, this was the highlight of their day. For most patients the cigarette was smoked and savored until the last possible puff, but a few patients like Rosie smoked the paper down until it burned the flesh between the fingers where it was held, leaving black charred calluses. An apparent staff favorite, Rosie was frequently pulled aside and offered extra cigarettes and candies for helping manage patients. Although making friends and caring for patients in need seemed like measurable progress, the staff doctors saw it as negligible at best. They considered another round of ECT, but they ultimately decided to meet with the only family of record before proceeding, in hopes that he might offer some fresh insight into her past history. After numerous attempts, the hospital abandoned these efforts. Because the only visitor of record was the family priest, the staff contacted him.

Father Greiner received the letter. As he opened it, he hoped the hospital was writing to tell him that Rosie was well and that his help was needed to find her a place to live. His mind quickly fantasized about getting a car, putting her in it, and then the two of them would take off for destinations unknown, disappearing for the rest of their lives. He would leave the priesthood and do what he should have done the day he took Rosie to Hawthorne House. This time he had the nerve. The more he read, the more distressed he became. Never did he expect that there was no improvement, no moves forward, nothing. He reread the letter several times over, hoping he might have misread some part of it in haste.

May 17, 1947

Dear Father Greiner,

As you no doubt know, your parishioner Rosie Gradel has been a patient at Woodside since October 12, 1943—nearly four years.

This young woman has been examined and evaluated by audiologists numerous times with inconsistent results. We remain unable to determine why she cannot or will not speak or whether she can or cannot hear. She remains a mystery.

As you may or may not know, her depression is severe. We have no record of how long she has suffered with this problem, nor have we any record of previous treatment. We know nothing about this young woman, and any help you can offer would be greatly appreciated.

We have tried numerous times to contact an Emil Gradel, but to no avail. The doctors need any help they can gather to further treat this patient. Any information regarding his location would be helpful and appreciated. Please contact this office at your earliest convenience.

Thank you,

Cecelia Lewis, R. N., Woodside Hospital

Father Greiner folded the letter and carefully put it back into the envelope. Dismayed by Emil's lack of interest and apparent unwillingness to help his sister, he decided to call Rose Dunnigan. After all, she was Rosie's aunt and knew far more about the family's dark past than he ever learned in a confessional. Besides, what he heard during confessions went no further than his ears, no matter how sick anyone was.

He removed his hand from the dialer, and decided that a face-to-face meeting was in order. What could she do—not let him in? He doubted that would happen, besides he wouldn't let her get away with it, not this time. Someone had to talk to her, and he knew that if he didn't leave right then, he'd postpone the errand indefinitely. This was not a call Father Greiner wanted to make.

It was a bright sunny day and he walked three blocks to the trolley, climbed onboard, bought a transfer token, and headed to Arlington Avenue. He got off the trolley and walked the remaining half block back to Rose's house.

The curtains were all drawn, and the house seemed eerie. There were holes in the bricks where the bronze plaque once hung, advertising to the world and all its passers-by that Emil Gradel, Instructor of the Violin, once taught here. The front yard, with its normally manicured garden, was covered with tall dead weeds that managed to poke and stick through packed leaves left over from fall and winter. Because Rose no longer attended his church and failed to ever call, he had no way of knowing what was going on other than that she clearly wanted to keep her distance.

The large brass knocker on the front door always shined so bright you could see it a block away. Today it was tarnished and ugly, like the rest of the house. He took hold of the knocker and hammered it to the door four times—*rap, rap, rap, rap!*—then waited. No answer. He tried again and again, finally hammering as hard as he could, six times. Surely someone would hear him. A few minutes later he saw the curtain pull back and was greeted by Pat Dunnigan's face looking back at him. It took only seconds before Pat opened the front door.

"Father Greiner, how are you? Come in, come in."

"Pat, when no one answered the first time I knocked, I began to wonder if you and Rose still lived here. How are you?"

"Not so good."

"What's the matter Pat?"

Pat paused, placed his hand on his forehead, and shook his head from side to side.

"It all started when Emil moved out. I always knew those two had something going on between them, but I had no idea what. Those two whispered about everything and shut up when I came round."

"Pat, you don't look well, in fact, you look terrible."

From the day Rose discovered a child named Emil, she transferred every ounce of life and love into him and Pat existed on his own. As Emil grew older and learned the essence of keeping secrets, Rose shared more with him and less with her husband. Pretty soon the distance and hostility between them mounted and Rose pushed him away, hoping he would finally leave, but he never did. Whether Pat stayed out of stubbornness or devotion remained an unanswered question.

After Emil had left, Rose found one reason after another to pick a fight with Pat, always coupled with endless threats of throwing him out of her house, but for some reason she never did follow through. This constant berating, reminding him of how he didn't own so much as one single brick in her house, had turned Pat into a beaten man who was unable to justify Rose's disdain and so turned to drinking so he could sleep without thinking. Afraid of losing his job, he minded his ways, worked hard, and lived for evening to come so he could drink his Irish whiskey and listen to his radio—wondering where on earth he had gone wrong.

"Guess everyone looks like me when they're marking time and waiting for the grim reaper. How about you, Father, how're you doing?"

"I'm waiting for lots of things, but not the grim reaper. Figure he'll find me sooner or later, so I just keep trying to keep one step ahead of him."

"Is Rose around?"

"Sure is. She's up in her room. When I take her meals up to her, I have to leave them at the door and get the hell out of there. She won't let me in."

"Pat, why do you allow this to go on without her seeing a doctor?"

"Father, I don't mean to sound disrespectful, but you don't have any idea how mean she is. She's changed into an ugly mean person, and I'm afraid of her. You wouldn't know she was the same Rose. Hasn't been right since her baby Emil left. She misses that boy so much I think she wants to die."

"Pat, this sounds like the same old game her family played all the time when someone got sick, like they're unwilling to spend the money or something."

"Father, Rose hasn't been out of this house since Emil left. I do all the shopping, all the cooking, take all her meals upstairs because she refuses to come down for anything, and take care of the house. Claims there are too many memories down here and they depress her.

"We no longer share the same bedroom. In fact, I can't even sleep on the same floor as her; my choices are the third floor, where you cook or freeze, or in the damp basement where I've spent my life ever since that boy came into her life. This is crazy, I know, but I can't stand the screaming so I let her have her way. Always did spoil that woman. If I didn't take her food up to her, she wouldn't eat."

Pat started crying, wiping his eyes with his fingers, pressing the inside corners trying to stop the flow of tears. "I love her Father and always will, but she hates me and I don't know what I did wrong. I keep trying to fix things, but nothing works. Every day I wake up and think, maybe today she'll change and the old Rose will come back, but I've come to one conclusion: The only thing to make her better is Emil. Have any ideas how I can get him back here Father?"

"No Pat, I don't. The only idea I have is for you to figure out a way and get Rose to see a doctor, or call one and have him come here."

"Father, I don't mean any disrespect, but you're crazy if you think she will agree to what you suggested. I already told her she needed to see a doctor, that she was sick just like when she found out she couldn't have a baby. You wouldn't believe the filthy words she threw at me, and when she got through doing that she stood at the top of the stairs and hurled dishes, shoes, bottles, and anything else she could get her hands on until the base of the stairs looked like a trash heap."

Pat was embarrassed but resolute; he was determined to tell all and get it off his chest. "This is the ugly part I'm so ashamed of. I was very drunk this one night and could hardly walk. When I bent over to clean up the mess Rose made, I never noticed her standing over me like some possessed thing, and by the time I saw her it was too late. She hit me over the head with an umbrella out of the umbrella stand and knocked me out. Not that that wasn't bad enough, but she beat on me and beat on me until I couldn't go to work for a week. I'm afraid of her Father."

"Somehow, Pat, you have got to get help before she has to be put away like young Rosie."

"What the hell you talking about Father? Put away like Rosie? This is the first time I'm hearing this. Where is young Rosie?"

"She's in Woodside State Hospital."

A deeply religious man, Pat blessed himself and began to cry.

"Please dear God, dear Heavenly Father, please dear Jesus, and all the saints in Heaven, don't let what I've heard be true. Please let this be one of my drunken stupors and let me awaken to find this is not true; please dear Jesus, please."

"I'm afraid it's true, every single word. It's the saddest thing I've ever witnessed. Pat, Rosie's had a complete mental breakdown. I'm here because the hospital contacted me and wants to talk with someone from Rosie's family, hoping to put together missing pieces of a puzzle that might help Rosie get well."

"Father, can I help? I'll do anything for that kid. I always liked her so much more than that brother of hers. What can I do to help? I'll do it. I'll do anything. What do they need—they want money?"

"Evidently there is so much about all of this you don't know because Rose never told you, and it's not my place to be the one to tell you what she hasn't."

"What do the doctors need to know? How she grew up? What she did in that store? What kind of mother that Elsa was? How Rose and Emil hid her away in some house they rented somewhere?"

"Pat, how do you know about all of this?"

"Rose and Emil were crazy. Not the kind of crazy like Rose is now, or the kind of crazy Rosie has where they had to lock her up. My Rose and Emil were a different kind of crazy. Those two always thought I was upstairs on the third floor drunk or down in the cellar passed out, but lots of times I wasn't. I was at the top of the stairs or over the register listening to them sitting on the couch, having these tea parties, her fondling him like her lover and him letting her. It used to make me sick and I'd get drunk because I was ashamed, and too afraid, to do anything about it. I went to communion and confessed what I saw and tried to ignore it, but I just couldn't block it out. I should have said something to Rose, but I was afraid of losing her for good and so I kept all of this to myself."

"I had no idea this was going on."

"That's not all I know, Father. I know about Rosie's baby, too. And the house where she lived."

"Does Rose know you know this?"

"No Father, she has no idea and I'm afraid to tell her because I snuck around and listened to everything she and Emil schemed up. They thought I was drunk and passed out and they'd talk freely. Please don't tell her I know all of this. I should have stopped them but didn't know how. Rosie wasn't my niece and wasn't my business, and Rose would have been the first one to tell me so. I know her better than anyone else in this world and would never want to cross her because I'm afraid of being left alone."

"Pat, would you be willing to go to the hospital and talk to the doctors and visit Rosie?"

"Sure Father, I'd love to see that kid again. You know, she was a smart little cookie, was reading when she was only three years old, always behaved and never bothered anybody. Please let me help her, that would make me feel good inside and maybe God will forgive me for being such a sneaky coward. When can we do this? When can I go see her?"

"I'm not sure, but I'll call and find out then let you know.

"That kid loved sweets, but if my memory serves me, her favorites at our house were Rose's imported chocolates her grandmother sent from Germany. Rose hid them from me, but it didn't matter none because I don't eat sweets. Only one she shared them with, Emil. Thought I didn't know about their little games, but I was on to all of them."

Pat hated the games Rose and Emil played all the time. So to get even, when Rosie came to visit he'd fill her little hand full Rose's favorite sweets by wrapping them up in a piece of paper before passing them off to her. His delight came in watching her bright eyes twinkle as she tucked them away and raced out the door. Pat knew it was wrong to sneak Rosie candy behind her mother's back, but he hated Elsa far more than Rose disliked his two maiden sisters who spent half their life drinking beer and smoking cigarettes while chewing bubble gum.

"I knew it was wrong, but Elsa was so frugal and stingy, only thing she'd buy that kid was a violin. Little Rosie didn't want a violin, she wanted what the rest of the kids wanted—candy and having fun like a kid's supposed to. Now mind you Father, if that kid wanted a violin, it could have any violin in the world. But the kid sure as hell better play that violin after Elsa bought for her, or she'd make the kid eat the guts off the strings. That was one nasty, mean woman who always treated me like I was less than human, and not smart enough or good enough to carry an empty violin case. But I was sure good enough to give her sister a good life and find Hans that job where he ended up owning the store. Never did like that miserable woman." Pat, unlike his wife Rose, lived by the golden rule with everyone but his sister-in-law Elsa. He avoided her at every given opportunity.

"Please don't change your mind and not go to see Rosie. Maybe if you took her some sweets it would remind her of the fun times you two shared, and this in turn would shake out something good and happy and turn her around."

"Would you go with me, Father?"

"Not this time Pat, but I'll find out when would be the best time for you to go; I'll give you a call."

"Father, I asked Rose why Emil left and she refused to talk about it. Told me it was none of my business. Another time I asked her about Rosie and she told me her family business was not my business and told me to keep my nose out of whatever happened with Rosie, but I already knew most everything and wanted to help."

"Pat, all this talk is serving no useful purpose, and because I'm no longer your family priest I have no business here. I came today as a family friend to see if I could help one of my former parishioners, who has no one except a brother and an aunt, and neither one seems willing to help. I've done as much as I can, and the rest is up to you, Rosie's extended family. Thank you for answering the door and talking to me, and for God's sake, please get help for your wife before it is too late."

"Father, I'll do my best."

As the days and months wore on Rose became a total recluse and went to great extremes to keep Pat from coming anywhere near her. What had been their bedroom was hers, and the remaining four bedrooms on this floor were to remain unoccupied and unavailable. Rose informed Pat that this was *her* house and he had to sleep on the first floor, either the sofa or floor itself if the sofa wasn't good enough. The other alternative was an old cot in the basement. Her feelings never changed.

"Take your pick, Pat. This is my house, and you're lucky I let you stay here at all. If it weren't for me and my house, you wouldn't have a pot to pee in. You're nothing but a lazy Irishman. If you don't believe me, take a look at that family of yours who still rent that old wooden shack they were living in the day we met. Were it not for me, you'd be just like the rest of them. When they die, what are they going to leave you? If you can't answer that question, I will tell you what you can count on from them: A cellar full of empty beer bottles and lost receipts from playing the numbers—that's what you'll have."

As evidenced by his daily routine, Pat had stopped living and had begun merely existing the day Emil came into his life and home. When he wasn't at work, he was home drinking alone or sleeping off the last drinks that had ended his day. The house had three bathrooms. One was on the second floor across the hall from

Rose's bedroom, and Pat was forbidden to use it. There was a toilet and sink on the first floor and the same in the basement. The one in the basement barely qualified as a bathroom because it had no place to bathe, except for a small corner sink next to the toilet and crowded inside a small wainscot stall. The original owners were avid gardeners and used the bathroom as a convenience when working in the garden to ensure minimal dirt tracking through the house. This had by now become Pat's bathroom and, because it had no tub, he improvised and bought a three-foot galvanized tub; once a week he carried pails of hot water to the basement and filled it. When he didn't feel like carrying pails of water, he skipped bathing completely or bathed at the Coke-Cola plant where he held a supervisory position. Eventually he took fewer and fewer baths, smelling worse all the time. Rose could always tell when he hadn't bathed in a while, especially after he brought her tray of food and left it in front of her closed door as per her instructions. She had a nose like a bloodhound and could smell the combination of Pat's body odor and stale whiskey, and this would set her off into a rage. She would take the plate full of food he'd left outside her door, go to the top of the open split stairwell, and throw it, sending it crashing to the wood floor below while screaming at the top of her lungs.

"You smell so bad, you've ruined my appetite you swine. How the hell am I supposed to eat this food when it smells like dirty old man? No one could eat this but you, or someone in your stinking family. It's spoiled. You got your smell on it and you eat it, you filthy stinking thing. Stay down there and don't bring me one drop of food until you bathe."

The china dish, covered with food, would invariably have broken, creating additional work for Pat. At one time this would have been the maid's job, but Rose had dismissed her the day Emil left, leaving all her eccentric madness for Pat to tackle. Rose generally went back into the room, waited until Pat had cleaned up the mess, and resumed screaming the minute he finished. These outrageous outbursts were never over—they just went on and on and on, and Pat had no idea how to put an end to them. The obedient husband poured himself a drink, downed it, cleaned up Rose's messes, and waited for the next one. Pretty soon there'd be no more dishes and she'd have to be served in pots, but at least those wouldn't break.

Sometimes as he cleaned up Rose's mess, he would begin to sweat, get a whiff of himself, and decide to take a bath. It was only then that he was able to prepare another meal for Rose and take it to the top of the stairs, walk down the hall, and leave it in front of her locked door. Occasionally he would knock and invariably Rose would blurt out or scream, "You awakened me you stupid fool. Get downstairs where you belong."

Pat distinctly remembered when this hell of living with Rose had begun, and to the best of his recollection it was the day after Emil left and he got home from work and found one of his unopened bottles of whiskey on the table and half empty. For reasons unknown to him she was gone all night, returning the following day with a gash in her head. When he inquired about the injury, she denied she had one, went up to her room, and never came downstairs again. Day after day she established new house rules—some written on paper, others spoken—and Pat honored them. Each time she'd give him one set of instructions, he could be certain the next time there would either be an addition or modification; all the same, he never fussed. It was easier to let her have her way and keep the peace.

Father Greiner provided a contact name and telephone number to the person at Woodside State Hospital responsible for Rosie's case so Pat could set up an appointment, but he never followed through.

October 1947 and life for Rosie Gradel seems to have gone as well as could be expected. The doctors vacillate back and forth as to whether or not she can hear and remain fairly certain that she has possibly had some kind of nerve damage to the inner ear. All testing has ceased. Her lack of participation in speech and failed attempts to cooperate and learn sign language remain among the reasons Rosie remains in the regressive ward of North One. For all intents and purpose, she appears happy, still biting her nails pitifully bad and absolutely addicted to smoking.

The doctors and staff have decided to let her remain where she is for the time being and not upset her routine of caring for patients who seem incapable of caring for themselves. Odors of any kind still remain her primary distraction, and she has no rest until things and people smell fresh and clean. So on any given day, when weather permits, Rosie pushes the windows up as high as they'll go to let the wind blow through.

***

June 1956

To handle the droves of patients wanting to go outside and escape the winter doldrums of confinement and still have their individual needs monitored, the state employs college students for the summer. These extras reduce pressure on the limited staff as well as assist patients in getting involved in outdoor activities.

These fresh new surroundings offer a chance to stimulate appetites, help heal minds, and adjust patient's attitudes. Everyone is encouraged to sign up for the various activities they may be interested in. Of course, many sign up and have no idea what they are signing up for, but when they see others doing this they mimic. Lists grow, but nowhere as fast as the staff, another reason for needing additional enthusiastic college students and therapists who come equipped with fresh ideas and determination to implement them with an abundance of energy and happy faces.

HELP WANTED

Kate O'Leary loved few things more than getting up early to brew a fresh pot of coffee and read the Post-Gazette from front to back before getting ready to head off to her job at Mercy Hospital. Once the pungent aroma of coffee perfumed the house, she'd pour a cup, grab a bear claw out of the bakery bin and put it on a plate, tuck the newspaper under her arm, and head for the living room to plop into her favorite chair.

She read every single article, including obituaries, to see if anyone she knew died, always hoping none among the column of deceased was a patient of hers. While reading the Help Wanted section she discovered an inconspicuous three-line ad. She tore it out and set it aside. It definitely had possibilities. After finishing her coffee and breakfast roll, she readied herself for work.

Meanwhile, across town, a group of five university day students were sitting around discussing final exam schedules when one of them brought up the subject of summer jobs. As soon as the idea was introduced, it became the topic of conversation.

"My dad's a judge," one of them said, "he assures me he'll land me a job filing legal docs at the court house."

"You lucky stiff," another one replied, "I have to beat the sidewalks and find my own job, and when I do, it'll probably be shoveling flour in some spaghetti factory."

"Hey, how'd you like to have my job? I'm going to be babysitting a bunch of spoiled brats at a summer camp in upstate New York all summer, while their parents sit around the pool and sip cocktails."

"Oh my God, I'd rather shovel flour."

The group got silly, throwing out odd jobs friends of theirs worked between semesters, and all of them found plenty to laugh about. Finally the group disbursed, but not before agreeing that a summer job was definitely desirable if you wanted happy parents.

Mary Cait O'Leary always got home before anyone else in the family and generally went right to her room to study, but having taken her final exam she felt justified lounging around and taking it easy.

Mary Cait tried to get home early on days her mother worked the midnight shift so the two of them could have teatime, something they'd done together since she was a child. Motivated by the discussion earlier in the day with her classmates, Mary Cait picked up the newspaper to see if she could find herself a summer job. An industrious and enthusiastic child, she had always found ways to earn spending money, even though her mother and dad preferred she not work.

Ever since Mary Cait began to talk, she insisted on calling her mother "Mama Ed." This name made no sense to anyone in the family, but everyone thought it was funny and, somehow, the name stuck.

The minute Mama Ed walked in the door, Mary Cait greeted her with a big hug and announced that she'd taken her final exam and was ready to hunt down a summer job. That's when her mother informed her about an interesting job opportunity she had torn out of the paper that morning.

"Mama Ed, unless they'd take into consideration those two years of psychology I've had, I'll never qualify for a job in occupational therapy."

"Honey, just wait until they meet you. I'll be willing to bet they hire you on the spot. After all, OT is nothing more than lots of arts and crafts, and you've had plenty of that as an Art and Design major. And who knows, maybe this will give you another career option—you just never know."

Mama Ed went into the kitchen to retrieve the brief three-line ad listing a job description, a phone number, the place of employment, and finally the name of the person to contact. Mama Ed handed it to her daughter who read it and then hesitated. This was not what she had in mind when she thought about a summer job, and she suddenly remembered what one of her friends had said: she'd "rather shovel flour." These same thoughts ran through her head, and shoveling flour began to sound awfully enticing.

"Mama Ed, I don't know about a place like that. Those people are crazy and might even be dangerous."

"I'm sure the dangerous ones are not ones they'd let inexperienced students work with. Trust Mama Ed, I've worked in psych wards and I know. The one's you're referring to are locked up, and you'd never get near them. So think about it, this could be a great challenge and eye-opener for you."

"I'll think about it, but I want to look at other options as well."

"You know how I read the papers, and since Easter vacation this is the first interesting job I've seen. If you hope to get a jump on the out-of-town college kids, I suggest you not wait too long."

"I still have plenty of time. Most of the kids won't be home for at least a couple of weeks."

"Honey, I have a suggestion. Why not call right now and try to get an interview. If you get the job, and decide you don't want to do it, you can always go back to what you did last summer."

The defining moment finally came when Mary Cait's mother reminded her of the job she'd had the previous summer. She despised taking census for the Polk Company, running all over the city, going to unfamiliar neighborhoods everyday, working out in the summer heat… all for what? To make three cents per person for each one she counted in every household who was over twenty-one. *No thanks*, she thought to herself. *Not this summer*.

"OK mama Ed, but I think it would take me a half a day to get there and at least five transfers."

"Young lady, I don't think it will be that bad. I'm sure our local bus service goes right to that hospital."

Mary Cait's mother handed her the want ad and she dialed the number. The operator answered and asked where to direct the call.

"I need extension 107 please."

After a few moments, an answer came from the other end of the line. "Hello, this is Dr. Green."

"My name is Mary Cait O'Leary. I am a student at Carnegie Tech and am calling in reference to the job advertised in this mornings Post-Gazette."

"What is your major, and what are your qualifications?"

"In the fall I will enter my last year as an Art and Design major, and upon graduation I plan to go on to graduate school."

"Do you know anything about occupational therapy, or have you had any psychology classes?"

"Yes, I'm familiar with occupational therapy and have considered it as a possible alternative should I change my career goals for any reason. I've had Psych 1 and 2, received A's in both courses, and am a dean's list student."

"Before we proceed any further, I'd like to meet with you in person to make certain you are the kind of candidate we are looking for."

"When would you like me to come there, Dr. Green?"

"Today at five o'clock." Dr. Green hated the interview process and additional paperwork the state required for the hiring of summer help, but if this candidate worked out it would be her last hire and half her battle would be over. "I'll expect you at five o'clock. When you get to the hospital and enter through the main gate, tell the guard to send you on to East Two, the administration building. It has a circular drive in front and is the only yellow brick building on the hospital grounds. Park anywhere in front, then go in through the main doors and tell the receptionist you're here to see Dr. Green. She'll ring my office and I'll come down and get you."

Mary Cait could hardly believe her ears when she hung up the phone. The first thing she did was to call her father and share the news, then ask if he could come home early to take her to the interview so she could be sure and be there on time.

"My schedule looks fine and I can leave early this afternoon. I'll try to be home around three o'clock so the three of us can talk and maybe practice answering questions you might get asked in that interview. Kiddo, you're something else. How did you find out about this job?"

"Mama Ed found it in the paper this morning. Next thing you know, I called and got an interview."

"Honey, I think you'll get that job. Let me talk to Mama Ed."

Mary Cait handed the phone to her mother and paced the floor. Her emotions ranged from excitement to apprehension.

"Oh John Patrick, I'm so excited. Just think of the exposure she'll get and what she'll learn. Who knows, maybe she'll end up being a doctor after all. Definitely has the brains to do it, and we have the money to see her through the process."

"Spoken like a true mother. I just hope it isn't dangerous and some sick patient doesn't hurt our little girl."

"Did you forget I'm a nurse? Hospitals don't put people in bad situations. I think you're worrying about nothing. Besides, she doesn't even have the job yet."

"Expect me sometime around three. And wifey, be thinking of questions we can throw out there for discussion that the interviewer might ask our girl. See you soon."

Mary Cait read and reread the tiny job description her mother had torn from the paper, making certain she hadn't misread any part of it. *College Students wanted for Summer Work at Woodside State Hospital OT Department. OT majors or art education majors in junior or senior year. No others need apply. Call Dr. Green at Browning 5-2821.*

Satisfied and confident that she was qualified to be applying for this job, she went up to her room and chose a conservative, straight, navy blue cotton skirt with kick pleat in the back, plain white long-sleeve blouse with small pocket sewn over the left breast front, a thin-quarter-inch wide grosgrain ribbon to tie at the neck after the blouse was buttoned, a garter belt, natural colored nylon hose, her favorite comfortable penny loafers, and, to finish it all off, a red cardigan sweater. The more Mary Cait thought about this job the more determined she was to get it. She picked up her rosaries, held them in her hands, knelt down by the side of her bed and prayed.

"Oh please dear Lord—please help me to think before I answer any questions today. Help me to stay calm and collected so that I give the best impression possible to that Dr. Green, whoever she is. Please have her like me and give me this job. You know I'll work hard and be the best person they'll ever find. Please, God, please be by my side and help me through this day. Oh, and thank you for listening. Amen."

The drive from their house to Woodside took about thirty minutes, and the three of them never stopped talking, her parents throwing out every possible question Dr. Green might possibly ask and Mary Cait doing her best to answer them all. When they arrived at the main gate, the guard stopped the car to ask them where they were headed and Mary Cait replied, "To see Dr. Green in East Two." The guard handed her father a pass to display on the windshield dash board, and waved them on through. John O'Leary parked the car. The three of them sat chattering wildly while watching the antics of the patients roaming the hospital grounds. Mary Cait's father had never been to a place like this and watched silently worrying about his daughter's safety. Difficult as it was, he kept opinions to himself. Mary Cait got out of the car, straightened out her skirt, and headed off for her interview.

Confidently walking to the front doors of East Two, she entered the building and disappeared from view. Her parents held hands, prayed silently to themselves, and waited patiently for their precious daughter's results of this her first big interview. No matter what occurred or whatever the outcome, this little family of three stuck together. They were extremely tight knit.

Mary Cait arrived thirty minutes early and waited in the lobby for her appointment. In what seemed like hours upon hours, when it was actually only an hour and fifteen minutes, the interview was over and out of East Two emerged this streak, grinning from ear to ear and talking so fast her parents could barely understand what she was saying.

"I got the job, I got the job. Did you hear me? I got the job. I got it."

Mary Cait jumped up and down and ran around the car acting so silly her parents just sat and took it all in. Their daughter was happy, they were happy, and nothing else mattered.

"Right now I am the luckiest and happiest girl in the world. Thanks to you, Mama Ed, I start June third and can work up until the day before going back to school. Because Tech starts later than most schools, and I'm a commuter who doesn't have to pack up and go off somewhere, I get to stay on and work an extra two weeks. I'm so lucky I got this job."

"Luck had nothing to do with this. You're one smart girl, and we're awfully proud of you."

"Mama Ed, I have so much to tell you. I really think I'm going to like working for Dr. Green. She's a large woman about five feet tall, must weigh three hundred pounds, and is one tough-looking department head. Bet none of those patients ever gives her a hard time because there's no doubt she could pitch them halfway across a room if they did. Also got a tour of the OT rooms and some other places I'll work in. Even got to look in various day rooms to see patients, and they all looked perfectly normal to me. Sure don't look crazy. In fact, I don't understand why they're locked up. Oh, I almost forgot to tell you, they filled the other slot this morning with a girl who goes to school in Kansas City and is an occupational therapy major. Now get this, she's getting credits for doing this as part of an internship program to graduate. If I had waited until tomorrow or later next week that job would have been gone. It's all your doing, Mama Ed. You stayed on me and I got the job because of you."

"No Honey, *you* got the job. All I get credit for is tearing a hole in the want ad section of the paper."

"Mama Ed, I was so excited I forgot to ask how much the job paid."

***

June 3, 1956

While waiting for the bus on the corner of Dormont Avenue and Elmhurst, Mary Cait stood tall in her snow-white uniform with natural colored stockings, admiring her handsome reflection in the storefront window, delighting in how much she resembled her mother.

Her thoughts were interrupted by the sound of screeching brakes. The driver had been barreling along Dormont Avenue, and because Mary Cait stood back from the curb a little too far, he didn't realize she was waiting to be picked up. Had he not spotted her she would have missed this bus. The next one would have made her an hour late for work. Not a good way to start her very first day.

The ride to work passed quickly, and before she realized, the driver announced her stop—right at the entrance gate. Before exiting she thanked him for spotting her and stopping back on Dormont Avenue. She told him he "saved her day."

A letter had come earlier in the week instructing her to report directly to the OT room on the lower level of North One. When she got there she found the door unlocked, the lights off, and the shades pulled down. Mary Cait hated dark rooms, and the first thing she did was turn on the lights and raise the blinds to look around at the various projects being done. This little investigation eliminated all self-doubt. The job would be a piece of cake.

Dr. Green arrived shortly thereafter, as did the other intern, Sue Dunster. Dr. Green took a seat at her desk and welcomed both girls. Introductions were made, and then the doctor stated her objectives and expectations for each of them. This first day, however, would be an introductory learning day, beginning with her boastful educational background of not only holding a doctorate in occupational therapy but also various and sundry associate degrees in everything from anthropology to music. She preferred to be called Miss Green in the presence of patients. The title "Doctor" was confusing for many of them, and "Miss" simplified things. The entire time she lectured the girls on the importance of supporting programs and ideas formulated by the psychiatrists and doctors, she did paperwork and stressed confidentiality in protecting each individual's circumstance. By this time she finished talking and showing the girls the three OT rooms, it was noon. The morning had escaped them, allowing only thirty minutes for lunch.

Today they were guests of Dr. Green in the staff dining room. In the future they were free to eat in this same place or bring lunch from home. After a disappointing plate full of institutional food with everything overcooked and tasting the same, except for the Jell-o, the girls decided that from then on they would brown bag lunch.

Later that afternoon Sue and Mary Cait were given keys to enter and exit various wards they'd have to go through to pick up and deliver patients for OT. The first few days were primarily spent learning the routine—where supplies were kept, what was and wasn't available, what you could and couldn't do, where you could and couldn't go, and in general to know limitations. Both girls were exuberant when they were handed schedules.

The daily routine began with a list of female patient names sent down to OT lab by ward nurses. Some wards allowed patients to volunteer and go to OT, but others were directed by the doctors. It was the intern's job to retrieve specific patients and take them to the OT lab where a group never consisted of more than ten women per two-hour session, five per intern. Progress charts were kept, attitudes rated, participation and completion noted, and remarks detailed.

The schedule varied, but to eliminate confusion patients who came on a Tuesday or a Thursday morning always followed that routine. Those who came on Tuesday and Thursday afternoons did likewise. The Monday and Wednesday morning and afternoon patients followed these same routines. Friday mornings were set aside to complete progress reports for the week. Friday afternoons were available so therapists could work one-on-one with patients who had special handicaps or specific anxieties requiring individual attention.

Weeks went by, and the schedules became second nature. Dr. Green delegated more and more responsibility to the interns, and their lists of willing participants from every ward grew.

Sue drove to work and, when she learned Mary Cait lived within three miles of her house, offered to stop every morning and pick her up along the way. Sue drove and Mary Cait's mother paid for the gas, which was a win–win situation.

One night after dinner, Mary Cait's dad excused himself and went into his office to do paperwork. Mary Cait and her mother loved when he had homework, because it meant they could go into the living room, share a pot of tea, and talk girl talk. Mother and daughter were extremely close and shared everything. There were no secrets.

"Last week I was assigned a patient named Lucy. She is so sweet, but all she wants to do is sit off by herself and pull hairs out of the top of her head. I don't even know how she gets them out because she bites her nails clear down past those little fat cushions at the tops of her fingers and has nothing to grab hold with."

"Bet she never gets hair in her food."

"Oh Mama Ed, you're terrible. If you saw how pathetic she looks you'd feel so sorry for her. All she does is sit real quiet and nervously run the tips of her fingers back and forth over her head with diligence, searching for the first sign of any new hair that's broken through the scalp. Her head is completely smooth on top like Daddy's face after he's shaved. It's so sad, breaks my heart. One of my assignments this summer is to get her interested in doing something with those busy little fingers besides pulling out those stupid little hairs. I chose knitting, and we're working on a baby sweater for her sister's baby. She seems pretty excited."

"What color is this sweater? "

"Blue, plain blue, it's her favorite color."

Mary Cait had noticed a woman on one of the wards who reminded her of an incident dating back to her childhood she'd forgotten. For the remainder of day it was somewhat bothersome, and when she mentioned it to her mother, she brushed it off as one of those silly things kids do. She gave her daughter a goodnight kiss and a quick reminder: "we're Irish through and through and we Irish are tough as nails and don't let dumb little things bother us. It's those dumb little things can drive you nuts." Mama Ed and her daughter could sit and talk all night long, but Mary Cait needed her rest as did her mother—both had early starts in the morning.

Chapter 30

Still Water

Two staff psychiatrists, Drs. Challis and Grey, scheduled a meeting with Dr. Green. They designed a pilot program involving the occupational therapy department, knowing that summer interns were available to enable their implementation of this experimental program. Dr. Green met with the interns. The idea was to start with one patient per intern to get some indication whether or not the program was feasible. Because the daily schedules were full except for Friday afternoon, the doctors discussed working the pilot program into Friday's time frame. Dr. Challis asked to have a meeting with the interns before implementing this new program. If successful, it could become a permanent program at Woodside, and it may even be utilized in other hospitals throughout the state. He explained how it would work. The program would be one on one, aimed at treating a specific problem. For Sue, this program would complete a summer internship requirement and earn her the necessary credits needed to graduate. Mary Cait, on the other hand, needed something to do during this same time slot and the staff decided she was qualified to participate in this same program. This inclusivity of participating in the new program included staff personnel who were instructed to avail themselves and cooperate with helping her wherever and whenever she needed them.

Dr. Challis suggested the interns observe patients on Wards A and B of North One for one week. At the end of that time frame he expected a patient's name and why they were chosen. Case histories were rarely discussed with anyone other than staff members, and depending on whom they chose, he may or may not divulge information or answer questions about that particular patient. Under the guidelines of Dr. Challis's program, he and the intern would set up an individual plan based on that particular patient's needs, and specific goals would be set with patience and perseverance as key elements, under no circumstances did he want the patient pushed.

To sum it all up, the program was based entirely on feasibility. The interns needed a patient choice and an exemplary plan, and lastly, Dr. Challis's approval. If the plan were not credible, he would not validate it. Compatibility between patient and intern was therefore a must, something he would oversee weekly. By the time he'd finished, both interns were thoroughly engaged and ready to participate. They returned to the OT room fully charged and ready to tackle this new challenge.

Dr. Green could see the girls' enthusiasm and asked whether there were any questions. This was Mary Cait's first exposure to mental illness, and she had several uncertainties and reservations that needed clarification. "Did Dr. Challis mean it when he said we could walk into Ward B for instance, and elect to work with anyone, no matter how bad they appeared?"

"That's what I understood when we had our meeting before he spoke to the two of you."

"What if my choice is one of the women sitting on a day room bench rocking back and forth, doing nothing but talking to herself all day long? What if she's the one I want to challenge? Think he'd approve?"

"According to what he said, I'd say yes. But I would hope you'd select someone who shows an interest in your being there. You can't create an interest in whatever you're trying to teach or work through if the patient isn't a willing participant."

The girls left to pick up their four respective patients to participate in the regular afternoon session of OT. Some, like Ellie, would practice using the sewing machine, whereas others, like Bessie and Annabelle worked at the looms from the minute they arrived to the minute they left. Those two could tie Turkish knots and finish rugs faster than the OT girls could re-string looms. They *lived* to make rugs. When they couldn't tie knots, they became obstinate and frustrated. Often patients who just completed ECT would come to OT to sit or do nothing but cut small pieces of yarn required for the knot tiers. Other patients would dig in their heels and refuse to go to OT, claiming all they do there is dumb baby stuff. That's when all the stops were pulled and the patients were told there would be treats served in the "dumb baby room," and suddenly, the resistance was gone and they were ready to go to OT. Once there, it was difficult to get them ready to leave and return to the wards.

The week passed quickly. Time had come for the girls to give Dr. Green the names of the respective patients they'd chosen to work with for the remainder of the summer. Sue went first.

"I've selected a patient from Ward B, a regular Tuesday-Thursday afternoon patient named Marcy Handly. I believe if I gave her individual instruction and attention, she could work the sewing machine extremely well and eventually learn to read and use patterns. I think she's talented, capable, and very smart. I also believe she could complete something for her brother's newborn baby and get beyond those feelings of anger she has towards him. I need to discuss this further with Dr. Challis."

"Sounds to me like you're heading in the right direction Sue, but don't be disappointed if she gets away from you and slips backward about the time you think you've gotten her over the hump. You don't know this, but Marcy went home once before and ended back here after a brief two-month stay with her family. Each time a patient can go home and stay there we consider it a positive step and look forward to the time they go home and never return. I think she's a good candidate, and I'm interested in what Dr. Challis has to say when you meet with him."

It was now Mary Cait's turn.

"I selected a patient from Ward A that I've routinely observed as I go through that ward to pick up my regulars from Ward B."

Nodding her head up and down in a positive fashion, Mary Cait looked directly at Dr. Green and said, "I know which patient I want."

"What's her name—and what if anything, do you know about her?"

"She's never been to OT, and I have no idea who she is or why she's here, but for some reason, I find her curious and interesting. Throughout this past month I smile and try to talk to her, but conversations are always one-sided. I say things like, 'it's a pretty day,' or 'looks like you're working awfully hard.' Lately she's been waiting on the other side of the door as if in anticipation of my arrival, and once I unlock the door, she comes up and touches me. It's a gentle touch and I'm not afraid of her, nor do I ever think she is waiting there to try to get out. It's strange, I know, but I think her reaction to me is a good sign. You've seen her do that, haven't you, Sue?"

"I thought it strange, but then, you talk to everyone and never give up until they talk or smile or say something. A lot of what's happening with her is you, you know."

"I don't agree. I think it's something else. Mama Ed always says, when things happen there's a reason and you accept it as 'a meant to be' kind of thing."

Dr. Green expressed her need for things to be either black or white, and suggested that Mary Cait stop at the nurse's station the next time she went to Ward A and talk to the floor nurses who are with this patient day in and day out, something said might trigger her to change her mind.

"Dr. Green, think the next time I see this patient I can tell her about OT and suggest or offer to take her to see the OT lab?"

"I don't think that's a good idea. Take the normal route, and do as I've instructed. You're nowhere near ready to discuss anything with a patient. I think you're getting ahead of yourself and once you do, it might be impossible to retract your position."

Mary Cait climbed the back stairs leading up to the second floor where the patients from Ward A would be waiting to go to OT and put her key in the lock. As she looked up, she saw two faces looking back at her through the small wire-meshed glass window in the center of the door. Tess and Annabelle's noses were pressed against the glass, and the minute she opened the door they began to push their way out of the ward while arguing about which colors they were going to use to tie knots. It was one of those days when they both decided to use the same colors of yarn, and that generally meant refereeing and breaking up fights for two hours.

Mary Cait ushered the two of them back into the ward and relocked the door. Leaning into the nurse she whispered, "Any excuse you have or can use to keep one of them here would be greatly appreciated. When these two start off fighting, it generally ruins everyone's day."

The nurse laughed at Mary Cait's request.

"These two have been at it since early this morning. Tess is scheduled for ECT tomorrow and this always puts her nerves on edge and makes life miserable for everyone. We had her all morning, now it's your turn." She paused, "Lucky you, you gals in OT only have to put up with her for two hours this afternoon, and we need a break up here."

"Guess we're ready to go then. By the way, where's Thelma today?"

"We have two getting ECT this morning, and Thelma's one of them. She's had some major setbacks and won't be going anywhere for a while. In fact, they're talking about putting her in that new wing of North One. Not good."

"Gee I'm sorry to hear that. While I'm here I would like to inquire about that patient cleaning the floor over there by your office, that tiny little one, what's her name?"

"Her?"

She pointed in the general direction to the woman on her knees scrubbing the floor.

"Oh, that's Rosie! Everyone knows and loves her. She's the sweetest gal on the ward. Never bothers anyone and never gives us a minute's trouble. Don't know what we would do without her."

"Dr. Challis is implementing a new program here at Woodside and he's allowing Sue and me to select any patient we want from any ward we want, to see how well it works."

"Oh yeah? Once a month that guy comes up with some new-fangled idea or the other. Good luck."

"I want to work with her—I want to work with Rosie."

"I don't know how you can work with her, there's nothing to work with. She doesn't talk, she can't hear, and no one knows why. Haven't you ever noticed that she never talks to you, she just smiles?"

"Yes I did, but I thought she was just shy, or quiet, or maybe didn't talk to people she didn't know."

"Boy you got that all wrong, hon. That little sweetheart can't talk. She's been here at least as long as I've been here. Everyone around here knows her as the old timer."

"How long is long?"

"I've been here eleven years and she's been on this ward the whole time I've been here, and I have no idea how long she was here before I came. Could be she's been here longer, you never know unless you look in the records, and none of us can do that. Doesn't matter, they're here and our job is to take care of them. One thing I do know, and that is, that she never has any visitors."

"Are you sure she never has visitors?"

"Positive. Not a soul. All of us on this ward think her family dumped her off like lots of them do, and then they forget they're even here. Sad, but happens a lot you know."

"I'd never do a thing like that to anyone, whether they were a family member or a stranger."

"It's not a nice thing when someone goes off, you know, loses their mind. Sad part is the family denies the person even belongs to them and is ashamed to have anyone know they're here. Unless you're here day after day and see how these poor things push us and push us until they nearly drive us nuts, too, you just don't understand how hard a job this is."

"Guess it's different in OT because we only see them two hours at a time, and that's a lot different from having them from sun up to sun down like all of you deal with on the ward."

"We're forced to fill these poor babies full of pills so they keep quiet and stay out of our hair. Guess we're as bad as their families, but in a different sort of way."

"I can't stop thinking about her family and how they never come see her. Maybe she doesn't have one."

"Hon, like I said, I have no idea, just hear rumors and gossip. One thing we all know, she keeps this place spotless, and keeps these patients spotless, too. She loves taking care of everybody, and I mean everybody. Hon, she doesn't care if they're fat, skinny, tall, short, black, or white, doesn't matter to her. All that matters is that this place and the people in it are clean. If someone comes out of ECT and messes themselves, it's 'Rosie to the rescue.' She babies everyone and gets upset if she can't run things and keep this place in order, so we let her go so long as no one hurts her."

"If she really can't talk, what does she do if and when she gets really upset?"

"She always has her pail ready with clean water in it and rags all neatly folded sitting next to it. No one ever touches those. Maisy's her best friend and guardian angel who loves her to death and you can see by the size of Maisy, no one dares cross her."

"Not only does she protect Rosie, she talks for her, and believe you me, she watches that pail like it was full of gold and doesn't allow anyone to touch it. Every ward has its own kind pecking-order, and in this one Maisy's at the top. I don't know what Rosie would do if anything ever happened to Maisy. Those two belong to each other."

"Does Maisy have any family?"

"Yes, she had a grandmother who raised her, but when she died Maisy ended up here because there was no-one left to care for her but an elderly aunt. Maisy's afraid of the real world and would never make it out there on her own. Like many patients, she feels safe here. She's gone home several times and has always ended up coming back. I suspect she fools her aunt and doesn't take her medication, then bingo—she has a setback and is returned to us. The last time she went home she tried to choke her aunt to death, and now the aunt won't even come see her. It's sad when that happens, but it does. Each time a patient goes home we hope it's for good, but when the brain is sick you never know what will trigger a negative action. But when it happens, they're sent back. It's tragic for everyone when this happens."

"I'm sure it is, but just think how horrible it would be if there wasn't a Woodside? What would happen to all the Maisy's and Rosie's out there? At least here they're safe—they have doctors, nurses, and other staff people to take care of their medical needs, and best of all—they have each other to look after."

"In spite of the fact that she can't talk, we all understand everything she wants."

"Has anyone ever tried to teach her sign language?"

"No, hon, I don't think so. If anyone ever did it was before my time, and obviously it didn't work or she'd use it. She has her own kind of hand-sign method of communicating. Believe me, she makes her self understood. None of us has any trouble getting her message. In fact, one of the rumors I remember hearing when I first came here was that they tested her to see why she couldn't hear, and the doctors could never put their finger on exactly why. I can't believe you think you want to work with our Rosie, but I wish you well, young lady."

"Thanks for telling me all of this. And by the way, what is her diagnosis for being here?"

"Depression, plain ugly depression, complete nervous breakdown."

"That was one of the things I was directed to ask."

"She is a dear soul and everyone loves her, but I doubt you'll get anything out of her. If her best friend Maisy can't get her to talk, I seriously doubt you will."

"How old is she?"

"Don't have any idea, maybe late-thirties early forties? Your guess is as good as mine. It's hard to tell with people her size because they're so tiny, you almost think of them as kids with an older face."

"I have to get going. I'm behind schedule and Dr. Green gets furious when we're late in returning with patients, because it cuts short the time they get to spend in OT.

Mary Cait tried to hurry the patients along through the hallways leading to the OT room, but they moved like a herd of cattle, unwilling to cooperate, preferring to straggle along and look about, or not move at all. Of all the days for patients to be uncooperative, this was not it. She knew a well-deserved lecture was in the pipeline and all because she got carried away yakking.

"Mary Cait you're late, and that's irresponsible. I wanted to get started on time but you have managed to wreck havoc with the schedule and cheat the patients of valuable OT time."

"Dr. Green, I'm terribly sorry this happened. First I had to wait for Annabelle because she didn't want to come make rugs today, then I began talking to the ward nurse about this project you're going to allow me to participate in with a special patient, and lost track of the time. I won't let this happen again."

Mary Cait wondered why Dr. Green never asked about her choice, but was glad she didn't, because there was no way anyone was changing this stubborn little Irish girl's mind. Five minutes to count-down time. The minute her watch hit the twelve, she knocked on the doctor's door.

"Come in. So Miss O'Leary, have you selected a patient with whom you would like to work?"

"Yes sir, I have. The woman's name is Rosie on Ward A. Today when I picked up my regular patients, I spoke to the one of the long-time ward nurses and she told me that Rosie doesn't speak and no one knows why."

"Explain this to me young lady. Why would you knowingly and willingly choose to take on such a challenge?"

"Day after day I go through Ward B to gather my patients for OT and I find it rather curious, if not interesting, to see her standing on tiptoes, barely able to see through the glass in the door in Ward A watching me as I approach. Once inside, I'd look over at her face behind the glass and realize she'd kept a vigilant eye on me the entire time I was lining up the patient's in Ward B who were going to OT. At first I'd smile, give her a little wave, get the group, and go. This made me think of a gang of friends sharing treats—and how sad it is when an onlooker-kid, who is not part of the clique, looks at them with hungry eyes just coveting a taste and the brats tell the loner to get lost. I see her as that onlooker kid, who wants very much to be included, not left out."

"I think you're being melodramatic and reading something into her condition that doesn't exist."

"I'm sorry to disagree with you sir. I've observed her tend and care for patients like she's their mother, and from what I understand, no-one ever does the same for her. It's her turn, and I want to be the person to show her that she has worth. Please Dr. Challis, please let me do this. If I don't accomplish another thing but polishing nails and getting her to stop biting them clear down to the nail bed, then I'll consider myself successful."

"I was of the understanding Dr. Green explained to you what I wanted done, but it's obvious to me you missed something. I'm looking for success in the area of confidence building and independence that enables the patient to leave here permanently. You've already failed by doing what you want rather than what you were told to do."

"Dr. Challis, please allow me to do this."

The doctor realized that Mary Cait's training in the field of occupational therapy was nil and limited to two years of psychology, but he also recognized this intern's intelligence and basic intuitive instincts as keenly polished and decided against better judgment to allow her to go ahead with her selection despite it's being a poor choice with every chance of failure. He'd been at Woodside far longer than he'd originally planned and was very familiar with Rosie's case—it was a true anomaly.

"Young lady, listening to you, I gather you haven't been impulsive in this choice, but have thought and planned your argument well. Better judgment tells me this is going nowhere. I'm no fool. I've been around a long time and recognize when I'm being sold a bill of goods by one hell of a saleswoman, so now you'd better deliver on those goods you've just sold me."

"Thank you Dr. Challis, wait 'til you see what we do."

"Before we go any further, let me do something."

Dr. Challis buzzed his secretary. "Do you need something sir?"

"Yes, Mrs. Grady, call Ward A over in North One, and get me the full name of a patient there named Rosie. After that, have the folks in records deliver her case-file here for me to review."

Dr. Challis wanted to make certain there weren't any recent negative notations on this particular patient that could possibly cause more harm than good, ultimately reflecting badly on him. In the meantime, his discussion with Mary Cait continued.

"Have you any other ideas or plans you hope to carry out with this patient besides playing beauty shop?"

Raised by a strong independent-thinking mother, who encouraged forthright honesty above all else, she spoke from the heart with no exceptions or deletions.

"Are you poking fun at me, Dr. Challis?"

She hesitated and waited for an answer, but the doctor remained silent, knowing this wisecrack remark signaled determination to be heard.

"I don't know exactly what I will do with Rosie, not yet. First we need to get acquainted, then I plan to win her heart, and lastly, I'll earn her trust. From there, who knows, she might even talk for me. What do you think of that Dr. Challis? Is that the kind of goal expectation you are looking for from me?"

"Yours is certainly an unusual approach and not one normally taken here at the hospital. I don't see the harm in what you want to do, but neither do I see that this will bring any change or progress to a patient who can't hear or doesn't talk."

"Can you tell me why she doesn't speak, Dr. Challis?"

"If memory serves me right, I believe she's the one who's never been positively diagnosed or analyzed."

Mrs. Grady returned with the file and handed it to the doctor. He opened the folder to re-familiarize himself with this case. He perused the general information—full name, year and place of birth, names of parents, name and address of older brother who signed papers committing his sister to Woodside. Under the column of visitors, there were no check marks noted in the family column, but three were noted in the "no relation" column. A brief, sloppily handwritten single page of notations had been made, noting that a priest had visited the same day she mysteriously went missing and that hospital officials had tried to locate him. However, the name he left did not exist or belong to any of the local dioceses; there was no such priest. File marked *closed*, no further notations were made until her mysterious return. Hospital officials believed this mysterious priest had everything to do with both her disappearance and her return. She had been found wandering the hospital grounds after she had vanished two years earlier, confused but otherwise healthy, and the case was closed. Because no one had ever heard the patient speak, there was no way of knowing anything additional about her except what was assumed, or presumed. The hospital noted that they'd tried to contact the elusive brother, who for all intent and purpose, evaded all means of communication and requests for meetings to try and help his sister. A collection of unopened hospital letters remained in the case jacket marked *return to sender*.

During this time, Mary Cait waited, silently seemingly lost in her own thoughts. After long minutes of each seemingly lost in their own considerations, the doctor finally looked up at Mary Cait and spoke.

"Looks like our hands have been tied in trying to dissect the probable underlying cause or causes related to Rosie's complete mental breakdown. From the day she arrived we have been powerless with this patient, having no records from a family doctor, and without records we have virtually nothing to go on. We determined that her severe depression was more than likely exacerbated by being poorly medicated or not medicated at all, likely poor diet. Could be any number of reasons, none of which we know anything about. From all I've read, apparently she won't or can't talk and the uncooperative brother refused official forms giving permission to treat his sister's illness. At one point during her stay here there was a problem that endangered her health and the welfare of other patients on the ward, and the hospital proceeded with administering ECT. The problem no longer persists."

"What was this problem she had?"

"I don't care to discuss the particulars at this time, but should cause arise in the future—where necessary, I may be willing to divulge some information not otherwise available to anyone other than family, physicians, and staff." He neatly rearranged the papers inside the folder and pushed it aside, the discussion was over. "Do you still want to work with this patient?"

"Absolutely, I have no second thoughts, and no reservations. As a matter of fact, while you were leafing through her file I came up with my plan and have it all mapped out in my head."

"When a tough old doctor like me can't sway your opinion, I suppose it can't be done.

"I want you to understand why I want to work with Rosie and why it doesn't matter if we play beauty shop. The apparent way she's been dumped here convinces me not to change my mind because I have this unwavering, haunting voice inside me demanding I help this poor soul."

Dr. Challis rarely saw this kind of determination in the staff, and he was positively drawn to her spirit. "The papers needed for keeping accurate records of how and what you plan to do, as well as progress charts I want kept, are on my secretary's desk ready for you to pick up on your way out. Good luck, young lady. Remember, I'll scrutinize your every move to prove my point and why you've chosen the wrong direction. However, nothing would delight me more than if you were to prove me wrong."

"Wait 'til you see how we squeeze six hours into three every Friday afternoon. By summer's end, I'm going to show you the miracle everyone around here says never happens."

Mary Cait stood up and walked around the side of the desk where Dr. Challis sat and reached for his hand. As she did that, he stood up and she firmly took hold and shook it enthusiastically.

"Thank you, sir, for spending your valuable time with me, I truly appreciate it. I'll bet if your name were Rosie Gradel and you were a patient in this hospital, you'd want me working with you. I make things happen."

Mary Cait picked up the stack of papers from the secretary's desk and headed back to the OT room. Her feet barely touched the ground, her mind exploding with ideas and ways to fashion and integrate them into positive changes. One way or the other, Mary Cait had one goal in mind, and that was to improve the life of a woman named Rosie.

An impish smile came across Mary Cait's face knowing Mama Ed would fully approve the way she'd struck her mark and held her ground in refusing to back down from Dr. Challis when he challenged her choice. It's how her take-charge-head-strong mother with a doctorate in nursing got to the top—she believed in making things happen, and taught her daughter well.

In the meantime, Dr. Challis had called Dr. Green and apprised her of the situation regarding Mary Cait and Rosie and how this intern had sold him on the idea of allowing her to work with "one Rosie Gradel" from Ward A. He spoke of Mary Cait's reasons as sound, valid, and not made in haste. As a doctor he knew her reasoning was uncharacteristic and medically invalid, but instinct told him that this young lady was packed with so much electricity she could recharge the dead. He ended their conversation by complimenting Dr. Green on hiring two great interns and remarked how sorry he'd be to see them leave.

***

The days, from July through the second week of September, flew. Both interns completed their respective programs with individual patients, as well as, those they saw daily, receiving accolades from the entire staff.

Drs. Challis and Green studied the graphs, charts, and files the interns maintained on each patient to see whether or not they achieved their respective goals and outlined those areas where they showed weakness or failure. Each intern then had a scheduled review.

Sue's meeting came first and went very well. By knowing from past experience how to select the right patient and formulate a no-fail procedure to follow, she earned the necessary credits to satisfy all of her internship requirements.

It was now Mary Cait's turn to face the man of many doubts. Confused, she went to the administration building as Dr. Green had directed her.

"Dr. Challis, I was told you wanted to see me but I'm not sure why."

"I was certain you would fall short of your goals, but what you managed to achieve is rather remarkable. Young lady, I don't know what career path you will end up on, but one thing I do know, whatever it is—you will be a force to be reckoned with."

"These results you're addressing came from a combination of three—you, my ego, and Rosie. You were the motivational force behind how well I did, because you challenged me by saying 'I made a mistake in choosing Rosie.' My ego proved you wrong, and Rosie fooled us all."

"Is it true she says words?"

"Yes, it is."

"When I read your weekly progress reports and got to the final section where you wrote about her saying words, I questioned Dr. Green, and she assured me Rosie was talking. Tell me how you got her to do this."

"Do you have time right now?"

"Yes I have time. The beginning would be a good place to start."

Mary Cait sat down across the conference table from Dr. Challis and paused briefly before starting. She wanted to give herself time to mentally recount the painstaking planning and preparation done daily to implement the montage of goals she'd set for herself and Rosie. Fully confident she had all her ducks in a row, she was ready to begin.

"Sessions would begin by picking Rosie up promptly, utilizing every precious minute I had with her, and not returning her to the ward until the last possible second. It only took a couple of times before I saw this tremendous change in her behavior. When I arrived she would be waiting by the doors all freshly groomed.

"The night before the day I was to get her for the very first time, I'd gone to the store and purchased two bottles of hand cream, one smelled like lily of the valley, the other like roses. Because her name's Rosie I figured it was worth a try to test and see if she'd associate the smell with her own name or maybe give me some sense about her likes and dislikes.

"I took her to the beauty shop, just as we had discussed. When we got to the OT room I took one look at her fingernails and almost threw up. She had none. What barely remained looked pitifully disgusting. I decided to focus and tackle the crusty black calluses between her fingers.

"Since we had no way of communicating, I opened both bottles to let her smell them, and then I asked her to select the one she liked best. Bingo, you got it. She picked the rose one. I poured some in the palm of her hand, which was as rough as sandpaper, and asked her to rub it into her skin. She chose to do nothing but hold it in the palm of her hand and look at it.

"There's a record player in the OT room, and I thought it might be nice to listen to music while I rubbed lotion into her dry rough hands, but before turning on the record player I asked if she liked music. There was no response.

"I flipped through Dr. Green's assortment of records to make a selection, but in the end I decided to give the choice to Rosie just to see what she would pick. I was astounded to see her pull out a classical recording of Bach, and that's when I became suspicious—could she hear? I didn't get excited or act any differently, I put the record on the turn-table, turned up the volume some-what, and casually continued massaging lotion into her hands. When that side of the recording finished, I flipped it over and played the other side. Whether or not she heard the music doesn't matter, what mattered to me was the fact she chose the recording.

"I waited a few seconds and put some lotion on my own hands, rubbing it into my skin and said, 'Rosie, be sure and rub this in real good.' Again, not sure if she could actually hear or if she was just mimicking me because she followed my instructions, even managing to smile at me a couple of times. You have no idea what that meant to me. I felt right then and there that I had wings on my heels and could fly. I was so excited to have been able to raise her to that level of expression. It was like I got her to talk. I didn't need to hear any words. That's all we did that first day, listen to music and play beauty shop. I talked out loud to myself and massaged each finger with more lotion and kept asking her not to bite her nails. I told her that I would come get her every Friday afternoon. I wrote down on a piece of paper the time and the day, and then I told her I had more treats and surprises for her if she could quit biting those nails. I returned her to the day room and the first session was over—as simple and easy as that!"

As Mary Cait spoke, Dr. Challis occasionally made notations on a pad of paper in front of him. "Please go on. You have my undivided attention for the next hour, and when you're through, I have something I want to tell you."

"The next time I went to get Rosie, the same things happened and in the same order. There she'd be, waiting at the door, all set and ready to go. I'd ask who made her look so pretty, but she never acknowledged me. She knew where we were going and led the way to the OT room where we'd spend the time alone.

"One of those times we spent together, I took out a small bag I'd hidden in the table drawer. In it were two hair barrettes I'd purchased because I saw how annoying the hair was that kept falling in front of her eyes and couldn't stand it. I wondered how anyone tolerated not being able to see, but I figured the ward nurses wouldn't allow her to keep the barrettes, so at the end of our session I removed them and put them back in the drawer for the next time. She never objected and once again I wondered, *Can she hear, or can't she hear? Is she reading my lips? What's going on with this woman?* This woman fidgets constantly. In her seat, out of her seat, stand up, sit down, out of the chair, back in the chair, she practically drove me nuts. At this point we were still trying to establish trust with one another so I let her do what ever she wanted.

"On the third day we spent together she did something unusual and interesting. She walked over to the record player, lifted the lid, and turned it on. It was exactly as she'd seen me do, and I wondered if she imitated or heard.

"I don't know what's going on with her. I wondered if I'd be able to handle what she was beginning to do to my mind, not to mention what she was doing to my nerves on the third day. What damage would she do to me in a month? The Irish side of me said *dig in those heels and don't let her get your goat.*

"Rosie proceeded to select a record, put it on the player, turn it on, then follow through by sitting down as though ready to listen to the music. Again she chose classical music, which I want you to know, is beginning to grow on me.

"I assume by now you've gathered I'm one hundred percent Irish, and I love and know Irish music very well and one of these days I plan to bring in some recordings of it for her to listen to. It's sure a lot happier than that serious and heavy classical music she always selects. Maybe that's what's wrong with her—she's too serious.

"To this day I still don't know whether she heard any of the music or put it on for my benefit because it was what I'd done with her the first session. I do think she's very smart. She definitely wants to please and do the right thing. I'd give anything to get inside that head."

"Do you recall how many sessions the two of you had before you got her to say the first word?"

"It's in the progress report. I think about the end of the third week. I have it right here." Mary Cait immediately reached for the file.

"That isn't necessary right now. I have a copy of your report and can look it up myself later."

"I was now picking Rosie up from the day room regularly, every Friday afternoon, and each time I noticed her nails were slightly longer. Although she was still biting them, there finally appeared to be enough to paint with nail polish. Earlier in the week I'd purchased a light colored polish and put it in the drawer, just waiting for this day. Before starting, I decided to massage her pathetic looking sandpaper hands with the rose-scented lotion. At first those little things were stiff as boards, but as I worked the lotion into them, I could feel the tension leave, and tight hands became limp. It was not melodramatic like you said, and not my imagination, but she definitely relaxed and seemed to revel in all the attention.

"Once I reached this comfort level or trust level, not sure what to call it, I opened a magazine and began flipping through it. We sat quietly. I turned pages and she sat with her hands folded in her lap, fastidiously observing the magazine.

"Periodically I'd take the opportunity to point at pictures and tell her what they contained, just as you would with a small child who's learning to talk. One time I looked at Rosie and felt like I'd seen her before, but I realized she was the face of every patient in the hospital. After a while they all look alike. Adults stuffed inside child-like minds—twisted and gnarled and jammed into grown-up bodies by who knows what and why? I see adult Rosie as a good kind soul residing in a child-like mind.

"I took the small worn-out right hand and placed it on my throat. I thought, if this woman is deaf, maybe she feels vibrations, so I'll let her feel mine as I formed words and leafed through the pages randomly selecting pictures. Coincidentally it happened to be a picture of a baby. While she was looking at the picture I said, *baby*. I looked at her, kept her hand at the base of my throat, and said it again and again. *Baby*, Over and over. *Baby. Baby. Baby.* Then I told her to say it after me, but I used a harsh and direct tone. I said, 'Rosie, say *baby*.'"

"The next thing you know, she said *baby*. It was clear, no stuttering, no hesitancy, the word rolled right off her tongue like she spoke all the time. I'd have to say speaking for her seemed effortless. Dr. Challis, I almost flooded the room. I jumped up, grabbed her by her small shoulders, and began screaming so she and the rest of the world could hear me.

"'You did it. You did it. You talked for me. I heard you and you talked for me!' I have to tell you Dr. Challis, I don't know if she's aware of talking or not. You can't read her." He asked her to proceed, he wanted to hear more.

"After all this happened she showed absolutely no signs of emotion. None, nothing, just a blank dead-pan look as if thinking, *what did you expect me to say when you asked me to say 'baby?'* I tell you, she's as hard to figure out as looking into a lake of still water on a perfectly beautiful day trying to figure out what's beneath the surface."

The question then became whether Rosie *is* aware that she's talking, does she know what she is saying? Or, is she in fact just repeating what she heard Mary Cait say. If she is repeating what she said, did she read her lips, did she hear her voice, did she pick up the vibration in her throat, or—in looking at the picture, did she know what that was and know what to call it? Or can she in fact hear perfectly well?

"What is she all about? In my report I didn't elaborate or tell anyone any of this for fear someone might begin to put her through tests that could upset her, which in turn would cause me to lose her trust. I wanted to take her as far as I could before leaving for the summer. Her vocabulary has grown immeasurably for someone who purportedly can't hear. Furthermore, I know she knows these words because when I point to things, she names them.

"My only fear is what will happen to her once I'm gone. Who will spend the time and care to keep her moving forward?"

The doctor hesitated in giving her the answer to this question knowing full well what he was about to say was not, nor would be, what she wanted to hear.

"Your fear of what will happen when you're gone is a valid concern. There will be no one to carry on what you have begun. Unfortunately, state hospitals have limited resources, which fall under the dictate of minding a budget. Because of these stringent budgets, staff is targeted first. Individual attention, such as the kind you provided Rosie, is impossible to provide. Now if Rosie were in a private mental hospital, you could walk away and know someone would pick up where you left off.

"But here we are required to do our best to help as many patients as possible return to a so-called 'normal' life. Perhaps now you can see why I was concerned about your patient choice—what was and was not realistic. The choice you made needed to have reasonable expectations and not unrealizable goals, which is where I classify Rosie. Because you're leaving her now at summer's end, she will more likely than not revert back to where you started.

"I have some papers I would like you to sign, giving the hospital permission to film you with Rosie before you leave. The hospital staff is interested in what you have done and would also like to take several still photos of you with Rosie for a national publication printed exclusively for state hospitals around the country. There will be a condensed write up from the records you kept of how you were able to get her to cooperate and work with you to regain the use of speech. Would you be agreeable to having this done for us today before you leave?"

"Of course I would. I will be happy to do whatever it is to further help the hospital and Rosie in any way, Dr. Challis. Should I want to return next summer and pursue work with Rosie in the OT department—can I have this job back?"

"If I'm here, I would certainly recommend you, and if Dr. Green is here she'd probably give you a raise to come back. In fact, her comment to me—'that girl belongs in OT.' I want to give you a commendation letter to keep in your résumé file for future use. It has been a pleasure having you run our one-customer beauty shop. I applaud you on a job well done!"

"Thank you for giving me the opportunity to do something special with someone as special as Rosie. We both learned a great deal."

Dr. Challis' phone buzzed. "They're waiting for you in the OT room to take photos and record your achievements. I'll see you down there. The nurse from Rosie's ward will be bringing her down to meet us there as soon as they get her into some new frock they had made for today. Apparently the nurses wanted her to have something new to wear for this special occasion. Whatever they do, I'm sure they'll have her as dollied up as you can make someone dressed in a fancy printed hospital gown."

Mary Cait sprinted down the hall towards the stairs leading to the OT room. Her feet barely touched the ground as she raced down the stairs two at a time. The rush of knowing she'd reached the pinnacle of success in spite of all the "Debbie Downers" who doubted she'd even get to touch the golden ring at the beginning of the summer much less end up with it in her hand when she chose the woman without a voice. Mary Cait and Rosie entered the OT room at about the same time. They exchanged smiles and it appeared as if Rosie knew something was about to happen. Never before was there a bath with pretty perfumed soap, a new dress, hair primped for no reason at all, new shoes that fit—ones that didn't cause her to trip when she walked, and sparkling new white anklets. Mary Cait figured the nurses would have her looking as good as they could with what the hospital issued, but never expected what she saw.

"Rosie, you look absolutely beautiful today. Looks like they opened a new beauty salon up on your ward?" Mary Cait talked all the time, the girl was a walking-talking-talking machine, and when excited, she just talked faster, then for sure, no one could even get a word in edge-wise. "We're about to get some pictures taken together that are going to be printed in a magazine that will get circulated all over the country for other doctors to see and read how great you did. We did it Rosie, you and me! You learned a lot this summer and so did I."

Mary Cait took Rosie by the hand and led her over to a bench on the far side of the room where the two of them then sat down. She gently took Rosie's chin and turned her head so Rosie could see her face when she spoke.

"This is the last time we'll be together. Tomorrow I clean out my desk here in the OT room, and I'll be done with my summer job. On the fifteenth of September I start my last year of college. After that I plan to go on to graduate school."

The photographers were through setting up the equipment and asked Mary Cait to move closer to Rosie so they could begin. "Mary Cait, could you open some magazines and act just as the two of you have done in the past weeks, so we can take these photos and let everyone get back to their routines?"

The photographer didn't like the lighting and Dr. Challis didn't like the position of the two women and asked them to reposition themselves at Dr. Green's desk so that Rosie sat in the chair and Mary Cait leaned over from behind, pointing to the pictures in the magazine. Mary Cait tapped Rosie on the shoulder and urged her to get up and move into the desk chair where she took a standing position behind her. In five minutes the entire session was over. The doctor thanked everyone and the attendant was ready to take Rosie back to the ward, but before she left Mary Cait promised her she'd come by the following day to say goodbye, and she reminded Rosie not to mess up her pretty nails by biting them.

The nurse and Rosie headed back to the day room, the hospital photographer went to the lab to develop the photos, Dr. Challis returned to his office for a staff meeting. Dr. Green rearranged the OT room and got ready for fall sessions without the two interns. Mary Cait, all alone now, began the departure process. Tomorrow she would box up her personal effects in the top drawer of the temporary desk she'd been assigned, and then she would go to the main office to sign out and turn in all keys before picking up her last paycheck. It turned out to be a great summer job and she looked forward to her senior year, but the question remained: What did she want to do the rest of her life?

The pride and satisfaction in what she'd done to make a difference in one person's world raised Mary Cait's ego to new heights. Wow, life was wonderful! The next day was not considered a workday, but a day specifically set aside for summer help to return all hospital property and formally check out.

Mary Cait remembered telling Rosie she would come to say good-bye, and she knew full well, that Rosie would be waiting with baited breath. When she walked down the hall leading to Wards A and B that same head bobbed up and down, it could be none other than Rosie's. In Mary Cait's pocket were two bottles of hand lotion she'd bought to give Rosie, which were identical to the kinds they'd used at various sessions throughout the summer. Mary Cait unlocked the door to Ward A, and she found herself greeted by Rosie and the ward nurse. The first thing she did was hand the lotion to Rosie in front of the nurse.

"Rosie, I thought you might like to have these as a reminder of all our fun times in OT. Maybe you can use them after you get your work done everyday and remind yourself not to chew those nails. Hopefully, it will last for a while and help keep your hands nice and soft. I'll give them to the nurse and I know she'll give you a little everyday until it's all gone. I'll try to come back and see you some time, but can't promise when because I don't know what my schedule will be like this year. But if I get a chance, I will come see you."

The nurse let Rosie hold the two bottles, and she stood there clutching them in her small hands staring at Mary Cait as if unable to believe she, too, was leaving her behind. Mary Cait leaned over and hugged Rosie. "Please don't be sad today, and try not to forget all the things we did together. You hear me? I'll keep you in my prayers, Rosie, and thanks for being a great student and for working so hard for me. You're a smart lady, and you've made my summer a real pleasure."

Mary Cait turned around and started to walk out the door when suddenly she felt a frantic tugging and pulling on her skirt. At first she thought she'd gotten the edge of her uniform skirt caught in the door as she was walking out, but it was Rosie and she was practically pulling her skirt off by hanging on.

"Rosie, please let go of my skirt. I have to go. I can't stay any longer. I have to be on the corner in fifteen minutes to catch the bus, and buses don't wait for anyone."

Rosie began pulling Mary Cait towards the nurse's station and wouldn't stop. This seemingly irrational behavior confused Mary Cait, but she knew that Rosie had something in mind that was obviously important, and had no choice but to follow her.

Rosie knocked on the glass at the front of the nurse's station and the nurse on duty opened the door.

"What's the matter dear? What's wrong? What do you want?"

Rosie pointed to the locked metal drawer in the nurse's office and motioned for her to open it. The nurse obliged and opened the drawer. In the drawer was a long white envelope with Rosie's name on it. The nurse said, "Rosie, I'll give you the envelope after you give me those two bottles of lotion you're refusing to give up. We'll keep them safe in here for you and you can have some for your hands anytime you want. You know you can't have anything like that on the ward. Someone might drink it and get sick."

That said, Rosie handed the nurse the lotion bottles, "That's our girl, thank you Rosie. Now, why do you want your envelope?" Rosie kept pointing at Mary Cait.

The nurse attendant, who was very fond of Rosie and generally understood anything she wanted, hesitated at first, but eventually she got the envelope and handed it to Rosie.

"You know you can't take that envelope on the ward Rosie, you can only look at it in the office with one of us present. You want to show it to Mary Cait before she leaves, is that it? Is that what you want to do?"

Rosie grabbed Mary Cait's hand and placed the envelope in it, firmly closing her fingers around it as if making sure that Mary Cait held onto it tightly and wouldn't drop it. The nurse watched Mary Cait's reaction to Rosie's placing this in her hand while pushing her towards the door, as if wanting her to go.

"Rosie, I can't take this, whatever it is, it's yours. It has your name on the envelope and it belongs to you. I don't want to take something that's yours. You keep it. I have all kinds of treasures at home. You keep this so that when you leave here someday you'll have something to take with you. It's so sweet of you, wanting to give me something, but you already did that in the OT room, a bazillion times over. Please don't give this to me."

Despite Mary Cait's refusal Rosie would not relent, she kept pushing Mary Cait, until finally Maisy saw what was going on and came over to help her friend give Mary Cait the final shove out the door. The nurse attendant followed them to the doors used to enter and exit the dayroom, but Maisy blocked the nurse's intervention. Mary Cait tried to speak, but Rosie put her hand over her mouth and stunned everyone standing nearby. That's when the attendant spoke up. "I think you best take the envelope like she wants you to, and leave. I have never seen her act like this in all the years I've worked here. I have every reason to believe she knows what she's doing, and obviously it's important enough or she wouldn't keep this up. There is no doubt she wants you to have it. This is her only possession besides a bible we keep here in the office she comes to read every once in a while. It's obvious to all of us, she wants you to have this, so please accept it and make her happy."

The entire time the nurse attendant spoke Rosie shook her head up and down and smiled, and Maisy applauded until another nurse stepped in and told her to stop so she could talk to Mary Cait.

"The treasure inside this envelope, as you might call this, can be an excuse for you to come back and see her. No one ever comes to see her, and maybe that's what she hopes you'll do if you take this with you. She is a complex puzzle and we know not what she thinks or wants, so let's make her happy and you accept her gift. You've given her more time, attention, and love than anyone has since the day she came here." Here the nurse paused to consider what she's just said. "Well that isn't entirely true. Maisy loves her like she's her own child. Take the envelope, and keep it safe for her. I know this will make her happy if you do."

Mary Cait lifted the flap of the previously opened envelope and quickly glanced inside. "Rosie, thank you from the bottom of my heart for the best present anyone ever gave me—their one worldly possession. No one has ever made such a sacrifice for me and you can bet I will protect this gift like Maisy protects you, and I will keep you in my heart and always in my prayers. Don't worry Rosie—I'll be back. I could never forget anyone as loving and kind as you."

Mary Cait turned away and walked toward the locked double doors, unlocked them, and as soon as she got on the other side, she heard the automatic door lock click, imprisoning every patient behind them, just as they were eternally trapped and locked inside their heads. Halfway down the corridor Mary Cait turned around to look back and see whether her friends were still there. Her eyes filled with tears as she tried to distinguish the three faces fixed behind the meshed glass staring at her. There they were, the three of them—the nurse, Rosie, and Maisy, silently waiting for Mary Cait to exit their world and return to her own.

Mary Cait approached the final door leading to the first floor, inserted her key, and unlocked the double locks for the final time. Once on the other side, she heard them automatically click and relock.

Back inside, the nurse put her arms around Rosie and Maisy and led them back into the day-room, towards the windows where they'd hoped to get one last glimpse of Mary Cait. The three of them stood at the window for some time before the nurse said, "You girls have to excuse me, I have important work to do and medicines to get ready or none of you will get them this afternoon, and we can't let that happen."

After a few minutes Rosie followed the nurse back into the office and pointed to the lotion, motioning the need to have some on her hands. The nurse obliged, squeezing several drops onto each of Rosie's hands before rubbing them together and putting them up to her nose so Rosie could inhale the perfume. The nurse delighted in seeing Rosie so happy over something as simple as sniffing her pretty lotion.

"You'd better not use that all up today or you won't have any left and you'll be sorry. I know you like it, but let's take it easy with the lotion, honey."

It was as though Rosie understood what had taken place that afternoon, but no one could ever be certain but Rosie, and she wasn't talking.

Chapter 31

Sealed Envelopes

It was ten-thirty and Mary Cait was home alone, studying for an exam. She hated nights like these when Mama Ed worked late and the family didn't have dinner together..

John Thomas was a devoted husband and father, who also hated it when his wife worked the late shift and ceaselessly nagged her to quit, but she loved nursing and wanted no part of giving it up just to stay home all day long doing nothing but wait for him to get home.

The routine at the O'Leary household never changed. Those nights John Thomas's wife worked late, he'd pick her up so she wouldn't have to ride the trolley, and they were always home by eight thirty. It was now well past ten-thirty and there was no sign of them. Mary Cait was so entrenched in her studies that she had lost track of the time. When she realized how late it was, she immediately began to worry.

Earlier in the evening an unexpected early March snowstorm had blown through and the weathermen were calling for more snow before midnight. Mary Cait assured herself that her parents would be along shortly, assuming they must have stopped off at Finnegan's Café so Mama Ed could have a bowl of "the best Irish stew in town." They did this frequently on cold nights when Kate worked late.

The only muddling thought she couldn't shake was the one reminding her that they didn't call and tell her their plans. She tried to console herself with every possible explanation, finally settling on the fact they were afraid she might be asleep. Even though she reminded herself time and again that her parents were fine, none of this malarkey worked. Finally, the phone rang. Mary Cait's timid "hello?" was answered by an unfamiliar voice.

"Are you Mary Cait O'Leary?"

"Yes I am. Who's this?"

"This is Mercy Hospital. Your mother and father were in an accident. Is there any way that you can get here as quickly as possible?"

"Where, what, who are you? This must be some kind of mistake."

"No, miss, this is not a mistake. Is your name Mary Cait?"

"Yes, I'm her."

"Then you are who we want, and you must get here right away."

Mary Cait hung up the phone and frantically ran from room to room screaming for her mother and father as if hoping one of them would answer. She ran outside looking for their car as if hoping to see them standing in front of the house. Surely this was all a mistake. From there she ran screaming to the neighbor's house, pounding on their front door and screaming at the top of her lungs until she managed to awaken them.

"Help me please, someone help me please." The porch light went on and the neighbor apprehensively opened the front door.

"Mary Cait, what is this all about? Is something wrong?"

"It's Mama Ed and Daddy. Mercy Hospital just called. They've been in accident and they said I have to get there as soon as possible. Can you take me there, Mr. Beck? Please! Please take me to them. I have to get there. I have to see them!

"Of course I will. Come inside, you'll freeze out there in the cold and catch your death of pneumonia without a coat on in this kind of weather." Mr. Beck reached for his coat, which was hanging on a hall tree next to the front door. "Here, put my coat around you and keep warm until I get dressed."

"Mr. Beck, please hurry. You don't even have to get dressed. Just take me to the hospital right away and drop me off."

By now Mrs. Beck had heard the commotion and had rushed downstairs to see whether she could offer any consolation while her husband was dressing. She saw Mary Cait standing by the front door with her husband's coat wrapped around her, looking pale as a ghost. She had heard the entire conversation and was without words, afraid of what the outcome could be, and remained silent, waiting for her husband to return dressed and ready to take Mary Cait to the hospital.

"Mother, do want to come along with us?"

"No Dear, I think it better if I stay here, less confusion that way. Mary Cait, rather than run home for your coat, wear mine and give Mr. Beck his. It'll save you some time not running back home. You two get going. And be careful, looks like everything's freezing up out there. I'll pray everything is alright."

They rushed to the hospital in what seemed like one of the worst snowstorms of the winter, at times moving along at a snail's pace. Both were visibly shaken, not knowing what awaited them at the hospital. Mr. Beck dropped Mary Cait off in front of the hospital emergency room doors and went to park the car.

Once inside, Mary Cait raced to the front desk and gave her name to the person sitting behind it, and was told to take a seat while the receptionist notified the emergency room. Within minutes a nurse appeared at the desk then walked over to Mary Cait. "I understand you are Mary Cait O' Leary."

"Yes, I am."

"Please come with me."

As the two of them walked to the emergency room, the nurse explained that her parents had been in an accident while driving over Mt. Washington. She informed Mary Cait that her father had died instantly at the site and that her mother, now lying still and silent in the bed as they approached, had clung to life, uttering nothing but Mary Cait's name.

Mary Cait stood looking at her mother in total dismay, unable to comprehend how such a dreadful thing could have happened from something as pretty and soft as snow. "Why did this happen to you? You're such a good person. You've dedicated your life to caring for the sick and you were such a good mother to me, Mama Ed. And you were such a loving wife to Daddy. Please don't die and leave me all alone. Please Mama Ed, please don't die and go with Daddy. He'll be alright without you. Stay here with me and love me and take care of me. I'm your little girl and I need you."

Her mother never opened her eyes, but she managed to open her mouth as if wanting to say something. But no words came—she took one deep gasp, and then she was gone. Mary Cait sat immobile, unable to call for the nurse. Her request for Mama Ed to stay had been denied.

One of the nurses, who had known her mother and worked with her, remained in the background to give Mary Cait all the time she needed to say good-bye. Mary Cait remained at her mother's side, holding her hand for nearly two hours, sometimes stroking her face, all the while sobbing and refusing to leave. Finally the nurse convinced her it was time to go home. A devastated Mary Cait stood up, and when she turned around, Mr.

Beck was waiting by the door to take her home. Neither one said a word the entire drive home.

Mr. Beck had called his wife earlier to inform her of the circumstances and suggested she call Kate's sister Aine, explain what happened, and have her there when they arrived so Mary Cait wouldn't be left alone in the house.

When they got home, Mary Cait's Aunt Aine and her husband were waiting inside the house, and they remained by her side until after the funeral. They even tried to get her to spend a brief time living with them, but Mary Cait refused.

The devastating blow of losing both parents, made concentration impossible, and Mary Cait decided not to try and complete the term. Weeks went by before Mrs. Beck decided to give her a visit.

A soft-spoken, gentle woman, who never had any children of her own, but had surrounded herself with them through teaching, decided Mary Cait's suffering and mourning had gone on long enough. She looked like something out of a children's fairy tale as she approached Mary Cait's house carrying a small basket of fruit, freshly baked cookies, and an assortment of teas.

The two of them sat in the kitchen and discussed whether or not Mary Cait had taken care of her mother and father's personal effects and whether or not she needed any help. It was then that Mary Cait admitted to suffering from serious bouts of depression that had left her unable to eat, and interrupted her sleep throughout the night. The two of them continued to talk through the afternoon, and before Mrs. Beck left, she had convinced Mary Cait to see their family doctor and get some medication to help get through these difficult times.

"Thank you for forcing this issue today, Mrs. Beck, and thank you for not interfering earlier. I wasn't ready then, but now I think I am. I truly appreciate the time and space you've given me, and I apologize for never properly thanking you and Mr. Beck for all you did that night. I hope you know how much I appreciate everything you and your husband have done for me."

"Of course we knew then and we still do. You take good care of yourself, and if you change your mind, or if you need anything, you come get us. We're right next door."

Right after Mrs. Beck left, Mary Cait phoned her family physician and went to see him. He gave her a brief physical, then sat and talked to her for an hour, which helped a great deal. Before prescribing a mild sedative to ease anxieties and help her sleep through the night, he emphasized the importance of eating properly, and getting plenty of rest, and he scheduled a follow-up appointment in a month to check her progress to make sure she did everything she was supposed to. On the way home she refused to think anything other than accepting what happened to her parents as an unfortunate accident.

After she left the doctor's office she thought more about what he had said, and promised herself that when she unlocked the front door, things would be different. It was no longer Mama Ed's and Daddy's house, it was now her home.

***

Only months before, Mary Cait had watched nurses force patients to take pills to calm them down, help them sleep, and behave, and now she held a glass of water in her hand and was getting ready to take a similar kind of pill to steady a confused mind and a bad case of jittery nerves. She waited anxiously for its effect, but she knew that it wasn't a knock-you-over-the-head one like she anticipated. Instead, it actually did nothing at all, at least nothing she could definitively put her finger on. She did think she felt less anxious, but she credited that to the lecture the doctor had given her and the talking-to she had given herself.

Whatever it was, it was the best she'd felt since the death of her parents, but nothing prepared her for entering their room or, for that matter, even opening the door. Their room was off limits, and for the time being it didn't matter whether anyone ever went in there. The important things were the two of them, and they were gone. So be it.

Mary Cait went to bed and slept through most of the night for the first time since her parents died. The following day, she awakened and decided not to miss taking the pills as per doctor's orders and held to the prescribed schedule. For the first time since the night her parents were killed she allowed herself to think and say aloud, *they're dead*, and *they were killed in an unfortunate ugly accident*. With the help of medication, the improvements to her whole psyche became significantly noticeable with each passing day.

A lawyer from Mahoney and Shaw called demanding she stop postponing and canceling appointments and get into their office as soon as possible to review her parent's last will and testament so he could file the necessary papers the law requires when someone dies.

Mr. Mahoney wanted her to come first thing the following day, with no excuse short of death.

"Is nine o'clock tomorrow morning a good time for you?"

"I'll be there."

"In case you didn't remember, our offices are still where they've been for the last twenty-six years, 2708 Larchmont Boulevard, second floor."

"I told you, I'll be there. Is there anything I'm supposed to bring with me?"

"No. Everything you'll need to sign is here. Your parents have always kept their affairs in order. All we need tomorrow is for you to be here. Shouldn't take long, and we'll manage to have you out of here in no time."

"Thank you, I'll see you in the morning at nine o'clock."

The next morning, Mary Cait scurried about selecting the right outfit. This was an important meeting and she wanted everything about it to be in order. If she was to conduct adult affairs and be responsible, she wanted to look the part and accept whatever came her way this day.

She arrived at the law offices fifteen minutes early. The outer office was empty and she tried to read a magazine, but she couldn't concentrate for wondering why her parents never discussed personal affairs and what she should do in the event something like this should occur. The idea of moving out of the house upset her when she thought about the memories there, but the difficulty of not being able to face going near her parent's room, made the threat of being forced to move out of the house more palatable and easier.

Life was simple. There was no boyfriend, no one to worry about except herself. The thought of living with anyone was out of the question, especially her aunt and uncle. It was fine for the summer, but after two weeks, staying with them got old, because they smothered her more than her parents, and she hated that. The other thought racing through her mind was whether money had been set aside so she could finish graduate school. Mary Cait was so deep in thought she never saw the secretary enter the outer office.

"Mary Cait, Mr. Mahoney is ready to see you."

The secretary opened the door to a large formal-looking conference room where Mr. Mahoney appeared to be organizing several stacks of papers. He stood briefly, introduced himself, and instructed her to sit to his right. Being blind in his left eye made him sensitive to the placement of people, but by putting them to his right he could see when they did and did not understand him.

Mr. Mahoney was all business, and there was no time for small talk. Mary Cait didn't care for him and wondered why her parents had chosen him as their attorney.

"I have papers you need to sign, young lady. Hopefully, everything can be finalized today so you can begin to reconstruct your life. These first documents will legally transfer ownership of the house and its contents to you. Sign on the bottom line and put today's date under it."

Mary Cait felt extremely uncomfortable with him, especially with his unwillingness to look at her. When she finished signing, he took the papers and turned them upside down, forming two separate piles.

"Your parents routinely purchased savings bonds, which they preferred to keep here. This document individually lists each bond with date of purchase. Bottom line gives both total number of bonds and total value. The manila envelope contains the physical bonds. The attached sheet acknowledges that you have received everything and that you are satisfied everything is in good order. Don't rush to sign and date anything without fully understanding what it is you are putting your signature to."

He advised her of the negotiability of saving bonds and the importance of keeping them in a safe place. There were three substantial savings accounts requiring new bankcard signatures naming her as the account holder. Her eyes nearly popped out of her head when reading the amounts.

There was a stack of stock certificates with hundreds of shares in corporations like Koppers, General Electric, Bethlehem Steel, Westinghouse Corporation, Zenith, Standard Oil, and AT&T, all transferred to her name. Burial and hospital expenses were paid out of a large insurance policy. The balance was given to Mary Cait in the form of a check. Documents flew back and forth with no semblance of order, and she signed with no semblance of thought. Mr. Mahoney knew exactly what was going on to his right, and the reason her parents hired him, he was a detail man.

"I almost forgot this last remaining piece of personal business for which you will not have to sign. When I first became your parent's attorney, I was given this envelope for safekeeping along with specific instructions and what was to be done with it should you out-live them. Should you have pre-ceded either of them in death, the envelope and contents were to be destroyed. The signing of these papers today fulfills their wishes as stated in their will. Please sign this last document that you fully understand everything you've signed here today, and you can be on your way. In life they lived everyday for you. In death they've done the same by leaving you financially independent. Hopefully, you will move forward. That's what they wanted."

"Thank you Mr. Mahoney. I will try. I want to be everything they would expect me to be. I bear their name and will try to live up to it just like the two of them did."

It was ten thirty. In less than an hour and a half, a lifetime of work was disposed of with simple signatures and the day's date. The bounty of those years now belonged to someone else. It was just that simple.

Mary Cait left the office overwhelmed. She was proud of how well her parents handled their affairs, even in death, still taking care of their little girl. How fortunate she was to have had them as parents.

Each step up the stairs to the front porch reminded her that the house and everything in it were now her responsibility. She thought about her parents and the three of them as a family, and how one snowy night took it all that away. Just like that—all gone. She unlocked the front door, set the stack of papers Mr. Mahoney had given her on the arm of the sofa, and took off her jacket.

Today, she thought, I'll get Mama Ed's favorite cup, sit down in her favorite chair, and we'll have tea together. She selected her mother's favorite bone china cup with gold-tipped rim and little green Irish four-leaf clovers all over. Daddy had bought it as a birthday present years before Mary Cait was born, and it was by far Mama Ed's favorite cup.

After boiling water, she poured it into the teapot and let it steep a few minutes before pouring a cup and retreating to the living room where she planned a chat with Mama Ed to reminisce about all the fun times they shared.

There were pictures everywhere of the three of them, from the day they brought Mary Cait home from the hospital to the most recent one taken this past Christmas. It would be the last picture of them together as a family. In time, this photo too would fade in color and memory. Her eyes filled with happy tears holding it.

After finishing her second cup of tea, she took Mama Ed's cup into the kitchen and carefully hand-washed it, dried it off, and placed it back in the china cupboard where her mother kept it. After hanging up her jacket she went up to her room and changed into her robe and pajamas. The house seemed chilly and she turned up the thermostat, which was directly above the stack of papers Mr. Mahoney had handed her as she was leaving his office. There were so many papers to sign it was disconcerting and overwhelming, and when she thought about things he'd said, she couldn't remember a thing but "sign here."

With nothing planned for the rest of the day, she decided it might be a good idea to review what she'd signed in the event any questions needed addressed with Mr. Mahoney before it got, too late, to do anything about it.

Opening one of the large brown manila envelopes, she removed the stack of papers, and because it was early and she had the entire day to read what she considered boring papers she started with the one on top—their last will and testament. She quickly put it down. The language made no sense, and she was happy for people like Mr. Mahoney who could decipher this legalese, explaining to her what it meant in words she could understand, like "sign here."

Basically familiar with the pile of papers signed earlier, her eyes drifted to the sealed envelope he had given her last. Did she understand him correctly, something about a sealed envelope? Looking through the stack she thought she remembered something about a smaller envelope inside a larger one and something about securely sealed. She went back through the pile and found the large sealed envelope with nothing written on the front of it and opened it.

Inside was an assortment of loose-leaf papers and one white letter sized envelope that appeared to have never been opened. What was all of this about? The first paper she removed had a heading sprawled across the top in dark fancy print which read *Notification of Birth Registration*. Directly above that in broad plain letters kept within an ornate ribbon border, *THE UNITED STATES OF AMERICA*. Whose birth certificate was this any way? Convinced it must have belonged to one of her parents, she read on. *Department of Commerce. Bureau of the Census of Washington. This certifies that the following Record of Birth is Registered and preserved in the office of the State Registrar of Vital Statistics at Harrisburg, Pennsylvania.* All this was very interesting because she had never seen a birth certificate before. Name—The space had been blank but was filled in longhand with the name, Mary Cait O'Leary. Date of Birth, blank again but filled in with, August 14, 1935. Place of birth, Pittsburgh, Pennsylvania. The next line read *Name of Father*. The long blank line had had something written at the head of it, but someone scratched out what was written and put in the name, John Thomas O'Leary. The last line read *Maiden Name of Mother*. There again someone had blotched out with scribbling the birth mother's name and filled in the name Kate Muldoon. This was a birth certificate, but instead of belonging to one of her parents as she had thought, it belonged to her. Confused by all of this, Mary Cait began to scramble through the remainder of papers in this mysterious envelope.

There was more. Adoption papers all appearing to be legally documented and signed by Kate Muldoon O'Leary and John Thomas O'Leary. The signatures were authentic and those once belonging to her parents. They were unmistakably recognizable. *Mama Ed wasn't her real mother. She was her adopted mother*. The formal-looking legal adoption papers that had been neatly signed and filed with the Commonwealth of Pennsylvania explained why all the secrecy and confirmed that she was in fact adopted. Scrutinizing the birth certificate to see whether she could decipher anything under the deliberate scribbling someone had done as an afterthought, she read the word *none*. Handwritten in its stead was her father's name. She tried to read the name under the scratched and scribbled lines covering the woman's name as originally written and, it too, was obliterated and impossible to make out, even with the use of a magnifying glass.

Not this, not anything could ever change her love and devotion to them, but why did they keep this secret so guarded? In an unemotional moment she thought they might be ashamed of who she was, a bastard child, and wondered if in their hearts they believed they could keep this secret indefinitely.

If they believed that, they must have believed they could change who Mary Cait was. For a split second or two she felt it obviously bothered them she wasn't part of them, just part of their lives. After all, she wasn't born *to* them, but born to be *with* them. That wasn't enough. They pretended she was theirs until it became real to them, where in reality she was the product of another love. A love validated by conception and birth.

Mary Cait couldn't help wonder why her parents were so threatened and afraid of a mother they didn't know, or wouldn't even recognize if they bumped into her. She felt sorry for them. She picked up the last remaining oversized envelope on the sofa cushion and decided to open it to see what other secrets had been kept from her.

Inside was a plain white envelope with something inside. It appeared sealed and written in the lower right hand corner were three words. Three words that meant nothing to her, *Mein Liebes Kind*. After opening the envelope, she discovered a letter written in perfectly meticulous and minuscule penmanship.

It began—

> *Good-bye, dear child.*
>
> *For nine months you were mine, and through my flesh I touched your soul and shared my deepest love.*
>
> *In birth I gave you life, and in giving you away, am giving you life again.*
>
> *I want you to know I am alone and unable to give you what you deserve, and if I had any other choice, I would not be giving you away.*
>
> *With our parting I want you to have half of the only possession I own, these rosaries. The stones are Alexandrite's and each one was carefully selected by my maternal great-grandmother in Germany, and given to me when I was confirmed. I've been told there are no others like these except for those belonging to the women in my family. Your great-grandmother's name is engraved on the back of the crucifix along with her date of birth, and I believe this rightfully belongs to you.*
>
> *I am keeping the other half to pray the rest of your mortal life is blessed with love and faith in almighty God. Remember to hold Him in your heart as I will always hold a place for you in mine. You will always be my child first, the child of your new family second, and a child of God's forever."*

As she read these final words, time seemed to stop entirely. Beads in hand, Mary Cait frantically raced up the stairs, as if racing against time to get to the dresser before it disappeared. Tears poured from her eyes and virtually created one huge visual blur, but that didn't stop her from finding the other half of rosaries in the top dresser drawer. Carefully placing the beads next to the ones found in the envelope, she could see where they had once been joined before deliberately being cut apart. The match was perfect. There could be no mistake—these two sections belonged together. Rosaries a young mother separated to unselfishly give the child she couldn't keep with her but always kept in her heart. Just like the letter read, this all fit together. There was no mistake.

Mary Cait looked at the time, it was two o'clock, and by now the patients would be through with lunch. Because the hospital wasn't more than thirty minutes away, she could be there for mid-afternoon visitation. Rosie had to be there, and her mind had to be awake to help sort through all this confusion. Question after question spun through her mind. Was she this child? Was she the reason Rosie's heart was silenced, or was Rosie's giving her the beads pure coincidence? Were they really hers, or had she taken them from another patient or had she perhaps found them? A sick mind like Rosie's was capable of anything. Maybe she didn't steal them at all, maybe she found them when she was cleaning the day-room, and maybe one of the patients got them from a relative. The possibilities were endless, the combinations numerous. Mary Cait's mind was spinning. Nothing made sense. The entire day made no sense. In fact, the last two months made no sense.

As she frantically raced to get dressed, ideas ran loose like cannons going off inside her head. She grabbed the two sections of rosaries, along with keys to her father's car, and ran outside.

The car hadn't been driven much, and the possibility remained of it not starting right up—and it didn't. The first two attempts failed, and she could hear her father saying, *"you flooded it, turn off the ignition and wait awhile."* A combination of patience and Dad's warning had her off and running within minutes. Now all she needed was to find Rosie.

In the past, visiting hours were from one to four in the afternoon, but not on all wards. Surely the staff would remember her and make an exception. No one would deny her time alone if she explained the reasons for wanting to talk to Rosie. This was important. But what if after she explained her reasons for wanting to see Rosie, the nurses or doctors saw the visit as damaging? They could refuse to ever allow her visitation privileges. After all, she wasn't family. She thought about that last day when Nurse Nelson told her not to forget Rosie, to come back and visit. Quietly she begged God to have her on duty when she got there.

Mary Cait drove up to the guard station, signed in and got a valid visitors pass, then continued on to the rear of North One. She parked the car and got out. The drive was so intense that when she took her hands off the steering wheel, they cramped up from gripping so tightly. She nervously approached the reception desk and signed in.

"Who are you here to visit?"

"Rosie Gradel in Ward A."

"Is she expecting you?"

"No, she is not."

"Please take a seat while I call upstairs to the ward nurse and see if it's possible for you to see her today."

Mary Cait swallowed hard, the lump in her throat kept urging her to cry, but she fought back the tears and tried to think about what she was going to say when she saw Rosie.

The volunteer receptionist spoke in a surprisingly loud scratchy voice and everyone in the room heard what she had to say. No secrets here.

"Miss O'Leary honey, just spoke to Nurse Nelson, and she said she'll bring Rosie down to see you as soon as she can get her cleaned up. Shouldn't take long! Maybe you'd like to go to the coffee shop and grab a cup of coffee while you wait?"

"I don't drink coffee, and besides, I don't mind waiting."

In spite of her remark about not minding the wait, Mary Cait fretted, fidgeted, and paced the floor for what seemed more like twenty hours than twenty minutes. When the double doors finally swung open, Rosie appeared along-side Nurse Nelson. Mary Cait panicked and considered running out the door, believing she'd made a serious mistake by involving Rosie in something that had all the ear-markings of being one huge misunderstanding over a gift simply given in exchange for kindnesses shown.

"Mary Cait O'Leary. How wonderful to see you. I was beginning to wonder if you forgot about your old friends back here at Woodside."

"Nurse Nelson, I could never forget any of you, it's just that I've been really busy taking care of family matters, but now maybe I'll have more free time to come visit."

"Well enjoy your visit. I know you came to see Rosie so I'll leave the two of you alone, and besides I need to get back on the ward. Have any idea how long you'll be staying?"

"No I don't. Does it matter?"

"Nah, the receptionist can ring me when you're ready to leave and someone will come get her. When I told Rosie you were here to visit she paid me no mind. But when I took her hand and motioned putting hand lotion on it, this little lady wasted no time getting ready. I wish you could have seen her face light up, racing to put on a clean dress and wanting me to comb her hair. Sure makes me happy to see her finally get a visitor."

Mary Cait took Rosie's small hand in hers and led her to a bench at the far end of the visitor's day-room where no one would interrupt them. The sun was shining through the long tall windows, casting jumbled patterns of rainbows and shadows that danced randomly across the granite floor, much like the questions inside her head. All of it was distracting.

As she'd practiced and had done many times before, Mary Cait gently took hold of Rosie's chin and turned her head so they were facing each other and she began to talk. "Rosie, I came here today because I need to talk to you about something very important." She waited a moment, not knowing whether or not Rosie read her lips, heard her voice, or even gave two hoots that she was even there. She waited hoping for some reaction, nothing. Mary Cait opened her purse and took out the gift Rosie had given her when they parted. She thought by holding them up and jiggling them back and forth might draw a reaction. The reaction came, but not as she had expected. The awe struck reaction was her own when the stones caught the sun's rays from behind, and as if by some stroke of magic, the granite floor beneath their feet and the wall across from where they sat became scattered with what looked like fire-flies dancing without music. Mary Cait couldn't hold her tongue, "Rosie, do you see what I see?" Of course Rosie knew the characteristics of the stones, so there were no surprises there.

Without any kind of a response, Mary Cait put her hands on each of Rosie's knees and swung her whole body around, forcing Rosie's body to turn so the two of them were face to face. With having Rosie's full attention, Mary Cait placed the gifted rosaries in Rosie's hand.

This definitely got her attention and she immediately handed them back to Mary Cait, shaking her head from side to side as if she didn't want the gift returned.

In Mary Cait's purse was the other half of the rosaries, which she slowly removed and held together with her fingers so Rosie could see the completed circle, but Rosie made no attempt to respond or look up from the floor.

Mary Cait put the rosaries in her left hand, and with her right one, firmly but lovingly gripped Rosie's chin, gently forcing her to look up at the rosaries. As she released Rosie's chin she noticed how the facets in the beads once again caught the sun's rays and the color changed. For a split second she imagined, or thought she saw, something in Rosie's eyes that recognized that same color change.

Carefully and slowly, she placed both sections in Rosie's small hands. Still nothing! Those reoccurring thoughts she feared most played over and over in her mind. The rosaries meant absolutely nothing to Rosie because they never belonged to her, they were simply found somewhere in this hospital and she had somehow ended up with them.

Rosie appeared frightened and confused, and to make matters worse, Mary Cait was running out of patience with having tried repeatedly to communicate with someone who was no better than talking to the wall. Out of frustration, she grasped Rosie's face with both hands and looked intently into her eyes, but forcing her to look at her instead of the floor was not easy.

Speaking slowly, choking on each word she said, "I know who you are."

Rosie tried to pull back and away from Mary Cait's firm grip but was powerless against the forces of her need for answers.

Mary Cait repeated herself but this time spoke more slowly, not knowing for sure what was going on inside Rosie, but none of that mattered any more. "I know who you are! Look at me, *Mein Liebes Kind*!"

Mary Cait's eyes pooled so heavily with tears they blinded her entire field of vision, making it impossible for her to see Rosie clutching the completed circle in her small hands. The inscription on the back of the crucifix read *Rose Hedwig Kuenstler, June 14, 1820.*

Chapter 32

Home Sweet Home

The ultimate self-punishment had begun years before the day Father Greiner took it upon himself to work up the courage to physically go and remove Rosie Gradel from the only safe haven she had known for the greater part of her adult life.

He secretly lusted for her from the time she began to blossom into a young woman, but he knew the ridiculousness of thinking she would be anything more than a sinful obsession presented by the devil to torture him in mind and strength of faith.

The 1950s were a time when some Catholic priests were leaving the priesthood for love and marriage, and, in some cases, even to have families. Father Greiner, the inveterate dreamer, saw these happenings as a perfect time to leave the priesthood and transform his life. The impetus to make this final decision and purchase a house in a small town in North-western Pennsylvania took several years of shrewd and careful planning. He wanted no one to know anything about him.

No one could have predicted the outcome of fate's mastery in dealing with the likes of Father Greiner, whose plans began with the purchase of a house in an undisclosed location for nefarious reasons, or falsely choosing to use the name Father Spero—guest visiting Rosie Gradel, or falsifying his intentions of ever bringing Rosie back. In Father Greiner's case, fate chose not to be on his side.

Nothing he could say or do ever made a difference. Rosie remained the same. She refused to look directly at him. She refused to talk or eat at the same time he did. She left the room when he entered and went to another part of the house to avoid any contact. Other than working all day long and sometimes working on into the night cleaning the house over and over again, she had no other physical activities and refused to leave the house with him.

Impotence replaced lust, and what he once thought of as love gradually evolved into bitter resentment. He tried everything from gifts to music, hoping something would help, that somehow she'd be so happy to be out of Woodside and living with him, that she'd get better. Nothing seemed to work. It finally became evident to him that his being with Rosie was never in God's plan. Two years gone with nothing to show but two years of absurd dreams, wasted time, and two people who were never meant to be together. A beaten man, he turned to God, knelt down, and prayed.

"Dear God, I find that if we mortals suffer failure in life, there is never an excuse we can offer ourselves that is adequate, and right now I desperately need to talk, please hear me. For some unexplainable reason my mind keeps slipping back to one Saturday evening in the middle of December when Rosie's destiny was predictable. What is it about communion that purges the soul and sets us free to redesign our future plans with positive hopes of change—when our mind and body lack discipline, and over a period of time destroys those well intended promises made to ourselves, leaving us with empty words of 'I'm sorry' and 'I promise.' Yet none of us has an inkling of their respective meaning or we would be strong enough to maintain those promises and not be blinded by those same desires that led us astray in the first place. Dear Heavenly Father, I have dishonored and offended against your holy laws and humbly beseech your forgiveness for this cowardice act I am about to do."

The following morning when Rosie came downstairs he was dressed and waiting. He fed her then forcefully put her in the car, and together they took the long ride back to Woodside where he deposited her at the entrance before driving off without ever looking back.

The guard at the gate saw the whole thing and immediately notified the central desk. He asked to have a couple of male attendants sent down to the main gate to pick up what looked like a woman in distress. Someone in a black car had dumped the poor thing off along-side the road.

When the attendants arrived, Rosie refused to speak or acknowledge them. This behavior ended up getting her shuffled from one ward to the other until she eventually ended back in North One. There she was readily recognized and immediately returned to her old ward.

When Maisy saw Rosie, she began to weep. She raced to where Rosie was standing— swooped her up in her arms, and for the first time since Rosie disappeared, began spinning her around, clutching onto her friend while singing arias from Massenet's *Thais*. The ward nurse asked her to put Rosie down before she dropped her or one of them got injured. Maisy gently set Rosie down, took a step back, and looked at Rosie to make sure this all wasn't just a dream or a bad dose of ECT.

"I asked them stupid's where you went and they gave me a buncha' bullshit. Where'd them stupid's hide you all these two years?"

Rosie tugged at Maisy's dress and pulled her shoulder down so she was within earshot.

"Maisy, want me to teach you how to tango?"

"Hey all you stupid's, Rosie can ta—."

With that Rosie cupped her small hand over Maisy's mouth.

"Shh."

CPSIA information can be obtained
at www.ICGtesting.com
Printed in the USA
LVHW040713221221
706908LV00003B/60